BOUND TO THE ABYSS

BOOK ONE: INTO THE WORLD

A THREE MOONS REALM NOVEL

JAMES R. VERNON

JUST A FEW PEOPLE THAT DESERVE A SPECIAL THANKS.

My immediate family for supporting all of the time and effort I've put into this story.

My excellent beta reader, C.D. Verhoff, for helping me shake off the bad habits of a new writer. I am becoming an adequate adverb killer and plot streamliner thanks to her help.

My cover artist, Mominur Rahman, for the amazing work he creates that helps draw both my readers and myself into my world.

And certainly those that backed me in a big way to get this book whipped into shape;

Jim and Frances Vernon
James and Kim Logan
Caitlin G.
Charlie and Amy Metz
Angela Q.
Mary Elizabeth Gaige
George Windsor
James E.
Linda Aben-Kralowetz

BOUND TO THE ABYSS

CHAPTER 1

A SHARP PAIN EXPLODED in the back of Ean Sangrave's leg, tripping him up and stopping his mad dash for safety. He stumbled forward, bounced off the side of one of the village's small, wooden homes and landed face down in the dirt alley. The copper and silver coins he had been carrying flew from his hand, jingling as they struck each other before hitting the ground with a splat in the mud. *How did they find me so quickly?* he thought as he tried to rise. The plan had gone perfectly that morning. For once, Krane Erikson had been on the receiving end of some punishment, and Ean had been spared another horrible morning of abuse from the other eighteen-year-old and his two lackeys. He had felt so confident, in fact, that he had sent his only trusted friend away. The rock, or whatever they had hit him with, killed that thought. Footsteps squishing into the mud behind him made Ean wish Zin were around, even if his only true friend couldn't help.

"You really thought you could get away with it, didn't you?" Krane's voice was like a second blow, this one filling him with dread instead of pain. "Even as educated as you should be as a healer's apprentice, you should have realized that whatever tricks you pulled wouldn't scare me off."

A foot stomped down on Ean's back, and he splayed out on the dirt. Expecting a follow-up blow, he chose to roll over onto his back, tucking in his knees to protect his body and raising his arms to protect his face. In a back alley of his village, between homes and away from the farmlands, Ean had little hope of someone coming to his aid. In his eighteen years of life, fending for himself was the only way to survive. When a few moments without an attack passed, he lowered both his arms and legs to look.

Krane stood a few paces away. His lackeys, Gall and Dansh, stood on either side of him. The thickest in size of the three, Krane tried his best to smirk down at Ean. The bandage wrapped tightly around his head took away from the boy's attempt to look tough though. Krane's two friends seemed nervous at least, both of their eyes were locked on Ean's gloved hands. If Zin were still around, he could throw a stone or branch at the two of them without being seen, fooling the two superstitious bullies into really believing that the Lord of the Abyss protected Ean. He mentally cursed the decision to send Zin away as Krane took a step forward.

"You might have these dopes believing you are something special," Krane said, pointing a thumb over his shoulder at the other two boys, "but I know you are too worthless for any of the gods or goddesses to waste their time on. All you are is the son to a pair of dead drunks that got what they deserved."

Krane always tried to get a rise out of Ean by mentioning his parents, as if talking about two people he had never really known would stoke his ire. The looks of disappointment and disgust he received from most people in the village on a daily basis had dulled any feelings he had over the loss of his parents. But Krane continued to think one of these times it would get under Ean's skin. Letting silence be his reply, Ean stared back at Krane as he moved into a sitting position.

"Luck was the only thing that saved you this morning," Krane continued on, his frown hinting at his disappointment that his comments had yet to strike a nerve. That tile was probably loose and you saw it was about to fall off the inn roof. You just tricked me into moving underneath it so it would hit me on the way down. It wasn't an act of one of the gods trying to protect you, especially not Ze'an."

Ean hadn't needed to maneuver Krane. Zin just happened to have excellent aim from where Ean had told him to wait. Their mistake was feeling confident that after the two lackeys carried Krane off, that there wouldn't be any retaliation later that same day.

"Don't say his name!" Gall whispered in a harsh voice. "You'll curse us all, or at the least, get us whipped if anyone else hears you say that name."

"Quiet, you dope!" Krane replied, spinning and pointing a finger at both boys in turn. "Bunch of superstitious fools you two are. I'll prove it was a fluke right now."

As Krane turned back around, Ean got to his feet. Dansh juggled a rock in one hand, eliminating the choice of flight. Bracing himself, Ean stared Krane down.

Krane was as fat as Ean was lanky, with a wide nose and dark, beady brown eyes. His clothes had the look of someone that came from outside of their village; different colors marked his shirt and pants, his boots, a dark red leather. If it wasn't for all of the different food stains blending into the colors of his shirt, Krane might actually look imposing. The boy took a step towards Ean, but stopped as Ean raised two fists.

"Oh?" Krane replied with a laugh. "Have to defend yourself now? No god to come to your aid and drop another tile on my head? Or is that just because all of the homes around us have thatched roofs?" Turning slightly towards his companions, Krane gave a dismissive wave in Ean's direction. "See boys, nothing to fear. He is still just a weak little—"

Krane's words cut off as Ean's shoulder slammed into his chest, sending both of the boys tumbling to the ground. When they

3

stopped rolling, somehow Ean ended up on top and began raining down haphazard blows on the larger boy. Ean had never been on the offensive before and was not going to let up now while he had an advantage. Unfortunately, it was only for a few moments before his arms were seized, and he was flung off of Krane.

As soon as he hit the ground, the assault by the other two boys began. Kicks came from every direction. Ean curled up into a ball. He lashed out with a kick of his own when he could. Twice, his foot connected with something solid, but most of his kicks hit open air and he resigned himself to staying on the defensive. When the blows stopped, Ean moved his arms away from his face enough to see why.

Dansh and Gall stood on either side of him, breathing heavily and staring him down. A few paces away Krane had gotten to his feet, his hand covering his mouth. A new red stain had appeared on his shirt and sleeve. When Krane pulled his hand away from his mouth, Ean could see a large gap where two of the boy's top teeth should have been. Despite his pain, a barking laugh escaped Ean's lips before he could stop it. That was a mistake.

"You think this is funny, you worm?" Krane growled, spittle shooting out of the gap in his teeth. Glancing around for a moment, Krane moved over to the side of one of the houses. With an evil smirk in Ean's direction, he reached down and picked up a thick branch from a pile of firewood. With slow deliberate steps, Krane moved towards Ean, smacking the branch in the palm of his hand.

"Alright, healer's apprentice," he said with a laugh that held no warmth. "Let's see how long it takes you to recover from this."

Ean blocked the first blow with his forearms. The pain lanced through his arms and shook his entire body. As the second blow fell, the telltale crack told him something was breaking, although at this point the pain was so intense he had no idea if it was the branch or one of his arms. As the blows continued Ean tried his best to separate his thoughts from the pain, but the sound of Krane's laughter made it impossible. When the pain became too much, Ean happily welcomed the loss of consciousness.

EAN SPENT THE NEXT nine days recuperating in bed until he was tired of lying around feeling sorry for himself. Rising, he got dressed as quickly as his bruised and battered body would allow, then moved over to the chest at the end of his bed and started routing around in it. He pushed the odd piece of clothing and empty bottle out of the way as he searched the chest until he found his small carving knife and a few small pieces of hardened clay. It had been long enough for Zin to accomplish what he needed to do. Time to bring his only real friend back from the Abyss.

Ean gathered the materials he needed for the task at hand: a few hardened pieces of clay, a carving knife, and most important of all, the focus to carve the necessary runes onto the clay piece. With everything he needed, he sat down on the wood paneled floor, propping his back up against the side of the bed. Piling the blank, medallion-sized clay pieces next to him, he chose a round piece and picked it up with his left hand. Moving around was difficult with his right arm in the sling, but thankfully at this point, moving his hand around didn't cause him much pain. It had been strange during his recovery to think of his scarred left arm as his more useful arm. Taking the carving knife in his left hand, Ean began the slow process of carving the summoning rune into the clay that would bring Zin, an imp from the Abyss, back to this world.

Compared to the more simple runes that represented individual words, summoning runes were the most intricate of them all; the complex shapes and letters twisted together in a manner that was difficult to get perfect. One slip or misspelled word and any number of creatures could crawl out of the Abyss, if the spell didn't simply fizzle out of course. It took him three tries before he was happy with his work. Ean examined the completed rune.

"Perfect," he said and set the finished piece on the floor with the rune facing up.

Taking a deep breath, he mentally prepared himself for the pain that came with a summoning. After a few moments of peace, Ean braced himself. Placing his left hand on the rune, he activated it by tracing a finger along the proper symbol set in the center of the design.

An iron-tight grip began to squeeze his chest as the spell took hold. The rune carved into the clay began to glow with a dark blue light that bathed Ean's entire room. As the light grew in intensity, the piece of clay began to dissolve into the floor. Once the glowing rune actually touched the floor, it flared once, causing Ean to squint. Then it was gone, replaced by a pinprick of blue light shooting into the ceiling. The small speck grew into the size of a coin and continued to grow. When it finally stopped expanding, a circular opening twice the size of a dinner plate rested on his floor. A dark blue, purplish mist made seeing into the hole impossible, but Ean knew what was on the other side.

Ean couldn't help but grin a little bit through the pain at the sight of the knee-high imp rising out of the gateway. Claw marks and burns covered his light brown, humanoid body. His cheeks and small pointed nose looked bruised. His normally erect, long pointed ears flopped forward like bent blades of grass. Out of the eight nails at the end of his four fingered hands, six were broken. The worst injury appeared to be a broken toe bent at an odd angle. Zin had a large smile on his face, though; Ean imagined the imp was just as relieved to be free of the Abyss as Ean was to see him back in one piece.

As soon as the imp's body was completely free, the gateway closed on its own, shrinking back into a tiny beam of light before winking out. The pressure vanished from his body, signaling that the spell had run its course. Reappearing at the end of the spell, the clay piece was slid into Ean's pocket as Ean collapsed onto his side. "Welcome back," he said to Zin in between heavy breaths.

"Why, thank you. It's good to be back," Zin said, that mixture of a half grin and half smirk he usually wore showing off his rows of razor-sharp teeth. "It looks like you had just as rough of a time up here as I did down there." Moving over to Ean's side, the imp dropped his little pack onto the ground and sat on the floor. "I'm glad you decided to bring me back a day early. It only took me half the time to get what I needed, which meant I spent the rest of the time either getting kicked around or doing my best to hide."

"Yeah well, as you can see, I got kicked around quite a bit as well. Almost right after you left, in fact." Ean used his good arm to push himself slowly back up into a sitting position. "Krane didn't waste any time getting his revenge for making him look like a fool."

Zin's eyes opened wide. "So quickly? That's a surprise. I swear that boy is slightly insane." A mischievous grin appeared on his face. "But we won't have to worry about him much longer. Time for your present!"

The imp reached over and grabbed his bag, opening it up and digging around inside. When he pulled his hands back out, he held what looked like a writing utensil, but it also could have easily been a severed finger from some large creature with blue skin and red nails. "Here is the key to your future," Zin gave an elaborate bow as he presented the hard won prize. "May it help us to finally get out of this armpit of a village. The only other thing we need now is The Abysmal Tome."

Ean smiled, but said nothing. Feeling underneath his bed, his fingers touched the rune carved into the planks of his floor. On instinct his finger moved to the activating symbol, the sudden glow coming from beneath his bed signaling the activation of the rune and effectively opening up his Pocket. A miniature gateway into the Abyss, it connected him to a small, secure area that held his most prized possessions. His hand dissolved through the floorboards for a moment before he pulled out a rough cloth bag. He pulled out a book from inside, its cover a thick black leather about as wide as his leg. Since the cover had no distinguishable markings, he had started calling it The Abysmal Tome, or just 'The Tome'. Ean deposited the book in front of Zin before he tossed the bag aside.

"All right, what page are we looking for?"

"Look for a hand with a rune inscribed on the palm," Zin said. "I'm pretty sure I saw it towards the back."

After a couple of moments flipping through the worn pages, Ean found an illustration of a hand with one of the most intricate runes he had ever seen drawn on the palm. The number of different shapes and inscribed letters was astounding. He let out a low whistle.

"This looks pretty complicated. Are you sure I'm up for it?" All Ean could make out were the simple words for "abyss" and "rune." The majority of the rest he had never seen before. He started to shake his head. "I don't even know if I can figure out which parts are the activating words and which are just descriptions of what the rune does."

Zin's finger floated over the book as he scrolled over the words. He was careful not to actually touch the Tome lest his hands burst into flames again. The imp scanned over a few of the passages and then stopped at what appeared to be the middle of a paragraph. "That's it, right there. This won't put you in the kind of pain that summoning does. All you have to worry about is getting the rune perfect on your right palm."

Shrugging, Ean reached down and picked up the finger-like item. "Whatever you say." Ean moved the Abysmal Tome from the floor onto his lap so he had a clear view of what he was doing. He stared at the drawing, trying to take in everything, all of the curves and lines, trying to see it as one continuous rune as opposed to a series of interlaced ones. When he was finally comfortable with the design in his head, he dipped the strange nail down into the ink. As soon as the tip touched the ink, the fingernail drained the ink bottle and the entire finger began to pulse with an eerie blue glow. Ean glanced over at Zin, eyebrows raised. The imp simply nodded back and then waved him on to continue. With a shrug, Ean took the item and placed the tip against his palm. When nothing happened, Ean relaxed a bit and started to draw.

A jolt of pain lanced through Ean's entire body as soon as he moved the nail even the tiniest bit along his skin. Dropping the finger, Ean shot Zin an angry look. "What in the Abyss was that? Are you trying to play a joke on me?"

"Of course not," Zin replied. "You didn't think a powerful spell like this would be painless, did you?" The imp flashed him a smile, showing off his tiny, jagged teeth. "Trust me, from what I've gathered, the new power you will acquire will more than make up for what little pain you endure now."

"Little pain?!" Ean almost yelled but controlled himself. The last thing he wanted was Cleff coming up to check on him at this particular moment. "It felt like I had stuck my hand in a hornet's nest and then gave it a good shake."

Against his better judgment, he picked up the finger and tried again. The pain returned as he started to draw, but Ean kept reminding himself that the pain would be worth it in the end. Hopefully. He had gotten the first major design finished, a swirl of lines that curved around and back on itself so many times it became difficult to follow, when a particularly nasty jolt made him drop the finger again. As soon as the nail left his palm, the entire rune he had been drawing disappeared.

"Oh, you can't be serious."

"Well, look at that. I guess you have to finish it in one go." Letting out a little laugh, Zin climbed up on the bed. "I guess I can take a nap until you actually get it right." Taking a few moments to glare at Zin, Ean turned his attention back to his hand and tried again.

Ean had no idea how long he attempted to get the rune inscribed on his palm. Each time he would get only so far, when a jolt of pain made him mess up again. After a round of cursing, he started again from scratch. As the sun started its downward descent towards the mountains to the West, Ean finished. The completed rune stayed on his palm, giving off a slight glow and the tiniest bit of heat.

Ean showed it to Zin, who was lounging on his side. "Looks good, doesn't it? This better be well worth the effort."

"Oh, it will be. You'll see," Zin said. He climbed down off the bed and looked down at Ean's book. "All right, you remember which parts to read, correct? Is there anything you need help pronouncing?"

"No, nothing too difficult there. Should be easy compared to actually getting it drawn on my palm." Looking down, he slowly went through the passage in his head twice and then began to recite the words aloud. The language of the Abyss was strange, with many of the words consisting of noises that sounded more like a person clearing his throat than an actual language. He had gotten quite good at pronouncing the words; it was just unfortunate that he did not know what most of them meant. When he finished, the rune on his palm grew cold and started to dim. For a moment, Ean thought he had failed and would have to start all over again, but then the light of the rune sprang back to life, bathing his tiny room in a dark blue glow. Proud of his accomplishment, Ean glanced at the imp expecting him to look impressed. His smile froze when he saw worry lines etched into Zin's brow instead.

"This part is going to be bad," Zin said. "Just do your best to ride it out."

"Wait, you said—" He lost his words when pain suddenly dropped him to his knees. Molten lava coursed through his veins. His arms and legs flailed violently. Muscles contorting, he writhed on the floor, trying to escape his own body. Sweat drained out of his pores. Was that his heart pounding in his ears or a war drum?

The sound was blighted out by the force of his scream that could not be contained. He had never known such agony.

The light from the rune disappeared, and with it, the pain. Ean's body went limp, a few aftershocks of the agony he had been in making parts of his body twitch randomly. His mind was blank, his body exhausted. The door crashed open and a moment later he sensed someone kneeling beside him. "Nightmare," Ean breathed out, although how he had thought of the lie so quickly, he'd never know. He clenched his right fist to hide the rune. The figure at his side wordlessly picked up Ean's limp body and put him back in bed. Ean was out soon after.

WHEN EAN AWOKE, THE green light from the first moon cast the room in a soothing glow. He stretched out his free left arm, feeling tired but good. Actually, he felt pretty great. Taking off his sling, he moved his right arm about, bending the elbow and twisting his wrist and forearm about. It wasn't even sore! Next, he checked out the rune on his palm.

The rune was still there, giving off a faint glow that mixed with the moonlight and turned his room a faint purple. However, there was more now. Small, dark blue lines ran out of the rune, moving along his palm and up his fingers. The lines wrapped around his hand and seemed to converge on the back, creating a swirling design. From there, smaller lines shot out and moved up the back of his fingers as well, ending at his fingernails.

"Well, that's new," Ean said to himself, turning his hand over and back repeatedly as he inspected the new addition on his hand.

"That's just the beginning." Ean looked over and found Zin sitting on his dresser. "The longer that rune is on your body, and the more you use your power, the faster your strength will build. At least that's what I gathered it was supposed to do. Oh, and sorry about lying to you about the pain. I figured it would just make you nervous if you knew it was coming."

"Oh, yeah. It was much better not knowing," Ean half-heartedly threw his pillow at Zin, which the imp easily snatched out of the air. "So what's different now? What can I do, summon stronger creatures? Actually be able to control the creatures I summon?"

"I have no idea. Let the magic settle into your body and then we can see what happens. Remember, all I know is that your power and tolerance should increase." Zin jumped down off the dresser and made his way over to the bed. "There is one thing you can do right away." He reached under the bed and pulled out Ean's bag. The Abysmal Tome was still sitting on top of it.

"Wait!" Ean exclaimed. "Cleff didn't see this stuff, did he?"

"Nope, thankfully, when your body started jerking around, The Tome landed on the bag and I dragged them both and the finger under the bed before he broke in. How about you hide these things away again?"

Ean grabbed The Tome and the finger, carefully placing both into the bag. He was about to start crawling under the bed to access the rune to his Pocket, when Zin's raised hand stopped him. "No. Just use your hand. You should be able to create runes now just from your power alone. Just try visualizing your finger as a knife carving the rune."

Ean cast a funny look at Zin but went along with the imp's suggestion. He sat on the floor and started to trace the same designs he used to open his Pocket onto the floor. As Zin predicted, the design began to glow with a faint light, rising a few inches off of the ground, before dissolving into the floor. When he had finished, the rune light grew, rising a few inches off of the ground before disappearing as the gateway to Ean's own personal storage space opened up before him.

Ean couldn't believe it. He hadn't even needed to retrace the activating rune at the center of his design. This would be much more convenient in the future. He grabbed his bag with his scarred left hand and slowly lowered it into the Pocket. Once it was inside, he instinctively placed his right hand on the edge of the portal and tried willing it to close. As he expected, it closed on its own, replaced by the rune used to summon it. With a brush of his hand, the rune disappeared as well. The only light now came from the rune on his hand and the green moonlight coming through his window, the two mixing into a hazy combination of both colors.

"That is amazing," Ean said, shaking his head. "Not sure if that alone was worth all of that pain, but still a handy skill to have."

"Like I said, your power will grow with use," Zin replied. "It's not just a handy drawing tool. More handy skills will come with time. I think. You just have to be patient."

Ean didn't even hear Zin's words; he had already started to practice drawing different runes. He practiced long into the night, with Zin watching apprehensively. When the first rays of the morning sun peaked in through his window, Ean was both physically and mentally exhausted and crawled into bed. Zin crawled into his usual sleeping spot underneath the bed.

"Thanks a lot, Zin," Ean said quietly, "I really needed something good to happen for a change."

"Don't get all weepy on me now, you little girl," Zin replied. "But you are welcome. Now let's get some sleep; it's been a long night."

Ean flipped his back to the window and chuckled. "Fair enough. Sleep well, Zin. I have the feeling that when we wake, our lives are going to start to take a turn for the better."

CHAPTER 2

PRACTICING THE CRAFT

THE SOUND OF MEN shouting woke Ean out of a deep sleep. He moved to the window and glanced outside. The morning sun cast a blood-red light over the empty ground between his home and the Skyfall Mountains that circled his village.

A group of four people were making their way towards the house, carrying a fifth person between them. Cal Halhan and his son, Ted, were on one side while Chris Tanner, moving with a limp, and Allie Bale was on the other side. It looked like all four were carrying Allie's husband, Lane. They were all splattered with blood, and from the looks of it, most of it was probably Lane's. His clothes were torn to shreds and stained dark red, his hair was matted in blood. Worst of all was his right leg. From about the middle of the shin down, his leg was gone, the open wound exuding blood. His face was pale, and his eyes had rolled back into his head. If he wasn't already dead, he would be soon.

Bear attack, Ean thought as his stomach sunk to his knees. Lane had never been nice to him; most members of their small village had never been nice to Ean because of what his parents had done. But no one deserved to be hurt because of how he had been treated, and they certainly didn't deserve to die.

Ean watched for a moment more and then ran out the door of his room, grabbing his gloves as he went. He hurtled down the stairs, his long gloves covering both arms before he hit the bottom step, and headed straight towards the front of the house. He was about halfway down the hall when Cleff slammed open the front door.

"Ean, grab my bag out of the office, and get a bottle of Flashseal from the closet. The key is sitting on my desk. Hurry, now!"

Skidding to a halt, Ean spun around and sprinted back down the hall. Entering the office, he ran_over to Cleff's desk, grabbed the keys sitting there, and moved over to the one closet that was always locked. The key turned with a loud click in the heavy lock, and Ean pulled open the door. Scanning the shelves full of bottles and containers, it only took him a moment to locate the one Cleff needed. The bottle labeled "Flashseal" contained a silvery powder, the stopper sealed with wax. He picked up the bottle with both hands so the contents did not shake and then made for the door. He was just almost out of the office when he stopped again. The bag! Turning around, he saw Cleff's bag sitting on the floor next to his desk. He reached it in one giant step then sprinted to the front door and then outside.

The scene just outside the front door was out of a nightmare. They had put Lane down, splayed out on the grass, his leg turning the ground a bright crimson color as his life bled out. Allie was kneeling down next to her husband, sobbing, and holding his left hand in both of hers. Cleff was kneeling on the other side, examining the deep slashes on the man's chest through the holes in his shirt. Ted was just standing there, his clothes covered in blood, his mouth wide open as he simply stared at the carnage in front of him. Cal was gone, already on his way to inform the the Mayor. Lane was comatose; the only sign that he was still alive was the slow rise and fall of his chest. Moving to Cleff's side, Ean placed both the bag and the bottle of Flashseal down, in between Cleff and Lane.

"The slashes on his chest aren't too deep," Cleff said, his eyes locked on the bleeding man. "Get some of the smashed up Rottwealth out of my bag and rub it into the wounds."

Ean switched places with Cleff on the ground, placing himself closer to the man's chest. Pulling over the bag, he pulled out both a bottle of Rottwealth and one of Cleff's cutting tools. Using the tool to cut free what was left of Lane's shirt, Ean got a better look at the damage underneath. There were four gashes, the first starting just below the man's shoulders and the last one just above his hipbones. This was certainly not a bear attack. Judging by how deep and wide the cuts were, the claws of whatever hit Lane must have been huge!

Getting over his shock, Ean dumped out the whole bottle of Rottwealth onto the man's chest and began to spread the brownish powder out over the wounds. As his hands pushed the smashed up plant into the gashes, Lane let out a weak groan. Well, that was a good sign, at least. While Ean worked, Cleff was spreading out the Flashseal over the stub of the man's leg. When it was covered, the silver powder an odd contrast to the dark red wound, Cleff stood up.

"All right, everyone take a step back."

Everyone complied, although Ted, just barely out of his stupor, had to pull Allie away from her husband. Reaching down, Cleff struck a spark near Lane's stump of a leg. With a flash, a small green flame flared up on the wound, accompanied by the smell of burning meat. Lane sat up for a moment, letting out a horrible scream, and then fell back again. What little strength he had to stay conscious fled his exhausted body. His leg, however, had stopped bleeding. The wound had turned black from the flame and sealed close from the intense burst of heat.

Allie looked at her husband in horror for a moment, and then turned to Cleff. "Is he going to be all right? Is my husband going to live?"

"I honestly don't know, Allie," Cleff replied with his usual gruff-sounding voice. "He lost a lot of blood. It all depends on how much he lost and if the Rottwealth does its job." Turning his head, he regarded Ean. "Take Ted and grab the stretcher out of the house. We need to move him inside and keep him warm. These next few days will be vital in determining if he lives or not." Nodding, Ean grabbed the older boy's arm and dragged him into the house.

The sun was almost straight overhead by the time they had gotten Lane inside and laid out in one of the visitors' rooms on the first floor. Cleff and Ean worked on the man for hours, sewing up where they could and cleaning off the wounds while his wife waited outside. By the time they were done working on him, the sun was just starting to set over the mountains to the west. Cleff sat down by the man and waved Ean off, telling him to get something to eat. He just had taken a single step out into the main hall when Allie jumped up out of one of the waiting chairs and ran over to him. She looked haggard, her hair a mess and face dirty.

"How is my husband? Did Cleff say he would make it?"

Ean shook his head. "We don't know yet, Mrs. Bale. It's too early to tell. We've done all that we could, but he has lost a lot of blood. Only time will tell."

She looked at him, tears starting to flow from already red eyes, and then she flung her arms around him in a grateful hug. "Thank you," she said in between sobs, her voice a whisper in his ear. "I know most of us treat you something horrible, but I know having you there to aid Cleff helped my husband's chances."

Ean blushed, not quite sure how to react. Cleff had never been one to show emotion, and the other villagers often reacted to him with disgust. This unexpected show of gratitude was a bit more than Ean could take. Patting her on the back twice, he pushed the older woman away.

"It was nothing, really. Just doing what I've been taught most of my life, and Cleff is an excellent teacher." He frowned a second, trying to think of what to say. "Thank you, though." Allie nodded, seeming on the verge to say more, but they were interrupted as the Mayor stomped through the front door.

"Is he awake?" the Mayor said, looking concerned. He was a large man with a powerful voice that commanded the attention of an entire room. "Did anyone see what attacked him? Where are the foreman and the other men that did not return? They'd better tell me it was a bear, because I'll be damned if I'm going to close the mine." He was staring at Allie, expecting some kind of answer.

"Lane is in a bad way, Mayor." As always, Ean had to force his tone to remain civil. "It might be some time before he is conscious, if he even survives at all." He wished he could take the words back as he watched Allie's face go pale, but he had to keep going now. "Didn't Cal or Ted let you know what happened?"

The Mayor shook his head, his attention still on Allie. When he responded to Ean's question, he directed his response to the distraught wife. "Both were babbling away, and all I could understand was that they had gotten to the mine late. Tell me, what happened today, Allie?"

"It was horrible!" Allie burst out, the tears flowing freely now. "Lane and I got to the mine right before dawn. Lane went into the foreman's home and was talking to all of the other miners for a time while I started setting up the cooking station, being that it was my turn to feed the men lunch later in the day. A short time later, all four of the men left the house and entered the mine with their picks. They were only in there for a few moments when ... " Her body started to shake at the memory, but she continued on. " ... when I heard this horrible roar. It was followed by some shouts from the men, and then suddenly the foreman and Wes, one of the other miners came rushing out, carrying my husband between them."

She paused, taking a breath. She held the complete attention of both the Mayor and Ean; Ean, at least, was curious to what happened next.

"I immediately ran over," she continued, "and helped support my husband and was about to ask what had happened when I heard another terrible roar. We all turned to look back at the mine, and what came out was something out of a nightmare."

A shudder went through Allie's entire body, and she closed her eyes for a moment before continuing on. "It was a mass of scales and claws, taking up most of the mine entrance. Dangling from the left corner of its mouth was a partially chewed foot, part of the boot still hanging off of it. Poor old Glen's boot." Her face took on a greenish hue and Ean was about run off to get her a bucket in case she got sick, but the woman continued on. "I screamed at that point, and the beast started to make its way towards us. The foreman dropped my husband and ran off towards his house. Wes turned to me and said, 'Allie, get him as far away as you can. I'll try to slow whatever that is down.' A real hero, Wes was! He took his mining pick and set himself between the beast and us. I did my best to carry Lane; at that point, he still had enough strength to walk on his one leg. We went as fast as we could. At one point I heard Wes scream …"

She paused again, tiny sobs escaping from her mouth. "But … but … I didn't turn around this time. I just moved as quickly as I could. When Lane's strength finally gave out, we both collapsed to the ground. That was where Cal and Ted found us."

She stopped, collapsing into one of the chairs, unable to control her emotions as she buried her face in her hands. Ean and the Mayor stared at her, overwhelmed by what they had heard. Nothing like that had ever happened in their valley before. Sure, every now and then, the men that made up the town guard would have to scare off a bear or the rare mountain troll that wandered down close to the village, but the beast she had described was like nothing that had ever appeared in the village before.

"I have to go inform the town," the Mayor said, his tone neutral. "Let everyone know that the southern area of the valley is off-limits. Inform the town guard in case this was something more serious than a bear attack, and it makes its way towards town." Spots of sweat began to appear on the larger man's clothes. "I don't want to start panicking the entire town for nothing, though. We'll see if this creature is really as horrible as you say before we take more drastic actions. Either way, this is a terrible turn of events, just terrible. So much work to do now ..." The man mumbled the last few words, walking out of the house.

With a scowl, Ean watched him go. The Mayor always seemed to find a way of making Ean think even less of him. Moving over, he took a seat next to Allie, his hands fidgeting as he sat there next to the crying woman. He really was horrible at these types of things. Despite how awkward he felt, Ean reached over and patted her on the back twice.

"I'll set up the room next to Lane's so you can sleep here tonight. Cleff won't let you into your husband's room tonight, I don't think. He'll just want Lane to rest and let the medicine work."

The woman nodded, her head still buried in her hands. Standing back up, Ean fetched a blanket to put around her shoulders before moving into one of the side rooms and setting up a bed. Allie was still crying when Ean came back out. "The bed is ready whenever you want." She didn't even acknowledge him this time, but Ean didn't take it as an insult. Instead, he walked over, patted her on the back again, and headed for the stairs.

Little light remained in the day by the time Ean entered his room. He stripped down to his underclothes, removing his blood-soaked clothes. Even after he had dropped them outside the room and closed the door, he could still smell the blood. Shaking his head,

Ean walked over to the dresser and changed into a fresh set of clothes.

"You're not planning what I think you're planning." For the first few years of knowing the imp, Ean had always jumped at hearing Zin's voice before seeing him. He was used to it now, always expecting the imp to be around. From the sound of his voice, Zin was sitting on the windowsill. Ean wasn't sure, of course, because the small imp had a habit of turning himself invisible.

As far as he knew, Ean was the only one able to make out a blur that marked where the invisible imp was located, like heat rising off of hot stew, but it was easy to miss if he wasn't looking for it. At the moment, it was hard to see that blur in the darkness of Ean's room. Without much light, Ean just had to guess where the imp was based on the sound of his voice.

"It doesn't sound like anything I've ever heard about before," Ean said, slipping on his gloves. "I need to see what it is."

"You've lived in this valley your entire life," Zin replied. "I'm sure there are many things out in the rest of the world that you haven't heard of before. Doesn't mean you have to go out and get yourself eaten because of it." Zin made himself visable and hopped off the windowsill before walking over. "If the thing is like a lizard, then it could have a strong sense of smell, which means if it catches you, it will probably catch me and eat me too."

Smiling, he reached over slowly and patted Zin on the head. "Well, while he is chewing on me, you'll have plenty of time to get away then, won't you?"

"That's hardly reassuring," Zin grumbled, walking away. He stayed quiet the rest of the time as Ean got ready. Once dressed, he did his best to remain silent as he headed out of his room, Zin right behind him. The imp had turned invisible as he passed through the doorway. Ean moved down the steps, pausing every few steps to listen for any other sign of life in the house. When he got to the bottom of the stairs, he peeked out of the doorway into the main sitting hall. Allie was still there; she had stopped crying and was just staring at the door to the room her husband was in. Cleff was either in there as well, watching over his patient, or had gone to bed. Moving backwards, Ean went in the opposite direction into the back of the house.

He passed through the main storeroom first, which contained all of Cleff's lesser healing plants and mixtures. The room itself smelled like the outdoors, the various aromas coming off the plants left out to grow or the open bottles of ground up material, giving the room an earthy smell. The most powerful smell was the fresh Rottwealth, its sour aroma permeating everything else in the room. Moving through, Ean reached the main living area and kitchen. The kitchen was his goal as there was a doorway out to the backyard. He eased the old door open, trying his best not to let it make too much noise, and waited until he felt Zin brush past him before heading out and closing it behind him.

Since the sun had set and none of Cleff's outside lanterns were lit, it was difficult to see. Even the green light of the First Moon and stars were blocked out by dense clouds, eliminating what little light they provided at night. Ean took a moment to get his bearings and let his eyes adjust then began to inch his way along the wall.

"You know," he heard Zin say behind him. "Your hand is now a permanent source of light. You could whip it out instead of having us stumble around in the dark. I doubt we will run into anyone, and it would be nice to at least see the beast coming before it eats us."

Ean responded with a simple grunt, then reached over and pulled off the glove on his right hand. Sure enough, the rune on his palm gave off enough light so that they could see a few paces away. Holding his hand up in front of his body, Ean moved around the back of the house until he found the dirt path to the bog. Best to head there first then follow it around to where the mine was located. That would give them a good escape route. Plus, Ean knew the bog like the back of his hand, and if they did have to run, he could cut through the bog since he knew where the more solid patches existed. A beast as big as Allie described would get bogged down and move much slower in the muck

Heading south down the path, a light breeze blew in from the north. On it, Ean could still smell blood in the air. It turned his stomach. Lane had lost so much blood from his wounds that it was doubtful the man would survive. It was a shame. Ean had liked being on the receiving end of gratitude for a change and didn't want to ruin it by telling Allie that her husband had little chance of living. Best for Cleff to tell her; let him take the grief.

They walked in silence all the way down to the bog, with Ean thinking about how Allie had acted towards him while Zin kept up behind. Once Ean started to smell the harsh odor of the Rottwealth that grew in the bog, he knew they were getting close. The bog itself was huge, taking up the majority of the southern end of the valley. It was a large section of land covered in water, pieces of mossy earth sticking up here and there. The glow from his hand gave the place an eerie light, and it made Ean think of his parents, buried somewhere deep within the water and mud. Strange how the bog had never made him think of them before. He spent most of his time working for Cleff down here, trudging around, collecting the Rottwealth once it had flowered, and looking for any other herbs or flowers that might be useful to the apothecary.

No, there was never a need to think about them before; Ean had never felt a real attachment to them, only anger. It was because of their actions, after all, that he was despised by the majority of the townspeople. Well, that would change. He would do something great, so that many more people would show him the appreciation that Allie had shown and respect him. And he would have his revenge too: teach Krane, the Mayor, and anyone else who had gone out of their way to make his life horrible in the past. He just had to become stronger first.

Before he knew it, they were at the east end of the bog, the foreman's squat log building and the area around the mine just visible in the darkness. The smell of blood was stronger here, much more obvious than the smell back near the house. Ean stood still, trying to listen for any kind of movement around the area, but it was dead silent. "Do you smell anything other than all that blood, Zin?" Ean whispered.

"Yeah, death. It's all over this place." Zin's voice came from his side. "Death and rotting meat. Can we get out of here, please?" Ean nodded, not caring whether Zin could see him or not. This had been a bad idea. Ean was about to turn back around, when he caught a bit of movement coming from one of the windows of the foreman's home. Ean paused, wondering if it had just been a trick of the light, but sure enough, after a few moments, he saw it again.

"I think something is in the foreman's home. Let's go check it out."

"You must be crazy!" Zin's words were still a whisper, but just barely. "For all you know, it could be the beast."

"Not a chance," Ean replied. "No way could the creature Allie saw fit into that house without creating some kind of damage to it, and the house looks fine from here. It could be the foreman in there. Allie said she had seen him run off."

Slinking down low, Ean made his way around the edge of the bog to where the mountains rose off into the haze above him and then walked along them towards the house. He couldn't tell if Zin followed along, which made him more nervous than he already was. Although Zin couldn't do much if it came down to a fight for their lives, it was still more reassuring to have the imp there than to be alone.

Moving towards the building seemed to take forever as he inched along the mountainside, before he reached the side of the house. He paused there, trying to calm himself so that he could hear more than his own heartbeat and breathing. The area still smelled of blood and something worse. Ean was starting to get the faint hint of rotting meat in the air now as well.

"I smell something else now..." Ean almost jumped out of his skin at the sound of the imp's voice. Zin had followed after all. "Smells reptilian, but doesn't have even the hint of the Abyss on it. Whatever it is, I've never encountered it before."

Ean couldn't decide whether that made him feel better or worse. Well, he had made it this far. Peeking around the side of the house, he still didn't see anything moving about, and he didn't have a clear view of the front windows now either. Staying low, he moved along the wall, pausing every couple of steps to make sure nothing else was moving about. Once he made it to the door, he pressed down on the latch. The door opened without a sound. Ean held his runed hand in front of his body, providing a little illumination to the inside of the building. The single room of the foreman's building was filled with various tables, chairs and cabinets. Serving as both the organizing point and the dining hall, the room was a mess; plates and wooden cups on some of the tables, maps of the mine and reports on others. Ean didn't see any sign of life.

"Hello?" he whispered. "Is anyone in here?"

A small scraping noise came from behind the door of one of the cabinets. A moment later, the door opened a crack and part of the foreman's face could be seen peering back. From what Ean could see, the foreman looked haggard, the blue light mixing with his pale face to make him look almost like a ghost, and his eyes were darting around as if he expected the creature to jump out at any moment.

"Is it gone?" The man's voice was gruff, but it wobbled, exposing his fear.

"I'm not sure," Ean replied. "But it's not outside at the moment."

That seemed to be enough for the foreman, who opened the door the rest of the way, climbed out of the cabinet and moved over to Ean's side. The foreman stopped a moment to stare at the light coming off of Ean's hand but said nothing. So much for keeping his new talent a secret from the village.

Moving with careful steps, the two exited the house with Ean in the lead. Moving back along the wall the way he had come, Ean led the frightened man back in the direction of the bog. Once they reached the edge of the house, Ean turned to look at the man, then pointed to the bog and made a circling motion with his finger. The foreman nodded, a small bit of color returning to his face. Returning the nod, Ean was just about to step out away from the house when Zin's voice cut through the silence.

"Look out!"

It was pure instinct that made Ean listen and dive down to the side as a huge blur swiped the air where his face had been moments before. The blur connected with the building, creating a loud crunching sound as what Ean now saw was a huge claw smashed into the wooden wall. Rolling to his feet, the light from Ean's hand gave him a good view of what had almost been his end.

The creature was much worse in person than how Allie had described it. A little more than three persons tall with a reptilian head and tail, the creature hissed at him, its tongue poking out between its pointed teeth. Its body was covered in what Ean first thought was dead skin, but realized it was some kind of leather armor. As the two locked eyes, the creature seemed to speak, its mouth moving in a series of hisses as the sounds came from between those horrible teeth. Then it started to move in his direction, its eyes still locked on him, but squinting against the light coming off of Ean's hand. Not knowing what else to do, Ean did the only thing he could. He drew a rune.

His hand moved with a life of its own, his index finger leaving a bright blue light wherever it cut through the air. The beast slowed as Ean's rune grew in brightness, raising a giant clawed hand to shield its eyes. Meanwhile, Ean was working on instinct, not even thinking about the rune he was drawing, working purely from memory of something he had done the night before. When the rune was finished, it hung there in the air, its light exposing everything in the immediate area: Ean, the beast, even the poor foreman, who was still huddled against the side of the house. Then it vanished, returning the area to darkness that was only broken up by the dim glow from Ean's hand. The beast stared at him for a moment, then let out a horrible hissing laugh and continued forward again.

Ean stood there frozen, the fear overtaking him. Were these his last moments? The beast had moved close enough now that Ean was within reach of its giant clawed hands. With another hiss, it reached for him with those terrible claws reeking of blood. Too scared to run, all Ean could do was cover his head as he waited for the blow that would end his life.

Without warning, an explosion of bright blue light appeared from where Ean's rune had been, like a flash of lightning but a hundred times brighter. The creature reared back, making an agonized noise as both of its hands shot up to cover its eyes. Ean, on the other hand, was not affected, although he stood there in shock. Only for the briefest moment, though. A tiny weight smashed into his side and got him moving.

"Run, you giant idiot!" Zin's voice broke him out of his daze. Ean took off, heading straight back for the bog. Once he reached it, he sped around the edge, ready to cut into it at even the slightest hint of pursuit. He didn't have to worry about that, though.

Just moments into his run, Ean heard a blood-curdling scream from behind him. The beast had found the foreman.

"Better him than us," he heard Zin say from somewhere behind them. Ean was happy to be alive, but did not feel good about leaving the foreman behind.

He kept running, not slowing down or looking back. When he reached the path back to his home, he kept on running. Ean made it all the way back to his house without stopping, surprised at his endurance. He had never even been able to jog from the bog home before, and tonight he had full out sprinted the entire way. Was it the fear that had given him the extra strength, or something else? The glow of the runes on his hand made him think it was the latter.

Ean entered the house, moving through the kitchen, careful not to make too much noise, and then up the stairway and into his room. He noticed Cleff's room was dark as he passed, meaning he was already asleep or was sleeping downstairs, keeping watch over Lane. Either way, Ean hoped that Cleff hadn't noticed his late-night departure.

Once inside his room, Ean changed out of his clothes and into something suitable for sleep. He kept a glove on his right hand to block the light, hoping to get a good night's sleep for a change. Although after tonight, he doubted that was possible. A vision of the creature and the sound of the foreman's scream echoed in his head. But he had survived. Climbing into bed, he heard Zin crawl underneath, bumping the bottom of the bed once or twice.

"Quite the adventure, huh?" Ean whispered, trying to calm himself down.

The room was silent for a long time before Zin responded.

"You're still an idiot. Let's not ever do something that insane again."

"Agreed." But deep down, a part of Ean had enjoyed the thrill and the danger. In his mind, tonight had just cemented the fact that he needed to get out of this village and see what else was out there in the world.

Luckily for him, although he wouldn't see it as lucky at first, his opportunity to leave would come very soon.

CHAPTER 3

A HERO VISITS

LANE NEVER WOKE UP from his wounds and died the next morning with Allie and Cleff by his side. At dusk, the entire village gathered around a funeral pyre in the valley. The Mayor gave a speech first, praising Lane as a standup member of the village. He spoke about his own memories of Lane and Allie together, as well as recounting stories of the two provided by others in the community. Allie stood off to the side, surrounded by both her and Lane's parents. She smiled occasionally at the tales, but the smiles were short-lived as she often broke down into sobs that shook her entire body. Her family stayed by her side, ready to place a reassuring hand on her shoulder or hold her up when the anguish made her legs weak.

Listening from the back of the crowd, Ean became swept up in the stories of their lives. He hadn't known the two well; he didn't really know anyone in their small community very well, but for the first time, a small sliver of regret at that fact began to form. Here were two people, clearly in love, that had worn their hearts on their sleeves for all to see. And Ean had missed it. The regret grew to a knot in his stomach. How would he find what Allie and Lane had if he kept himself separate from everyone around him. Isn't what they had exactly what I want? To have someone understand me completely and still want to be by my side? The regret spread to his chest, seeping into his soul. As the Mayor finally finished his speech and grew quiet, Ean realized that maybe all of the walls he had created to protect himself were starting to isolate him from everyone else. The thought weighed heavily on him as the next part of the funeral began.

A few more people were given the chance to speak after the Mayor, just a few of Lane's closest friends and family, and then the fire was lit. With the sun almost set, the light of the flames covered the crowd in a warm orange glow. Complete silence fell over the crowd as many members of their small community knelt and offered up their silent prayers. Most would be offering their prayers up to Kaz'ren, goddess of the Soul and Afterlife, but it wasn't uncommon for anyone to pray to their patron god/goddess as well. Ean wouldn't have been surprised if each of the six gods/goddesses received at least one prayer that day. None of them would receive a prayer from him, though.

It wasn't that he didn't believe in them. With his connection to the Abyss, a place created by the god, Ze'an, he would be a fool to believe that the others did not exist. No, Ean wouldn't be praying to the gods, BECAUSE they exist. They exist, and do nothing. How often did prayers to the deities go unheard when the fields produced little food? Or when a child died of a sickness that not even the Rottwealth plants could heal? Or when someone's parents drank too much and ended up almost ruining an entire village? Ean didn't bother praying to the gods and goddess, because in his mind, they didn't bother to listen.

Five members of the village guard wouldn't be giving their prayers either. This very morning, the monster had snatched up a few of the sheep that grazed in the southeast fields, terrifying the two villagers that had been tending them. The description they gave of the monster matched the one Allie had given, making the Mayor finally agree that it was more than a bear that had taken up residence in their valley. The members of the village's guard were absent, having been placed by the Mayor in a position to the south to keep an eye out for the creature. None of the guards had gotten close enough to try looking in the mine or foreman's cabin, but the complete lack of any remaining bodies told its own tale. The foreman certainly wouldn't be receiving the same funeral rites as Lane. As a precaution, the Mayor had declared the entire southern section of their valley off limits, which included the bog. That didn't exactly sit well with Cleff. Most of the plants they used came from the bog.

When the fire started to die down, the villagers got up and started talking amongst themselves. It was a somber affair, with all of those gathered moving about and talking in small groups to those with whom they were closest. Allie stayed close to the fire, talking to anyone that came over briefly but spent most of her time staring into the flames alone. Ean was alone as well, standing in between various groups of people, not sure what to do. No one was going to come up to speak to him, after all. He could sneak away and get home, maybe spend some time with the Abysmal Tome or just get to bed early, so he would be nice and rested for a change. Even with the bog closed, Cleff was sure to have a variety of chores planned out for him.

Letting out a silent sigh, Ean began to walk in Allie's direction. She had shown him that small bit of compassion, something that he certainly wasn't used to other than from Jaslen and Bran. She more than deserved to receive his condolences. Of course, he received dirty looks from other members of the village as he approached her but he ignored them. Let them think what they wanted.

"I'm sorry about your husband," he said as he reached her. Allie had her back to him, her full attention on the fire. She didn't respond at first, and Ean was about to turn and leave when she spun around and immediately embraced him.

"Thank you, Ean. Thank you for trying your best to save him."

Ean felt the blood rush into his cheeks. "Yes, of course. I mean, Cleff did most of the work. I was just there to help."

"I still appreciate it." She squeezed him once then pulled away. They both stood there for a few moments in silence until another villager walked over. The man shot Ean a dark look before stepping in between him and Allie. The man probably thought he was saving her from Ean. That was fine. Ean knew the truth.

Turning his back on Allie and the diminishing flame of the funeral pyre, Ean headed home.

EIGHT DAYS AFTER THE funeral, word reached the Healer's home that a man calling himself "Hero" had arrived in the village. The appearance of anyone from outside of their valley was a rare thing in Rottwealth, and so the whole town was abuzz with excitement. Ean heard that the Hero had arrived in the middle of the night and took up lodging in the Mayor's inn. Ean had wanted to go see this new visitor right away, but of course, Cleff had him performing various chores around the house that took up most of the day.

The old man had been difficult to deal with since the bog had been declared off-limits, his main source of income from the various healing items he could make from the Rottwealth plant and others found there being cut-off. Of course, this meant that Ean took the brunt of the man's frustration, which in turn meant he was put to work both in menial tasks around the house and had to spend more time studying the intricacies of being a Healer. The studying he didn't really mind, but there were only so many times you could wash the same set of empty jars.

The sun was already high in the sky by the time Ean was finally set free. Zin had already left earlier in the day. Most days the imp lazed about in Ean's room or wandered around the village looking for a stray rat to eat, leaving Ean alone for most of the day. When Ean was finally finished with his chores, he left his home and followed the village's gravel road north past the small amount of open space to where the edge of the village actually began. A collection of a few dozen small wooden homes, Rottwealth village would probably be considered quaint by outsiders. The main gravel road ran north from Cleff's home and casually curved east as it divided the village in half. Cleff's two-story home and shop, as well as the inn owned by the Mayor, were the only distinguishable buildings in the village; the rest of the homes looked relatively the same, lining both sides of the street. There were two or three rows of homes on each side, one row behind the other, with the last row on either side almost completely surrounded by farmland. Ean moved down the street as fast as he could, passing the open field of the town square on the right as the road curved and finally reached the end of the village where the inn resided on the left.

The inn, named The Golden Coin by the Mayor's grandfather, was a large two-story building made of simple stone and wooden planks and painted a light yellow. Two small steps at the entrance led up onto a porch where many of the villagers could often be found, enjoying both a drink and a cool breeze that blew down out of the mountains. The inn was the first building a traveler would see following the road into the village, if the village received visitors. Its large sign depicting a few coins spilling out of a mug was hard to miss.

As Ean approached the large building, he could hear the sounds of merriment coming from inside. The actual appearance of a visitor was such a rarity that it wouldn't be surprising if many of the villagers had put off work for the day so that they could take a look at a new face. Hopping up the steps, Ean crossed the porch and pushed his way through the swinging doors that led inside.

On the inside, the main entrance opened into the tavern where the Mayor's wife was most often behind the bar along the far wall.

From her central position, she served drinks, directed the servers to the various tables that littered the room, and directed Togh, the inn guard, to remove anyone attempting to catch a nap at a table or cause trouble. A stairwell sat in the back near the bar, leading up to rooms that were never used. Three doorways led out of the main hall: one going back into the kitchen, another leading into where the Mayor and his family lived, and the last being the doorway leading out to the back where patrons could relieve themselves.

Just as Ean expected, the tavern section of the inn was overflowing with people. All of the circular tables were full, as were the seats at the bar, with the majority of people crowded around one particular table. Having the advantage of being thin and lanky, Ean moved in and out of the crowd until he was almost right next to the table where he assumed this Hero was sitting. What he found there was certainly not what he expected.

The "Hero" was a large fellow, although not in a muscular sort of way. His size seemed to strain both the chair he was lounging on as well as the one on which his feet were resting. He had short stubby hair, a large nose, and a beard that contained flecks of food and was soaked with ale. His leather armor barely seemed to fit his body, as pieces of fatty skin seemed to poke out at every opening, and his round stomach extended past the bottom. He wore two short swords on either side of his waist and a sheathed knife across his chest. All in all, he looked more like a common thug, a grown up version of Krane, except for a strange sparkling green stone on a necklace that hung around his blubbery neck.

The Hero's name was Lathan Riley. By the time Ean was able to maneuver close enough to hear what was being said, the man was in the middle of a story about how he had faced down five bandits by himself in order to protect a caravan of helpless women. As Ean listened half-heartedly to what he believed to be a vast exaggeration of what probably actually happened, he looked around at the other villagers.

Every face of those gathered around was clearly caught up in the story; their eyes locked on the man, expressions turning to awe as he described the battle and his victory over the bandits, with both the men and women chuckling as he went into detail about how the women of the caravan rewarded him for his efforts. The only expression on Ean's face was disbelief. All of these people that he had known the majority of his life were looking at this stranger as if he was some kind of king!

"Caught up in the story, too?" said a female voice that Ean instantly recognized as belonging to Jaslen. "It is quite exciting to have an actual Hero here, isn't it?"

"Uh," Ean's tongue froze whenever Jaslen was around. The way her bright red curls fell about her shoulders, in contrast with her forest green eyes, stunned his senses. Come on, Ean. She is one of the few people in this town that's always been nice to you. Don't act like an idiot. Heat rose to his cheeks as he pulled himself together. "I...he...the Hero doesn't seem all that impressive to me, Jaslen."

Realizing he had stopped talking and was just staring at her, he blushed. "I mean, uh... he barely fits into his armor," he said, trying to recover. "How is he going to fight something as horrible as the beast looking like that?"

Jaslen laughed in response, the sound happy and full of life. "Oh, Ean, you always look at the negative side of things. So what if he doesn't look like the way a warrior is expected to look? I, for one, don't care if he eats the mayor out of house and home as long as he can get rid of the beast. My poor father has been a wreck worrying about his crop. You know our plot is in the area the Mayor has said is off limits. If the Hero kills the beast and Father can get back to work, hopefully there won't be too much damage to our first harvest this year."

"Well, of course, that would be great. I wouldn't want your father to lose the harvest. Maybe I am wrong and this Hero is more than he seems."

"I hope so," she replied, turning her attention back to the Hero's story. "Bran has been talking about trying to take the beast down himself." Ean wasn't surprised; any conversation with Jaslen eventually turned into one about Bran. "From the story I've heard from poor Allie, I don't think Bran would have a chance to survive against that creature. A shame, her losing her husband that way." She shuddered, wrapping her arms around her body. "I couldn't imagine what I would do if I lost Bran."

"I'm sure Bran would be fine. After all, if I was able to escape the creature, then I'm sure someone as wonderful as Bran could as well." Ean had meant the comment to be a backhanded insult towards Bran, but his mouth snapped shut after he realized what he had actually said.

"Ean, stop making up stories," Jaslen said, giving a little laugh afterwards. "You know you don't need to act all tough around me." She looked at him for a moment then her eyes opened wide. "You didn't really see it, did you?"

Now Ean was stuck. He could lie and say she was right and that he hadn't seen it. If she believed him, then she would go back to thinking of him as her weak little friend. Or he could tell her the truth, well, most of the truth and possibly impress her. Unless she didn't believe him and then would just pity him more for feeling, in her opinion, the need to lie. Either way, he could possibly make things worse. After a moment of thought, his heart won out.

"I did, the very same night that Lane was attacked." Pausing to look around the crowded room, he gently took a hold of her arm. "I don't want to talk about it here in front of other people. Can we go outside? I promise to tell you what I saw."

She nodded, her wide eyes and slight grin showing her excitement. Ean led her back through the crowds and outside of the inn. They moved across the main street, finally stopping in one of the alleys between a few homes. From their spot, the roar of the crowd in the inn could barely be heard.

"All right, we're alone." Jaslen said, pulling her arm away from Ean. "Now tell me everything! And I swear, Ean, if you are just making this up, I am going to be furious at you!" She placed her hands on her hips and was looking at Ean as if she already expected him to lie.

Ean took a quick look around, more for dramatic effect than actually thinking anyone would be close enough to hear. Then he told her what had happened that night, leaving out the parts about Zin and his magic. Jaslen listened until the story was finished then shook her head. "I don't know, that sounds a little hard to believe. Plus, how you described the creature was different than how Allie described it."

"She was frightened at the time," Ean said defensively. "Plus, she was a good distance away from it. I actually got up close to it, well…" Stuttering a bit, he ran a hand through his dark hair. "It got up close to me, but either way, I was still close."

Jaslen shook her head at him. "I don't know, it's still hard to believe that this thing could kill a few of the other villagers and swipe up some sheep so easily, but you were able to get away…" She frowned as she trailed off, and Ean's heart sank. He had to do something to prove to her that he was telling the truth, but what?

"I'll take you to see it! When the Hero goes to fight it!"

Ean immediately regretted the words as soon as they left his mouth. What was he saying?! He should have stopped there and just accepted that she wasn't going to believe him. Accept the increase in pitying looks she sometimes gave him. It's not like he had a chance with her anyway; she was head over heels for Bran. Ean should just let this go… but he couldn't.

"When the Hero goes, I can sneak the two of us around the edge of the bog so we can get a good view. No one will know that we're there, and if things go bad, we can easily escape through the bog. Then you could see for yourself that I was telling the truth." The last few words left his mouth in a rush. When it was done, he just watched her, hoping for any kind of positive reaction.

She continued to frown, then turned and started pacing in front of him. "We could get in a lot of trouble, Ean. Whether or not you're telling the truth, if we get caught out there, we'll be in a cart full of trouble." She continued pacing, seeming to be talking more to herself than to him. "Plus, if you haven't been telling the truth, then who knows if we would be able to safely get away if the Hero were to fall to the beast."

"I am telling the truth, Jaslen!" Ean blurted out. "Please let me prove it to..."

His plea was interrupted by a laugh he quickly recognized. It filled him both with a mixture of anger and dread all at the same time. Turning around, he found Krane leaning against the corner of one of the buildings, laughing at him.

"You, Ean? Tell the truth? What a fantastic joke." Krane continued to laugh, although the humor was not reflected in his squinting eyes. "You never tell the truth. You're just trying to impress my brother's girl, but even she sees right through your lies." Pushing himself off the wall, Krane approached them.

"Knock it off, Krane," Jaslen growled, stepping between Ean and the other boy. "I won't let you go around bullying whoever you wish. Especially someone much weaker than you." That caused Ean's shoulders to slump in disappointment. Did Jaslen really think he was weak? Ean had to do something to prove he wasn't a weakling, even if it ended in another beating. Stepping around Jaslen, he glared at Krane while clenching both of his hands into fists.

"I'm not scared of Krane, Jaslen." Ean said, slightly turning his head to see her, but keeping one eye on Krane. "He's not so tough without his friends to back him up and without a weapon. He's just a giant windbag."

"I'd watch what you say, rodent," Krane said between clenched teeth. "I wouldn't mind spending a few more days in the stocks if it meant I got to break some more of your bones."

"You can go ahead and try, you fat piece of..." he stopped as Jaslen placed a hand on his arm and yanked him backwards.

"Enough of this!" she yelled, looking back and forth between the two boys. "I expected this kind of tough-guy attitude from Krane, but don't you start as well, Ean." She turned completely now to face Ean, looking him straight in the eyes. Oh, how Ean could get lost in those eyes. "Don't sink to his level; you're better than that."

Ean looked at her for a time then looked away and nodded. "I guess you're right, I..."

A sudden blow to his stomach doubled Ean over and forced him to his knees.

Jaslen, who still had a hold of his arm, sank with him as Krane pulled his back from Ean's gut. Once Jaslen regained her balance, she turned on Krane from her kneeling position. "You're nothing but an animal. I'm going to let Bran know what you did then we'll see how tough you are."

Krane grunted then gave the girl a smirk. "You're not going to tell him anything. I promise if he hears one word of this, I'll make sure that little Ean is recovering in bed for an entire season next time I get a hold of him. So you just keep your little mouth shut."

"Hear one word of what?" a new voice said, one that made Ean cringe. Just perfect, this is all I need. Turning his head slowly, his stomach still burning and his breath struggling to return, he saw the town's golden boy.

Bran was what you would expect a real Hero to look like. Tall, lean and muscular, Bran was considered handsome by most, with every feature of his face, from his short and shaggy brown hair to his chiseled chin, considered perfect by all of the girls in the village.

A few years older than Ean, Bran had been training to be an expert with a blade since he was a young boy. He spent hours every day practicing with the sword he had received before his age was in double digits, making him more than proficient as well as keeping him in great shape. A few years ago, he had even been appointed as one of the protectors of the village. Unlike his brother, he wore a simple white shirt, opened in the front, and gray pants. His sword swung in its scabbard from its usual place on his belt.

To say that Ean was jealous of the older boy would be an understatement. An excellent fighter, beloved by the village and adored by Jaslen, Bran had everything that Ean wanted and more. The worst part about it was that Ean couldn't even despise him. Bran was a model of virtue, always doing what was right and standing up for the weak. Of course, that mostly meant standing up for Ean. Other than the last time, Bran often was there in time to keep Krane and his underlings from doing Ean much harm. Bran had even gone so far as to try and befriend Ean, but that simply couldn't happen. As much as Ean wanted to have people he could trust and talk to, he just couldn't see himself in the constant presence of someone that reminded him of all of the things he was not. Also, it was difficult to watch how close he and Jaslen were growing every day.

Bran walked with a casual stride into the alley, his eyes moving between Jaslen and Krane, completely overlooking Ean for the moment. Stopping at Jaslen's side, he gently placed a hand on her back, and then leaned down to give her a kiss on the cheek. Ean knelt there, feeling like he had been punched again. Standing back up, Bran regarded his younger brother.

"I've had it with you bullying the weaker boys of this village." Ean cringed. If one more person called him weak, he would explode. Staring down his brother, Bran continued on. "From now on, every time I hear about you hurting someone else, I'm going to give you an even worse beating."

Sneering, Krane laughed in response. "You wouldn't dare. Father wouldn't allow..." Faster than Ean would have expected, Bran moved right up in Krane's face, grabbing his shirt roughly with his left hand and holding his right fist in front of the now terrified boy's face.

"Father won't do a thing, and you know it." Bran's face was red now with anger, a sight that Ean had never witnessed before. Apparently, Jaslen hadn't either as she was looking at Bran with a look of both awe and adoration. Ean's heart sunk even further.

"Now," Bran continued. "Have I made myself clear?"

Krane glanced at Ean with hate-filled eyes, but then turned back to his brother. "Yes, fine, fine, I understand. Now let me go." Seemingly satisfied, Bran gave his brother a not-so-gentle shove away from himself. The two brothers stared each other for a moment longer then Krane took off down another alley. Turning back around, Bran faced Ean and gave him a half-hearted smile.

"Hopefully that will settle things between you and my brother now, Ean. If he gives you any more trouble, you just let me know. Here, let me help you both up." Extending both of his hands in their direction, Bran moved over to their side.

Jaslen took his hand immediately, while Ean moved a bit more reluctantly. "I could have handled that myself, you know," Ean said as Bran pulled him to his feet, "I'm not as weak as everyone seems to think I am."

Bran frowned a bit at the response, but Jaslen simply laughed. "Oh, it's true Bran. Ean is quite strong. Apparently, he fought with the beast and survived!" On her feet now, she wrapped an arm around Bran's waist.

At her comment, one of Bran's eyebrows raised, and he regarded Ean skeptically. "That sounds a little hard to believe. Have you been telling my girl stories, Ean?"

Brushing himself off, Ean shook his head. "I never said I fought the beast. All I said was that I had seen it up close and had been able to get away. Jaslen is the one that is over-exaggerating what really happened."

"Perhaps," Jaslen responded, a faint smile still on her lips. "But Ean did say he could get us close enough to watch the Hero fight the beast. Isn't that right, Ean?"

Ean simply looked at her and scowled. He had said that the TWO of them could get close enough to watch. Ean hadn't meant for it to be an opportunity for Bran and Jaslen to spend even more time together while he became the odd man out. They both were staring at Ean now, which made him realize he had no way out of it now.

With a sigh, he finally nodded. "Yes, I can get us close if we cut around the bog. Like I told Jaslen, if anything goes wrong, we can escape into the bog. I know the more solid areas, and a creature as large as the beast would have a hard time following."

"Excellent! The Hero is set to go after the monster right after my father serves him dinner, so we can sneak down there now and find a good spot." Bran was grinning as he spoke, his left hand moving involuntarily to the pommel of his sword. "Maybe I could even go and help if the Hero needs it!"

"NO!" Ean and Jaslen yelled out in unison. They both looked at each other for a moment, and then Ean took the lead. "If we're going to do this, you can only watch, I don't want you running in and bringing the beast down on all of us." Shooting another glance at Jaslen, he continued on. "Plus, you really wouldn't want to put her in any extra danger, would you?"

Bran's frown and downturned eyes made it clear that Ean had hit a nerve. "You're right, of course," Bran said, running a hand through his hair, "I wasn't really thinking. Best to just watch, and see what happens. At the very least, I'll get to see how a Hero from outside the village handles a blade and how dangerous the creature really is."

Both Ean and Jaslen nodded, this time Jaslen being the first to speak. "That is a very wise decision, I think. If the creature is strong enough to kill this Hero, then I don't feel that you would be able to aid him anyway." She nodded matter-of-factly, then pulled him closer and placed a kiss on his cheek. Ean cringed. "Someday though, you could be one of these Heroes, and creatures like the one terrorizing our village will all run in fear."

The two stood there, staring longingly into each other's eyes, while Ean stood forgotten next to them. Ean stomached the situation as long as he could, then let out a loud cough. "We should probably get going if we want to see the fight. If we get caught up in the crowd as the Hero leaves, we'll never be able to sneak past everyone and get to the bog." The other two nodded, but made no sign of moving. With a grunt, Ean turned around and started walking without them.

"I'm not waiting for you!" he yelled over his shoulder as he marched back out onto the main street. Eventually the two caught up to him, and they walked back towards Ean's house and the bog in silence.

CHAPTER 4

UNWANTED ATTENTION

BY THE TIME JASLEN, Bran and Ean had made it to the edge of the bog, the sun touched the tips of the mountains to the west. They continued on in silence until they reached an area within view of the stone mine. Ean raised his hand to signal them to stop and then crouched down behind a large patch of reeds. The other two followed suit, and they all huddled together.

"Alright, this should be a good spot," Ean whispered. "We're close enough to be able to see what's happening, and far enough away to be able to escape through the bog if the creature manages to see us."

"Can't we get a little closer?" Bran said, an eager look in his eyes as he scanned the area in front of the mine. "If the thing is as big as you say, it's not going to be able to sneak up on us." His one hand had drifted to his sword again, and he looked like a man ready to attack, not flee. Ean turned to Jaslen with a silent plea for help. Their eyes met in mutual understanding.

"Please, I'm not as fast of a runner as you and Ean," she said, placing a gentle hand on his shoulder. "And think of the Hero. If the creature sees us, there goes his chance to take it by surprise, making his job all the more difficult, not to mention dangerous."

Clever girl, Ean thought. For someone so head-over-heels over Bran, Jaslen had a good idea of how to steer him in the right direction.

"You're right, as always." Bran flashed her a warm smile, and the two seemed to get lost in each other's eyes. Ean felt the sudden urge to dunk both of their heads into the bog. As much as he adored Jaslen, Ean knew his chances with her were not existent as long as Bran was around. And the two were around each other all the time. Pushing his own frustration down deep inside, Ean turned his attention back to the mine.

By the time the hero came into view, the sun was half hidden by the mountains with long shadows starting to stretch across the valley. A strong wind had started to blow down out of the mountains as well, which sucked the warmth right out of the area. The three observers huddled by the end of the bog, watching the Hero as he approached the entrance to the mine with large confident strides. He had both swords drawn, twirling one in each hand as he approached the entrance. He stopped a few short paces from the mine and yelled into the entrance, but the howl of the wind drowned out his words.

But not even the wind could drown out the creature's reply; a roar that echoed from deep in the mine shook the earth.

"By the gods," exclaimed Bran, "what was that?" His hand moved down to the pommel of his sword. A quick glance at Jaslen found that her expression mirrored Bran's words. Her mouth hung wide open, and she clung to Bran's left arm with an iron grip. The older boy looked like a man ready to charge.

Ean placed a restraining hand on Bran's sword arm, shaking his head. "Don't even think about it." He held tight until Bran's arm relaxed and fell to his side. One crisis avoided, Ean turned his attention back to the mine.

The Hero had moved back a bit, realizing that killing this beast wasn't going to be an easy feat. He stood there, face locked in the direction of the mine, the wind blowing the grass at his feet. Another roar came from inside the mine. The three of them flinched. It was much closer this time. Ean almost jumped out of his skin when Jaslen grabbed his hand as well. It was a shock at first then gave him courage as he squeezed her hand back. And then the beast emerged.

In the fading sunlight, the creature seemed larger and more terrifying than it had before. Ean's first instinct was to run, but the pressure of Jaslen's hand on his own rooted him to his spot.

Twice the Hero's height, the beast seemed to hold itself up in a more human fashion than Ean remembered. It was also wearing some kind of armor that seemed patched together, with the rest of its exposed body covered in red scales that shimmered and reflected the sunlight.

It moved toward the Hero with slow and deliberate steps, its tail swaying hypnotically like a huge snake. Even though it was nowhere near the Hero yet, it reached out towards him as if it could snatch him up even from far away. The Hero was back peddling with slow, measured movements, but still appeared confident as he returned to swirling the swords in his hands. He moved with the grace of a dancer at the Harvest Festival, which Ean hadn't expected from the robust man. The Hero might have a chance if he could out-maneuver the beast.

The beast lunged for the Hero. The distance between them closed in an instant, its giant right claw sweeping towards the Hero's armored body. The claw passed over the Hero's head as he ducked and rolled to his right. Ean had underestimated the overweight man's ability. A spark of hope flared up deep inside of Ean's chest, and he found himself rooting for the man.

Coming out of his roll and springing to his feet, the Hero slashed the creature with both of his swords in a cross pattern. The blades glanced along the scales of the creature's left leg with a grating sound but didn't seem to cause any damage. The beast didn't even flinch. It swung its entire body to the right. Its tail aimed at the

Hero's chest. This time the Hero dodged just in time and leapt away.

"The creature is fast for its size," Bran said in a whisper, his eyes locked on the fight. "But the Hero seems to be handling himself well."

Ean turned and glared at him. "Quiet. Just watch and be ready to run." He kept his gaze on him until Bran nodded again then turned his attention back to the battle.

Instead of waiting to dodge whatever the creature threw at him, the Hero had taken up the tactic of staying on the move. He rolled and dodged when the creature was facing him. Darted in whenever he could to slash or stab at the large beast. Then retreated and watched for another opening. Unfortunately, none of his attacks seemed to be doing any damage to the creature. By the time the sun was just a slash of light peaking over the mountains, the Hero had returned to the defensive. Even from a distance, Ean could see the large man breathing heavily, his breath creating a mist in the cool dusk air. Turning to his companions, Ean nodded his head back the way they had come. "I think it might be a good idea to get out of here. It doesn't look like our Hero is going to last much longer."

Bran ignored Ean and took a step towards the fight.

"What are you doing?!" Ean whispered, rising as well. "You see how the Hero has failed to even hurt the beast. You can't possibly think that you can do better than him or that your blade would have any better luck." He grabbed a hold of Bran's arm and tried to pull him back. Instead, Ean found himself pulled along as Bran took a few steps away from the bog.

"You're right. It's clear I would have no chance against the beast." Despite his words, Bran continued forward, dragging Ean behind him. "But maybe I can do something to distract it so that the Hero can get away." Stopping suddenly, he turned his head to look Ean square in the eyes. "It's the right thing to do, Ean. We can't just stand here and watch the man die."

"Oh, I have no plan of watching the man die." Ean let go of the larger boy's arm. "I plan on getting out of here before he becomes dinner and we become desert." The look Bran shot him was all Ean needed to understand what the boy was feeling. Taking a step back towards the group, Bran poked an accusatory finger into Ean's face.

"I cannot in good conscience walk away and let the man die." Bran's voice was rising now as his convictions overrode his common sense. "When even the smallest possibility exists that I could have done something to help him."

Ean knew Bran to be an honorable guy, but he didn't know that he held his ideals higher than his own life. Ean hoped Jaslen could talk some sense into her boyfriend, but the look of horror on her face made him follow her gaze back to the right. The Hero was pinned to the ground by a giant clawed foot planted on his chest.

The poor man was squirming beneath the beast, his arms and legs flailing about, both of his swords out of reach. The creature was looking at him like a dog slobbering over a bone, its tongue darting in and out between its teeth.

"We have to do something," Bran said, then started back towards the beast.

Ean watched him take two steps, looked at the Hero still pinned to the ground, then let out a frustrated growl. "Fine, fine. Let's all get killed saving a stranger. I hope it eats you first." Ean hoped the anger in the voice masked his terror as he stomped off after Bran.

They hadn't even cleared the bog when Jaslen's terrified pleas froze them both.

"Please don't leave me," she said, her voice low and strained. "Don't leave me alone."

Bran looked back, his face conflicted. Ean felt conflicted as well, although he doubted it was for the same reasons. Part of him wanted to continue on and try to be the hero in front of Jaslen and Bran. The other part wanted to run screaming back into the safety of the bog.

A growl from the beast made them all turn their attention back to the area in front of the mine. The creature had reached down and plucked the Hero off the ground with one large clawed hand. The man looked like a doll in the hands of an adult. Still showing signs of life, the Hero beat at the creature's hand with both fists, but his fate was already sealed. He let out one spine-shivering scream. Then the creature opened his mouth wide and bit down, its mouth covering half of the large man. When the creature pulled its head back, the hero's top half was gone. Along with the chance for Bran and Ean to do something to help.

As the creature chewed on the upper portion of the Hero, Jaslen made a retching noise as she lost her last meal. Despite their horror, Ean and Bran stared as the monster continued its meal. It chewed on what was left, pieces of bone and flesh hanging from its maw.

Bran began mouthing something, probably a prayer, although he kept his eyes locked on the carnage.

Ean only pulled his gaze away when a tug on his pant leg got his attention. Glancing down, he saw the telltale shimmer of his invisible imp. Ean turned to Bran, grabbing his arm.

"We really need to get out of here."

As Jaslen finished getting sick, Bran reached down and picked her up in his arms. She buried her cheek in his shoulder and quietly sobbed.

Ean watched them walk off for a moment before turning his attention back to the beast. The sun had taken refuge behind the mountain, as if it couldn't bear to watch what was happening to the deceased Hero. All that was left of the day was a sick yellow glow over the horizon. Zin gave his pant leg another tug, but Ean remained transfixed by the sight of the creature feasting on the Hero's torso. The sounds of bones breaking made him cringe, but he refused to look away. He wasn't sure why, but he felt that it was important that he stayed until the end. Important that he watched what horrors this world could hold.

A SECOND HERO ARRIVED at their village a few days later. Another self-proclaimed master swordsman, this one was much more impressive. He wore leather armor engraved with the outlines of a variety of different creatures, all of which he claimed to have killed. Unlike the previous Hero, he carried a single long sword, its hilt inlaid with jewels and the hand-guard carved with intricate designs on its surface. He had wide shoulders and a trim waistline. At the inn, Hero number-two leapt from tabletop to tabletop without losing his balance, showing off his athleticism for the delighted crowd. What an arrogant buffoon, thought Ean, but he had to admit that the physically fit second Hero showed more promise than the first one had.

And at the bog he lasted twice as long before the creature made a snack of him. Ean watched the whole battle from the same spot, this time without Bran and Jaslen. He hadn't seen the two since the night they had watched the first Hero die. He had to admit it hurt, and he felt abandoned, but he was used to them only making brief appearances in his life.

The third Hero arrived about twelve days after the beast made a home in the mines. He came into town on the wagons of an unknown trader, which in itself was something special. For the added visitor, the villagers set up their stalls in the town square like it was the Harvest Festival, hoping to sell the little crafts they made in their spare time. The few families that had produced a good harvest brought out a variety of different meals to serve to the trader. All of the meals were made of different types of beans, since it was one of the few edible plants that grew in the valley, but the villagers had learned enough over the years to spice them up in different ways to make them interesting.

The Hero appeared to have magical abilities of his own, thus also considered a Magus. After the wagons had settled in around the village square, he leapt out of the back, throwing sparks of different colored energy into the air. Then, in a shower of red lights, he was gone, appearing again on the other side of the square as more sparks flew from his fingertips. The crowd that had gathered around by that point cheered and followed along after the Hero as he bowed once and sauntered his way back towards the inn.

While the villagers laughed and cheered as they followed along after the man, Ean found the whole situation ironic. The fact that the gruesome deaths of villagers and Heroes at the hands of a horrible creature would bring the town to life was funny in a sad sort of way. He looked forward to the day he could leave this cruel town more than ever. The only thing keeping him here now was his complete lack of money, since Krane had stolen most of it from him. He had no idea how long it would take to save up enough money to leave. But he was here now and curious to see what this new Hero was capable of doing.

Ean frowned as he passed the two men the mayor had posted at the entrance to the inn. Their mere presence kept the town folks on their best behavior. Ean managed to weave his way through the crowd gathered on the porch and reach the front doors. The thugs guarding the door were only being paid to toss people out, not keep paying patrons from coming in, so they let Ean pass through the swinging doors.and he weaved his way through the crowd gathered right at the entrance.

The place was packed. He had to muscle his way through the crowd to find a place close to the new visitor. With the inn so packed, it took him a while to figure out where the Magus was sitting. The failures of the previous two Heroes had made the town cynical. People had come here to socialize and get drunk, not to dote on some pompous windbag who would probably be dead this time tomorrow. Nonetheless, the third Hero had found a small audience. Ean spotted him at a table in the far corner of the room, leaning back in his chair with a mug of ale in one hand. By the time

Ean wormed his way over to him, the man seemed to be in the middle of a story.

"I found half of the loggers dead, ripped apart and fed upon. The beast was nearby, a horrible creature three times the size of dog and twice as mean looking. I recognized it right a way; the steam coming off the ground and bodies where the saliva of the beast had landed marked it as a Hound from the Abyss. Its back was to me as it feasted on one of the unlucky men. Not wanting to risk a lengthy battle, I unleashed all of my magic on it before it knew I was even there."

"Where does your power come from?" a voice called out from the crowd.

The Hero's eyebrows furrowed in annoyance. With a visible effort, he forced a smile before answering.

"An excellent question, even if it did interrupt the story." He cast another glance around the room before continuing on. "We Magus or Magi, that's what my kind of magic user call ourselves, draw the energy for our magic from our bodies, a sort of well that the older Magi, from days long past, called a Sal-Eum. Now, it doesn't matter the size of a man or woman's body; the depth of each person's Sal-Eum is as different as each person's nose in here tonight. Most of you might even be able to hold a small amount; it just might be so small that it's not noticeable."

He waved the serving girl back over. The Magus snatched the pitcher of ale she was holding and held it up along with his cup. "This pitcher is a good representation of my own ability. A decent amount, but nowhere near the capacity of the most powerful Magi. Thankfully, the most intelligent Magus of the past found a way to increase all of our capacities." Raising his free hand, the Magus showed off a variety of rings on each of his fingers.

"These are called Wells. Let's say my cup here represents the Wells that I wear on my fingers. Once my own Sal-Eum is full, it begins to overflow." The Magus tipped the pitcher over, pouring the golden brown ale down into his cup. "The Wells catch and store the overflow, allowing me to draw power from them later." He paused, taking a long swig from his cup. "Or from my Sal-Eum." Tilting his head back, he took a longer swig from the pitcher. "See." He paused again, this time to belch. "Nothing complicated about it."

Ean found the whole explanation enlightening, but he was more curious about the Hound. The scars on his left arm were a testament to his own experience with one of the creatures, and that one had looked like a pup. Pushing his way closer to the Magus, he called out to him. "What happened with the Hound?"

The Magus glanced at Ean briefly, then turned his attention back to the crowd and continued on with his story. "Well now, as I was saying, the Hound was focused on his meal and didn't know I was there. I drew on all of my power, both my Sal-Eum and the power in my rings, and unleashed upon the beast streaks of pure energy." He shot a little bolt of yellow energy out of his finger into the air. It fizzled out before reaching the ceiling. "The savage beast didn't have a chance. Its body was torn to shreds by the energy before it hit the ground."

"Did you see any distinguishing marks on its body?" Ean was leaning in further now, his interest peaked. The Magus paused a moment underneath that stare, then let out a laugh.

"I was too busy worrying about ending up like the rest of the loggers to notice, boy," the Hero slurred. "Why does it matter anyway?"

"No reason," Ean sighed in disappointment. "Just curious is all."

"No problem at all, boy," the Magus said, leaning back in his chair again. "It's only natural for a simple village boy to be curious about the rest of the world. Now how about I tell you the story about how I killed a whole pack of–?" But Ean was already making his way out the door.

The sun had reached its midday position in the sky, which gave him plenty of time to make it to the bog ahead of the Hero. Ean wanted to find a prime spot to watch the idiot Magus get eaten. As he started making his way down the street, he couldn't help picture the cocky man getting scooped up in the creature's huge hands and made a meal. Of course, part of him felt a little bad about the thought; maybe the Magus would succeed after all. Deep in thought, Ean made it about halfway down the road when something struck him in the back. He was about to defend himself when Zin's voice whispered in his ear.

"What was all that about in the inn? You might as well have come out and said you've seen a Hound before." Zin spoke in hushed tones, making his whiney voice difficult to hear. "The villagers are always looking for an excuse to punish you, so you better quit asking about the Hound. They'll run you right out of the village if they even suspect that you have a connection to the Abyss."

"They were all focused on the Hero's stories" Ean brushed off his comment with a wave of his hand. "Besides, I wanted to know if he had killed my Hound. It would have made me somewhat upset."

"YOUR Hound?" Zin shouted. Thankfully, most of the village was out of earshot. "I wouldn't exactly call that mangy beast a puppy—an acid-slobbering killing machine is more like it. Even as young as it was, that creature was a menace."

"He wasn't all that bad."

"Not that bad?" Zin let out a harsh laugh. "He chased me around the room, trying to make a meal of me, and he did a number on you when you tried to send him back."

Ean rubbed at his left arm. "Yeah, well, I wasn't strong enough to control him at that point. But that's not his fault. He was just acting out like any puppy."

"Except most normal puppies don't leave you burnt and scarred from their saliva."

Ean shook his shoulders about, trying to dislodge the pesky imp clinging to his back, but failed as usual. Unable to persuade his friend, he changed the subject. "So, what do you think— this Magus fellow have any chance bringing the creature down?"

"Nope, but watching him try is sure to be fun." Zin said then held up a dead rat for Ean to see. "I even brought a snack."

CHAPTER 5

SURPRISES

AND ZIN HAD BEEN right.

From his usual hiding spot, Ean watched a real magic user battle the beast. The Magus sent bolts of blue that sizzled and lit tiny flames on the creature's scales. Bolts of orange and yellow crackled with electricity but bounced off the creature and into the night. Whenever a bolt hit, it would explode in a dazzling display of light, illuminating the mine and nearby bog. This always seemed to blind the monster for a few moments but nothing more. Eventually, the creature would make his way through the bolts to within striking distance of the Magus, only to find the man far to its left, right, or back.

Ean was fascinated to see a different kind of magic at work. His own magic relied on runes and the language of the Abyss, where the slightest mistake could result in disastrous consequences. The night he had created light out of thin air had happened more on instinct than Ean having an idea of what he was doing. Seeing the Magus launch the magic out of his fingertips at will opened up a whole new realm of possibilities.

The Magus's spells, on the other hand, leapt from his fingers on command. He moved across the field in the blink of an eye without any elaborate motions or fancy words. It all seemed so simple. Ean would be lying to himself if he said he wasn't a little jealous of the ease of how the Magus's magic seemed to work.

The Magus started to show signs of tiring. His bolts began to dim, and the previous rainbow of colors he had used before was reduced to only blue. He also wasn't able to teleport himself as far, each jump seeming to put him closer to the beast than the last. After one last burst of energy to the beast's eyes, the Magus teleported back in the direction of the town and took off running. By the time the creature had oriented itself again, the Magus was far out of its reach.

Ean watched the man run towards the protection of the village until he was a gray dot on the horizon. It had been the second best possible outcome. It would have been great if the Magus had succeeded, but watching him fail and survive to live with that failure was an acceptable outcome. He crouched there, laughing, until Zin tugged on his glove. The imp pointed to the mine with a wide-eyed expression. Following Zin's finger, Ean's stomach dropped when he realized the monster was looking straight at him with those awful, yellow eyes. A strangled sound escaped from Zin just before he turned invisible.

The creature was still in the same spot as before, but it had turned and was now facing Ean. He hadn't realized how close the Magus and the creature had gotten to his position, but he was aware of it now. It was close enough that he could make out its blood-stained teeth and black claws.

Ean froze. It had every opportunity to catch him while he had been laughing and not paying attention. Why hadn't it attacked? If the thing charged now, he should be able to lose it in the bog, maybe blind it with the same rune he had used before.

A dozen different possibilities raced through Ean's mind. A moment later, the creature turned around and stomped back to the cave. Afraid to move, Ean held his breath, expecting it to change its mind at any second and come storming back out. When it didn't, he let out a long breath. His limbs were trembling, but he was grateful to be alive.

Zin shimmered then reappeared, looking just as confused as Ean. "I have no idea what that was all about," Zin said, his eyes locked on the mine entrance. "But let's not press our luck." Not waiting for a response, the imp started heading back the way they came.

After a few moments, Ean jogged to catch up, slowing down once he reached his friend and matching his pace. "After not catching its meal and being riled up by all of those blasts from the Magus, why wouldn't it at least try to come after us?"

The imp waved his question off with a clawed hand. "Who knows, and who cares? I'm just happy not to be a meal." He shuddered and continued walking.

There had to be something more to what happened than simple indifference by the beast. They returned to the house without answers. Zin crawled into his sleeping spot beneath the bed, while Ean climbed onto the mattress and burrowed into his sheets. Staring up at the ceiling, he couldn't stop thinking that there was more to the monster's retreat than apathy. But the answer continued to elude him as he drifted off to sleep.

WAKING UP EARLY, EAN headed downstairs to see if there was news about the Hero. Cleff informed him about the Magus's embarrassing departure. While Ean had been making his way back home the night before, the Magus had run all the way back through town. He didn't even stop to collect his things from the inn as he ran out of the village and towards the pass out of the valley. As unfortunate as it was that the Magus hadn't taken down the beast, Ean was glad that there hadn't been another death.

Later that morning, while Ean was busy cataloguing and organizing Cleff's various bottles and containers of potions and plants, a villager stopped by the house. Cleff greeted him at the door, while Ean hovered behind in case Cleff needed his aid. The villager was only there to deliver a message, saying that the Mayor had called for an emergency village meeting. The entire village was to meet in front of the inn before midday.

Ean worked twice as fast at finishing his chores so that he could make his way down to the inn early. It was rare for the Mayor to gather the whole village for a meeting. Usually the man preferred to make all of the decisions himself. That was, after all, the best way to ensure that any decision made was the most beneficial to him.

After finishing up his work, Ean jogged up the road to the front of the inn, which was already packed with people. It seemed like the whole village was already there. The Mayor wore an arrogant smirk as he gazed over the gathering crowd. Bran stood at his side looking confident as usual. Krane stood on the opposite side of the mayor with a superior scowl. What a threesome, Ean thought. I'm surprised the porch doesn't collapse under the weight of so much pride.

Ean was stuck on the edge of the crowd, his small frame no help for how packed the villagers were gathered around the front of the inn. The Mayor cleared his throat and stepped forward. The crowd grew silent as they waited for him to speak.

"My fellow villagers! Thank you so much for meeting together here on such short notice. These are troubling times, I know, but I believe I have come up with a solution to rid ourselves of the beast that has taken over our mine!"

Ean pushed himself as close as possible in order to listen as the Mayor continued on. He received a few dirty looks for his efforts but ignored them.

"The worry I have felt for the well-being of our fellow villagers has kept me awake most nights, and I have spent many days thinking about what can be done. Our fallen Heroes had strength, skill and courage, so I keep asking myself the question: Why did they fail?

My friends, I have found the answer to that question: Ignorance. They did not know what they faced--the monster's habits, strengths or weaknesses. Everything the gods put on this earth has a weakness; we just need to know how to find it, which brings me to the solution of our problem: Knowledge."

A murmur from the crowd started, but the Mayor silenced it with a raised hand. "How are we to discover the way in which to beat the creature? The answer is to send one of our own to the capitol, to ask the very leaders of the temples for help." The Mayor lifted his hands in triumph as if just his idea had already saved the village. He stood there, hands raised until the crowd applauded. When the applause died off, he continued.

"And who should we send? Who should we task with such an important mission?" He grew quiet then, glancing around at the crowd and trying to add to the suspense. Reaching back, the Mayor wrapped a giant arm around Bran and pulled him forward. "My own son, of course! Intelligence and skilled with the blade, he will set out on a quest to bring about the end of the beast, one way or another!"

The crowd cheered. The village viewed Bran as their own beloved son. They were eager to get behind any campaign that heralded him as their personal savior. Bran allowed the applause to last for some time then raised his hand, which silenced the crowd.

"I feel honored to be chosen for such an important task." Bran's face had grown serious now as he addressed the villagers. "But for such an important quest, I should not go alone. I will be going out into a world where dangerous creatures and brigands prey on unwary travelers. If I am to survive, I will need someone who is skilled at bandaging wounds, healing broken bones, and dealing with poisons."

The crowd started to chant Cleff's name. Despite his advanced age, he was the obvious choice to go on a long trip. As thoughts of all the freedom he would have with Cleff out of the house ran through his head, the crowd quieted down.

"Cleff, of course, would be a valued addition in any circumstance." Why was Bran staring at Ean as he spoke? He started to get a very bad feeling as Bran continued. "But can we afford to take Cleff away from the village? What if others are hurt and need his skills?" Shaking his head, he continued on. "No, I cannot take Cleff with me, but there is another who knows the ways of a Healer, and who deserves the chance to prove himself."

Ean seemed to be the only one that understood where Bran was going with his speech. He started to turn to leave but only made it a few steps before Bran pointed right at him, confirming his fears.

"Ean will be going with me." Bran smiled as he looked at Ean, lost in his own speech and failing to notice the look of horror on Ean's face. "He has trained with Cleff for most of his life and has an extensive knowledge of the healing arts. With the two of us going together, nothing will be able to stop us!"

It was clear that Bran had expected a rousing applause when he finished speaking. What he got instead was stunned silence from both the crowd and his family. A low murmur started in the crowd, as all of the villagers turned to face toward Ean's direction. Ean's heart pounded in his chest. Sweat dripped down his forehead. He gave a weak laugh and shook his head, unable to move. After what felt like an eternity, Cleff broke Ean out of his stupor. The old man had made his way over and placed a hand on Ean's shoulder.

"Ean would be proud to be of aid to Bran on his mission." Pride painted Cleff's face, something Ean had never seen. "May Alistar guide and protect these two young men as they go out in the world."

Cleff gave his shoulder a light squeeze as he turned back to the crowd. Ean could only stand there, wondering how things had gotten so out of control, as the crowd began to nod in approval. He turned to look at Bran, who was grinning at him like a fool. The slight narrowing of his eyes and a twitch at the corner of his lip gave away that his expression was forced. How had this happened?

Bran began speaking again. "With the three, uh... I mean two of us together, we will be able to reach the capitol and find the answers or the help that we need. Please pray for our safety and wish us luck, for we leave today!"

As the crowd shouted Bran's name, Cleff draped an around Ean's shoulders and steered him towards home. They walked in silence for a time, the noise of the cheering crowd following them as they moved down the road. Ean's knees wobbled as he was led away. It felt like he was carrying the mountains on his shoulders. As they passed the field of the town square, Cleff spoke up.

"This will be a good experience for you," the old man said, still leading Ean along. "You will see more of the world, learn new things." He shot Ean a withering stare. "And do some good instead of causing trouble." Cleff let out a grunt. "I think you have gotten all that you can from me and this village. The mistakes of your parents have blinded the people here to your true potential. Better for you to get out now, grow as a man. Then someday, if you wish to return, these close-minded villagers will see the man you have become and come to regret the way they have treated you all of these years."

All Ean could do was nod as all control over his own future was torn away from him.

CHAPTER 6

THE START OF A JOURNEY

ON THE WAY HOME, Cleff confessed that Bran had told him about the plan to bring Ean along on the journey earlier that day. "From what I understand," Cleff said. "You and Bran will reach the base of the mountain tonight. You'll camp there and begin the two-day journey through the mountains in the morning. It's cold up there this time of year, so pack a few heavier pieces of clothing. I'll take care of packing up the medical supplies, and Bran will have all of the provisions you need."

By the time Ean and Cleff made it back to the house, he had just enough time to pack before having to head out again. He stuffed his bag with a few changes of clothes, his carving knife, and other odds and ends.

"Zin?" he called out to the empty bedroom before leaving. "You here?"

No reply. The imp was probably amused by Ean's predicament, laughing it off somewhere. It was better he wasn't around to rub it in anyway.

At the bottom of the stairs he found the old man waiting with a bag twice the size of his own. "I tried to pack a little of everything," Cleff said, the pride still clear in his voice. "If you run out or need anything else, you will have to find it as you go. You do remember your lessons on identifying plants and fungi, I hope? There is a much larger variety of plants outside of the valley than what we can find here. None of it as good as Rottwealth, of course, but still useful."

Waving Cleff off, Ean leaned down to grab the other pack. "Yes, yes, of course, I remember. You had me looking at pictures of..." Ean lost what he was saying as he struggled to lift the bag of supplies. The pack was twice as heavy as his bag of clothes. Cleff must have packed everything he could. Ean wouldn't have been surprised if the old man had left little of his stores for himself. With a great deal of effort, Ean moved the second pack to his shoulder, adjusting both packs around to be as comfortable and balanced as possible. As soon as he was settled he turned back to Cleff.

"Well, Sir, wish me luck. I suppose I wouldn't object if you sent the occasional prayer to Alistar my way." Ean knew he would; Cleff was a devoted follower of the God of Justice. The older man had never tried to push his beliefs on Ean, though.

Cleff moved in close, placing a hand on each of Ean's shoulders. He struggled to maintain his balance under the extra weight and shifted his bags around as Cleff spoke.

"I can certainly do that. You take care of yourself, boy. I want you to make it back here safe and sound. I truly am proud of you for doing this." Without another word, the old man released him, patted him once, and headed back towards his office.

Ean stared after Cleff as he walked away, conflicted between following him to give a more meaningful goodbye or simply leave it as is. The man was one of the few people that had kept Ean's best interests at heart. After a few moments, he decided to leave things be. He might be back after all. Ean had plenty of people here that he wanted to show up for how they had treated him, with Krane sitting at the top of the list.

Wobbling along as he tried to get his balance, Ean couldn't wait to unload the bags on the Mayor's horse. A wave of nostalgia hit him as he left Cleff's house. He had spent the better part of his life, the parts he had been old enough to remember, here. Part of him had never expected to leave, and certainly not so soon. The afternoon air had a bit of a chill in it, the cold of the Chill season sticking around longer than usual. The gray fog that often clung to his village like the gray fingers of death filled Ean with a sense of foreboding.

He made it about halfway to the inn when a hot breeze caressed his skin, but there was no heat on this cool afternoon. Pausing, he tried to figure out where the strange feeling was coming from. There was a force to it now that went along with the warmth. It pulled at him, a feeling both familiar and new, like being unable to put a new name to a known face.

Ean tried to focus on the force affecting him. There was a direction associated to the pull--behind him. There, between two houses. Straining his eyes to see in the late afternoon light, he was surprised to make out the telltale shimmer of his invisible friend.

This was certainly new. He had always been able to see something of the imp when he was invisible, but he never felt him before. Ean hurried to the alley, straining under the weight of his luggage. The blur that was Zin started to move away as he approached, slinking back into the shadows of the alley between the squat houses.

"Not so fast!" Ean growled, trying to keep his voice as quiet as possible. Ean didn't want to take any chances of being overheard.

The blur stopped, the form of the imp shimmering into view. "You have better eyes than I thought," the imp said. "I was going to wait until we got out of the village, but I suppose we can come up with our plan now."

"Plan? What plan?" Ean's questions about the strange feeling left his mind at the imp's odd suggestion. Zin's plans often ended in Ean getting into trouble, and that was inside the village. They could lead to much worse outside of it.

"Our plan to ditch the do-gooder as soon as we get out of town, of course."

"I can't ditch him now! The whole town expects me to go with him, and even though I couldn't care less what most of the people here think..." Ean paused to shake his head. "I can't do that to Cleff. Not after everything he's done for me. The pride I saw in that man's eyes...it would destroy him to hear I had abandoned Bran."

"You really care what that old man thinks?" The imp let out a laugh, then dodged out of the way of a clumsy kick from Ean. "Fine, fine, we go with him all the way. It's not like you had the money to get out of this mud pit on your own. So now we get to leave, and the Mayor is going to pay for it, so it still seems like a win-win situation to me."

Ean grunted, then turned and continued his walk to the inn. It was annoying, but Zin was probably right. This was an excellent opportunity to get out and see the world. And Bran wasn't all that bad, especially when Jaslen wasn't around. Of course, Ean would never admit to the imp that he was right, so he kept up his scowl as they walked on in silence.

Sounds of merriment drifted out of the open doors and windows of the inn as they approached, but not a single person sat on the porch. The Mayor's brown horse was tied up outside, loaded with bags in a variety of different shapes. Bran was standing there as well, checking the bags with a huge grin on his face. As Ean approached, the older boy stopped what he was doing and jogged over to greet him.

"Great, you're here!" Reaching out, Bran started taking Ean's bags off his shoulders.

Ean was surprised at the ease with which Bran could handle the heavier bag. "Thanks," was all Ean was able to get out, not trusting himself enough to say more.

"No problem. It's the least I could do after blindsiding you like this." Glancing over his shoulder, Bran flashed him a sheepish look.

"I hoped that if I caught you off guard, you would have trouble saying no. Guess it worked, huh?"

Ean returned his expression with a fake one of his own. "Yea, I suppose it did. Are we all set to go then?"

"Yup, all set. I've loaded old Claire here with everything we need." Bran said, pausing to pat the horse. "I've packed rations of food, two tents for us to sleep in while we're on the road, and a few other things that we might need along the way." He placed his hand on the pommel of the sword hanging from his waist. "And of course, I have this in case we get into any trouble. But I don't think we'll have any problems. No one from outside the valley has ever mentioned anything dangerous on the path out."

"Of course I'm sure the rest of the world is perfectly safe," Ean said, not able to hide the sarcasm in his voice. "The abundance of these Heroes that seem to roam the realm is quite reassuring."

Bran gave a slight frown and changed the subject. "Well, the gods willing, we'll have a pleasant trip east through the mountain to the village of Rensen, and then an easy journey north through Rensen forest to the capitol city. Those are the directions my father gave me, at least. It's exciting, isn't it? To see what we've only heard about all these years?"

Even though he hated to admit it, Bran's enthusiasm was contagious. A twinge of excitement went through him at the prospect of escaping the confines of the village. "Yes, it will be great to get out of here and see the world. And the sooner the better. Like now." Without waiting to see if Bran was ready, he started to head up the road towards the mountains.

Bran was quick to follow, leading the pack horse behind him as he hurried to catch up. It was strange. Ean had expected some kind of fanfare or send-off party, at the very least, a few people to watch them go. But it was only Ean, Bran and the horse--and Zin who was somewhere nearby--that moved from the edge of the village. Jaslen wasn't even there to see them off, which was strange. She and the rest of the village appeared to be too busy celebrating their eventual success to bother giving them a nice send-off.

The two moved along the road without comment from that point on, which Ean took as a blessing at first. Bran was known for being chatty, talking about whatever came to his mind. He was happy to find Bran in a thoughtful mood as the sun moved over the tops of the mountains behind them.

About halfway between the town and the mountain pass, Ean caught sight of Zin's mostly invisible form climbing up onto their horse. The lazy imp! Shaking his head, Ean turned his attention back to the road. He had never been this far outside of the village on this end of the valley. There was nothing really to see; all of the farmland stopped a little past the last house, which meant no one else would be found this far east. Even the area where the ashes of the dead were scattered looked the same as the rest of the land.

As the sun sank behind the mountains, their tiny convoy reached the base of the mountain pass. Bran was still silent as the two set up camp, which at this point was starting to make Ean a little nervous. The other boy looked about sporadically and avoided making eye contact. Maybe it had finally occurred to Bran that his companion hadn't appreciated being drafted into this journey against his will. Ean started a fire, set up a tripod, and hung the pot of beans he had prepared. Stirring the embers with a stick as they waited for their meal to heat up, Bran broke the silence.

"Well, Ean, we are off on our own." He gazed into the fire as if it were the most fascinating thing in the world. "As much as I'm enjoying the freedom, I'm glad to have someone like you—a skilled healer—at my side."

"Yes, well, I'm nowhere near as skilled as old Cleff, but I should be able to handle the occasional injury." Why was Bran still refusing to look at him? "Bran, it's clear something is bothering you, so let's hear it. As nice as the silence has been, I don't want it to continue for the entire trip."

Dragging his gaze from the fire, Bran regarded Ean quietly for a few moments, the only sound being the crackling of the embers. When he spoke, the words came out of his mouth in a rush. "I'm sorry I didn't tell you before we left, but I didn't want to risk having you tell either of our parents."

"Tell me what, Bran? Ambushing me to come on this little trip was enough of a surprise. I don't need any more."

"Well then, hopefully, this one will be a pleasant surprise?" The sound of a familiar female voice behind him made him jump to his feet. He turned around to see beautiful, forest-green eyes staring back at him.

"Jaslen!" he gasped.

Used to seeing her in long skirts, it took a minute to adjust to her more masculine attire—a short-sleeve, green shirt with a brown vest, form-fitting brown trousers, and black leather boots. A bow and quiver were slung over her shoulder. She walked past him, patting him on the back a few times before sitting down next to Bran. All Ean could do was stand there dumbfounded, his mouth hanging open.

"See, I told you he wouldn't take it well," Bran said, turning to look at Jaslen. "He can't even say anything, he is so upset."

"Nonsense!" she replied, placing an arm around Bran. "He is just shocked to see me, is all. Once the shock has worn off, he'll be happy to have another person to talk to while we travel. Isn't that right, Ean?"

Shaking himself out of his stupor, Ean let out a grunt. "You really think you are coming with us?" Turning to face Bran, he gestured towards Jaslen with his left hand. "You can't really think it's a good idea to take her, do you?" Bran tried to respond, but Ean didn't give him the chance to answer. "I can understand how you might think it fun to have your girlfriend along, but this trip is going to be dangerous. How can we worry about keeping ourselves safe while we have to worry about her?"

"Now wait just a moment!" Leaping to her feet, Jaslen moved right in front of Ean, leaning forward and jamming her face almost into his own. "Out of the three of us here, YOU are the one least likely to be able to do anything in a fight!"

"If I remember correctly, you were the terrified one at the bog," Ean retorted. "Bran had to carry you all the way home."

"I had never seen anything that terrible in my entire life," she shot back. "You're a healer. Blood, guts and bone are your life. Excuse me for being momentarily overcome by the horror of it all."

"Who's to say you won't be overcome if some other horror comes along?"

"Give me the chance to prove myself. I'm pretty good with a bow and staff. And Bran is the best swordsman in the village. You're only useful after the fighting is done. I'm useful during, unless you have some other skills that neither of us know about."

Well, let's see. I can summon creatures that I have no control over, and I could cast spells if I knew at least a tiny amount of how to read the runes from the Abyss. Not comfortable going with either of those answers, Ean decided his best course of action was to just shrug and look disgruntled.

"That's what I thought!" Jaslen said, a self-satisfied smirk appearing for a brief moment before she returned to her seat next to Bran. The boy had just sat there and poked at the fire during the entire exchange. "So, I don't want to hear anything more about having to worry about me. Now, with that out of the way, we can enjoy our little trip together."

"Whatever," Ean said, turning his back on the two. "I'm going to head to bed. All of these surprises today have destroyed my appetite." He walked over to his tent, opened it up and placed one foot inside before turning back around. "It's... nice that you'll be with us, Jaslen," he said in an attempt to make peace. He received a warm smile as a response before he moved into his tent.

He set about inside getting himself changed and ready for bed, a hundred thoughts running through his head. It was one thing to stomach seeing the two cozying up in the village every now and then; it was another thing entirely having them sleeping together only a few paces away. But what could he do? And how could he keep his secret from both of them? That was going to be the bigger problem. It was going to be hard enough with just Bran around, but now with Jaslen too, did he have any hope?

He shook his head, trying to knock free the questions plaguing his mind. Wrapping a blanket around his body, he was just about to nod off when he felt Zin draw close. It was going to take some time getting used to, having the ability to feel the imp's presence. A few moments later the imp's mostly invisible form crept through the opening and moved to sit down by Ean's head.

"I don't want to talk about it," Ean whispered, hoping to cut off the inevitable conversation he knew was coming. "Let's just get some sleep, and we can figure things out in the morning."

"Fair enough," was the reply, and he felt the imp moved down to his feet and curl up beside him. With a sigh Ean kicked a bit of his own blanket over the invisible form then turned his back to the imp. His last thought as he drifted off to sleep was how he hoped having Zin around would balance out traveling with the happy couple.

CHAPTER 7

TRAVELING IS HARD WORK

THEY WOKE JUST BEFORE dawn. As they packed up camp, the first rays of the sun peeked over the mountains. Grassland surrounded them, making the smooth path cut into the mountain easy to find. Their goal for the day was to follow the trail until they came to a clearing halfway through the mountains. It was where the Merchant camped on his way into and out of their village the one time of year he visited. With that goal in mind, they broke camp and headed up the mountain.

The road through the mountain was an interesting piece of work. Less of a road, it was more a carving into the natural formation of the mountain itself. Decades ago, Cleff's father had hired miners to cut a travel-able path to connect their small village to the outside world. They had worked with the natural formations of the mountains instead of against them, carving into the rock wherever it was most convenient. This led to long winding sections that rose and fell, curving at spots and making sharp turns at others, often doubling back on itself. The only convenience the workers had provided was a flat, narrow surface for travelers to access.

The small group spent the first part of the day traveling in silence. While Ean, Bran and Jaslen moved on foot, Zin had returned to his seat on top of the packs. Ean could just imagine the imp lying back and enjoying the ride. The group ate as they walked, not bothering to waste time cooking breakfast. Ean made sure to slip Zin a dried piece of meat for him to eat. It was strange, not only being able to see the imp while he was invisible but also to actually feel his presence whenever he was nearby. It could have something to do with the tattoo he had painted onto his hand, but there was no way to know for sure. Zin had seemed just as surprised, which made Ean nervous. What other side effects would start to spring up?

As the sun started to reach its apex in the sky, Jaslen broke the silence. "Ean, there was something we, I mean, I wanted to ask you. If you wouldn't mind, of course." Her hands were folded across her chest and she sounded nervous, which could mean any number of things.

Ean gave a noncommittal grunt.

"It's about a rumor that we've heard about you," she continued. "One I've been too nervous to ask about." She looked at the ground for a moment, before continuing on. "Do you really follow Ze'an?"

Ean remained silent for a time as he tried to figure out how to answer. In his village, the fact that people thought he followed a cursed god made them less likely to bother him. Was she one of those people? Should he continue his lie and tell her that he did follow the forsaken god or deny it? He had no idea how either of his companions would react either way. A quick glance at Jaslen and Bran found them both staring at him with blank expressions. Bran's opinion he didn't care that much about, but Jaslen's was a different story. If she already thought he was a follower of Ze'an and came on the trip anyway, he might as well go along with it.

"Yes, I worship the Lord of the Abyss."

"That's great!" she said, clapping her hands together in excitement.

It certainly wasn't the reaction he had expected.

"We've been trying to learn more about him, and of course we couldn't ask around our village. The rumors about you are the only time Ze'an's name is ever mentioned. When we heard you had actually spoken to him, we saw this trip as the perfect opportunity to--"

That caused Ean to stop in his tracks. "Wait, what? Who told you I've actually talked to a god?"

She must have heard the panic in his voice, as she raised her hands in a soothing manner. "You don't have to hide your beliefs from us, Ean. We both are interested in Ze'an as well. That's another reason why we wanted to make sure you came. Knowledge about the other gods and goddesses are practically forced down our throat. We want to learn everything you know about the Lord of the Abyss."

She stopped, looking at him with wide, expectant eyes.

He had no choice now but to make something up. "Of course," he said, standing straight and trying to look impressive. "If you want to learn about Ze'an, I clearly am the best choice to instruct you in...ah...our beliefs." He placed a hand on his chin as if deep in thought and resumed walking down the path. The other two glanced at each other once then moved after him.

Ean let them follow along in silence as his mind raced in an attempt to come up with something to say. He knew little about the Lord of the Abyss. Zin, of course, could provide a wealth of information, but he couldn't exactly ask him at the moment. Bluffing his way through the day was his only option. While he struggled to come up with something interesting to say, Jaslen caught up to him.

"So what questions do you have about Ze'an?"

"Well," she hesitated for a moment. "Bran and I wanted to know if you have actually spoken to Ze'an before." Ean grimaced, which caused Jaslen to rush on before he could speak. "I'm sorry if that was too forward. The rumors we've overheard all mention you speaking to thin air. We figured that he must speak to you. Or you're crazy." The laugh that followed couldn't have been more forced.

So much for not getting caught speaking to Zin, Ean thought. "Oh...well. To be honest, no, I have never spoken to him. And I have no idea why people think they saw me talking to thin air. That would be crazy."

When she remained silent, he pressed on. "I just believe what Ze'an stands for, is all. That's why I worship him."

A smile lit up her face. "Great! That's how we feel too, although Bran and I have our different reasons. I believe that Ze'an is misunderstood. The creatures he creates in the Abyss are meant to be a benefit, not things to be feared. After all, he does keep most of the dangerous ones contained."

"I believe," Bran said, calling up to them, "that he creates dangerous creatures in order to test humans and make us strive to be stronger."

Jaslen let out a small laugh, casting Bran a fond look before turning back to Ean. "As you can see, we believe close to the same thing, that Ze'an is helping humans in the long run. We try not to worry about the small differences in our opinions. How about you, Ean? What do you believe Ze'an stands for?"

"Me? Well, actually, I believe the same as you. Why would a god create things if not to help us, right?"

Behind them there was a burst of laughter that lasted only a moment. Jaslen turned around and shot Bran a dirty look.

"It wasn't me!" he replied, a confused look on his face. By Jaslen's expression, it was clear she didn't believe him, but Ean did. He knew that laugh, and Zin would pay for it later.

Casting Bran one last annoyed look, Jaslen turned her attention back to Ean. "I'm glad you feel the same way I do. It makes me feel better about what I've believed all along. I mean, the stories we hear from our parents have all been about horrible monsters that eat people and destroy farms and villages. I'm surprised our village hasn't blamed the monster's appearance on the Abyss." She gave a sniff before continuing on. "Enough about that. Tell us about the Abyss, Ean. You must know a lot about that."

This was one topic that he did know quite a bit about. Zin had told him a great deal about the terrors of his home.

"Yes, I do," he replied. Jaslen's eyes brightened and she waved him on. Even Bran picked up his pace and moved closer to hear. "From what I understand, the Abyss consists of eleven levels, each level containing different creatures and areas. The further down you go, the stronger the creatures you will find. Resting at the bottom is Ze'an himself."

Jaslen frowned before replying. "Yes, we all have heard those stories, Ean. I want to know MORE, though. Do you know more?" Her voice was a mixture of hope and doubt.

"Yes, yes, I know more." Ean said, not bothering to hide the frustration in his voice. "Have the stories you've heard mention the types of creatures and where they are? Have the stories told you about the Imps that reside on the first level, simple creatures hunted by every creature stronger than them for food or slaves? Beasts like the Hounds live on the first three levels. They are huge black dogs, three times the size of a normal dog with intelligence, that have acidic saliva that can burn through most things. Or how about on the fifth level, where scores of rock-like creatures called Maruks reside, their only purpose is to forge weapons and armor infused with the energies of the Abyss. Do you know what resides on the seventh level? Spirits. The souls of those too filled with rage or somehow corrupted by the energy of the Abyss lie trapped, unable to be taken by the Goddess Kaz'ren. Or the tenth level where there are creatures so terrible that they are simply referred to as the Nameless Ones. Have you heard any of those in your stories?"

By her flushed cheeks, it was clear that she hadn't heard any of it before. Bran also looked impressed, walking along behind them with the horse still in tow.

"I'm sorry I doubted you," Jaslen said breathlessly. "You know more about the Abyss than the entire village combined."

"We'll have plenty of time to talk more during our trip." Ean did his best to look stoic, but inwardly he was sighing with relief. Jaslen and Bran would give him some space now if they thought he was upset. He could use that time to try and get some more information to feed them from Zin tonight.

They returned to walking along without saying much for the rest of the day. Both Bran and Jaslen hung back with the horse, which was fine with Ean. He had grown uncomfortable after the conversation had ended. It had become natural for him to lie in the past; it kept him out of trouble and on occasion kept trouble from finding him. But it felt wrong now. Bran and Jaslen were being open about a subject that was taboo in their village, and as far as he knew the rest of the world. Didn't they deserve honesty in return? The thought put him in a sour mood.

CHAPTER 8

SECRETS

WITHOUT CONVERSATION TO LIGHTEN the mood, the path through the mountain felt even more cold and barren. Few trees grew up out of the rocky ground and cliff faces. A chill wind constantly whistled through the pass. They gathered what few branches and sticks they found along the way so they could make a small fire when they stopped for the night. Unexpected bursts of wind would howl through the pass like the cry of a wounded animal. At twilight they reached the halfway point of the path, putting them that much closer to the village of Rensen.

Twice as wide as the rest of the path but just as barren, the halfway point was as welcoming as the bottom of a boot. It made the lack of trees and plants all the more obvious. The added space also gave them less protection from the wind, which blew constantly and put a chill in Ean's bones.

They moved about the area, setting up their meager camp. They each took their time as there was little else to do once the sun had set. Ean and Bran focused on their tents while Jaslen set up the fire and got to work on their dinner. Ean was glad that Bran refrained from asking any questions about the Abyss. It had been a long and tiring trek up the path. Ean was looking forward to a quick meal and then off to bed.

Jaslen had a stew of beans and potatoes simmering over the fire by the time the tents were set up. The group gathered around, still silent, as they waited for the broth to warm. Every now and then, the wind would shriek through the pass, overwhelming the crackle of the fire. The three, now used to the sound, would look to each other and let out weak laughs, which relieved some of the tension that had crept into the group.

While they waited for the stew to cook, Bran moved away from Jaslen and took out his sword. Taking a piece of stone from his pocket, he began to run it up and down the blade's edge while she continued to monitor the stew.

"I can't believe we're actually out of the village," Bran said. "I never imagined I would leave at all, let alone one season after my twentieth birthday."

"I didn't think I would have the chance to leave for years, especially after..." Ean glanced at Bran then quickly looked away. "Krane stole most of my money."

Bran's face reddened, but he did not look away. "Ean, I truly am sorry about my brother. I have no idea why he holds such a grudge towards you. I promise when we get back and the monster is taken care of, I will make it my mission to have all of your money returned."

Ean dismissed the comment with the wave of a hand. "I would worry less about my money and more about what other horrible things—" he paused a moment as a particularly loud shriek of the wind interrupted him. There was something different about it this time, something that made Ean glance around the clearing. Bran and Jaslen paused at what they were doing and scanned the cliff faces.

When the sound failed to repeat, Ean's muscles relaxed until he noticed his right hand had gone numb. Clasping and unclasping his fingers, he wondered if his glove had cut off his circulation.

Jaslen let out a light yelp. She was staring up behind Bran into the mountains, her one hand on her mouth and her other pointing in the direction she was looking. Both Bran and Ean turned in unison, trying to focus in the direction she was pointing.

Poking its head out over a ridge not so high above them was one of the ugliest faces Ean had ever seen. About twice as wide as a normal human face, its head was covered in scars and pockmarks. Its skin looked like someone had stretched a normal person's face out and then stuck it into a hornet's nest. Its narrow ears stuck out, pointing away from its head, and its chubby nose was just as long. The creature's eyes were hidden deep in their sockets.

"What in the blazes is that?" Ean said, slowly getting to his feet.

Bran was frowning but didn't seem too concerned. "It looks like a mountain troll. They come down into the valley on occasion but are timid and easy to scare off. I've had more trouble with mountain bears than with trolls the past few years of patrolling the village."

"Looks like a troll or is a troll?" Ean wasn't about to relax. There was something in Bran's voice, a slight question in his tone that kept him on edge.

"Well, yes and no. Something about it isn't quite right. It looks...bigger than the ones I've had to scare off." He shrugged and kept his eye on the troll. "They usually aren't much of a problem. Simple creatures with simple needs. It probably just caught the smell of our stew and thought it might find an easy meal. I doubt it will come close now that it's seen us."

He returned to sharpening his blade, but every now and then he would glance in the creature's direction. Jaslen returned to her task of stirring the stew, her eyes repeatedly flickering at Bran.

Not feeling the least bit comforted, Ean watched the creature. Bran was right; there was something strange about this troll, but not because of its appearance. Ean could feel it. In the same way he could feel Zin a few paces a way without even looking for his telltale blur. What did it mean? Lost in thought, he didn't notice when the creature's head disappeared from view.

"See?" Bran said, a little bit of tension leaving his voice. "Nothing to worry about. It's probably moved on to find an easier meal."

"Well, that's good," Jaslen said, a forced laugh accompanying her words. "I only made enough stew for the three of us." She lifted the ladle out of the pot, bringing a small amount to her lips. "Shouldn't be too much longer now, and then we can eat."

Ean could still feel the thing out there in the mountains. It was moving, circling around their camp and steadily making its way closer. He stood, keeping his body facing in the same direction as where he felt the creature. He felt Zin move too, away from the tents and towards where Ean was standing. Ean frowned, not sure what to make of any of it.

"You're sure the troll isn't anything to worry about?" He directed the question to Bran without looking in his direction.

"Of course. Someone even younger than us could scare one off with a little effort. I'm sure seeing the three of us will keep it away. You really don't have to be afraid, Ean." He said the last part with a chuckle, Jaslen joining in a few moments later.

Ean ground his teeth, anger washing away any concern over the creature moving about. "I am not scared!" It came out as a yell even though he had meant to simply state it. They both stopped laughing, Jaslen looking at him with pity while Bran looked down at the ground.

"Ean, I was joking. Really." Bran said, the sincerity clear in his voice. "You really need to learn not to take things so personally."

"Maybe you shouldn't be calling people—" Ean was on the verge of yelling again when a loud thud cut him off, followed by inhuman screams. Spinning towards the noise, Ean saw a gruesome sight.

The troll had taken their horse to the ground and was crouched over it, its right side facing them. The horse was flailing around in an attempt to get up, but the troll had it pinned with its large, muscular arms. The troll's face was buried in the side of the horse, great tearing sounds coming from it, mixing with the whinnying of the horse and the wind's howl.

Bran leapt to his feet, his sword gripped tightly in his hand as he rushed to the horse's aid. Jaslen remained motionless. She seemed frozen in a sitting position on the ground, soft sobs escaping her throat as she watched the horse being devoured. Ean was frozen in place as well, his emotions a mixture of fear and curiosity.

"Stay here; I'll get rid of it." Bran said over his shoulder, the confidence in his movements not matching the tone of his voice. He was at the horse's side in moments, his blade slashing out and catching the troll on its right arm before it even knew he was there. The blade cut deep. A thick substance similar to blood spurt into the air. When the troll let out a familiar howl, Ean realized that they had been mistaking the sound of the wind throughout the day. It stood to its full height and moved back a pace or two, allowing Ean to see the troll completely.

The troll stood twice as tall as Bran. Strips of fur hung from its muscular yellow body. The troll's face was cratered with scars and pockmarks. Lumps and boney protrusions grew out of its skull and shoulders in random patterns. Its long arms hung down at its sides, the hands swinging at its knees, long claws extending from each finger. Where Bran's blade had hit, there was a large gash with a reddish-blue liquid that Ean assumed was its blood dribbling down the arm.

"Stay back!" Bran yelled, his sword weaving about in front of his body. "I think this one is sick!"

The troll's attention was locked on Bran now, its dark, yellow eyes now visible in the firelight. It moved into a crouching position, its knees bent and the knuckles of its large hands resting on the ground. With a growl, it launched itself at Bran. The speed of the creature caught the three of them off guard. All Bran could do was dive out of its way.

The troll landed with a crash between Bran and where Jaslen and Ean were standing. Its limbs were splayed across the ground in every direction, but it was back on its feet in an instant. Bran was on his feet as well, his eyes locked on the troll and his sword waving slowly about in front of him. The troll let out another growl but this time did not charge. Instead, it took slow, careful steps towards Bran.

While Ean was still locked in his position, unable to take his eyes off the battle, Jaslen finally started to move. Racing to the tent she shared with Bran, she grabbed the bow and quiver of arrows that were resting beside it and moved back to the fire. She had an arrow nocked and ready to go.

"I can't get a good shot! It's too close!" Her voice wavered as she spoke, but she kept the bow steady.

Bran circled to his right as he waved his blade in a slow and deliberate manner. The troll followed him, loping along on both its hands and feet to his left. It limped slightly whenever it put any weight on its right arm, but otherwise it seemed to ignore the wound. Jaslen slowly started to move around the beast in Bran's direction, the arrow in her bow still ready to fly.

The troll charged. Bran dodged and scored a long slash across its back with his blade. The troll let out a moan, stumbled, then fell forward onto its face. It scrambled to rise, falling over once or twice, before finally regaining its feet. It turned about, its eyes scrunched together and a snarl touching its lips, as it started towards Bran again.

The twang of a bowstring sounded behind Ean. Something whizzed past his ear. As if by magic, an arrow appeared in the troll's left leg. Way to go, Jaslen, he silently cheered.

The troll stumbled from the impact. With a grunt, it swatted at the shaft with one large hand, breaking most of the shaft off, leaving the arrow head imbedded in its yellow flesh. It looked around for a moment until its eyes fell on Jaslen at the same moment she notched another arrow. Those yellow eyes, set deep into the sockets, narrowed as the beast charged towards Jaslen.

Caught off-guard by the beast's change of target, Bran did his best to get in front of the creature. It shouldered him out of the way. Jaslen let loose the arrow she had ready, but it flew wide. With a scream, she raised her bow, swinging it about in a feeble attempt to stop the troll's charge. The bow caught the creature across one of its arms, but it barreled right into her anyway.

The two went to the ground with a crash, legs and arms intertwined. Jaslen's small frame made her look like an infant compared to the size of the troll. Ean leapt into action. He grabbed the end of a burning branch out of the cooking fire on his way to help. As fast as Ean moved, Bran was faster. He reached the troll just as Jaslen and the creature stopped tumbling along the ground. He thrust the point of his blade with measured movements, careful that his attacks stayed clear of Jaslen's body.

Unfortunately, the jabs seemed to do little more than enrage the troll even further. It lashed out with a thick foot, catching Bran directly in the stomach and launching him into the air. Ean got there before Bran hit the ground. He slammed the flaming branch down onto the back of the troll. The blow did little harm, but the flame started to light the animal skins the troll was wearing on fire. Ean received a large backhand to his side and across his body by the beast for his troubles, but it did roll off and away from Jaslen. Ean stumbled backward from the blow, the branch dropped from his grip before he fell to the ground.

As soon as Ean hit stone, he tried to rise back up but a shiver of pain shook his body. Looking down he noticed three slash marks cutting through his shirt, stomach high. A faint seepage of red starting to moisten the edges of each tear.

The troll was busy trying to smother the flames. It rolled about violently, past Ean and Bran, before it stopped near Jaslen. She was still lying on the ground, face down, arms and legs splayed out and not moving. Her red hair was covering her face and matted together in places. Ean's vision blurred with his pain as he tried to focus on the fight.

The troll was back on its feet, snarling at Bran. Its eyes settled on the weakest prey, Jaslen, and it charged straight at her. Bran charged, aiming to cut the beast off before it could reach their fallen friend. His sword did not waver as he sprinted to intercept the beast.

Ean started to draw a rune onto the stone of the mountain path. Instinct and concern controlled his actions. The lines lit up as his fingers traced them across the ground, his hand moving faster than he thought possible. Time seemed to slow down as he drew the rune along the ground. He glanced up for a moment. Bran had somehow gotten between the beast and Jaslen. The troll had come to a halt in front of him, both of its clawed hands raised and ready to strike. Bran looked as if it was taking all of his strength just to stand, the sword in his hand dipping slightly in front of him.

Behind Ean, a shout rang out. "No, you fool! You can't control him!"

Ean vaguely recognized Zin's voice but ignored it. Jaslen was badly injured, Bran was only delaying the beast until his body gave out, and Ean was next to useless. He had to risk it.

The rune was nearly finished when he felt Zin grab his arm. "You don't understand," he screamed into his ear. Was he screaming? It was hard to tell. "It's been four years since you tried this. Do you know how big it will have grown in four years?!"

Ean had no clue and didn't care. He completed the design then activated it. The dim glow of the lines grew bright, brighter than the campfire, brighter than even the fading sun. They grew in intensity until, with a flash, they were gone, replaced by a dark, glowing hole in the ground as wide as a wagon wheel.

Ean risked a quick glance and saw both the troll and Bran staring at him, both frozen in place, their mouths hanging open. He watched as the opening in the ground pulsed with a dark light. It was hypnotizing; the soothing blue glow, the light pulsing steadily like a heartbeat. Just the slightest bit of warmth flowed out of it and dulled the chill of the wind. Ean's body started to relax in that warmth...

Then, the pain came—like a dull knife carving up his insides. He had expected the pain, but this was a dozen times worse than the last time. Doubled over, he fell onto his side. Then he saw why the pain was so much greater than he had expected.

When he had first tried summoning an Abysmal Hound, the creature had been the size of a puppy, although a large one. What came out of the portal now was far from puppy-sized.

Its front feet emerged first, huge paws the size of a man's head, with four claws just as large on each one. They reached out of the hole and latched onto the stone, the muscles in its legs straining as it pulled at the ground. The rest of the Hound's body quickly followed. It was covered in thick, black fur that shimmered with grease; the oily substance dripping off its fur gave off a sickly-sweet smell. A short muzzle and dark purple, pupil-less eyes glanced in every direction at once. Its body was slightly muscled, its tail short and stubby. What Ean had remembered as being the size of a puppy was now the size of a young bear. It towered over Ean.

As the Hound stepped completely into their world, the pressure and pain wracking Ean's body ceased, replaced by a dull ache. The portal to the Abyss closed, the complex summoning rune returned in its place. The Hound was practically right on top of him, its opened mouth showing off razor sharp teeth. Its breath was hot in Ean's face, the smell of decaying meat overwhelming his senses. The small singular rune on its neck was his doing. It marked the beast and allowed him to summon it instead of pulling a random one from the Abyss.

It sniffed at him a few times, great intakes of breath that seemed to draw him towards the Hound's mouth. The Hound continued to stare at him for a few moments, its head tilted to the side, those dark purple eyes measuring him while its tongue hung out slightly over its pointed teeth. Ean hoped that whatever it decided to do with him did not involve those teeth. A familiar howl sounded from behind the Hound.

Ean glanced under the Hound's thick body and frowned at what he saw. The troll had recovered from the shock of the summoning and had turned its attention back to Bran, who was still staring at Ean and the Hound. He didn't even react as the troll swept a huge fist into the young man's side. Bran went tumbling to the ground with a grunt, the sword flying free from his hand. It clattered along the rocky ground, finally coming to rest a good distance away. The troll let out a low growl and started to stalk towards where Bran had fallen.

Ean quickly pointed at the troll and yelled out, "Attack!"

The Hound stared at him.

"Go! Get it! Uh...kill!"

Still nothing. Maybe it couldn't understand him? Over the years, Ean had learned pieces of the language of the Abyss from Zin. He frantically searched his brain for the equivalent of attack.

"Li'atch!" he yelled. Zin had taught him that word once a long time ago. It meant "to eat."

The Hound spun and took off in the direction of the troll, kicking up dirt and stone as it sped towards the other beast. The troll had just enough time to put up its arms in defense before the Hound crashed into it, knocking the troll onto its back.

The troll batted at the Hound's side with both hands. Each blow rocked the massive beast to the left and right but it kept its balanced on top. Bits of saliva began raining down on the troll, most scorching the raggedy clothes, a hiss escaping as each drop fell.

The Hound bit down hard into the other creature's right shoulder. With a howl of pain, the troll began to thrash harder, its feet kicking into the dirt, its fingers and nails digging into the sides of the Hound. But the Hound held on.

As the two beasts fought, Ean began a slow and painful crawl over to Jaslen. It took an extreme amount of effort for him to just to keep from collapsing. The summoning, combined with his own wounds, had left him weak. On the way to Jaslen, he sent a glance in Bran's direction see the boy trying to get back to his feet. With Jaslen's boyfriend not looking too injured, Ean continued to crawl. He alternated his attention between Jaslen and the two beasts.

The troll made one last effort to buck the Hound off, letting go of its grip and heaving its body. Releasing its bite on the troll's shoulder, the Hound sank its teeth into the troll's neck. What had been a terrible howl coming from the troll before turned into a gurgle as its thrashing tripled.

By the time Ean had reached Jaslen, the troll gave one last shudder and then remained still. The Hound kept its strangle hold for a bit longer, its tail wagging now, then released its grip. It sniffed at the troll, looked it up and down and then began to feed.

Trying not to gag at the sight and sound of the Hound tearing into the troll, Ean turned his attention back to Jaslen. Her breath came at normal intervals, and her eyelids fluttered when he touched her head. He checked over the rest of her body, flushing as he examined her chest and thighs. Other than a number of scrapes and a thin cut on the side of her head, Ean didn't find any cause for worry.

"Jaslen, wake up." He patted her face with a few fingers as he tried to be as gentle as possible. She stirred, a whimper escaping her mouth, then her eyes opened. "Bran? Is that you?" Ean wished his own name was the first thing that crossed her lips.

"Uh, no. It's Ean."

Her eyes opened wide. "Oh, Ean. I'm sorry, I just thought..." She blinked a few times, her expression changing from confusion to concern. "Where is Bran? Is he alright?"

"He's fine," Ean said, pointing over her shoulder. "A little bruised maybe, but in much better condition than you." Bran was limping his way over to them, but he got there before Ean could say more.

"Jaslen! I was so worried!" Bran placed a hand under Jaslen's head and lifted her into a sitting position, leaning her slightly against his own body as he crouched next to her.

A twinge of jealousy forced Ean to look away.

Ean took the opportunity to slide back a few paces, trying to put some distance between himself and the couple. "I'll go get my medicine bag," he murmured before getting up and walking away.

Bran nodded in acknowledgement and continued to talk to Jaslen in low tones. Ean did his best to ignore what they were saying, which wasn't too difficult since it took all of his effort to stand and walk. He had only gotten a few paces before the sound of a scream made him spin around. The movement nearly brought him to his knees, his stomach afire with pain. Jaslen was pointing at the Hound while Bran seemed to be trying to calm her down.

"What is that?!" Her voice was trembling, and she clutched at Bran with one hand. The Hound was still chewing away at the dead troll. It had taken a bite out of the troll's side and was now munching away on one of its arms, its short tail wagging along behind it.

"Don't worry, dear," Bran said, holding her close, "That creature is on our side. I don't know how Ean brought it here, but he did, saving us all."

They were both looking in Ean's direction now, their faces hard to read with the only light coming from the small fire and soft glow of the summoning rune. The sun had set, and the first moon had yet to make an appearance in the sky. Ean just stood there, feeling like an awkward fool.

"Well, I guess there is no need for me to keep hidden anymore." Zin said, appearing without warning in between the three. He scratched at his back and kept his eyes on the Hound.

Both Bran and Jaslen turned their attention to the small imp, the shock written clear on their faces. It was almost comical to see, except Ean felt like he was about to get sick. Years of effort at keeping his secret from everyone, ruined.

"You truly are a servant of Ze'an." Bren said, a note of wonder to his voice. Jaslen continued to stare.

"No, well..." Ean grunted, both from pain and frustration. "There will be plenty of time to explain while I patch us all up." He turned back around and stalked to where his medicine bag was sitting.

"I can't wait to hear this." Zin mumbled, loud enough for Ean to hear. It took all of Ean's will power not to turn around and kick at the imp.

CHAPTER 9

QUESTIONS WITHOUT ANSWERS

EAN RETURNED TO BRAN and Jaslen with the medicine bag. They watched the Hound, a mixture of wonder and revulsion painted their faces as it continued to eat away at the corpse of the troll. Jaslen was sitting up on her own now, Bran close by her side. Zin was sitting off a few paces from everyone, still visible, and eating what appeared to be part of a rat or mouse. When Ean sat down next to Bran and Jaslen, they barely acknowledged him.

"We'll start with Jaslen's head first, I think." Ean said, his sour mood worsening when neither replied. He took out a small length of cloth and one of the thick vials that contained ground up Rottwealth from his bag. Applying a small bit of the Rottwealth powder to the cloth, he began to wrap it around Jaslen's head.

"Ean," she whispered to him while he worked. "Can you...can you make it go away?" She gestured slightly to the Hound, her hand barely moving in its direction.

"Once we're all bandaged up I will. It seems busy at the moment."

She nodded, not looking convinced. Finishing up the bandage on her head, he put a calming hand on her shoulder. "It's alright, I promise. I've handled him before. There is nothing to worry about." He tried to make his voice sound reassuring, but it wasn't something he was used to doing.

"If you say so, but I'll be happier when it's gone." Her body relaxed at his touch but she kept her eyes locked on the Hound. "And what about that other thing? The thing that talks. Is it dangerous as well?"

"What, you mean Zin?" Ean couldn't help but laugh, even though it made his wounds throb. "He's just an imp. Harmless for the most part, although he talks way too much."

Finished with Jaslen, Ean lifted his own shirt and examined the gashes the troll had caused. Not too deep, they wouldn't need stitching. Dumping a small amount of the Rottwealth onto his hand, he began to gingerly apply it to the wounds.

"You sound as if you've known...Zin, for a long time?" Jaslen asked. She was watching Zin now with those beautiful forest-green eyes.

"Uh...yes. Zin has been with me for years. I guess you could call him my friend."

"That thing is your friend?" A hint of surprise touched her voice. "Wait, years? How come we haven't seen him before now?" Jaslen was looking at him as if seeing him for the first time. Ean wasn't sure if it was a good or bad thing.

"Zin can turn himself invisible, although I can see a slight blur." Ean winced as he touched a slightly deeper wound, growing silent for a moment as he examined it again. When he looked back up, Jaslen was watching the Hound again. So much for holding her attention.

Wrapping his own wound with a bandage, he looked at Bran. "Are you cut up badly or bruise—" Ean wasn't sure what it was about Bran's expression that made him stop. The normally jovial guy was staring at him with an expression that Ean had never seen before. Was that anger?

"Nothing too serious, thankfully." He was grinning now. Had Ean imagined it? No, Ean had definitely noticed something strange in his expression. Bran continued. "It seems like you received the worst of it. That was pretty brave, coming to Jaslen's rescue with just a lit stick." There it was again! Only a brief flash of an emotion that Ean couldn't make out, but it was there.

"Uh... well...I had to do something, I guess." Ean dropped his eyes. Why did he feel so uncomfortable all of the sudden?

Bran barked a laugh. "Do something? You certainly did something." He gestured over towards the Hound. It had eaten most of the meat off one arm and moved on to the other one. "If you had done that in the beginning, none of us would have even gotten a scratch."

"I only summoned the Hound once before," Ean said, still not looking at Bran. "And the last time didn't exactly go that well." He rubbed at his left arm.

"If you say so."

A hand on his shoulder made him jump. What was wrong with him today? Jaslen was looking at him again. "If we're all bandaged up now, could you please send the Hound away? I can't stand the sounds it's making while it eats."

"Yes, yes, of course." Rising, he walked over to where the summoning rune was still glowing with a faint light on the ground. Kneeling next to it, he placed his right hand on the edge. The rune had activated before without actually saying the words, maybe it would close the same way. He pictured the rune activating in his mind and instantly it flared to life. A portal back to the Abyss opened up in front of him, its purple mist swirling around below him.

The Hound's body jerked away from its meal as if pulled by an invisible leash. Its body began to slide backwards as it struggled against the invisible force. Its large claws dug into the stone, raking long scars into the ground. Realizing that wasn't working, it whipped its head around, a low growl escaping its throat as it looked directly at Ean.

Ean blinked a few times as a spike of fear ran up his spine. The Hound would be next to him soon. His left arm itched as the memory of what the Hound could do when it was annoyed leapt into his mind. And that had been when it was a young pup! While his attention wavered, the opening started to close.

With the pressure released, the Hound started to move towards Ean with a more determined pace. Its head was low, but its eyes burned. Ean tried to focus and the portal grew. The Hound jerked again as the magic took hold, and it slowed as it tried to dig its claws into the ground.

"Maybe you should let it finish its meal," Zin yelled from somewhere off to Ean's side.

The Hound was moving again, slowly, but it seemed to be the one in control. Maybe Zin was right. He could release it and let it go back to eating the troll. Or the Hound could hold a grudge for the interruption and turn Ean into its next meal. Either way it was clear that the Hound was not going back without a fight. Ean decided to let it go and hope for the best.

Taking his hand off the rune, he raised both into the air and pointed back towards the troll. Stumbling as it was released, the Hound recovered and bounded the last few steps to Ean. Expecting to be a meal, Ean closed his eyes and cringed. When a few moments went by and he didn't feel the creature's teeth sink into his neck, he opened his eyes. The Hound was standing in front of him, its dark purple eyes staring into his own. It continued staring at him for a moment, then not so gently nuzzled the side of his face.

Ean blinked in surprise. The Hound sniffed at him one more time, snorted, then sauntered back to the troll. Surprised he was still alive, Ean sat in shock as the Hound sat and resumed its meal. A burning sensation on his neck knocked him out of his stupor, as he realized a drop of saliva had gotten on his neck. He brushed it away with a gloved hand.

"Never a good idea to come between a Hound and its meal," Zin chuckled. The little imp walked over to Ean while he continued to wipe at his neck. "And I would have thought that you had learnt your lesson last time about a Hound's saliva."

Ean's neck felt hot and irritated, but the pain was gone. He was about to let out a string of curses at Zin but Jaslen spoke first. "You're really just going to let it roam about free? What if it decides that we look as appetizing as the troll?"

"I'm sure he won't turn on us," Ean said, trying to reassure her. "He isn't completely under my control, but I believe that he is somewhat loyal to me. We'll just wait, and when it's done eating, I'll try to send him back again. At the very least he'll keep any other trolls away."

His little speech didn't seem to alleviate Jaslen's fears. Her hands were rolled up together in nervous balls, and she flinched every time the Hound's teeth crunched on the troll's bones.

"If Ean says it will be alright, I'm sure he believes it. After all, it looked like it was about to make a meal of him too and didn't." Bran's expression changed to one of concern. "I have never heard of a troll attacking anyone so viciously before."

Forgetting the Hound for a moment, Jaslen nodded slowly against Bran's chest. "I've scared a few off our farmland myself, and it's never taken anything more than shouting at it." Her body shudders slightly. "But I've never seen a troll that looked that way before either. He seemed...sick. And his body was so deformed." She shuddered again, one hand reaching over to grasp at Bran's shirt. "It was horrible."

Ean nodded along with them. He had never seen a troll before, but it looked like what he had expected. Big and ugly. How was this one any different?

"Well, regardless, it's dead now," Ean said, trying to sound relaxed. "Who cares if it was sick or rabid or whatever?"

He got up slowly and carried his medicine bag back to the rest of his belongings. He could hear Jaslen and Bran still whispering to each other behind him, but he ignored it. What he couldn't ignore was the feeling of Zin walking up behind him. It was strange. Sometimes he could put the new feeling of the imp out of his mind and other times, it pulsed like a drumbeat that was impossible to ignore.

"So, how much are we telling them? I just want to know now so that I don't say anything that will get me kicked later." Zin said the last part with a smirk. Ean couldn't remember a time he had actually been able to catch the imp, and Zin knew it.

"We won't be telling them anything." Ean let the medicine bag drop to the ground. He regarded his other companions with disapproval. "Those two already think I have a special connection to Ze'an. The last thing I need is you adding to their delusions, so keep your trap shut and let me do any explaining. Got it?"

"Oh?" Zin said. "I thought you would say anything to impress the girl." That did earn Zin a kick, but the imp easily dodged to the side then continued on as if nothing had happened. "Just think, if you had told her you were a prophet of Ze'an, she would probably do anything you wanted. ANYTHING."

Ean grabbed a rock and threw it as hard as he could at the now chuckling imp. It missed, of course, and the effort earned Ean a flash of pain from the wounds on his stomach. "You will NOT talk to them about me or the Abyss. I swear, if I even think you've told them anything, I'll send you back. Then we'll see if you're still laughing after a few days down in the Abyss."

Zin threw his hands up, his cocky expression replaced with frustration. "Fine, fine. I didn't know you were going to get this worked up about it. I won't say a single word. I promise. No need to threaten me."

Ean stared at the imp until he was certain that Zin wasn't lying, then nodded and got back to his feet. "Good, I'm glad that's settled. Now, I have a question for you. Since I tattooed this rune on my hand, I've been--" he paused a moment, trying to figure out how to put into words what he had been feeling. "I've been able to, I guess the best word would be 'sense,' when you are near. And that's not all. I think I could sense that troll as well. And the Hound. At the moment, the Hound is like a burning beacon in my mind. I think I could find him if he were a day's journey away. Are my tattoo and the feelings connected?"

Zin's head tilted to the side as he regarded Ean. A slight frown touched the corners of his mouth, and when he spoke his tone was guarded. "Yes, the two are connected."

Ean stared at him until he realized the imp wasn't going to say more. "That's it? No explanation? Not even a—"

He was cut off by a scream. Spinning around, he found Bran on his feet, sword in hand, standing in front of Jaslen. He followed both of their gazes and found the Hound. It had already finished its meal, a pile of gnawed bones and discarded limbs marking where the troll had been. The Hound was now walking towards them, its head low and teeth bared.

Ean moved to place himself in between the beast and his companions. Raising both hands, palms out in front of the beast, he started to move towards it. The Hound stopped, raising its head.

"Time to go home now." Ean spoke slowly, doubting the Hound understood a single word. To help emphasize what he was saying, he gestured towards the still glowing summoning rune. The beast looked at the rune, then at him, and back at the rune. It seemed to think for a moment, and then to Ean's surprise, made its way over to the rune.

Feeling more confident, Ean moved so close to the Hound that he could smell the rotten stink of troll guts on its breath. Suppressing a gag, he picked up the rune. When he locked eyes with the Hound, it was as if he were sinking into its watery purple eyes. Images of a dim gray cavern floated in his mind. The floor was made of a polished sheet of black granite. There were stalagmites everywhere, reaching high into the air and disappearing into the darkness.

There was movement as well. The slither of scales came from in front of him, the whisper of padded feet brushed behind him, the flap of wings on either side buffeted him with air. The crackle of their camp fire faded away as his body went numb. As the two worlds seemed to mix in his mind, the darker world became everything as his consciousness faded away.

EAN TRIED TO YELL, call out, but nothing escaped his lips. He had no control over his arms, legs or body. Even his eyes wouldn't travel to where he wanted them. His body moved of its own accord. At first he thought he was crawling around on his hands and knees, as his head swiveled about. There was movement in the darkness, movement away from him. He suddenly felt an excitement that was not his own. His eyes, no, the eyes he was seeing through, seemed to lock on something in the darkness.

He took off, sprinting along the ground and into the darkness. The strange, dim glow that lit the small area around him seemed to follow along as he moved. Onward he plunged while dark shapes skittered away in the darkness. He ignored those shapes, or to be more accurate, whatever eyes he was seeing through ignored them. His attention remained fixed on something in the darkness, something that dodged around stalagmites and leapt over dark holes in the ground.

Ean was starting to feel the excitement as if it was his own now. He caught sight of a clawed foot or paw as he ran, but ignored them. The flap of wings above him sounded as if flocks of birds were flying just out of sight. The cries and whimpers of the creatures dodging to get out of the way just seemed to drive him on even more. Most pronounced of all was the scrape of claws on stone.

Was he seeing things through the eyes of his Hound? That brought up an even more worrisome question: Had something gone so wrong that he had become part of the Hound? The thought rocked Ean to the core, but the Hound bounded on. His own fear began to mix into that feeling of excitement that rolled around in his mind. There was so much he didn't know about the magic he used. Had he caused this? Was this going to be the rest of his life, trapped in the mind of a beast?

The excitement he felt changed to exultation, and the Hound put on a burst of speed. Time seemed to slow. In front of him, a form started to take shape in the darkness. It was small, the head of the creature not even reaching as high as the Hound's head. A moment later, and the form took on an actual shape. It was humanoid, with thin arms and legs, its skin a muddy brown color.

The Hound was only a few steps away now from the unlucky creature. Ean could feel a rumble in his stomach, no, the Hound's stomach. It seemed that the longer he was a part of the Hound, the more their sensations merged...which caused Ean to panic more.

Taking a few bounds, the Hound leapt into the air. Ean's terror was washed away with an overwhelming sense of triumph. The Hound's prey let out a scream and spun around, giving Ean a clear view of the potential meal. Its face had a look of horror, mouth wide open showing tiny pointed teeth, beady black eyes squeezed shut behind its long, pointed nose.

Zin! Ean screamed in his mind as the Hound's jaws snapped shut.

CHAPTER 10

EAST TRAVELS

"ZIN!"

"What?" Ean heard the imp's voice behind him. "I'm not doing anything!"

Ean blinked. In front of him sat the Hound, its dark eyes still staring back at him. He looked down to find his hand hovering above the rune, its faint glow a contrast to the stronger light coming from the fire. He looked up and found the stars still in the sky, the three moons now visible this late at night floating along high above him. Behind him, he could feel Zin approaching.

"Are you alright?" The imp's voice was hesitant, almost worried.

"Yes...uh, I'm fine. Completely fine."

"Alright, if you say so."

Ean took a better look at everyone. Zin stood in a tense pose as if he was expecting to be kicked. Bran and Jaslen were still huddled together, both looking at him with calculating eyes. Great, now they probably think I'm crazy. Returning his attention to the Hound, he tried not to think about the three pairs of eyes he could feel drilling into his back.

"Alright, boy, time to go home."

The rune tripled in brightness, bathing the area in a dark blue glow. It disappeared, replaced by a gaping hole in the ground that seemed to drop off into nothingness. Ean stared into the hole, trying to look past the purplish-blue light but couldn't make out anything past the haze that swirled around just inside.

"Go ahead, boy," Ean said to the Hound.

He used his head to motion towards the portal. The Hound complied and placed its front paws into the hole. Instead of dropping straight down, it sank like a cart sinking into a bog. When the entire Hound sank from view, the portal closed and was replaced again by the rune. The rune flashed one last time, then faded away into nothing.

Ean got back onto his feet. His mind continued to swim from the experience of seeing through a Hound's eyes and feeling its hunger. Had he imagined it all or had it been real? Had he been looking through his Hound's eyes or had it been the eyes of something else? A mountain of questions piled up in his mind. He really had to get Zin alone at some point so that they could talk about everything he had experienced since painting that rune onto his hand.

The rustle of clothes brought his attention back to the here and now. He found Bran and Jaslen rising to their feet as well. Bran steadied Jaslen as she found her footing and went over to Zin.

"You are much less intimidating than that other creature...Zin, is it? Can you speak?" Jaslen's voice had taken on a friendly tone, but she kept some distance between herself and the imp. "My name is Jaslen."

"Yeah, I know who you are. I've been around Ean long enough to know all about yo...uh the people of your village."

"Oh really? Then how come we have never seen you around? Does Ean keep you locked away?"

In answer, Zin vanished from sight. Jaslen fell back, a small squeak escaped her mouth. "Where did he go?"

Zin reappeared, exactly where he had been before. Jaslen stared at him for a moment then began to clap her hands and laugh. Her joyful laughter made him smile.

"That was wonderful! Can you do it whenever you want?"

"Yes. It's helpful in your world, but most things in the Abyss can hunt by smell, so it's not as useful there."

Knowing that Zin tended to shift a lot whenever he felt uncomfortable, Ean knew the imp must be a complete wreck. All of Jaslen's questions, and her unwavering attention, had Zin fading in and out like candle light in a breeze. If the cuts on Ean's stomach didn't burn so much, he'd be splitting a gut at the poor imp's plight. For now, he kept a stiff back and snorted out a barely controlled snicker.

"Well, you won't have to worry about hiding with us around now," Jaslen said, giving the imp a friendly smile, "at least not while we're traveling outside of villages and towns. I can't wait for a better opportunity to sit down and ask you all about your home."

"Yes, that sounds like it would be oh so much fun." The sarcasm was clear in Zin's voice, but Jaslen's expression never changed. She either missed it, or chose to ignore it. Zin continued to shuffle his feet, his hands clasped together behind his back.

Jaslen opened her mouth to say more but Bran interrupted. "The horse is dead," he said glumly. "We'll have to fashion some kind of splint to carry our things into Rensen. It will probably be slow going. It might even take us two or three more days to reach the village."

Jaslen's expression dropped for a moment but then brightened as a thought seemed to strike her. "Is there anything you can do, Ean? With your magic? Maybe make our things lighter somehow? Or how about summoning something that could drag or carry our things at least through the mountain? Something that isn't as scary as the beast you just sent back."

"Well, I guess there is one thing I could do."

Ean knelt down and began to draw a rune with his finger. He had to draw it a lot bigger than usual, but it was the attention to detail that mattered, not the size. The lines and symbols flared to life as he drew them along the ground, casting that now familiar blue light on the surrounding area again. As soon as he finished the complex design, the rune disappeared, replaced by another gaping dark hole in the ground.

"What are you summoning now?" Jaslen's voice was a mixture of awe and fear.

"Nothing."

She squinted her eyes, clearly expecting more.

"It's a storage space, of sorts, my own private storage space. Zin calls it a Pocket. I can fit a certain amount things in there and open it back up somewhere else."

Jaslen's expression bordered on adoration. Ean felt heat rush to his cheeks. The blush embarrassed him, but having the positive attentions of a pretty girl was inebriating.

From the corner of his eye, he saw Bran's eyes narrow, while the corners of his mouth turned down in disapproval. Realizing that in an unguarded moment he had let his feelings for Jaslen come to the surface, he turned his face to an impassive expression. Ean pretended not to have noticed the other boy's angry glare. All he could do was hope that Bran would chalk up what he saw to his imagination. They had a long road ahead of them, and it was essential that they learn to trust one another. Ean vowed to be more careful in hiding his true feelings in the future.

"Bran," Ean said, trying to sound casual. "We can fit most of our things in here, but we'll still have to carry the tent materials."

Bran was silent for a moment, still regarding him with that same expression. Ean shifted about until he finally spoke. "That's fine. The posts and materials are not that heavy. They shouldn't slow us down at all."

"That's good."

Ean felt uncomfortable. He looked up at the sky, trying to get an idea of how late it was at night. "Well, I don't expect to get much sleep tonight. Should we pack everything up and head out now, or do you want to try and rest a little before we leave?" He had directed the question to Jaslen, but Bran answered first.

"We should probably get going. We can rest for a day or two once we get to Rensen. It will give us time to try and find a caravan going to Lurthalan. My father said that would be the best way to travel."

"Yes, I doubt I could sleep tonight," Jaslen said with a sigh. "My head is still sore, and I expect to have bad dreams of trolls trying to make a meal of me for at least the next couple of days. If I'm going to have nightmares, I would prefer to wake up from them safe in an inn than out here on the ground."

"It's decided then," Bran said, placing a gentle hand on Jaslen. His normal, positive demeanor had returned. "You stay here, love, and rest. I'm sure Ean and I can handle packing things up. Unless, of course, Ean needs to stay near...that." He gestured towards to the still glowing hole in the ground.

"No, I can leave it there. It won't close up unless I go too far away, and even then it's simple enough to open up again."

"Good." Bran squeezed Jaslen's shoulder then walked off towards their tent. Rising gingerly, a hand holding his stomach, Ean started to move back towards his things. He had only taken two steps, when he heard Jaslen speaking and immediately stopped.

"So, Zin, we have some time now to talk while the boys pack things up."

Ean tried to subtly lock eyes with Zin. The imp was nodding at the girl, but his eyes were locked on him. Ean returned to his tent, hoping the imp would be smart about what he said.

"Not much to tell," Ean heard the imp say loud enough for him to hear. "Imps like me live on the first level of the Abyss with all of the other minor creatures."

Satisfied Zin would watch his tongue, Ean began to pack up his supplies and take down his tent. When he finished, he dragged his bags and the tent pieces over towards where Jaslen and Zin were still talking by his Pocket.

"No, I have never seen Ze'an," Zin was saying as Ean approached. "As far as I know, he never comes up to the top level of the Abyss, or any of the higher levels for that matter. Oh look, Ean's back."

When Zin got up to join him, Jaslen's lower lip formed into a pout which spread into a superior smirk, making Ean nervous. What information had she pumped from Zin? No time to ask him now. Reaching his rune, he set the tent material down on the ground and knelt down next to the hole. He tossed his bag of clothes down into the portal without a thought but was much gentler with the medicine bag, which he carefully lowered down until he felt it come to rest on top of something.

"How much can your storage space hold, Ean?" Jaslen asked as she stared down into the Pocket. The smirk that had previously adorned her face was gone. Ean couldn't figure out if that made him feel better or worse.

"I'm not sure," he said. "I usually only keep things that are important to me in there. This is the biggest I've ever made the opening, and I don't think I could make it much larger."

"Interesting..." Jaslen trailed off, her attention drawn to the swirl of color and lights.

Bran tossed his and Jaslen's things down in front of Ean. "That should do it." He placed his tent materials down next to Ean's and then looked at him expectantly.

With a grunt Ean picked up their bags and lowered them down with the others. Pulling his arm free, he focused his attention on the Pocket and willed it to close. Both Bran and Jaslen were looking at the Pocket with wonder on their faces. They would expect answers to so many more questions now that they saw his connection to the Abyss, or what they perceived as his connection. When the portal closed, the four remained silent for a time until Zin broke the silence.

"Well, if we are just about set to go, would anyone mind if I snacked a bit on the horse before we leave? The mountain path hasn't had a great deal of small vermin for me to eat, so if I could fill up now, I think I could make it the rest of the way without eating again."

"No!" Bran and Jaslen shouted in unison. Ean had been in mid-shrug but froze as he heard the other two. Zin took a step back in surprise and shot a confused look at Ean. When Ean kept his mouth shut, the imp scowled at him, then spoke to Jaslen and Bran.

"And why not?" the imp said, scratching at his head. "It would be a shame to let all of that meat go to waste."

"Claire was practically a member of my family!" Bran said. "Father bought her almost ten years ago, a special order from The Merchant that he had to place the year before. She isn't going to just be another meal for you or anybody else. We'll..." he looked about for a moment. "We'll bury her."

At that, Ean did speak up. "Bury her?" He waved his hand around, taking in the area. "This is all rock and stone. Unless you brought a pickax with you, there is no way we could ever bury her. Best to just leave her be and move on."

Bran shook his head violently while Jaslen took over the debate. "No, we can't just leave her to be scavenged." She placed a hand on Bran's shoulder. "It just wouldn't be right. We'll cover her with stones; that shouldn't take too long."

"Fine, fine," Ean said, surrendering to the two.

This was probably how the rest of the trip would go—him always getting out voted by the other two. He doubted they would start letting Zin weigh in on any decisions either. Mumbling to himself, Ean got back to his feet. He stumbled a bit as he rose, his right arm giving out as he tried to use it to push himself up.

That was strange.

If anything he would expect his stomach injury to cause him problems. Once on his feet, he began to rub his arm with his left hand, trying to rid himself of the numbness that had crept up it again. Very strange.

Bran was already on his feet, in the middle of helping Jaslen up as well. Jaslen wavered, almost falling back down, a hand going to her head as she tried to keep her balance. "Maybe you should rest a little longer," Bran said, concern clear in his voice. "Ean and I can handle covering up Claire."

"I'm well enough to help," she waved him off as she spoke. "Anyway, Ean was hurt as well, and he is up and moving around." She flashed Ean a small half smile which he tried to return.

"Better to just let her help, Bran," Ean said, trying to put some humor in his voice. "We'll be here all night if you try and arg—"

PAIN.

It shot through Ean's body faster than he could react. His eyes popped as his head shot back. A scream burst out of him. As the pain rushed through every fiber of his being, he closed his eyes to shut out the world, but it didn't help. His body hit the ground. His head bounced off a rock, but it was nothing compared to the river of agony that raged inside him. Curling up into a ball, he screamed again.

It washed over him like a sudden downpour, soaking him to the very core of his body. One moment it felt as if his entire body was aflame, a scorching inferno that cooked him to the bone. The next moment he was freezing, a cold that froze his lungs and stopped his heart. After that, it was as if he was being crushed and ripped apart all at the same time. And it kept repeating.

For moments.

For days.

For years.

A cycle of pain.

And then emptiness.

WHEN EAN AWOKE, THE first thing he remembered was the pain, but it was gone now. *Am I dead? No one ought to have survived the* kind of agony he had gone through — as if his body had been torn inside out. Now, he felt only comfort and peace as he snuggled inside a patchwork quilt upon a soft mattress. He rubbed his stomach — the wounds from the troll were gone.

He opened his eyes. A light blinded him at first, and he had to squint as his eyes adjusted. Above him, once he could make anything out, he found a wooden ceiling high above his head. So he was inside! But where? Certainly not his own room at home. The one lamp there couldn't cast nearly enough light to keep him squinting. Ean let his head flop to the side and tried to make out more of his surroundings.

The wall running behind him was the first thing he noticed—the wooden boards dyed a dark red color, a single window placed in the center. The window was dark, but that told him nothing. From where they had been camped, it was at least a day's journey to Rottwealth or Rensen. Arranged about the room were other pieces of furniture: a few dressers, a table with a couple of chairs and two other beds.

It was the person sitting on the bed across from him, though, that made him smile. Jaslen was sitting on the edge with her legs folded underneath her. A book was in her lap, and she was nibbling her lower lip as she read from its pages.

Ean remained still, looking over at her. The questions about what had happened went from a hornet's nest in his head to a mild buzz. She had always had that effect on him, even when they were little. She sat there wearing the same clothes as before his little blackout, strands of her dark red hair falling across her face, which she occasionally blew out of her eyes.

As always, Zin's voice disturbed his peace. "Welcome to the world of the living. See anything you like here in Rensen?"

Ean found Zin sitting on top of a bed post. The imp was looking down at him with that mocking little smile, half grin, half a show of his pointy little teeth. Blast the imp! Pushing the covers off his upper body, he inched his way back so that he was sitting up against the backboard of the bed.

"Ean! You're awake!" Jaslen moved off the bed, the book she was reading forgotten as it fell to the floor. She moved over next to him and knelt down. "We were so worried about you! Well, Bran and I were." She flashed the imp a grimace. "After you fell silent, Zin didn't seem worried at all."

"There was no need to be worried," Zin replied. "He survived the growth, which was the dangerous part. After that, it was only a matter of time before he woke u..." He trailed off as two sets of eyes locked on him. Shuffling about on the post, he remained quiet for a time before continuing. "It wasn't like there was a strong possibility that he would die."

Jaslen's full attention was on the imp now, her hands on her hips as she stared up at him. "Zin, during our entire trip here, you said that you had no idea what had happened."

"No," Zin said, shaking his head. "I said that I couldn't tell you what happened. I knew exactly what caused him to black out and where all the pain came from. I just wasn't allowed to tell you." The imp was looking directly at Ean now. That traitor!

"Why would you keep something like this from me?" she said looking at Ean, a tinge of hurt touching her voice. "I mean, us. Especially if it's something as serious as what I saw happen to you."

"Uh," Ean replied as he tried to get his thoughts in order.

"Ean, we had no idea what was going on. Your arm looked like it was on fire, and when you screamed ..." A shudder ran through her body. "You should have told us that would happen." She was quiet for a few moments. When she spoke again, her voice was low. "I thought you were dying. I thought that I was going to have to watch you die."

Heartbreak. Reaching over, Ean put a hand on her shoulder. "I'm sorry Jaslen, I really am sorry. My situation is, well, complicated, I guess is the best word." She still wasn't looking at him. "In all honesty, I don't even understand most of what is happening either. Zin apparently knows the most, but he has told me very little."

He tore his eyes away from Jaslen, and focused on Zin. "And it sounds like he knows more than what he has been telling me."

The imp tried to put on an innocent face. It didn't exactly fit with the beady eyes and multitude of sharp teeth that peeked out between his lips. "I have told you everything I know. I warned you about the pain." At Ean's harsh glare, he continued on faster. "Fine, after the first time it happened I did, at least. I have as little idea as you do as to when it will return. It's simply part of the process." He clamped his mouth shut.

"What process?" both Ean and Jaslen asked in unison. While Ean had directed the question towards Zin, Jaslen was looking at Ean again. Now it was his turn to look innocent. It wasn't difficult, since he had no idea what the imp was talking about.

"I don't know what he is talking about either," Ean said to her before returning his attention to the imp. "A process? I figured the pain was a one-time thing. You mean the pain is going to keep happening?"

"Yes." The imp was looking away now. "Putting the tattoo on your hand was more of a start to the process then actually being the entire process."

"And you were going to tell me this when?"

Jaslen cut in, snatching Ean's hand into hers as she spoke. "What does it do?" Her voice was hushed as she stared at the designs. Reaching out slowly with her free hand, she placed a finger on the runes that grew around his wrist, tracing along one of the designs. Her touch sent shivers up and down his body.

"I don't even know," Ean replied, "for the most part. Zin says that it will increase my strength in using the energy from the Abyss. As of now, summoning anything feels like I'm getting my insides ripped out. These designs are supposed to gradually lessen that pain. What he didn't warn me about was the random bursts of unbearable agony." Ean cut off as he took a better look at his right arm.

The tattoo that had extended from the rune on his palm to his wrist now stretched all the way to elbow, the lines twisting around each other to the point where it was impossible to follow one path all the way from beginning to end. Intermixed in the black curving lines were little lines of blue, almost like veins.

That was certainly new. Returning his attention back to Jaslen, he shrugged.

"Other than that, I have no idea what else these tattoos will do. I don't actually know what many of the runes mean." He tried looking up at Zin again, hoping Jaslen didn't catch the embarrassment that he was sure was written across his face. "And Zin has told me practically nothing about it since I inscribed it onto my hand."

"I tell you what I can!" With a snort, the imp leapt down to the floor. "The lack of trust you have ... after all these years ..." He stormed towards the door, muttering to himself. Just as he reached it, Zin spun back around. The glare he shot Ean was less than friendly.

"I'm going to find something to eat. Maybe by tomorrow you will have realized that I've always been looking out for your best interests." And with that he disappeared from sight. The door opened and then slammed shut.

Ean slumped down against the backboard. "I suppose I owe him an apology."

"Yes, probably." Jaslen said matter-of-factly. She rose to her feet and moved back to her bed, picking up the book as she went. "If you had any smarts about you, you would apologize to Bran and me as well. If we are going to travel together, we shouldn't be keeping any secrets from each other." She sat back down on the bed, and returned her attention back to him. "Especially ones as big as that." She gestured with the book towards his exposed arm and hand.

"I am sorry, Jaslen. I just ... I've been so used to keeping secrets, that it's almost second nature for me. It was stupid of me to think that I could keep this and everything else a secret while we traveled together."

Ean moved to the edge of his bed and sat there without speaking, his eyes on Jaslen. He tried to think about what he could say to make things better. Coming up empty, he got to his feet and moved over to the one window in the room.

Looking out, he found a village much different from his own. Across the street were houses densely packed together. Most were only one story like the houses in Rottwealth, but they were all made of planks instead of densely woven sticks, their bases stone and mortar. Each was also roofed with planks of wood, each roof painted a different color that made the rooftops look like a dark colored rainbow. Lights could be seen through many of the glass windows, fending off the darkness of the night.

A few streets back sat a larger building, four levels high, built of heavy logs instead of planks. There were a number of windows on each level, and even at this distance, Ean could see a large number of people moving about through the windows on each floor. Behind that building was an area of clean cut trees that eventually ended at the edge of the forest.

"Just promise me one thing, and I suppose I will forgive you this time." When he nodded, she continued on. "Promise me that from now on, you won't keep anything from us that you know is important or will affect our trip."

"Of course, I absolutely promise," he said.

"Good. Now, while Bran is downstairs in the common room having a few drinks, you get to keep me company. I think you should entertain me by telling me all about the trouble you and Zin have been up to back at home. I'm curious to hear about what you two have been doing right under everyone's noses."

He gave a short laugh and sat down on the floor in front of her. Maybe telling her MOST of what he had been up to wouldn't be so bad. He would just leave out the little things that involved her.

CHAPTER II

NEW EXPERIENCES

EAN WOKE THE NEXT day to find the room empty. Both of the other beds were already made, and a quick glance around the room confirmed that Zin wasn't present either. The imp hadn't come back before Ean and Jaslen had gone to their separate beds the night before. He had probably stayed out all night, hunting for food and trying to make Ean feel guilty about doubting him. Well, the imp certainly wasn't telling him everything he knew, so let him sulk.

Climbing out of bed, Ean moved to the window first. Judging by the small amount of light filtering in through the glass, it was still early morning. Down on the streets below, a few people moved about, but for the most part, the village looked empty and peaceful. Turning his attention back to the room, he noticed a piece of paper resting on one of the clothes drawers. The handwriting was clearly Jaslen's, the lettering flowing on the page. Sitting on his bed, Ean began to read,

Ean,

We thought it was best to let you rest. We've gone out to see the village and try to find passage to Lurthalan. Bran was talking to a few workers last night that work for a caravan that might be

heading north. We're going to try approaching whoever is in charge to see if they are heading to the city and if we can arrange passage. It would make the trip that much easier since we've never traveled the path through the woods before. Plus, after our experiences already with that troll, it would be nice to travel with a bit more protection. We'll meet back in the common room around lunch and let you know what happens. Have fun looking around!

—Jaslen

Tossing the note to the side, Ean got dressed and moved out of his room. Having been unconscious when they arrived, Ean had no idea how the inn was arranged. The floor he was on consisted of one long hall with wooden doors to either side. It ended with steps going down, which Ean followed down two flights that ended in a hallway that ran left and right. Towards the right, a sign marked the door at the end as the living quarters of the owners, so Ean went left and through a door that led out into the common room of the inn.

The common room was what you would expect from any inn, except that it was completely windowless. Long tables surrounded by wooden stools or benches took up most of the floor, very similar to the setup of the Golden Coin back in Rottwealth. A few of those stools still held people, some enjoying a morning meal while others were slumped over a table or against a wall. A single serving girl moved about the room, delivering food and drink to those awake, occasionally poking those passed out to make sure they were still breathing. Not wanting to have anything to do with that kind of crowd, Ean moved through the room as fast as he could and passed through the double doors that led out of the inn and into the street.

Stepping outside, he stopped dead, amazed at what he saw. In front of him, across the street and on the other side of a huge grassy clearing was the largest building he had ever seen. Constructed only of large logs placed on top of each other in a staggered pattern, the building towered over the rest of the village. A pair of square doors twice his height sat smack in the middle of the side facing the inn while the rest of the wall was windowless. Ean couldn't even imagine how something that huge could have even been constructed.

Shaking his head, he tore his gaze away from the building and looked around the rest of Rensen. Just like the inn, he had no idea what the layout of the town was like. Down the street to his left, he found what looked to be the residential area that he had seen from his window the night before. Sure enough, a few streets back he could make out the top of that large building that had been full of activity the night before towering over the other houses. Behind the building was a thick forest of evergreens. A road cut a path through it, spiraling towards the mountains looming in the distance. That must have been the road they had come in on.

To his right, he found a building with a sign hanging above the door that designated it as the town store. It sat on the corner of the street, while across from it further down the road was a large two-story house. Past that house was a field populated with different sized and colored wagons. That must be where the traders were, which meant it was also where Bran and Jaslen had gone. Not wanting to interrupt whatever the two were up to, Ean decided to head in the opposite direction. He was curious about the large building that sat in the residential area and even more curious about the monster of a building to the north. Why would anyone even need a building that big?

As Ean moved away from the inn, the streets were more or less empty. Being a logging village, he assumed the majority of workers must already be out in the forest chopping down trees or hunting game. He only saw two people as he moved towards what looked to be the residential area. Both carried large bows in their hands with full quivers strapped to their waists. Hunters, setting out for the day. They didn't give him a second glance.

He continued on, passing a side street on his left that was filled with similar sized homes, and then another block of houses after that, before reaching the street where the larger building he had seen last night sat. He walked up to the building, his curiosity growing the closer he got to it. Not a single mark or sign indicated the building's purpose. Every window that had been lit and filled with movement the night before was now dark and devoid of life. Dim morning light filtered through the windows, allowing Ean to make out the vague outlines of chairs turned upside down on tables.

With a grunt of disappointment, Ean headed back towards what he figured was the center of the village. Maybe the even larger building would produce something more interesting. Retracing his steps he walked down the street, glancing in the occasional window out of sheer boredom.

Ean had expected life outside of the village he had grown up in to be different, but he was surprised by this logging town's quiet streets. At this hour, the village back home would already be bustling with activity. Maybe the loggers were already awake and were deep in the forest. Then again, maybe everyone was asleep. What were the hours that loggers kept anyway?

He brushed the thoughts out of his mind as he reached the end of the street. Straight ahead of him, across the large open field sat the massive wooden building. The side facing him and the rest of the town gave absolutely no hints at what the building could possible contain.

The road slowly curved left around the clearing and then back to the large building. Instead of cutting across the clearing, he decided to follow the road around to the building's side. He hoped that searching the entire perimeter would yield a clue as to its purpose. Was it a saw house or storage facility?

Sitting slightly back and off to the side of the building was a large stack of tree trunks. Each one was two or three stories tall with wide trunks. The logs were stacked on top of each other, about six logs high.

"How is that possible?" Ean mumbled to himself. One log that size probably took a dozen men or horses to drag out of the forest alone. What could they possibly be using to lift the logs and stack them like that? Magic? The more he explored the village, the more interesting it became.

As he continued to move around the building, he saw a smaller set of double doors, just tall enough for him to walk under without having to duck. On the next story up, there was a giant rectangular opening in the wall that went almost all the way from one side of the wall to the other.

With the sun still creeping up in the east, Ean squinted into the dark opening but couldn't make out anything more than a few vague shapes. As his curiosity swelled, a movement in the building's backyard—the pine forest to the north—caught his eye.

Four people emerged from the trees carrying a huge tree trunk. A team of eight horses couldn't drag a log that big, yet these men were carrying it on their shoulders as if it were no trouble at all. The trunk had been stripped of all of its branches and most of its bark, with both ends cleanly cut. The four were positioned two at the front and two at the back, with the trunk itself sitting on their shoulders. They carried the trunk to the stack of other logs and maneuvered it up on top of the pile. It was only after they had placed the log and stepped away from the pile that Ean was able to see that they were not really human at all.

Ean had never seen a Taruun before, but he had heard about them from Cleff and read about them in many of the books he had studied on the healing arts. The four he saw stood easily twice the height of Bran, their long arms and legs almost twice the size of Ean's own limbs. While most of their bodies were long and gangly, their facial features were hard and precise, more harsh angles than curves. Each Taruun's head looked as if it had been stretched out slightly and then had all of the curves filed down to sharp edges, from their small eyes and noses to their pointy cheeks and chins. Their skin, which was an ivory white, looked as if it had been stretched tightly over every bone and muscle of their bodies. Each one had long, gray hair that hung just above their shoulders.

Their bodies looked thin and frail, at least the pieces Ean saw that were not covered by their loose fitting shirts and baggy trousers. Their appearance was deceiving, however. Ean had been taught that they were the strongest race in the land, and seeing four of them carry a log that even a dozen men would have struggled to lift confirmed it.

When teaching Ean about the Taruun, Cleff had even shown him where their amazing strength came from. The old man had shown Ean a jar containing the preserved remains of a Taruun arm muscle. The mass of it had three times as many strands as the average human muscle, densely woven together so that it was impossible to follow a single strand for very long. The muscles were also incredibly hard to cut. Cleff had taken a cleaver to the muscle, chopping at it with all of his strength and failed to put even a nick in the old muscle.

His curiosity getting the better of him, Ean started making his way over to the four looming figures. They were huddled close together now, talking to each other softly. Ean got within twenty paces of the group before they noticed. They stopped talking, and the one in the group that had noticed him first stepped forward, raising a large hand, palm out towards him.

"Only workers are allowed near the factory," the Taruun said. The way he spoke was strange, the pitch of his voice changing with each word. "It is dangerous for any to be too close, but especially dangerous for young ones."

With the funny way he spoke, it took Ean a few moments to comprehend what was said. A grimace crossed his face as the words sunk in. Young one? He wasn't some foolish child that would run around their legs while they carried the logs and get in their way, and he certainly wouldn't go near the stacks regardless of how stable they looked.

"I will be careful," he said. "I'm a Healer, so I know better than most of the kind of damage logs of that size could do to a human body." The four simply stared at him.

"And I'm not that young. I've handled people that have lost limbs or had bones crushed. Once I even hel—" Ean cut off with a squeak, falling backwards as a monstrous form reached out of a large opening in the side of the nearby building.

A hand emerged, larger than any of the Taruuns' entire bodies. It seemed to be made of wood, or at least a wood-like material. Each finger was made up of different sections connected by what looked to be solid metal joints. But no metal Ean had ever seen could bend to the degree that the fingers were bending. The thing moved as freely as if it were made of flesh and bone.

Ean sat there, too stunned to move. It lifted up the top log on the stack in its fingers as easy as he might pick up a toothpick and then retracted back into the darkness of the building. Moments later, a loud buzzing sound came from the opening, louder than anything he had ever heard before. Ean continued to gape at the opening until the buzzing stopped. It was then that he heard laughter coming from the Taruuns.

Embarrassment quickly overrode the feeling of shock. Climbing to his feet, Ean rounded on the Taruuns. "What was that?" He had meant his words to come out as a yell but instead he squeaked the sentence.

The Taruuns continued to laugh. They turned their backs to him and began to head into the forest. Ean wanted to yell after them, but fear of his voice cracking again kept him quiet. He resigned himself to glaring at their backs as they left.

Once the Taruuns had disappeared back into the forest, Ean turned back towards the building. Some kind of hatch had dropped into place where the huge hand had come out, blocking any view of the inside. Maybe there was another opening he could peak through around back? He stood there for a time trying to decide what to do when a low growl escaped from his stomach. Looking to the sky, Ean figured it was still well before mid-day by the position of the sun. If he gave up for the moment on this mystery, he could head back to the inn and grab something to eat, maybe ask one of the locals about the building. Maybe the building would be open again later in the day, and he could try back before he was supposed to meet Bran and Jaslen.

He cut across the field, his pace increased the more his stomach growled. As he moved, he noticed that the rest of the town was starting to come to life. Men and women were coming outside, going about their daily chores, errands or moving about the village. The lazier of the town's hunters were heading out as well; an irritated wife was even chasing one out with a broom. A few folks were gathered in other places while children began to play in the large field in the center of the town he was cutting across.

Trying not to be noticed, Ean kept his head down until he reached the inn. Ducking inside, he paused to look around the common room for a place to sit. In the short time that he had been gone, the room had cleared out. The single serving girl remained, cleaning up the tables and righting overturned stools. She waved Ean over with a tired smile.

"Have a seat over here, and I'll get you something to eat and drink," she said, motioning him over. "Your friends already paid for your breakfast before they left this morning, but you snuck out before I could tell you." The girl patted the top of stool she had just placed next to a table.

Ean hadn't paid much attention to the waitress when he first walked in, but this time he noticed the cute dimples in her cheeks when she smiled in his direction. Disheveled coppery brown hair, sky blue eyes, tiny button nose — she reminded him of a porcelain doll the mayor's wife proudly displayed on her fireplace mantel. The doll was one of the most refined things in his village; to see this lovely living embodiment in the flesh both intrigued and amused him.

Ean hesitated for only a moment before heading over to the table next to the woman. Mumbling a thank you, he sat down.

"Now you just wait a bit, and I'll be right back with your food." She patted his back the same way she had the stool then turned and strode away. Ean watched her go as she weaved in and out of the tables and then through a door next to the bar.

The girl returned with two plates of food balanced on one hand and a pair of mugs gripped in the other. She still wore a smile this time, though, there was quite a bit more life behind it. Reaching his side, she sat herself down next to him and deposited a plate and mug down in front of him and herself.

"My shift is up, so I figure I could give you some company. My name's Paige, by the way."

"I'm Ean," he stammered, a bit taken back. "Nice to meet you." Even with her hair disheveled and ale stains on her plain brown shirt and pants, Ean found her easy on the eyes. Which, of course, made him nervous.

"So, um, have you worked here long?"

She took a swig from her mug before answering. "Most of my life. My parents are best friends with the owners, and my mom works back in the kitchen, so I practically grew up here waiting tables."

She paused only long enough to rip off a small piece of bread and put it in her mouth. She didn't even bother chewing, simply washing it down with a drink from her mug before continuing on.

"So where are you from? Lurthalan? Halyquain?" Ean tried to answer but never got the chance as she continued on. "You don't look like one of the usual crowd that comes with the caravans. No, not part of the caravans. A boy setting out to prove himself maybe? Yes, that's got to be it! Ean the future Hero!" She clapped her hands together enthusiastically, her mouth finally closing for the first time since she sat down.

The words had come so quickly that it took Ean a bit to finally catch up in his head. And which question should he answer? "Actually I'm from Rottwealth, but my friends and I are heading to..."

"Rottwealth?" she cut in, a hint of skepticism touching her voice. "No one ever comes here from Rottwealth. And I rarely hear about anyone ever going there." She leaned forward, her elbows on the table and her head resting in her hands. "Is it true that everyone in your village is related?" She looked him up and down, her eyes lingering on his gloves. "Are your hands disfigured because of the inbreeding?"

Feeling insulted, Ean tried to keep the annoyance he felt out of his voice. "No, most of the people in the village are not related. And I wear the gloves because I burnt my hand working with dangerous plants and herbs. I'm a Healer. Maybe you shouldn't be so quick to judge a person by his appearance."

Paige grew quiet, her blue eyes narrowed as she looked at him. Avoiding the hurt look in her eyes, Ean focused on his plate, telling himself that the girl had deserved the harsh words, whether she had meant to be insulting or not. Leaning forward, he shoveled some ham slices into his mouth and then took a long sip from his drink. He kept his eyes locked on the plate because he was hungry, he told himself, not at all because he felt bad about snapping at her.

Well, maybe he felt a little bad.

Back at home, few people bothered to speak to him at all, especially not someone as nice-looking as the talkative young waitress. He should be happy she seemed interested in him at all. His guilt at lashing out started to grow, giving him indigestion and making his stomach growl for a reason besides hunger. If he wanted to enjoy his meal, he might as well apologize and be done with it. Pulling his gaze away from his food, he tried to look her in the eyes.

Paige was actually smiling at him! There were no signs of anger or annoyance anywhere on her face.

"You are an interesting one, Healer Ean." She emphasized Healer in a sarcastic, yet joking way, that smile never leaving her face. It was a pretty smile. "How about you walk me home. You can tell me all about the things you can do to heal people. And maybe I'll even understand some of it."

She rose and grabbed his hand, pulling him up as well. He tried to protest but she pulled him along anyway. As they reached the door, Ean glanced back at the table. While Paige's plate sat empty, his own was still had plenty of ham and biscuits resting on top of it. So much for getting a decent meal. With a dejected sigh, he gave in and let Paige pull him out the door.

Paige slowed down as they got outside, letting go of his hand as she moved to walk beside him.

"How long have you studied healing? Could you identify any plant in the world? Have you ever had a person you couldn't save?"

Ean answered each question easily, except the last one, as they walked down the street. What had happened to Lane and the mine foreman was still too recent and painful of a memory to talk about. The blood, the crying, the screams; he hoped it was a long time before he had to experience anything like that again. Thankfully she quickly changed topics.

"If this is your first time away from your home, you must have as many questions for me as I've had for you," she said. "Have you seen our saw mill? That is one of a kind, I promise you that."

He nodded. Finally, something coming out of her mouth that I'm interested in! Best to keep her focused before she moved on to something new. "Yes, I've seen the building. And a huge hand coming from it. What in the three moons is it?"

She gave a short laugh. "Oh, so you saw our Vithalos, did you? Amazing thing, that—really helped make the village profitable. I've also heard it's the biggest in the land, way larger than any other Vithalos created. Isn't that neat?" She stopped walking once she finished and stared at him with her hands on her hips. She must have expected some kind of reaction. Finding none, she gave an exasperated sigh. "You have heard of Vithalos before, haven't you?"

"No, I haven't, so it must not be that big of a deal." Ean said, trying to sound unimpressed.

"Vithalos are animated objects created by a magic user called a Thaljori." Her voice had taken on a lecturing tone. It grated on Ean's nerves, but his curiosity won out and he remained quiet as she spoke. "The Thaljori link a piece of a person's essence and mind, or something like that, to an object, giving it life. The person then has a limited control over what the object can do. In this case, the object was a humanoid construction taller than most buildings and can do the work of dozens of men in a shorter amount of time. The foreman of the mill, Efron Kale, is the one that controls it."

As soon as she finished, Ean cocked his head to the side and gave her a disbelieving look. Regardless of everything he had seen, it was hard to believe something like that existed.

"You must think I'm a real simpleton to believe a story like that. I know, I mean, I've seen my fair share of magic, and something like that just can't be possible." He smiled, hoping she took his words as playful teasing.

"It is true!" She stamped a foot like a child and frowned at him. "Just because there might not be any Vithalos in your tiny village does not mean they don't exist!"

"If what you are saying is true, then why haven't I seen dozens of the things walking around." He shot her a cocky grin. "Even in my little village."

It was her turn to laugh now. It was a quiet laugh, but the way she looked at him made Ean feel two inches tall. "Of course there aren't many of them walking around. There are very few born with the ability to be Thaljori. And from what I have heard, more often than not, they don't live for very long." Snaking an arm around his shoulder, she began to lead him down the street again. He tried to shrug it off but she was surprisingly strong for having such a willowy frame.

"Now, to continue your education, it is extremely dangerous for both the Thaljori and the person bonding him- or herself to the object. Apparently it takes a great deal of a Thaljori's energy to bond a person, and the bigger the object, the more energy is required. Now I was too young to remember when it happened, but my parents told me that the Thaljori that created the Vithalos in the mill was unconscious for a week after he had finished." Pausing, she shook her head before continuing on in a lower tone. "And poor Effron Kale has never been completely right since."

"You know a lot for a waitress," Ean said, still trying to sound annoyed. He still wasn't sure if he believed the girl or not. The story sounded too rehearsed and impossible to be real. But he had seen that massive hand with his own eyes. Of course, if he told Paige he had a friend that was an imp from the Abyss, she would probably think he was making things up too.

She gave a sad little sigh before answering him. "Yes, well, growing up here, there isn't much else to talk about. Other than our Vithalos or the occasional small bandit raid, nothing much happens."

She sighed again and grew quiet as she continued to lead him down the street. They were approaching the large building that had been so full of life the night before. The windows were still as dark and lifeless as they had been that morning. What had been going on there last night? A party? Ean was enjoying the pause in Paige's endless chatter when she stopped them in front of a house directly across from the party building.

"Well, this is my parents' house. Mom is still working in the kitchen back at the inn, and father will be out hunting for the rest of the day." She was looking straight into his eyes, a small smile touched her lips.

"Oh, well alright. I'll get going then. Have a good—"

"Wait!" Paige clapped her hands to her mouth after the outburst, laughing softly. "I thought you might want to, I don't know, come in and talk some more maybe?"

"I don't know ... I probably should get going." Ean did have questions, questions about the Vithalos and about their next destination, Lurthalan. And he knew for every question he had, there were dozens that he didn't even know to ask. But he had no desire to try and keep this girl focused long enough to answer them. "My friends are probably back at the inn by now."

"And I'm sure those two will be fine. They were holding hands and acting very affectionate towards each other. Is that something you really need to rush back to?"

No, he certainly had no desire to watch that, and Paige was an attractive girl. "I suppose I could stay a bit," he said, feigning reluctance. "But only for a little bit."

"Great! I promise you won't regret it." That smile had returned to her lips, and there was something of a spark in her eyes. She grabbed his arm roughly and pulled him through the doorway.

The inside of her house was dark, but that didn't matter as she didn't give him any time to look around. Before he knew what was happening, she pressed him up against the wall, felt her lips touch his, and then the rest was a blur.

CHAPTER 12

FAIR WARNINGS

WHEN EAN LEFT PAIGE'S home, the sun was well past midday. Had he really been in there that long? Shaking his head in an attempt to clear it and rid himself of the smile stuck on his face, he headed back towards the inn. For his first time alone with a girl, he thought he handled it rather well, despite the fact that he had been hurried out at the end. Of course, all they had done was kiss, for the most part, but that was good enough for Ean.

He was in such a good mood as he walked back that feeling Zin approach didn't put a damper in his spirits. Slowing down, he glanced around to make sure no one was nearby before addressing the invisible imp. "Where have you been?" he said in hushed tones. "I haven't seen you since last night."

"Oh, I'm surprised you even noticed I was gone." Zin's voice was laced with scorn. "Or cared. After all, I apparently have been hiding things from you all of these years."

"Don't be such a baby, Zin. And keep your voice down." All he got in response was a low growl, but the imp continued to walk with him. "Of course I trust you. Jaslen just brought up some interesting questions, is all. But if you say you don't know much more about the tattoo, then I believe you." This time he received a grunt. "Fine, pout if you want. You're not going to ruin my mood."

"Have a little fun with that waitress girl, did we?" A bit of humor touched his voice for a moment, but then returned to the harsher tone. "I noticed she tossed you out, so it must have been purely one sided."

Ean sent a weak kick in the imp's direction, but his heart wasn't in it. If the imp was insulting him, that meant he was starting to get over the night before. "I think I did alright, otherwise she would have kicked me out a while ago."

"Well, while you've been seeing what little sights are around here and messing around with girls with low standards, I've been keeping an eye on the happy couple. Those two are experts at finding secluded corners around the village."

"I don't need to hear about what they are doing in private," Ean growled. "Did they find us a caravan heading to Lurthalan or not?"

"They found one, but it doesn't leave for two days. Which means we're stuck until then. That should make your new girlfriend happy."

"How about we walk on in silence the rest of the way back to the inn." Ean picked up his pace, forcing the imp to scamper along faster on his shorter legs. He wasn't really annoyed with the imp, but Zin would keep needling Ean until he got angry, so best to play the part. Plus, more people were starting to appear on the streets. Hunters were coming in with their catches, farmers carrying their tools, and various others going about whatever else there was to do in the village. No need to make any of them think he was a madman for talking to thin air.

Walking into the inn, Ean was surprised at how much busier it had become. When he had left, all of the tables had been empty. Now, only a short time later in the day, they were almost completely full. Even more surprising was that the Taruun made up just as much of the patronage as the humans. Ean did a quick scan to see if he could find the ones that had made fun of him earlier, but they all looked the same to him—tall, pale creatures with sharp features and a similar taste in loose fitting clothes. He spotted Jaslen and Bran sitting at the back of the room playing footsie under the table as they made eyes at each other. With a sigh, he headed over to the "happy couple."

They saw him when he was about half way to them and Jaslen waved him over. Both had mugs in front of them on the table, but they did not look like they had been there long.

"There you are!" Jaslen said, a bit more energetic than usual. "We were just about to order some dinner. Are you hungry?"

"Only a little, but I could eat something." He was actually starving and surprised his stomach wasn't growling and giving it away. Licking his lips, he realized how thirsty he was too. He peered into one of their mugs. "What are you drinking?"

Grabbing the mug in front of her, Jaslen lifted it up towards him, some of the liquid sloshing out and onto the table. "It's called Burnbeer, and it's the most wonderful drink! It tastes slightly bitter, but makes you feel warm inside. Here, take a sip."

Ean took the cup from her and tilted it to his lips. He swallowed about half of what he got in his mouth before spitting the rest out back into the mug. She hadn't been kidding about it being bitter. As Ean tried to recover, both Jaslen and Bran burst into laughter.

"I had the exact same reaction," Bran said in between chuckles. "I promise it gets better, though, the more you drink."

Ean doubted that was true. The stuff had been horrible. He was starting to feel the warmth that they had been talking about though, and it did feel good. When he tried to hand the mug back to Jaslen, she waved him off.

"No, you keep that one. Most of what you spit out ended up back in that mug. I'll order a new one for myself."

Flashing Ean a brief smile and a wink, she turned and tried to wave the waitress over. Between the noise of the common room and the fact that there only seemed to be a single waitress working, by the time Jaslen got her attention, Ean had finished what was left in his mug. Bran downed his own mug as well, so Jaslen handed the waitress a few coins and she returned with three fresh mugs.

They all took a swig together, Bran and Jaslen grimacing and Ean coughing as he swallowed the strong liquid down. While Ean was still recovering, Jaslen took a quick look around before trying to speak loud enough to be heard over the crowd.

"Is Zin around? I haven't seen him all day." This caused Ean to cough again. It took Jaslen slightly longer to realize what she had said, her face reddening. Once she had, her hands shot up to cover her mouth as she let out a small squeak. Her hands left her face just as fast as they had risen, and she grabbed Ean.

"I'm sorry," she said, her eyes darting around. "I don't know why I blurted that out."

"It's fine, it's fine," he said. Her hand was warm on his arm, and he found himself leaning towards her. "It's not like anyone around here would know what Zin was just from his name. Plus, it seems that most people here are more focused on their own drinks than what we have to say."

He was looking right into her eyes. They seemed to sparkle in the light of the lamps lit around the room. She was looking back at him with a lopsided grin, and he leaned in closer.

The clearing of a throat made him jerk back. Bran was looking at him with a smile of his own, but Bran's was smug while Jaslen's smile was friendly. That annoyed Ean, but for some reason he couldn't quite understand why. His head was kind of fuzzy, as if he had just gotten up from a long sleep. Ean scowled at him anyway. Bran simply laughed, which angered him all the more. He was about to say something, but Jaslen's voice cut him off.

"Anyway, we should tell Ean what we have been up to all day, Bran." He waved a hand at her to continue, and Jaslen turned her attention back on Ean. "Well, I suppose I can tell you then. We met with a very nice man named Berek Soushade. He is in charge of all of the trade wagons in town at the moment. They are staying in town for another day or so to recover from some attack on their caravan before moving on."

"And here is the best news," she said, her eyes lighting up. "He agreed to take us to Lurthalan! He isn't even going to charge us to travel with him. All we have to do is help with the everyday chores until we get to the city. Isn't that great?"

Ean feigned surprise at hearing the news he had already heard from Zin. "That's great!" He wasn't sure why that excited him as much as it did. "That gives us another day to relax here."

Maybe he could see Paige again. Wait, why did he want to see her again? His head felt so heavy. And Jaslen was still talking. She was such a beautiful girl...

"... and then in a couple of days of travel, we'll be in Lurthalan and find someone who can help our home. Isn't that exciting?"

Ean found himself looking into her eyes again. Well, he started by looking into her eyes, but his gaze slowly dropped, taking in the rest of her. She certainly was much more beautiful than Paige. Why did that matter? And why was Bran still grinning and looking at him with that knowing expression?

He tore his gaze from Jaslen and looked down into his mug. When had he finished it? He waved at the serving girl, and after what seemed like a long stretch of time, she brought him a fresh mug. Before Jaslen had even finished paying for his drink, he had taken a few deep gulps. The drink didn't taste as bitter as it had before.

All of a sudden, the table next to them burst out into song. The table of five burly men were singing at the top of their lungs. The song had something to do with a man that did everything for a girl who wanted nothing to do with him. With a squeal of delight, Jaslen leapt to her feet, knocking over her stool and moved over to join the men. She was welcomed with open arms of course, the men not seeming to care that she had no idea what the words to the song were.

Both Bran and Ean watched her go, mouths hanging agape. Bran was the first to shake himself from the surprise, but instead of going after Jaslen he turned to Ean.

"We should talk," he said, his speech slightly slurred, "about Jaslen and us."

Ean stared at him for moment, then raised his hands in defense. "I don't know what you mean."

Bran laughed again, although there didn't seem to be much humor behind it. "Listen, I'm not as blind as you think. I've seen how you look at her. And I don't blame you, she is a wonderful girl, both inside and out. She can sometimes be a bit oblivious though, and I don't think she's realized how you feel about her. I just hope that it isn't going to become a problem with the three of us traveling together."

"Listen, Bran," Ean said, noticing his own words sounded funny as they tumbled out of his mouth. "I don't know why you think that, but I know Jaslen and I are just friends. Just like we're friends." That was the first time he had actually admitted Bran was his friend. It felt weird coming out of his mouth. "I think you are seeing something that isn't there."

Bran stood, unsteady on his feet, voice slurring. "To be clear, I'm not worried about someone like you coming between me and Jaslen. My concern is solely that it could cause problems between you and me, which could interfere with our mission."

"Someone like me?" Ean asked, a frown touching the corners of his lips.

"Don't get defensive, little buddy. I'm just saying Jaslen is out of your league, even if she wasn't in love with me. She deserves someone with a bright future—one that doesn't involve forbidden magics and dangerous creatures."

Bran patted Ean on the head as if he were a little boy. "But don't you worry—the right girl will come along, and you'll be just as happy with her as I am with Jaslen."

With that he wobbled over and joined the other singers, leaving Ean sitting there alone.

Anger and frustration starting to bubble up inside of Ean as he sat there. Bran acted as if he was nothing! And patting him on the head? The nerve! He shot the two of them a glare as he downed the rest of his mug. Of course they didn't see his face, wrapped up in singing as they were, but it made Ean feel a little better at least.

As the two continued to sing on into the night, Ean continued to drink. He couldn't believe that a day that had gone so well was ending so badly. Bran belittled him; Jaslen hadn't even bothered to ask what he had done all day; and Zin had disappeared again. Ean couldn't feel the imp anywhere nearby. Well, that was fine. He didn't need any of them to have some fun. He had proved that earlier in the day. Waving the serving girl over again, he decided he would find out how good this Burnbeer could make him feel.

CHAPTER 13

BUMP IN THE NIGHT

THUMP, THUMP, THUMP.

At first Ean thought the pounding was originating in his head. Lifting his face off his pillow, head swimming, he rubbed the sleep from his eyes. His tongue felt like sawdust. The pain behind his eyes made him wonder if an anvil had hit him. He had no idea how he had ended up in bed. Or why he was still in all of his clothes from the day before. Except for the light flickering through the window, the room was dark. Is it still night? For that matter, what day was it?

THUMP, THUMP, THUMP.

It took him a second to determine if the thumping was coming from outside his room or inside his head. When another round of pounding rattled his window, he realized it was coming from outside. Deciding to investigate, he rolled out of bed. His legs gave out, and he found himself sitting on the cold wooden boards of the floor.

"Is anyone here?" His words came out as a groan but didn't elicit a response. He couldn't even feel Zin in the room.

THUMP, THUMP, THUMP, THUMP.

If only the pounding would stop, maybe then he could figure out what was going on. With another groan, Ean climbed the side of his bed until he was back on his feet. He was able to stay up this time, although he swayed about. He could hear voices now, muffled shouts, but they seemed to be coming from outside instead of below. That was a blessing. Ean didn't think his head could handle the dulled roar of the common room below.

THUMP, THUMP, THUMP.

The voices might not be coming from below, but the banging was coming from the first floor. Wasn't the noise bothering anyone else in the inn? Well, there was no way he was going to fall back asleep now so he might as well go check it out. Maybe Bran and Jaslen were still downstairs as well. He would love to smack Bran for getting him to drink so much Burnbeer. At the very least he could get a mug of water.

With some effort, Ean made it out the door of his room and into the hall. The banging sounded even louder here. He slunk down the hallway, his legs still wobbly. Ean would much rather be in bed with a cold cloth across his eyes and complete silence. Reaching the stairs, he took each one with a slow, calculated step. As he reached the bottom of the stairs, the sounds of a subdued conversation reached him in between the pounding. What he saw in the common room caught him by surprise.

The room was in shambles. Tables and chairs were overturned, half-eaten food sat on plates and was scattered across the floor, and puddles of various liquids were everywhere. His first impression was that he was looking at the aftermath of a rowdy night of celebration. His eyes followed the path of destruction to the front door, where a number of tables and chairs had been piled up against it. A barricaded door sent up dozens of red flags.

The pounding continued. It was coming from the door. Someone or something was trying to get in.

"Get away from the door!" came a harsh whisper at Ean's right. Even low, the voice made him jump. It took him a moment to locate the origin of the voice.

Ean spotted the innkeeper, the innkeeper's wife and a serving girl he had never seen before huddled together behind a table. They were shaking and disheveled, making him wonder how long they had been hiding out. The serving girl was covered with flood splatters and drink, and her face was puffy as if she had been crying a long while.

"What's going on?" Ean whispered.

"She saw one of the regulars get taken down by an arrow right outside our door," the older woman whispered. "Poor Garrad — if only the warning had rang out earlier."

"Warning? A warning for what — whoever is outside that door?"

"Raiders," the innkeeper answered. "A larger group than we've see in a long time. Saw a dozen or so entering town from the south." Shaking his head, he reached out for Ean. "You don't look like the fighting kind, lad. Best for you to hide out here with us while the hunters take care of things outside."

Ean jerked away. "The two I was with, have you seen them?"

"I saw them sneak out a little after they put you to bed," the waitress whimpered.

"Is there any way, other than the front doors, I could use to get outside?" Ean asked.

The waitress started to cry out before the words were even out of his mouth. "No, no! He'll let them in. Please don't let him do that!"

The last few words were muffled as she buried her head in the chest of the innkeeper's wife. The older woman patted her back a few times before turning her attention to Ean. The look she gave him was full of scorn.

"I'm sorry about your friends, but I won't let you risk the few of us that are safe in here. We have a few families hiding upstairs, all women and children, with no way to defend themselves. The doors will stay closed until the bandits are either driven off or take what they want and leave."

"I can't just leave them," Ean tried to control the frustration in his voice, but it was difficult. "I need them. Open the door and then close it again once I'm out."

THUMP, THUMP.

The woman just shook her head. "Even if I wanted to help, you can hear them pounding on the door. They would rush in and kill us in a heartbeat. Sorry, son. Best if you just head back upstairs like the rest." Turning her attention back to the serving girl, she waved Ean away with a hand before resuming her attempt to comfort the girl.

Ean's hands clenched in anger. He was about to tell her exactly what he thought about her caution, when a small tug at his leg caught him by surprise, almost making him jump. Foolish. He had been so focused on the stubborn woman that he hadn't felt Zin approaching. The invisible imp gave his pants another tug towards the stairs and then started heading that way.

Sending one last frown toward the three cowering villagers, Ean followed the imp back towards the stairs. They walked on in silence back up to the third floor, at which point Zin became visible and rounded on him.

"There is no way you are going out into that mess! All I need is for you to get yourself stabbed by some bandit, which would send me right back to the Abyss. I'm sure Bran and Jaslen are fine. I saw them running off somewhere long before the raiders arrived."

"How do you ... wait, you were out there?" Ean got down so he could look the imp square in the eye. "Which means you know another way to get in and out of this building. Can you go find them and bring them back here?"

"Just because I'm invisible doesn't mean I can't still catch a stray arrow or get trampled. I'm not risking my life for them."

"Then you have to tell me how to get out. I'll go get them and bring them back."

The imp flashed him a wide grin, which showed off his pointed teeth. "We don't need them. Well, maybe we need their money. But that's not why you want to go off to their rescue and get yourself killed. You want to be the big hero again for Jaslen."

"Shut up. Did you ever think I might care about them?"

"I'm sure if Bran was killed tonight, you would shed hundreds of tears. It doesn't matter either way. Like I said, I'm not risking you getting killed, regardless of whatever excuse you come up with."

Reaching down the front of his shirt, Ean pulled out the clay piece that held Zin's summoning rune. The imp's smile slowly faded as he realized what was happening.

"Now, there is no need for that," Zin said, rubbing and wringing his hands. "What good will sending me back to the Abyss do?"

Ean ignored him, holding the clay piece between thumb and pointer finger of each hand.

Zin began to hop from foot to foot. "If you get killed tonight, the magic on that rune fails and I go back to the Abyss anyway, so breaking it isn't much of a threat."

Ean remained silent, instead applying a small amount of pressure to the clay piece. After a few moments a small crack appeared on the edge.

"Fine, fine!" Throwing up his hands, Zin began to pace back and forth in the hallway. "If you want to get yourself killed for a human girl, you go right ahead. What do I care? I was just trying to look out for you."

He stopped then and pointed a finger at Ean while glaring at him. "But if you think I'm going to help you out WHEN you get in trouble, you can just forget it." Gesturing for him to follow, Zin headed back towards the stairs.

Ean followed behind while returning the clay piece back under his shirt. He hated threatening Zin like that, especially when he knew how horrible of a place the Abyss was for imps. He would make it up to him if they survived this. A nice steak would do the trick. Hopefully the town butcher, if there was one, survived the night.

Zin turned invisible again as they reached the first floor, but his shimmering form continued down towards the basement. The inn at home had a basement for food and drink storage; it usually stayed cool which helped keep the food from going bad. This one was apparently no different, although as far as Ean knew, the inn at home didn't have an exit in the basement.

The cellar was about what Ean would expect in an inn. The room was dark, the only light coming through the doorway from the lit candles on the stairway. Barrels of what Ean guessed was food and drink littered the floor. Zin turned visible again and continued on towards the back of the cellar, finally stopping at the back wall. Ean looked around for a moment then scowled at the imp.

"What is this?" he growled. "Zin, if this is some trick, I swear I'll ..."

The imp rounded on him before he could even finish. "Oh yes, I understand how you can continue to threaten your only real friend."

The imp looked as if he would attack, and Ean backed off slightly, just in case. He had never seen Zin this angry before.

"This is no trick. There is a way out down here."

"And the raiders won't be able to use the same way to get in?"

"Not if you are smart enough not to lead them back to where this comes out. But before I tell you where I saw them last, I have a question for you. What exactly do you plan on doing if Bran and Jaslen are in trouble?" The imp glared at him, his hands resting now on his hips as he waited for an answer.

"Well, I could always summon something ..."

"Brilliant," Zin cut in. "What would you summon, your Hound? Because setting him loose in a village would be a great idea. I mean, you've had so much control over the beast in the past."

"Well, I could try something else, maybe a ..."

"Oh yes, even better. In the mess that is already going outside, you want to experiment? You don't even know what half of those creatures are in the Abysmal Tome."

Zin shook his head in disgust. "Do you know what makes a normally calm Cruxlum explode with a rage that lasts at least two days? Or how about what can cause a Vauropus to spawn dozens of children in just one day? Either one could end up destroying this whole village if left unchecked, and I bet you wouldn't even know which one you had summoned."

The imp's scowl was replaced with a self-satisfied grin. "So, do you have any other bright ideas? We know you have absolutely no skill when it comes to weapons or fighting. What does that leave? Am I missing anything?"

Ean just stood, stunned at his friend's tirade. Of course he had thought of all of those points. They had been running through his head as they marched down the stairs. It would be easy to just stay inside where it was safe.

But Bran and Jaslen were out there …

"We'll just have to be extra careful and hope we find them safe and sound. You said you knew where they ran off to, right? If you take me to them, we can try and get them back here to the inn without anyone noticing."

At this point Zin was shifting back and forth, his eyes on the ground. "They were out kissing behind that large building, the one that was full of lights and noise last night. When the trouble started, they ran inside."

Ean knew there was a lie in there somewhere. Either Zin was lying about where they were, or he was lying about knowing where they were. Heading towards that large building was as good a place to start either way. If they had gone out to find some privacy, as much as that thought made him cringe, they wouldn't have gone to the trade wagons.

"Fine, then we head to that building, and if they are safe there, we can join them. If not, we sneak them back here." He placed a firm hand on the imp's shoulder. Zin grimaced but didn't pull away. "Regardless of which ends up happening, the first thing is for you to show me how to get out of this basement."

Zin gave a defeated sigh and nodded. "Fine, right over here." Pulling away, he walked over behind a large shelf. Ean followed along although he didn't see anything right away.

"Good job, Zin. A dead end. You know, we don't have time for this. If you don't know a way ..."

"Sometimes I forget that your pathetic human eyes don't see well without the sun blazing over your head. It's right up here." The imp climbed up the corner wall and seemed to disappear. A few moments later, his head peeked out from what Ean could only guess was a small hole in the wall.

"Well?" Zin waved him up. "Are you coming or not? If you're going to get yourself killed, might as well be sooner rather than later."

Zin's head disappeared back into the hole before Ean could respond. The imp made a good point though. Better to get moving before he realized how stupid of an idea this was. An image of Jaslen sprang up in his head, and he quickly squashed it down. He was doing this for the group, not one person! Moving quickly, he climbed up the shelves and wall and into the hole.

As Ean crawled further into the hole, a foul stench like a sack of moldy meat smacked him in the face. Either this place hadn't been used in a while or something had crawled in it and died. His gloved hand went to his nose as he repeatedly gagged. As he inched along, it felt like the stone walls were closing in on him. Deciding he would rather be out of the hole than keep his dinner, he stopped holding his nose and used both hands to pull him along faster.

"I think I'm going to be sick," he moaned.

"Good," the imp growled, although he did put more distance between himself and Ean's mouth.

After what felt like an eternity of crawling in filth, Ean emerged on the other side behind a bale of hay. The air was stale and smelled like leather and grease. As his eyes adjusted to the dim light, he realized they had emerged in a small storage shed.

"This is your last chance to go back," Zin said in hushed tones. "Once we leave this shed, the odds of running into a raider are almost a certainty. They'll murder you sooner than you can say 'Zin is the smartest imp in the world.'"

"I'm pretty sure you are the only imp in the world …"

"Then again, you look kind of girly, so maybe they won't murder you right away," Zin shot back. He was trying to be funny, but there wasn't a drop of humor in his voice. Ean couldn't help but wonder if the imp's concern was for him or for the possibility of having to go back to the Abyss.

"Well, I guess you will just have to watch my back," he said, ignoring the insult, "because we're going out there."

Ean moved towards the light coming from underneath the door. Peering underneath, he saw a row of stables. This must be the storage shed for the horses of travelers who stayed at the inn. No wonder the bandits had left it alone.

He had expected to see bodies lying everywhere, homes on fire, and bandits running around the street. Instead the streets were empty, the homes across from him untouched, and not a single wounded or dead man to be found. Zin and those in the inn must have been mistaken. With a great deal more confidence, Ean stood up, pushed the door open and stepped outside. That, of course, was when he heard the first scream.

He stopped dead in his tracks. It hadn't come from close by. He squatted there for a few moments, and then he heard another scream followed by some shouting.

Staying low, he moved across the street and crouched in the shadows of a small house. He could hear a lot more shouting now; it seemed to be coming from every direction. Nothing he could do about that except hope the screams weren't coming from Jaslen.

Turning his back on the street, he began to carefully make his way through the alleyways between the closely built homes. He could feel the imp only a few paces behind him. Ean still hadn't gotten around to asking the imp about that, or how he had felt the troll as well. If he survived the night, Ean planned to press the issue with Zin.

The paths between the houses were dark, perfect for sneaking around. It reminded him of home—all the years of slinking around the village, trying to avoid the bullies. He walked on his toes, as silent as Zin stalking a rat, careful to avoid stepping on or bumping into anything that might give him away. Although the shouts could still be heard from different directions, the screaming had stopped. Whether that was a good or bad sign, he had no idea.

He was about to cross the alleyway when a tearing sound, like someone ripping a cloth, made him stop short. Curiosity won out over fear — he had to take a closer look. The alleyway to the left was clear. One house down, a dark mound moved to his right. Ean tried to focus on the shape, but it was difficult in the little moonlight that reached the alley. It could be anything—a hurt villager, an injured animal, or even one of the raiders. Better to just keep moving towards where Zin had said the two were hiding.

Continuing across the intersection, a frightened feminine whimper came from the mound, followed by a manly grunt. A dark thought crept across Ean's mind. Was a raider forcing himself on some poor woman?

What was the man doing to her? No, it was none of his business. Besides, what could he do unarmed?

But what if it was Jaslen? Wouldn't he want someone to step in and help?

Heart pounding, he found himself creeping toward the shrouded mound.

CHAPTER 14

TEST OF CHARACTER

WHY DID HE KEEP making such horrible decisions? He had always been so careful at home. Shaking his head in annoyance, Ean snuck along until he was only a few paces away from the figures. This close he could make out two distinct figures. The man seemed to be on top of the woman, his arms doing things that Ean couldn't see. It was clear though that the woman wasn't enjoying it. She thrashed around beneath the man, trying to escape.

Ean's breath caught in his throat, and he wished he had just walked on by and remained ignorant of what was happening in this dark alleyway.

But he hadn't.

Now he couldn't live with himself if he just walked away. But what could he do without a weapon? He could try to cast a rune, but which could he use? The wrong one could make things much worse. His mind raced as his eyes jerked around on to the rocks on the ground, to a loose shard of glass, to the stack of firewood against the building. That would have to do. He grabbed a piece of wood … causing the rest of the pile to spill down with a clatter.

The man immediately spun, drawing a dagger from his waist. He was an average-looking man, not much taller than Ean, with scraggly hair and a misshaped beard. Dressed in shabby brown clothes from top to bottom with an empty quiver at his waist, his face registered surprise at first. When he sized Ean up, a vile grin spread across his stubbly face.

"Come here, boy." His voice was harsh and gravelly. "Best if you don't make me chase you down like I did this little tart."

The man's free hand beckoned reassuringly while the one holding the dagger was held back a bit. The girl stayed where he had left her, either too scared or hurt to use the opportunity to flee.

It was all Ean could do not to bolt away. He believed the man could catch him; Ean certainly wasn't a fast runner, but if he threw the log at his leg, maybe that could slow him down enough so that Ean could get away. Or his throw could miss, which was more likely to happen, and he would end up angering the man. And what about the girl? If the girl would just get up and run, she might have a chance.

"Come on, come on," the man said impatiently. "I don't need to kill you, boy. A quick knock on the head and you get to sleep through this little nightmare. You wake up, me and the rest of my mates are gone, and you're none the worse for wear."

His voice dropped low, his grip on the dagger tightening as he inched forward. "But if I have to waste the time to catch you, when the villagers find you in the morning, it will take days for them to even figure out if the pieces I've left are even human."

Ean didn't believe the man for a second that he would just knock him out. He glanced at the girl, thinking he could maybe give her some kind of signal to run and then blinked in surprise. It was Paige.

Her hair was disheveled, but he could see sad eyes behind a dirty and tear soaked face. She was still wearing the same clothes as earlier in the day, although now they were torn and muddy, revealing more than a sweet girl like Paige would want to show. His mouth opened slightly at the sight, and that was when the man decided to pounce.

He hit Ean full force, knocking him off his feet. Sharp pain ran up his left side just before he hit the ground. The piece of wood flew out of his hand just as fast as the breath left his body. The man leapt on top of him. Locked together, they rolled in the street until the man pulled away. As Ean fought for his breath, the man got to his feet. The assailant's bloodied dagger glinted in the moonlight.

No time to think. The man kicked Ean in the side of the head. Stars exploded in his eyes from the pain. He brought up his hands to protect himself, but the repeated kicks sent him rolling along the ground until he splayed out on his back. Pushing himself up on his elbows, he struggled to focus. The man was walking towards him casually now, that wicked grin still on his face.

"This could have gone so much easier for you." He twirled the dagger in his hand as he approached. The man was taking his time now, not worried at all about either Ean or Paige getting away. "I would have just slipped the dagger into the back of your neck and you barely would have felt a thing. Now I'm going to peel your hide before I return to my fun with the girl."

He was standing over Ean now, that dagger spinning in his hand, flecks of Ean's blood spraying off of it. Ean tried to push himself back and away, but the man laughed and planted a boot square on his chest.

"Nowhere to go, worm." Kneeling down, he grabbed Ean by his shirt with his free hand and pulled him up so that they were face to face. "You should have minded your own business."

Ean expected intense pain to come next, but instead he was suddenly let go. The man screamed and stumbled back, the dagger dropping from his hand. Blood was dripping from the arm that had held the dagger, and he was waving it about wildly. It only took Ean a few moments to see the slightly shimmering outline of Zin latched on to the man's arm.

Ean rushed to his feet and snatched up the dagger. The man was still waving his arm around and beating at it with his other hand.

To Zin's credit he was holding his own. A few of those blows must be connecting. It was hard to tell with the imp being nearly invisible. Well, Zin had helped. Now it was time to return the favor.

Ean tried not to think too much about what he was about to do. Holding the dagger low, he relied on his knowledge as a healer to deliver the fatal thrust.

Before he could attack, the man slammed the arm Zin was riding into the wall. Zin fell motionless into the street. While Ean was trying to grasp what had happened, the man kept moving. Lashing out with a foot, he caught Ean in the stomach, knocking the wind out of him once again. Then, as Ean doubled over, the man kicked him again, this time in the face.

The blow almost made Ean black out. When he finally got his wits about him, he was on his back once again, the knife no longer in his hand. Before he could even shake the stars from his vision, the man was on top of him, both of his hands around Ean's neck. The stars in Ean's eyes changed to dark spots as he struggled to breathe.

"I don't know what you did," the man growled, spittle dripping off of his lips. "But I'm done playing around with you."

Ean grabbed the man's wrists and tried to pull them away, but they were like steel. Even if Ean was at his best, he wouldn't have had a chance against the stronger man. Fear and panic set in as his body demanded more air. He yanked at the man's wrists, but the bandit grunted and squeezed harder. Ean tried bucking around, but the man was too heavy. The black specks turned into a dark haze as he looked up at the man about to kill him.

Fear turned to anger, an inferno scorching away the unwanted emotion. He would not die at the hands of this peon, this thief and rapist. He was so much more than this man, this pathetic little bug that picked on women and children. He felt a power rush through his body and down his right arm. It seemed to explode out of him like a flood, leaving his hand and flowing into the hand of the man holding him.

This time the man screamed, but not the lower guttural yell of anger and pain, but the same screech of fear that Paige had made while the man had been trying to violate her. Throwing his head back, the man tried to pull away, but somehow Ean was the stronger one now.

Ean watched the man jerk to the sides and back, his vision coated by a dark blue light. This was real power; this was what he had wanted all along. He would destroy this man and any other that got in his way now. The glove on his right hand burst into a bluish flame and disintegrated just as quickly. The runes on his hands glowed bright, freed from the confines of the glove. He had thought that summoning strong creatures would make him powerful, but this ... energy was so much better. It made him feel strong. It made him feel alive. It made him feel ...

The bandit continued to try and pull away, his movements frantic. His skin was a sickly gray color now, his eyes completely black. His mouth hung open but no sound came from it. This wasn't what made Ean pause though. All over the bandit's face, his skin bulged, as if dozens of tiny creatures were moving about just underneath.

The sight of it snapped Ean out of his rage. He released the man's arm. The bandit flung himself backwards and grabbed at his face with both hands, clawing at it with gloved fingers. Inching his way back away from Ean, his mouth still hung open in that silent scream.

Climbing to his feet, Ean watched the man with a mixture of horror and curiosity. What had he done? He could still feel the power pulsing in his arm. He hadn't cast any kind of spell, yet the man had clearly been affected by something. Was still being affected right before his eyes.

The man was on his knees now, his hands covering his face. Ean couldn't be sure, but the man looked … bigger … now. Before, his clothes had hung off of him, but now they stretched around a body straining against the fabric. Not knowing what else to do, Ean glanced back to check on Paige. The girl was gone. He hoped she had taken off before Ean had done, well, whatever it was that he had done to the bandit.

A growl from the man made him turn around, and now it was Ean's jaw that dropped. The man still held his face in his hands, the gloves though were torn away, making his hands visible. They weren't human hands though, not anymore. Brown scales replaced human skin, three stubby claws where his fingers used to be. Pulling his hands away, the bandit moaned as Ean got a clear view of his face.

It was unrecognizable from what it had looked like only moments before. The same scales that had covered his hands also covered his head, his hair completely gone. His eyes were sunken back in his head. All Ean could see were tiny black dots peering back at him. His nose was longer and pointed as if it had been stretched out, while his lips were pulled back, revealing dozens of sharp little teeth.

"What have you done to me?" The man's voice was high pitched now, which seemed to shock the bandit just as much as it did Ean. "What have you done?!"

Apparently not interested in a response, the man, or what had been a man, leapt to his feet and ran off. Ean watched as the man went wailing into the night, disappearing into the darkness. Stunned, he stood there, having no idea what to do next.

The runes on Ean's body still glowed, making him a walking beacon. The last thing he needed with the raiders in town was to draw attention to himself. He looked for a glove, a cloth, anything to wrap his exposed and glowing hand in. He spotted a piece of familiar fabric on the ground. It was the same color as Paige's dress.

He wrapped it around his hand, hiding the glow while his mind raced with questions. But there was no time to look for answers.

"Zin," he said, voice cracking as he tried to rise. "Are you ok?"

He scanned the area until he found the still unmoving blur of the invisible imp on the ground. Kneeling, Ean gently placed a hand on top of the imp. He was still breathing, which was a good sign, and he didn't feel any signs of cuts or blood on the imp's body. Ean nudged at the imp gently.

"Zin, wake up. Come on buddy, I need you to wake up. We have to get out of here." After a few shakes the imp gave a soft moan and materialized into sight.

"I told you this was a bad idea," Zin said, raising his hands to his face while Ean let out a hiss of relief. "But you wouldn't listen. Now I have a massive headache, and I think I lost a few teeth in that cretin's arm." The imp's scolding was music to his ears.

"What happened to him anyway?" Sitting up, the imp took a look around. "Did he get tired of beating on you and carry that girl off?"

"No," Ean said slowly. "I ... did something ... to him."

"Did something? What did you do? I don't see anybody or smell any blood, so you weren't stupid enough to summon anything. Did you cast another rune randomly and get lucky?"

"No, this was something new." Ean paused, not quite sure how to explain what had happened. Just thinking about all that power running through him made him want to take it all in again. He could feel it now, sitting just in reach. It was in his arm. No, that wasn't quite right. It was coming from the tattoos on his arm, literally within his reach. What would it hurt for him to draw on it a little more ...

"I felt energy pass through my hand and go into the man," he said, a slight strain in his voice as he remembered the euphoria it had given him. Licking his lips, he almost tried to draw it in again, but restrained himself. "It was like a flood coursing through me. When it hit the raider, he transformed into something more horrible than he already was ... a monster."

Ean shuddered, remembering every detail of the horrible creature he had created. "How is that possible?"

"It must have been pure energy from the Abyss. Those tattoos are meant to be a direct connection to my home. That's why it's possible for you to cast runes by drawing them with your fingers now and why summoning should be getting easier for you. But for you to actually draw on the energy, I didn't think that would happen for quite some time."

"Wait, you knew this was part of what we did to me, and you didn't tell me? This is a big deal, Zin!"

"Quiet down, you idiot," the imp hissed. "We aren't exactly in the safest of places. Keep it down."

"Did you hear what I just said? The energy changed that man into a monster. Is the same thing going to happen to me?"

The imp shook his head. "No, I think the tattoos help channel the energy without letting it change you. You should be fine."

"Should be? Should be?" Ean kept his voice low, although it was difficult. "All you told me when we first decided to do this," Ean gestured to his arm, "was that it would increase my ability to summon creatures from the Abyss at a faster rate and give me some control over them. That was it. Now you're telling me I'm directly touching energy from the Abyss?"

"Basically, yes."

"Wonderful."

Ean turned and began to pace back and forth as the imp continued. "When you open a gate to summon something, you're punching a hole in the barrier that separates this world and the Abyss. Obviously, that is going to require energy from the Abyss."

"You mean, I've been using energy from the Abyss without even knowing it?"

"Yes. Every time you've summoned me or cast a rune, a bit of dark energy has flowed through you."

The fact that the imp sounded so calm made Ean even angrier. Not just at Zin, but at himself as well. He had been so smug thinking his ability to summon creatures would make him powerful, make all those that had bullied him run and hide or bow at his feet. All the while he could have grown horns, or his eyes could have fallen out, or who knows what else. This new knowledge knocked him down a peg, and Ean didn't know whether to focus his anger on the imp or on himself. He had been so foolish!

"But now I'm safe from it? How would you know?" Better to save his anger, he had gotten used to doing that over the years. "I'm tired of you letting me know pieces of information here, pieces of information there. I want you to tell me everything you know about what we've done to me. I don't want any more surprises."

"Listen, Ean. I'm discovering things right along with you. Most of the ideas I've mentioned are just educated guesses," the imp said, looking off down the alleyway. "I know that it protects you from the energy. I know that it makes you tolerant to summoning, and using that energy increases it at a much faster rate. And now I know that it allows you to focus that energy out of your arm. Other than that, I have no idea what else it might do. There may be other things we will discover later, or that might be it."

Throwing his hands in the air, Ean began pacing again. "Great." He wanted to scream. He wanted to kick the imp, kick himself. Why did he ever think things would work out in his favor?

"Well, Zin, if you truly don't know much about this then who does? Who can tell me for certain whether or not I'll turn into some freak if I keep using these powers?"

Zin simply shrugged. "I have no idea. The gods, maybe?"

"The gods?" Despite his anger, Ean couldn't help but laugh. "Why would the gods speak to me?"

"Hey, you asked. We're going to the capitol, so you can take your pick of which temple to visit. If one deity doesn't respond to your prayers, you can just get up and go petition the next one."

Ean shot the imp a contemptuous glare.

"What do you have to lose?" the imp continued.

"Alright, fine. Let's try to find the others and get somewhere safe."

Motioning for Zin to follow, he had just made it to the corner of the building when he heard the sound of running footsteps. Judging from the intensity of it, there was more than one pair as well.

Ean jumped behind the building and crouched low. Zin was already invisible and making his way over as fast as his little legs would carry him. It sounded like the footsteps were coming from the north. Had the man gone and brought back more of his fellow bandits?

Probably not. Ean would imagine as soon as the bandits saw what the man had become, they would have killed him on sight.

Seven men came running into view, each with half raised swords and daggers in their hands. A few had quivers and bows slung over their backs. They stopped as they reached the intersection where Ean had barely survived just moments before. One man knelt down and began looking at the ground.

"This was it, Cal," the man said as he scanned the ground. "There are still pieces of the girl's dress here." His hands pointed to various places on the ground. "And there was certainly a fight here. The dirt is kicked up in a few places and there is the occasional splattering of blood in others. The girl was unhurt, yes? So it must either be the boy's or the bandit's blood."

"Probably the boy's blood." The man that spoke stood shoulders above the rest, his body covered in a strange grayish armor that covered both his chest and arms in what looked to be a single piece. He held a long sword in one hand; held it like a man who knew how to use it. The other men were looking at him, waiting for him to continue.

"The girl said the raider stabbed the boy about here. When she fled, the boy was still alive and putting up a fight. Hopefully he got away."

"A boy against a raider?" one man asked. "Not likely."

"I know," the tall man replied with a grim frown. "The raiders don't show mercy. My guess is we will find his body stuffed in one of these alleys — Pen?"

"Yes, Cal?" A scrawny young man that had been examining the ground looked up.

"Did you find a clue as to what direction we should begin looking?"

The man on the ground shook his head. "No, the dirt's been disturbed in too many places, and there are no blood trails to follow." He paused a moment before continuing. "There is something else though. Come look at these footprints."

Cal walked over and joined the man on his knees. Ean remained motionless. Just because they sounded like they were members of the village didn't mean he was about to go rushing over to them.

"What are those?" Cal asked. "They look like animal tracks, but I don't recognize them."

"Cal, in my forty some years I have never seen their like. See how the toes are spread out? That makes it look more like a child's foot than an animal's. But these grooves at the end of each are clearly from some type of claw. Whatever it is, it's about the height of your knee and walks upright."

Time to put an end to those thoughts. Stepping out from behind the wall, Ean kept his hands raised so that he wouldn't spook the men.

"Hello? I think I'm the boy you're looking for." Eyes and weapons swung in his direction. "I was able to ..."

"Stop right there." Cal said, the point of his raised sword in Ean's direction. Ean immediately obeyed, keeping his hands in the air. "You look a little too scrawny and young to be a bandit, but I know you're not from here. What's your name, boy, and why are you wandering around in the middle of a bandit raid?"

"Ean, and I'm a man, not a boy." He couldn't help letting some of the anger enter his voice. He may be scrawny, but the man didn't need to point it out. "I came from Rottwealth with two others. We're just passing through while on our way to the capitol. The two I am with were caught out in the middle of this mess, and I was trying to find them."

The other men lowered their weapons, their attention moving from Ean to the surrounding alleys. Cal, however, kept his sword raised and his attention only on Ean.

"We ran into a girl who said that a boy had saved her from a bandit. Was that you, boy?" He put extra emphasis on the word boy. Was the man trying to get a rise out of him?

"That was me. I came upon the bandit assaulting the girl, Paige, and tried to help her." The man looked him up and down, frowning. "I recognized her from the inn. I couldn't let the man have his way with her, even if he was twice my size. I distracted him long enough for Paige to get away, and then I guess the man heard you coming and ran off."

"Do you honestly expect me to believe that a runt like you, without a sword or any help, fought off a well-trained and ruthless raider all by yourself?" Cal scoffed. "And lived to tell about it?"

Placing a hand to his injured side for a moment, Ean brought it back up for the man to see. Streaks of red ran across his palm. "I didn't exactly come out of it unhurt. I guess I just got lucky he didn't do more."

"Ah, well then ..." Cal's sneer dropped and he looked at the ground. "Sorry to question you then, uh, Ean was it?"

Cal's eyes began scanning the area, avoiding Ean's own eyes in his sweep. Good, the man should feel bad about giving him such a hard time. He had saved Paige after all.

"Why don't you head to the center of town," Cal said after he was done looking around. "That's where our Healer is attending to the wounded. I'm sure she could take a look at that wound and get it stitched up."

"No, that's alright. I'm an apprentice Healer myself, and I'm sure I could take care of my ..."

"Another Healer?" Cal cut in. "Wonderful, then, you can assist our own. We have many wounded, some who might not survive 'til dawn without a good deal of help, and we only have one Healer."

"Wait, I never said ..."

"Charles, Ven, escort this boy back to Mable." Cal was ignoring him now. "Make sure he makes it to her unharmed and stays there to help. The rest of you with me. I'm sure there are more scum to run out of our home."

With a nod, Cal and the rest of his men headed off down an alley, leaving Ean with the men that had been introduced as Charles and Ven. They were both looking at him, swords still in hand.

"Alright," Ean walked over to them with a tired sigh. "We'd better get going if I'm to be any help."

As Ean walked past them towards the center of town, the men fell in beside him, one on either side. So much for finding Bran and Jaslen on his own. If he had any luck at all, they both will be sitting at the center of town when he arrived.

CHAPTER 15

PUT TO WORK

EAN, OF COURSE, WAS not lucky. At the break of dawn, Charles and Ven escorted him to the open field at the center of town. Bodies littered the road around the clearing. Most of those in the road were already dead, but others sported serious and possibly fatal wounds. The ones that still showed signs of life were being carried onto the grass. Dozens of makeshift cots and blankets were spread about the lawn, each one holding a wounded man or woman, and tents were being erected as well. Looking over the wounded and dead, the only way to tell the difference between a villager and a bandit was whether or not someone was crying over the body.

In the thick of the carnage was an older woman wearing a dark cloak with snow-white hair down to her waist. She was bent over a man with a blood-soaked shirt. Cutting off his shirt with a knife, she tossed it aside and began to examine the man's chest. As Ean got closer, he saw a gaping slice that went all the way to the bone. The woman cleaned the cut first with a rag she rinsed into a nearby bucket. When she was done cleaning the gash, a boy ran up and took the bucket away without a word. With the wound clean, the woman took out a bottle and emptied out a yellowish paste that she stuffed into the cut. Ean couldn't help but grunt in disapproval.

"Problem with what I'm doing, boy?" she said without looking up from her work. Her silvery voice made her sound much younger than she looked. She kept her attention focused on her work as she spoke to him. "And what is that sound you are making? Can't handle the sight of a bit of blood? Don't get sick on any of my patients."

"I can handle the sight of blood," he replied. "I was just surprised that you would use Nevbane on a wound that bad. All that does is numb the pain. He'll be dead in a week from infection. If you're going to use that, you might as well just let him bleed out now. A real Healer would use Flashseal to close the wound and then cover it in Rottwealth. Then a week from now, instead of being dead, he'll just have a tiny scar to brag about."

"So you have some knowledge, do you, boy?" she said while unrolling a ball of clean white gauze.

"I've trained all my life."

"Seeing how our village has neither Rottwealth or Flashseal, and you've more or less told this poor man he's going to die, perhaps you need more training on beside manners, eh?"

"Well, I ..." he started, then shut his mouth. What could he say? He knew Rottwealth only grew in his valley, but Cleff sold so much of it to the merchant that came through town that he just imagined that every village had some available. And was Flashseal that rare as well? It didn't matter. He could make things right.

"I have some of each," he said when he could get his mouth to work. "Rottwealth and Flashseal. Up in my room at the inn."

"Do I look like I was born yesterday, boy?" She looked past him towards Charles and Ven. "I asked for help, not some spoiled brat. Get him out of here before I add another casualty to the total."

Charles ducked his head and kept his attention focused on his feet. Ven looked conflicted, but spoke up. "He says he is from Rottwealth, ma'am, and an apprentice to the Healer there. If he says he has Rottwealth, well ... maybe he does."

The woman stared at him for a moment, then waved both men away. "Fine, go to the inn and search his things for a medicine bag. If you find one bring it back here."

The two men spun and began to walk away until the woman's voice stopped them. "And either way, bring back a few small barrels of ale. We'll need it to clean some of the wounds, and I'll need a few sips to deal with all of you fools."

"Wait a second, you can't just take my things!" Ean called after the men but he was ignored. Mashing his teeth in frustration, he focused his anger on the woman. "You can't just take all of my supplies. I might need them."

"Why, are you hurt? I don't see any wounds." She gave a brief glance at the bloodstain on his side, but let out a snort that made it clear she didn't find it that important. "The people here need those medicines, if they exist, much more than you do."

"But I brought them in case I'd need them. Not to help out every emergency that I come across."

"We'll make sure you are compensated for whatever medicine you have that we use, and if you do have Rottwealth, well ..." Doubt flashed across her face and then was gone. "We'll figure out some way to repay you for however much we use."

Ean shook his head but remained quiet. What else could he do? He decided to stay with the woman and watch her work. If they were going to use up his medicine, he could at least stay and make sure he knew what they used. And made sure it was used properly.

As he watched Mable work, his thoughts wandered to what she had said about the rarity of Rottwealth. Ean knew that selling the plant had made Cleff a very rich man, but how rich? Most of his money had always been put back into improving the village, so it was rare that Ean saw him spend his money on anything else. If Rottwealth was as expensive as the woman was making it out to sound, Ean would have to be careful with what he said. If she knew he had no idea of its actual worth, she would probably try to take advantage of him.

Shaking his head, he let his attention wander away from the woman and injured man in front of him to the surrounding people. There were dozens of villagers, mostly women, moving about the wounded on the green. Every now and then, one of them would walk over to the old woman and ask a question before returning back to the person that they had been treating.

"I'm curious, boy," Mable's voice cut through his thoughts. "Would you have happened to learn your skills from a man named Cleff?"

Ean was about to snap back at her in a sarcastic manner, but the tone of her voice made him pause. It had been a casual question, but her tone had changed from sarcastic to dead serious.

"Yes," he replied. "Cleff has been my teacher for a number of years now. He's the one that gave me most of my supplies."

"Gave?" She barked a laugh, her head twisting up so that she was looking at him almost sideways. "I have never known that man to 'give' anything away. He sits in his little valley on top of the most amazing medicinal plant that exists and what does he do? Hogs most of it for himself, letting only a little sliver out of that cursed village for the rest of the land."

Ean could only gape at her. Part of him wanted to jump to Cleff's defense. After all, he had raised him well, if just a little strict. And the marshes did belong to him, so he should be able to charge whatever he wanted for the Rottwealth. It wasn't as if their village had a variety of goods to trade with the rest of the world. Most of the food grown was shared amongst the people, and whenever the trader did come to town, most people traded items that they made themselves in what little free time they had.

But then he took a look around at all of the people that lay injured, dying, or already dead. Doing a quick count in his head, he figured his supply of Rottwealth might be able help a third at most of those scattered about the field. And that was just for the ones that were in the worst shape. Many of the wounded will end up losing arms or legs because of their wounds or infection. Infection that Rottwealth could easily keep away. But if all they had was his supply, then that would be saved for the more serious injuries— head wounds, people run thru with a blade, shredded or heavily burnt skin or wounds that cut into the bone like the man in front of him. That fact tore at Ean's gut as the thought of so many dying overwhelmed him.

Charles and Ven were almost on top of them before Ean realized they had returned.

"It's true, ma'am," Ven said, clutching the bag with a broad smile. "This thing is plumb full of goodies — dried herbs, powders, and bottles full of pretty colored liquids."

Mable snatched the bag. Dropping it to the ground she dove in, routing around the clanking bottles until she pulled out one that contained some ground up Rottwealth. She dumped a small amount of the blackish powder into her hands and began to apply it to the man's wounds.

Ean moved to take the Rottwealth from her but froze as she turned on him. She shot him a glare but paused what she was doing, her hands hovering over the man. "Listen, boy," she hissed. "I told you we would find a way to pay you for what we used. I'm sure money is just as important to you as it is to ..."

"Would you please listen!" Ean shouted over her. "Applying Rottwealth to such a large area will save his life, sure, but it will damage his nerve endings. His arm will never work right again."

"What are you talking about?"

"Use some Flashseal first to close the wound, and then apply the Rottwealth. Even with the wound closed, the Rottwealth will sink into the burnt skin and fix the damage to the bone as well as the skin and muscles."

"And I assume you have some Flashseal as well?" Her voice still had a note of contempt, but it seemed forced now.

"I wouldn't have mentioned it, if I didn't have it."

Grabbing his bag back, he took out a much heavier vial. The silvery powder inside sparkled in the light of the torches as he carefully removed the lead stopper. He leaned over the injured man, sprinkling a tiny amount of powder along his gash.

"You at least know how the Flashseal works?"

The woman nodded.

"Good." He pushed the wound together with both hands and kept them there, giving the powder a chance to settle. "There is flint and steel in my bag. Light the powder and try not to get my fingers scorched."

Mable replaced the Rottwealth back into the bottle and pulled out the pieces of metal from the bag. She gave him one last questioning look.

"Do it," Ean said, holding the man down by his shoulder.

She lowered both pieces close to the wound and struck them together. On the first strike a small spark leapt off the metal and hit the wound. A small burst of flame erupted off of the wound and was gone followed by a low moan from the man. Ean checked to make sure that his gloves weren't smoldering before examining the man's wound.

A long patch of black, blistering skin covered the man's shoulder. The gash was gone, the skin fused together by the heat. The old woman grabbed up the bottle of Rottwealth and began applying small amounts to the burn. Within moments the blackened skin began to lighten, taking on more of a dark brown color. The Rottwealth wouldn't instantly heal the burn, but it would speed up the healing process. What would normally take two months to heal would be accomplished in a week.

With a nod of satisfaction, Ean rose to his feet. "There, now I'm sure you can handle things without me. I need to try and find my ..."

"I don't think so." Mable leapt up to clutch his arm. "You're staying right here with me, young healer. My people need you."

It only took a moment to realize she was right.

"If I stay, I'll need a couple of things. One, assistants to help with whatever I need …"

Mable motioned to Ven, who nodded and ran off.

"Done," she said. "What else?"

"Two, I need someone to fetch my missing friends — Bran and Jaslen. Last place they were spotted was the large building in the southwest of town."

She pointed southwest and gave a swat to the water boy's back. "Do as the healer asks."

"Yes, ma'am." The boy bowed and hurried down the street.

Mable turned to Ean with an impatient frown. "You happy now?"

"It's a start."

"Good, now quit wasting time and get to work."

Trying not to "waste any more time," Ean moved to the next seriously injured villager without saying another word to the old woman. The man's stomach had been run completely thru by what appeared to be a thin blade. The likelihood that the man would survive, even with Rottwealth, was hit or miss. Ven returned just as Ean prepped the wounds for the Flashseal. Ean gave him directions on what to do as he worked and then let his thoughts wander.

Cleff had always taught him it was better not to focus too much on the person you were healing. Emotional attachments lead to stress, which lead to mistakes. Of course, being thought of as scum by most of his village had made it easy not to get attached to any that he had helped heal at home. These were strangers, though, and hadn't done anything to him. Not yet at least …

No, best to keep to Cleff's teachings and not focus on the people.

The sun was high overhead by the time his supply of Rottwealth had run out. He had worked on a few dozen patients in that span of time. The majority would make full recoveries; a few would be permanently lame in an arm or leg for the rest of their lives; three still might not last the night; and one had passed away. Ean had been right next to the man as he passed. Even after successfully helping so many before him, that one death bothered Ean. It put a knot in his stomach that stayed with him the rest of the day.

He had kept his eye on the older woman when he could, mostly to make sure she wasn't making any mistakes. From what he saw, her rate of success with the villagers she treated was comparable to his own. Between the two of them, they had been able to treat all of the serious cases by midday.

That still left an even larger number of minor wounds to treat. Ean took a long enough break to eat half a loaf of bread, then went back to work. The task of cleaning and bandaging wounds, setting broken arms and legs, sewing slashes that did not require Flashseal, and applying soothing salves to villagers that had been burnt was easy compared to how the first half of his day had gone. All the while, villagers were helping those that could be moved off the green or setting up tents around those that needed to remain immobile.

Ean found himself enjoying the work as he moved from one person to the next. Most were overly grateful for the help, those that were awake, and seemed especially appreciative because he was a stranger. They would tell him about how they got hurt or about their families as he worked. He even got a few invitations to dinner, which he awkwardly refused. It felt nice to be appreciated but he was nowhere near ready to sit down with a bunch of strangers in a more social setting.

The sun was just starting to sink down behind the mountains to the west as Ean finished with his last patient. He was a much older man, the gray in his thin hair vastly outnumbered the black. A chipped and dirty knife sat on the ground not far away. He had been out in the thick of it, with the younger men, not quite as effective but still holding his own. He had received a nasty cut to his arm chasing after one of the bandits as he tried to flee. The old man was very proud of that.

Rising from the man's side with a smile, Ean took a good look around the green. He felt ... good ... about that and enjoyed the feeling. Sure, he had helped Cleff countless times, but that had mostly been for minor cuts and scrapes. These people he had healed on his own, without anyone looking over his shoulder or telling him what to do. There were men and women right now, sitting in their homes with their families, telling stories about how they had fought off a bandit attack, how they had received terrible wounds but were thankful for a boy in the village that had healed them. Ean didn't even mind if they called him a boy as they repeated their story. Well, not much, at least.

Ean slung his lightened bag over his shoulder. As he walked among the tents, he wondered where he might restock his supply. Since Rottwealth only grew at home and apparently cost a great deal, he might as well forget about getting any more. Flashseal, however, tended to grow near bodies of water. He made a mental note to keep an eye out for it next time he filled his canteen.

The atmosphere had been all doom and gloom when he had first arrived. Now people walked about, or limped about, in generally good moods. Ean even heard jovial singing from some of the tents. It felt good to be a part of that feeling. At home he had always felt it was him against the world. It was nice to find out that the entire world wasn't holding a grudge against him.

Instead of returning to the inn, Ean checked in on the worse of the wounded, those that couldn't be moved home. Most were surrounded by family, playing games or drinking Burnbeer. Grateful town folk asked him to sit down and enjoy a drink with them. Remembering his earlier battle with the after-effects of Burnbeer, he politely declined. As he exited a tent, someone tackled him from behind.

"You're okay!" Jaslen's musical voice only improved his mood. She wrapped her arms around him.

"Yes, and so are you. I was worried about you ... and Bran. Where were you?"

"Out amongst the trade wagons. The wagon guards held their own, but they needed help with their wounded and putting out fires most of the day. We only just left them a few moments ago to try and find you."

She spun him around and gave an impish smile. "I hear you've been rescuing girls in distress, healing the wounded and being an all-around hero."

He felt himself blush.

"Uh, well, I just happened to be in the wrong place at the right time, I guess." His thoughts went to Paige. Even if she was physically fine, he knew trauma like that came with emotional wounds that no amount of Rottwealth could heal.

"And as for the healing," he continued, "I was practically bullied into doing it by the local Healer. They were going to use my supplies anyway, so I figured I might as well make sure they used them right."

She playfully punched his arm.

"Whatever you say, hero. All I know is that everyone has been singing your praises. If you want to play it off and be modest, so be it. Just know I'm proud of you."

"Yes, well," he paused to readjust his bag, turning so she couldn't see his smile. "Regardless, we should be thinking about getting supplies for our trip and getting out of here tomorrow." He took a quick look around. "Where's Bran anyway?"

Her smile faded and she took a step back. "At the inn, but I don't think we're leaving any time soon."

"What? Why not?"

"It would probably be best to wait until we are back at the inn to discuss what we are going to do next." Something about her tone was strange, but Ean couldn't quite figure out what it could be.

"Alright. If you say so."

They headed off towards the inn, dodging around tents and people. More often than not, they were stopped so that someone's brother, daughter or other family member could thank Ean for everything he had done. Jaslen seemed to enjoy the attention he was getting, her grin growing whenever anyone stopped them. At some point, while Ean wasn't paying attention, she managed to snake an arm around his as they walked along. He was sure it was just a friendly gesture, but his cheeks still colored once he realized her arm was there. Once they had made it off the green, they were able to move on uninterrupted. They walked on in the fading light of the sun, arm in arm.

"So, what happened at the wagons while I was here saving the village?" Ean asked to break the silence.

"Well, after we put you to bed," she said, giving him another impish smile. "Bran and I were still wide awake. The leader of the trade caravan, Berek Soushade, had invited us to come back at night, so we decided to take him up on his offer. We stayed up talking and drinking for a time as they had a drink that was much smoother then Burnbeer, and were having fun … until one of their scouts came running into camp yelling about how we were about to be attacked. Then everyone leapt into action.

Guards drew swords, wagon hands gathered the animals together and then drew their own weapons, and even Berek, the head of the caravan, drew a weapon." She tilted her head slightly. "It was different than any weapon I had ever seen before. It was thin, like an enlarged needle and didn't look like it would do much to a man wearing armor. The way he used it though …" She gave a laugh. "I thought Bran had gotten good from all of his private tutoring, but the men that worked for the caravan had twice as much talent, and Berek had even more. He moved about the bandits as if he was dancing, but they all either fell or were disarmed before they could even get close to him. It was all very exciting." She smiled for a moment, then her voiced lowered.

"A good amount of Berek's employees were killed though. They had a Healer with them, but he couldn't help a lot of the men. They had been through another battle somewhere to the south, and the healer was low on supplies. It was horrible to have to sit and watch as some of them died."

Her voice trailed off, but she hugged his arm closer. Ean glanced over at her, but returned his gaze to the street ahead once he saw her crying openly. He had no idea how to handle a crying girl. For the first time, he actually wished that Bran was with them. He would know what to do to make Jaslen feel better.

Ean understood how she felt. In his own mind, he could still picture the man he had, well, transformed was probably the best word. That look of horror on the bandit's face as he realized what had happened to him … It made Ean shiver.

The pair continued to walk along in silence until they came to the inn. Jaslen detached herself from his arm.

"I don't want Bran to see me all a mess," she said, pulling out a cloth to wipe at her eyes. "You know how he worries about me." When she finished, she shot him a questioning look. "So, am I presentable?"

"Yes, can't even tell you were crying."

"Wonderful. Let's join Bran, yes?" Without waiting for a reply, she pushed open the doors and went inside with Ean trailing behind her.

CHAPTER 16

TROUBLE

AS SOON AS EAN pushed open the heavy doors, loud conversation and drunken laughter washed over him. He had expected a small crowd of somber diners but found a packed room full of men and women dancing in the aisles and falling over the tables and each other. Every table was packed with villagers, some of which he had helped earlier in the day. Ean was curious how the medicines he had given some of them would mix with Burnbeer.

A tug at his arm brought his attention back to Jaslen. She motioned over towards a far corner where Bran sat at a table alone. He waved the two of them over with the mug in his hand, the chair teetering beneath him. Even across the room, Bran's sloppy mannerisms made it obvious that he was nursing more than a light buzz.

As Ean tried to weave through the crowd, people pointed and whispered. Unlike at home, these people were smiling in recognition. Kindness shown in their eyes — something to which he was unaccustomed. People were reaching out to stop him, shake his hand, pat his back. It made him feel appreciated and claustrophobic all at the same time.

"Sit down, young healer," a crowd of boisterous men invited. "Let us buy you a drink while you tell us what it's like working with that sour crone, Mable."

"Uh," Ean said with a weak smile. "I'm sorry but my friends are expecting me. Maybe another time."

By the time they reached Bran, he was ordering another drink. He grabbed the serving girl by the arm as she was turned to leave, nearly yanking her off her feet.

"Make that three drinks, miss," he said, his words slurred. "My friend and my girl have just as much to celebrate as the rest of the people here. They both saved many lives today." Shooting him an annoyed look, the waitress nodded curtly then hurried away.

Not seeming to notice, Bran returned his smile back to Jaslen and Ean. "Sit, sit!"

Jaslen took a seat to Bran's left, pulling it close to him. Her usual smile grew as Bran wrapped an arm around her and pulled her in for a kiss. Ean didn't want to intrude on the couple's private moment but how could he not when they insisted on showing their affection in public? He shifted his gaze to the rest of the bar, thinking about how far he had come. The day's experience had opened his eyes a bit to the world. He didn't have to be against everyone or be jealous of what others had. Maybe he would even enjoy his time traveling with these two.

Probably not, but at least now he thought it was a possibility.

Bran must have sensed his good mood. "Look at our young Healer, all puffed up about his accomplishments." Reaching over, he patted Ean on the shoulder. "I heard all about what you did today. I always knew you weren't as useless as my father said you were."

That took Ean down a peg or two. The Mayor had always made his opinion about Ean known, but it was different to hear it coming from Bran's mouth. Well, it didn't matter. What mattered now was figuring out what Jaslen had been unwilling to tell him.

"As much fun as this is," Ean said. "We should prepare to leave as soon as possible."

Letting out a laugh, Bran took a swig from his mug before answering. "We'll leave in twelve days — give or take."

"Oh, so you want to vacation here a bit," Ean snorted, knowing Bran was joking. "Of course."

Jaslen narrowed her eyes and sent Bran a scolding frown. Without looking up, she said, "He's serious, Ean. We're not leaving — we can't."

"What do you mean can't?"

"Tell him about the Scar, Bran," she said. "And about the Seekers."

"The Scar? Seekers?" The temperature in the room seemed to plummet as a chill traveled down his spine. "Will someone just tell me what is going on?"

"Sure," Bran started, then paused. Lifting his mug to his face, Bran went to drink before realizing that he had finished it already. Frowning, he slammed it down on the table then began to look around. "Where is that waitress with our next round of drinks?"

Giving up on him, Ean turned his attention to Jaslen. "Please, just tell me."

"A Scar seems to be a ... well, Berek explained it as a doorway to the Abyss."

That got Ean's attention. "What? A doorway? You mean people can actually walk through?"

Shaking her head, Jaslen continued. "No, they say it's like a one-way doorway. Things can come out but nothing can go through. It also gives off some kind of energy, which apparently corrupts everything around it." She glanced at his arm for an instant before continuing on. "That's the main reason the caravans are waiting two weeks before trying to travel past it."

Ean let the glance at his arm go by without comment. Let her think what she wanted for now.

"The main reason? That seems like reason enough for these fools that know nothing about the Abyss." He felt himself growing angry, but he wasn't sure why. Even so he kept his voice low.

"Ean, it's not just the creatures that might come out of the Scar or what it might do to them that has the caravan workers scared the most. It's a group of people called the Seekers."

"Seekers?"

"Yes. They're a religious sect of the followers of Alistar that hunt out these Scars and close them." Her face went pale as she spoke, which Ean didn't understand.

"That would be even more of a reason to get going sooner. I would love to see one of these Scars for myself." The fact that he had never heard about them before, especially from Zin, annoyed him even further. Where was the imp anyway? "If we stick around here too long, those people will end up closing it before I get the chance."

Jaslen put a hand on top of his own. That stopped him from speaking.

"Ean, these Seekers," her voice was low and she was looking at him intently. "They kill anything that they even think has been touched by the energy coming out of the Scar. Anything." She gave his hand a squeeze, emphasizing the word.

So that's what had caused her so much concern. She was actually worried about him. The thought quelled his anger in a heartbeat, and he did his best to give her a reassuring smile.

"Even if that's true and these people exist, I doubt that they would be able to tell that I'm connected to the Abyss in any way." At least I hope.

Bran interrupted them with a bellow of excitement as the waitress finally returned with their drinks. As soon as she set it down, he snatched his up and brought it to his lips. Gulping a few times, he smacked the half-finished mug back down on the table.

"We don't need to fear these Seekers," he said, loudly. "We've turned into Heroes ourselves; we can handle them."

It took a few moments for Ean to realize that the whole room had grown silent. Jaslen's eyes darted about. The patrons in the tables around them had turned to face them, their faces blank. It took Bran a bit longer to notice.

"What's going on?" Bran asked, that stupid grin still on his face. "Did someone just die?" Ean watched as Jaslen cringed in unison with him. Bran didn't seem to notice. "Well, I guess a bunch of people died today, but many more lived. So you all should return to your celebrating!"

The faces around them weren't blank now. Open anger painted half of them while the rest had looks of disgust. People further away were mumbling now as well, occasionally pointing and frowning in their direction. Jaslen reached over and tried to get Bran's attention, but he was oblivious.

"I may not be part of this village," Bran continued on, "but I did my fair share of helping out. I didn't see these so called Seekers anywhere about." The scratching sound of a blade coming out of a sheath caught Ean's attention, and he stood so fast he knocked his chair over. He had no idea where the sound had come from, but the feeling of inevitable violence hung in the air.

"Now, now, no need to get all worked up," said a woman's voice from somewhere in the crowd. Ean tried to pick out the direction he had heard the sound from, but with everyone's attention on them, it was impossible to determine who might have drawn a blade. Almost everyone in the room now was looking in their direction.

Before anything could happen, the innkeeper's wife pushed through the crowd and planted herself next to Bran. She was built more like a solid block of stone, not like a soft doughy woman that had eaten too much of her own baking. She glared down at Bran from behind a mop of disheveled black hair.

"If you ask me, there should be an age limit on Burnbeer. The younger you are, the dumber it makes you. This one is too ignorant to be afraid of Seekers and lacks the good sense to respect the dead. I have a good mind to turn him over my knee and give him a spanking."

That got a few nods from the surrounding crowd, but just as many were still giving Bran looks as if they meant him harm. The innkeeper's wife continued on. "I'll escort our young trouble-maker back to his room and then the rest of us can go about celebrating in honor of those we lost today."

Bran had just been staring at the woman open-mouthed as she spoke, his face becoming redder with each insult. When she was done, he tried to speak. "Now wait just a second," he slurred. "I am perfectly fine ..."

A loud smacking sound cut him off as the innkeeper's wife backhanded Bran across the face. The woman moved so quickly, Ean didn't even think Bran would have been able to dodge or block the blow if he had been sober. The hit was hard enough to knock him out of his chair. A look of confusion crossed his face as he found himself on the floor. The crowd around them erupted into a cheer with many of the men and women standing to applaud.

With a satisfied nod in Bran's direction, the innkeeper's wife turned her attention on Ean and Jaslen. "Now, you better get him up to his room and keep him there for the night. I don't want to have to teach that boy a lesson again. I'll even help you get him there."

Without waiting for a reply from either of them, the woman reached down and grabbed Bran by the scruff of his shirt. Lifting him up, she held him out in front of her like a piece of rotten trash and began walking him towards the back.

There was nothing for Ean and Jaslen to do but follow after the woman manhandling Bran. The other patrons of the bar made room for the intimidating woman as she made her way towards the stairs.

As Ean and Jaslen followed behind, Ean heard the mumblings of some of the patrons.

"Just a stupid child that can't hold his drink ..."

"Last thing we need is the Seekers here ..."

"I heard everyone in Rottwealth is a little crazy. That's why they never usually come out of their valley ..."

Ignoring their words, Ean focused on keeping up with the innkeeper's wife. She moved through the crowd easily for such a large woman, especially considering Bran wasn't a lightweight either. Bran didn't seem to have his wits about him yet. He was moving his legs, but every time he got close to getting some traction on the ground, the innkeeper's wife just gave him a little shake. She ended up carrying him all the way up to their room, where she dumped him onto one of the beds. Then without a word, she dragged both Jaslen and Ean into the room, then slammed the door shut. Turning on them both, she jabbed a finger into Ean's chest.

"Now, I understand you probably know very little of what goes on outside of your village," she said in a stern tone, "but that should just make you and your friends more careful of what you say." She pulled over a chair and fell back into it, then motioned for the two of them to have a seat on the closest bed.

"If you learn nothing else while out of your village, you should at least know this: The Seekers are a horrible group that answers to no one but the Voice of their temple. Direct agents of Alistar himself, they roam about doing 'Alistar's work.' The things they do, though, make it hard to believe the god of justice would support them. Traveling around, dispensing their own form of justice, disregarding the mayors, village councils or whatever body governs a village."

"That sounds just like any other Hero," Jasmine broke in, "although a bit harsher than any I've seen or heard about."

"Heroes have their own rules, girl. They bend them every which way, but they never break them. If a Hero steps out of line, you can be sure a pack of them will arrive to put him or her in their place."

Letting out a long sigh, the innkeeper's wife fiddled with her dress before continuing. "The Seekers stand apart from everyone else. The only one that can call them out for their actions is Alistar himself, and I haven't heard of him ever making an appearance."

To Ean, the Seekers just sounded like another form of bully. "And no one is willing to stand up to them? They sound like a small group. If this village could defend itself from a whole pack of raiders, I can't see why they couldn't drive out a couple of holy men."

The older woman grimaced. "These three people, two men and a woman, are said to be the greatest fighters in the land. Blessed with skills and weapons by Alistar himself, so they say. They have only passed through here once. A group of hunters with a bit too much Burnbeer in their guts thought they could scare the group off. One Seeker killed six of the men on his own while his two friends simply watched. He probably would have killed more if the other man in their group hadn't stopped him."

"Well, of course he beat them easily," Jaslen replied. "I've seen how funny that Burnbeer stuff can make a person." Her eyes began to wander towards Bran, but she snapped them back towards the woman. "We might even be able to handle six men after they downed enough mugs of the stuff."

"No, girl, the men might have gotten a bit of courage from the drink, but they were not in any condition like your friend here. Those men were some of our best with a weapon, even when they were a bit tipsy, and he cut them down in a matter of moments. The other man said a prayer afterwards for them too."

She shuddered and rubbed her hands together for a moment before continuing. "The leader and woman seemed regretful that it had happened, but the other man ... well, he seemed to find the whole thing funny. Best not to even joke about people like that."

"Alright, we get it. They are dangerous," Ean said. "But what does that have to do with this Scar that we've heard about?"

The woman took a moment to mumble a prayer—Ean wasn't sure to whom—before speaking. "They say that the main reason the Seekers exist is because the god, Alistar, wants to destroy anything that has even the remotest connection to the Abyss. Now I've only heard this from a man that heard about it from his sister's husband, but apparently their leader has a weapon that can absorb and destroy the energies that come from the Abyss. The Seekers go about closing these Scars and then hunt around and kill anything that was touched by the energy that leaks out of it to stop them from spreading the corruption. Even if it's a person that made the mistake of getting too close."

Ean's thoughts immediately went to the man that he had 'changed.' The man had been a cold-blooded killer and rapist, and now he was something even worse. It was a callous thought, but he hoped the Seekers would track him down and take him out of this world.

"So, I hope you understand now how talking about them can stir up some bad feelings." Rising to her feet, the innkeeper's wife placed her hands on her hips. "Now, with that being said, this will be the last night you will be staying here."

"What?" Ean and Jaslen said in unison. "But with everything you just said, we can't travel north," Jaslen continued on. "The caravans won't be leaving for weeks."

"There isn't anywhere else we can stay in this village," Ean said, almost talking over her. "Where will we go?"

Stepping up almost directly in their faces, the woman's tone grew serious. "I suggest that you return home. You have no idea what the world outside of your little village is like, and you are probably better off. Better for you to return home and resume your safe little lives."

"Fine," Ean said, which earned him a silent glare from Jaslen.

"Glad to see you have some sense. Here." Moving to one of the dressers, she opened a drawer and pulled out a small sack. "Our healer sent this to you for thanks and said she would find a way to repay you more when she could. I already told her you were returning home so she can send whatever she thinks is right to your village. I've packed another sack downstairs filled with more than enough food for your trip home. I'll leave it at the bottom of the steps when most of the crowd leaves."

Tossing the bag at their feet, she headed for the door. As she entered the hallway, she turned, a small smile finally lighting up her face. "I know I have been a bit abrupt with you tonight, but it is for your own good. Our whole village is grateful for what you did and most want to make sure nothing unfortunate happens to you. So be safe and go home."

With that she closed the door behind her, leaving the three of them in silence.

Bran was the first to make a sound, a moan escaping his lips as he lay on the bed. He was on his side at this point, his eyes closed. Ean hoped he would stay asleep until the morning, that way he couldn't cause them any more trouble. He reached down and picked up the sack. Inside he found a variety of smaller sacks and carefully wrapped bottles. Searching through each, he found various herbs, powders and liquids. Of course none of them contained Rottwealth or Flashseal, but the medicine was far more plentiful than what Cleff had donated for the journey.

"Ean," Jaslen said as he examined each of the containers of medicine. "You can't really think we should just go home."

"Home? We are certainly not going home. We're going to Lurthalan like we planned."

"What? You just said that we were going to head home."

"I only said that so she wouldn't keep bothering us. That woman wouldn't have let us out of her sight if she thought we were going north." He gave her his best reassuring smile. "And you don't have to worry about the Scar. I can handle anything that has to do with the Abyss."

"Maybe," she seemed less than convinced. "But what about those Seekers? They hunt anything connected to the Abyss, which I would think includes you."

With a sigh, Ean got to his feet. He began pacing the room, pausing only to glance out the window. It was pitch black outside. The villagers must be making an early night of it, at least those that weren't still downstairs.

"The Seekers are three people," he replied. "I'm sure we can avoid them. And who knows how close they are. If we get near the Scar and it seems dangerous, we can turn around and head back or go around them."

A small frown tugged at Jaslen's lips, but she remained quiet. Ean pushed on, trying to reassure her. "I know you're worried, but I promise if we think it's the least bit dangerous, we'll turn around and head back."

"Fine," she said at last. "But I am going to hold you to your word. If I say we turn around, then we turn around. Agreed?"

"Agreed."

"Good." She motioned with her head towards Bran, who was sprawled out over the bed in his boots and snoring like a hibernating bear. "But what are we going to do about him?"

"We'll let him sleep it off while we pack. We had better get everything ready. I don't think Bran is going to be any help tonight."

Kneeling down, he started to trace the runes to open up his Pocket while Jaslen started pulling out their clothes. He did it without thinking now, his hand moving almost of its own accord. That left his mind free to think about all of the possibilities that these Scars could hold.

CHAPTER 17

MOVING ON

THEY TOOK THEIR TIME packing. Ean had no idea how Jaslen was feeling, but he was wide awake from the excitement of the day and what lay ahead. At one point she went downstairs to get their sack of food, leaving Ean alone upstairs with Bran. The other boy was still curled up on top of his bed, his loud snores filling the room. Ean smiled as he moved about, picking up his things. The start of the trip had been bumpy, but he felt that they had all grown from it. His experience helping the people of Rensen had given him a more optimistic view of the trip.

Sure, he might have started helping because he had been forced into it, but now he realized that he actually wanted to ease the suffering of people and save lives. The trust those villagers had placed in him, the gratitude he saw in their eyes, had filled an empty space inside of him. He couldn't explain it, but for the first time in his life, he felt peace about the path Cleff had chosen for him. As long as what he had done to his body and the powers that came with it didn't get out of control ...

His powers. Ean had never really thought about them as his before. Drawing runes, summoning creatures—they had all seemed like borrowed skills before. What he had done to that man, changing him the way he did, reinforced that it was a permanent part of him now.

It frightened him.

The ability to channel pure energy from the Abyss could cause a number of problems, especially if he found he couldn't control it. What if he was healing someone and accidentally changed them with the power? What if he was helping Jaslen up and changed her? He could never live with himself if he changed her. He would need to be careful.

A tingle at the back of his neck made Ean turn around. The door opened and the blur that marked Zin's presence slinked in. The blur paused in front of the door for a moment, and then the imp materialized into view. He flashed Ean a smile, his lips stained red. Bits of ... something ... were stuck in his pointed teeth.

"You really can feel that I'm near, can't you?" Zin phrased it more as a statement than a question. "Well, what's our plan now, oh great hero of Rensen? Are we off to another village to puff up our egos, or are we going straight to the city to find a solution to the monster problem in Rottwealth?"

Ean ignored the sarcasm in the imp's voice. "Filling yourself up with some of the local rat population, are we?" The imp simply gave him a mocking bow. "Well, regardless, I have a few questions for you."

"Oh joy, more questions that I probably have no answers to. I can't wait to be called a liar some more." Zin gave a quick glance at Bran and then motioned in his direction. "Are you sure they are questions that you want him overhearing?"

Shrugging, Ean took a seat on the bed. "He can hear whatever he wants; nothing I want to know matters that much. Besides, he's had enough Burnbeer to keep him out for a while longer, I think."

"Alright then, ask away. Just don't get mad when I don't know the answer." Taking a seat in front of the bed, Zin began to pick at his teeth with a clawed finger. When he dislodged a piece of meat, he stuck it back in his mouth and swallowed it down.

"I just love how positive you always are," Ean said. "What do you know about Scars? Rips in the fabric of whatever separates this world and the Abyss?"

The imp froze, a claw jammed deep in the back of his mouth. He looked at Ean unblinking for a few moments, then slowly pulled his hand out of his mouth.

"Listen very carefully, Ean," Zin rarely called Ean by his name. "A Scar is a very dangerous event. If you know about them, that means you heard about it from someone. Is there a Scar nearby?"

"The villagers have said that there is one a day or two up the road on the way to Lurthalan. They aren't sure how long it's been there."

The imp let out an uncustomary growl. Pacing back and forth, the imp's eyes were squinted and a small grimace showed off some of his teeth. He was mumbling something. When Zin stopped, he swung around towards Ean so fast that he almost leapt off the bed.

"We have to wait until it's gone," the imp said, a finger pointed right in Ean's face. "We can't go messing around one of those Scars; it is way too dangerous."

"I get they are a connection to the Abyss, but it's not like they could just draw a person in, right?"

"No, you don't get it," the imp said, clenching his hands together. "They are dangerous because of what they can do to the local animals. They are dangerous because of the men that will do whatever it takes to close them and kill anything else they find even remotely touched by them." His eyes closed for a moment, and he took a few deep breaths. "And most importantly, they are dangerous because it is possible they were created by something trying to come out of the Abyss."

Ean let it all sink in. The first part wasn't surprising; the innkeeper's wife had said as much, and he had witnessed first-hand how the energies from the Abyss could change something like the troll they had faced. The second must be the Seekers, but how did Zin know about them? Ean was pretty sure that no one in his village knew about them. Unless of course he was talking about someone other than the Seekers, which meant even more potential problems for them. He would have to figure out who Zin meant.

But it was the third thing that had him really thinking. Creatures could actually escape from the Abyss? His ignorance of the types of creatures that lived there was starting to become a problem. He would have to start prying more information out of Zin as they traveled. It wouldn't be easy, of course. The imp always found ways to change the subject whenever the Abyss came up. But time for that later.

"Let's start with the people you mentioned. The innkeeper's wife told us about a group called the Seekers. Are they the same people you are talking about?"

The imp shook his head. "Never heard about them before—they a religious group? I suppose it must be. Someone dead-set on closing a Scar has to be an Alistar fanatic. Anyone else would be too afraid to go near them, and with good cause."

"Zin," Ean cut in. "How do you know all of this? Have you ever come out of one before, when you lived in the Abyss?"

The imp waved him off. "No, of course not. It takes a group of beings of considerable power working together to open one, and they usually wouldn't let anything else through. As for random ones, I've never seen one in my entire lifetime. You have to remember, the Abyss is a huge place. The chance of being in the right place at the right time when a Scar naturally opens is practically nonexistent. The only way most of us creatures get out is by being summoned."

Zin was good at answering questions without actually answering them, but Ean was getting tired of getting the run around. "Then how do you know so much about our world? In all of the years I've known you, you haven't mentioned once how you know so much."

Another dismissing wave of the imp's little hand almost sent Ean into a rage, but he held himself together as the imp continued speaking.

"You're not focusing on the important things here. If something opened that Scar, it was probably a group of Nar'Grim, which would mean one of them could have escaped and could still be close to the Scar. Their kind are not something you would want to meet."

"What's so terrible about these Nar'Grim? You've never mentioned them before."

A tiny shudder ran through the imp. "The Nar'Grim control most of the levels of the Abyss, except for the lowest three levels. Immensely powerful beings, they manipulate most creatures through fear and pain. They are behind most of the different schemes that go on down there."

Zin let out a short laugh that was devoid of any actual humor. "I wouldn't be surprised if one or two didn't control a great deal of things up here as well. Even one loose in your world could be disastrous."

"How could they get away with anything up here? Wouldn't most people be afraid of something from the Abyss? Like you said, followers of Alistar would hunt them down."

The imp let a dark laugh. "It would take an army, or someone just as powerful as one, to kill a Nar'Grim. I would imagine most people wouldn't even realize what it was anyway."

Getting back to his feet, the imp took on a lecturing tone. "You see, Nar'Grim change themselves to look like your average human, although tall for your kind. They've spent decades mastering that deception down in the Abyss. They're jealous of your kind. The freedom you have, the power and authority you have over each other. Half of the things they do in the Abyss are their twisted versions of what you do up here. They have their own leaders and organizations, they build extravagant homes for themselves, and they just love to plot and disrupt the plans of others. Up here, without more of their kind to get in the way, a Nar'Grim could gain power quickly. It wouldn't surprise me if there wasn't one already in control of some town, or manipulating the temples in some way."

"Alright," Ean said, taking it all in. "But then why should I worry about one if it got out? It wouldn't have any interest in me. I can barely control what little I understand about my abilities as it is. I'm no threat."

"It would be interested in this." Taking Ean's right arm, the imp peeled back his glove enough that some of the glowing tattoos on his skin became visible. "A human tied by this to the Abyss? A human that can summon creatures, and is becoming stronger every day? Ean, to a Nar'Grim you are probably the most interesting human alive. Let's just hope that if there is one or two in this world, they have no idea you exist."

Wonderful. Now, he not only had to worry about the Seekers finding and killing him, he had to worry about becoming the plaything of one of the most powerful creatures in the Abyss. Enough was enough. Zin had to know way more about the tattoos. It was time Ean found out.

Lashing out, Ean grabbed the imp by the arm. Usually that feat was near impossible, but with the imp still holding onto Ean's arm, it was easy to grab him. Zin tried to bite down hard into his hand, but Ean's glove lessened the impact to a slight pinch. The imp shook his head a few times, then sighed and gave up. Sitting with his shoulders slumped, he looked up at Ean with questioning eyes.

"I want some answers, Zin." Ean was trying his best to sound intimidating, but the shock of actually catching Zin had caught him off guard. "I want to know everything you know about my tattoos, and don't try to lie to me again."

"I've told you everything a dozen times now! The tattoos help you channel the energy from the Abyss better and protect you from being changed by it. They will slowly grow and cover more of your body as your own power grows." He tugged at his arm trying to get it free for a moment, then gave up again. "And I guess they let you feel when anything else that's been touched by the Abyss is nearby. That's all I know, so let me go already."

"No, you're still hiding something. Why would these Nar'Grim take that much interest in me? It has to be more than the few things you've told me about the tattoos."

"Nope, that's more than enough to get their interest." The words poured out of his mouth while his eyes darted around. They mostly went between the still sleeping mound that was Bran and the door.

"They love collecting odd things," he continued on. "One even specifically hunted me down, because I could speak an actual language. Kept me around for I don't know how many years ..."

"Hold on a second," Ean cut in. "You mean to tell me that your kind can't speak? Not even some strange imp language?"

Zin shut his mouth, his eyes darting around faster now. Had he finally gotten the imp to slip? He gave Zin's arm a little shake.

"Start talking, Zin. Why can you speak and the rest of your kind not be able to?"

"It's nothing—I'm just a weird mutation." The imp's feet were squirming about. Ean was sure if he let go, Zin would be halfway across the room before he could blink. His speech increased in speed. "You saw what the energy from the Abyss does to creatures. I'm just a fluke."

Ean was just about to call him out for lying when the door opened and Jaslen walked in with the bag of food. Dropping it on the floor, she turned and gave Ean and Zin a warm smile. Which apparently was Zin's cue to let out a scream.

The imp began to whimper. Before Ean could open his mouth, Jaslen shoved him so hard, he almost fell off the bed. He caught himself but let go of the imp. Zin took advantage of the opportunity and jumped behind Jaslen and grabbed onto her skirts.

"What are you doing to Zin?" Jaslen scolded. "Look, you've scared him."

"Now wait a minute. I was just ..." The look she shot him made his jaw snap shut. She knelt down and patted Zin on the head.

"It's alright. I won't let that bully bother you anymore. You can just stay by me for a while until Ean learns to treat you better, ok?"

Zin nodded and flashed her a big, toothy smile.

This isn't over, Ean mouthed at him before climbing to his feet. Walking over to where she had dropped the food bag, he reached down and opened it up. It contained dried meat, vegetables and fruit. It was enough food to get them through a quarter of the season if they were careful, and the journey to Lurthalan was only supposed to take five or six days.

He closed the bag up and left it by the door to retrieve later. It would be one of the few items they would take with them on the journey ahead. They were also going to keep their money handy, Bran's sword and Jaslen's bow, of course, and a few other miscellaneous supplies. Everything else would go into his Pocket in the Abyss.

"Are your things ready?" He tried to make his voice as normal as possible, but he was slightly annoyed at Jaslen. She had jumped to the imp's defense without even attempting to find out if he had a reason to be grabbing the imp.

"I suppose so," she said in a flat tone, "although, I can't exactly ask him." As if in response Bran let out a loud snore. A small smile appeared on Jaslen's face for an instant, and she sighed. "We're ready, I suppose."

That small smile expanded into a grin. "Which means you get to show me again how you create that Pocket of yours."

"Of course."

Although Jaslen was quick to anger, she was just as quick to smile and offer forgiveness. That was one of the reasons he admired her so much. Ean took a seat next to the rest of their supplies piled in the center of the room. Jaslen and Zin joined him, with the imp keeping a safe distance away from Ean's reach.

Ean wiped the floor with a gloved hand to clear it of any dirt or stones they might have tracked in. Content with the space he was going to use, Ean placed a finger on the ground and began to mentally run through all of the runes he would use.

Without warning, a streak of dark blue light shot out of his finger and began snaking across the floor. He watched in stunned silence as the light moved faster and faster, eventually branching off into two and then three separate lights. In a matter of seconds, the complicated runes that opened up his Pocket were outlined on the ground, perfectly created and the exact size he had pictured. The design stayed for a moment longer before the runes activated and his Pocket appeared in the floor.

"No fair!" Jaslen said, a slight pout to her lips. "That was way too fast, Ean. I barely got to see it happen!"

"I ... well, sorry. It's open now, though." He began to toss their bags down into the mist that floated along inside the Pocket.

"Do it again, please."

Could he even try drawing them slowly again? Not if he was going to use pure energy, that was for sure. Maybe if he physically drew them with something, like he used to, but he really couldn't see himself doing that ever again.

"I don't think I can do it any slower. At least not anymore." He ran a hand through his hair, frowning at the hole. "I guess with my powers increasing, things are getting easier, like Zin said they would."

That earned him a cold stare from the imp, but he just returned it in kind. Just because the imp had been right about something, didn't mean he still wasn't holding things back. The answer did seem to placate Jaslen at least, as she nodded with a sigh.

"Alright then," she said, climbing back to her feet. "Let's get everything packed away so we can get some sleep. I'm guessing you want to leave early."

"Absolutely," he replied. "The innkeeper's wife was pretty adamant about us not heading north. Other people here might feel a bit stronger about it and try to stop us. The idea of anyone bringing the Seekers down on the village seems to put everyone here on edge."

"True."

Jaslen joined him as he stored their things, and together, they were able to get everything put away. Zin stayed by Jaslen's side the entire time. So much for getting him alone again in the near future. The imp would probably avoid him whenever they had the chance to be alone. The imp couldn't stay away from him forever, no matter how much he tried to be Jaslen's shadow. When they were finished, Ean placed his hand on the outside of the Pocket and watched as it closed just as easily as it was created.

With everything prepared, Ean and Jaslen said their good nights, put out the candles, and climbed into their own beds. Zin curled up at Jaslen's feet, one eye closed and the other watching Ean. The eye stayed fixed on him until Ean was completely under the covers. The imp was taking things a bit far. As a peace offering, he would let Zin have some of the meat in their supplies. Good food and not having to scavenge for a meal would make him feel better.

Tomorrow.

The Scar was certainly on the forefront of his mind. It was over a day's travel away, according to what they had heard and was somewhere off the path. Ean hoped that they could find it. It would be interesting to see something connected to the Abyss that he hadn't created. That thought swirled around in his head for a while longer until he finally fell asleep.

EAN WOKE TO THE feel of one of Zin's sharp claws between his shoulder blades.

"Knock it off, Zin!" he growled and burrowed deeper down into the covers.

A moment later, he found himself soaking wet.

Tossing off the blankets, he found Jaslen standing over his head with a pitcher.

"Sorry, Ean," she said, giving an apologetic grin. "If Zin's fingers poking you in the back wasn't enough to get you up, I figured I had to turn to something more drastic."

The only reply he could give was a grunt before he got out of bed and dried off.

Bran was just as difficult to get up. Jaslen pulled off his covers and jumped on the bed; she even hit him a few times with a pillow with no result. Eventually she just resigned herself to dumping water onto his head as well. That got him up quick. He mumbled a few words Ean couldn't hear from his side of the room and then climbed out of bed while the water dripped from his hair.

With everyone awake, once the men had dried off, they left. As they walked towards the stairs with their belongings, Ean took a look at his companions. Bran's hair was a mess, and he had stayed in the same shirt and pants he had slept in, both of which were riddled with stains. His eyes were half open, and he kept rubbing at them as he stood in the hall.

Jaslen was the complete opposite, wide-awake with her usual smile lighting up her face. She had put on one of her many brown dresses that she wore when she worked in her father's fields. She kept rubbing her hands together anxiously. Was she nervous about traveling again or excited? Hopefully the latter. If she suddenly decided that it was too dangerous to go anywhere near the Scar, Bran would take her side. Then not only would Ean not get to see the Scar, but they would add on a couple more days of traveling just to make sure they went around it.

Best not to worry about that. Glancing at Zin for a second earned him a dirty look before he turned invisible. Ean watched as his blur moved down the hallway. He was probably going to go hunt down some breakfast before they left. It was much easier to catch village rats than wild ones. Hopefully he would cool off a bit while he was gone.

With no one around, the three made their way out the front doors. Walking onto the main road, Ean got a clear view of the clearing where he had spent most of the previous day. There were fewer tents now, which he hoped meant the people that had been inside them had been well enough to go home. While he believed he had left most of those in good condition, without Rottwealth, it was impossible to say a person with a serious wound was ever out of danger.

Ean tried to stay positive as they began following the road east. The main road branched off to the north and southeast. The northern pass was the one they were going to follow, but it was what lay ahead, in-between the two paths, that made Ean pause.

A clearing similar to the one in the center of town sat off the road, filled with more wagons then Ean had ever imagined. There had to be over two dozen wagons resting out in the field. They sat some distance away from the road in no discernible order—wagons of multiple shapes, colors and sizes, some with wood roofs and others with canvas. Spaced out evenly about the wagon camp were small fire pits. Men and women moved between the fires and wagons, making the area around the caravan look like its own tiny village.

"Do all of those wagons belong to one caravan?" Ean asked as they turned and continued on north. Bran kept his head down and didn't respond. Jaslen gave him a disapproving look before turning her head slightly towards Ean.

"Yes, they all belong to Berek's family," she said, her eyes still on Bran. "They arrived a few days before us from the South. They had been trading with a group of people called the Shadaer Umdaer, some kind of tribal people that control all of the land a dozen or so days walk south of here."

"I couldn't imagine spending most of my life traveling around. I'm not saying I want to spend the rest of my life in Rottwealth, but I would like to have some place I could call my home."

As Jaslen's eyes narrowed and a small frown crept onto her face, Ean knew he had said the wrong thing.

"What do you mean you don't want to live in Rottwealth? Are you actually thinking about never going back?" She had slowed down now until they were walking side by side.

"Of course I'm going to go back," he said. "As soon as we figure out some way to help the village." Her features relaxed slightly, but she didn't look convinced. "I just meant that after we go back, and if we're able to get rid of whatever that creature is, I might leave to set up my own Healer's shop somewhere else, is all."

"What's wrong with Rottwealth?" Flipping her hair back, she glanced ahead at Bran for a moment then returned her full attention to him.

"It was just a thought, Jaslen," he said, trying his best to grin as much as he could. "I'm sure I'll end up taking over for Cleff and running things back in Rottwealth once he gets too old to keep working. It's just fun sometimes to think about other possibilities is all."

She sniffed at him and walked on in silence. So much for putting her at ease. Ean couldn't help but smile. If she was getting upset at him for talking about leaving, that had to mean she wanted to him stay, right? He didn't read into it as anything more than her not wanting to lose him as a friend, but even that felt nice.

They followed the road in silence from that point on until they reached the edge of the village and the beginning of the forest. Where most of the area around the road had been cleared before, as soon as it entered the forest, the dirt road became patchy and slightly overgrown. The trees were much thicker than Ean had first thought, making it hard to see very far. That combined with the low light of the morning made the forest intimidating. At least it felt that way to Ean, making him stop. Jaslen did as well, her face filled with doubt.

Bran didn't hesitate, although Ean couldn't tell if it was because of bravery or that Bran was in such bad shape that he simply didn't notice. He certainly didn't notice that Ean and Jaslen had stopped. They both watched him walk on a little ways before they turned and looked at each other. Jaslen broke the awkward moment first, giving him a sheepish smile before speaking.

"It can't be much worse than the mountain pass. As long as we stick to the road, I'm sure we will be fine. And after a night to think about it, I am curious about that Scar, and I'm sure you still have plenty of things you can tell us about Ze'an and the Abyss."

"Oh, right, of course," he said, turning away and readjusting the bag he carried. Sure he could tell them more, as soon as he could get Zin to tell him more first. Where was the imp anyway? He couldn't even feel him nearby.

"Well, we shouldn't let Bran get too far ahead," he continued on. "He might walk straight off the road and get lost without us to steer him. He looks like he's in really bad shape."

"Right." Jaslen nodded and set off after Bran.

Ean paused a moment longer to take a look back at Rensen. As crazy as his short time there had been, the people of the small logging village had been generous to him once they realized how helpful he had been. The possibility of settling down here was an attractive one. Of course, there were many more villages besides this one, most of which he didn't even know the names of. Best not to make any big decisions until he had been out in the world longer, and especially not until they had finished doing what they had set out to do. He had been honest about that with Jaslen. No matter how much he detested most of the people in Rottwealth, with the feeling being mutual of course, he didn't want to see the place where he grew up destroyed.

Jaslen had caught up to Bran and had put a decent amount of distance between them and Ean. Ean certainly didn't want to let Jaslen and Bran get out of sight, so he jogged after them. As he caught up, he decided to leave his thoughts about settling down behind him. A day or two ahead was an actual direct link to the Abyss, and he needed all of his attention to be focused on that. Closing his eyes, Ean 'felt' around to see if the imp had caught up with them.

Nothing.

CHAPTER 18

SOULS AND SCARS

THE THREE SPENT MOST of the morning traveling in silence. Bran remained in a sour mood, shooting Ean and Jaslen a pained stare whenever either one tried to strike up a conversation. So instead of talking, they took in the scenery, each lost in his or her own thoughts. Ean's thoughts flickered between the Scar that he hoped was still ahead, and all of the different plants and herbs he saw just off the path.

Surprisingly out of the two, it was the plants and herbs that monopolized his mind. The pure abundance and variety that he was able to spot in the forest was amazing. Back in Rottwealth, the most plentiful plants grew in the marsh and those were mostly Rottwealth and Oranganger, the plant used to make Flashseal. Most other types of plants that could be used in medicine and salves were difficult to find around his home. That wasn't the case out here, though.

There was Crimamon, a reddish-green flower which when ground up was commonly used to sooth burns and rashes. Mixed with Sunamir, a similar looking herb except for its lightly yellowish leaves, the two plants calmed the stomach and could even remove light forms of poison from the body. Then there was Viomane, a plant of the darkest purple, with slight barbs moving up its stem.

Once ground up and added to any liquid, the powder would put most people into a deep sleep. Very useful as a fever reducer, pain killer and sedative.

By lunchtime he had passed enough herbs to start his own store. He occasionally moved from the group to collect some of each, adding to the meager supplies that he had received from the Healer in Rensen. Each time, Jaslen and Bran would keep walking ahead, which forced him to jog to catch back up to the pair.

At this point, they had gotten so deep into the forest that the sun was blocked from view. Only small rays of light were able to break through the canopy of leaves, creating a pre-dawn level of light. Between the low levels of light, the silence of the forest, and the occasional dark blur of an animal darting about, the forest took on a creepy feeling.

When their stomachs growled in unison, they shared a chuckle. That was their cue to make camp, and they chose a spot just off the road. Ahead of them at a few dozen paces, the road curved to the right, quickly lost behind the dense trees. Jaslen went about finding firewood as Ean and Bran readied a spot for a fire. Bran's mood was starting to improve; a weak smile lightened up his still pale face. It was only a matter of time before idle conversation turned into questions about the Abyss. And of course Zin was still nowhere to be found.

Ean opened up his Pocket and retrieved their cooking pot and three bowls. Bran watched expressionless for a few moments and then turned his attention to starting the fire. On the menu for the afternoon was cooked vegetables in water. Ean closed the Pocket after getting their things and hung the pot over the fire that Bran had started. By the time they had the water and vegetables into the pot, Jaslen returned, her arms filled with more sticks and branches than they would need to keep the fire going for the short amount of time they planned to rest and eat.

With the food starting to boil, they sat around the pot in silence, a strange awkwardness hanging in the air. Jaslen and Bran were looking at everything except each other. Finally, Bran broke the silence.

"I want to apologize for how I behaved last night. I could have gotten us in a lot of trouble."

"And what about for this morning?" Jaslen said, folding her arms over her chest. "You've been acting like a horse's behind ever since you woke up. I've been too nervous to even talk to you."

"For that too — the Burnbeer paid me back though for how I acted, believe me. I'm sorry for taking it out on both of you."

He sounded sincere at least. Ean thought himself big enough to let it go, especially with how much Bran had stood up for him in the past.

Jaslen seemed to accept the apology as well. She reached over and pulled Bran's head close enough so that she could kiss him on the lips. Ean took the moment to reach over and stir the pot again. And kept stirring until he heard them come back up for air.

"That Pocket is a handy trick — wish I knew how to make one. It's all pretty amazing what you can do, Ean. Do you know that?" Jaslen asked.

He looked down at the ground, trying not to blush.

"More and more, I find myself thinking about Zin and Ze'an, and the Abyss. But most of all, I find myself wondering about you."

Ean swallowed hard. His words came out with a squeak. "Me? Seriously?"

"Yes, what are you exactly — a healer or a magus? What are those paintings on your skin? Are there others like you?"

Ean almost let out a sigh of relief but he did let himself relax as she continued.

A good question and one he could answer honestly. "No, I have no idea if there are others like me. I would love to say that Ze'an personally picked me to have these powers, but it really just came down to luck. I happened to find a book that was connected to the Abyss. It's possible that there are other copies of the same book out there somewhere, but I have no idea."

"Oh, I thought maybe Ze'an himself might have told you."

"Well, you see, Ze'an doesn't tell me anything, probably because he doesn't want to influence how I spread his, uh, teachings. Being a god of randomness and chaos, it's only natural that he would want me to ..."

He trailed off as a familiar feeling rose in the back of his head. There was something coming, something tied to the Abyss. It took him a few moments more to realize that he was feeling Zin. He was coming from the direction of where the road curved to the right. How had he gotten so far ahead of them?

And he was coming in fast.

Ean tried to move to his feet nonchalantly, but there must have been something in his manner that gave away his nervousness. Maybe it was the combination of how his voice had trailed off and then risen just as suddenly, or it could have been his sudden change in expression. Either way, both Bran and Jaslen were on their feet right behind him. Bran had his sword in his hand while Jaslen readied her bow, head pivoting as she tried to figure out where to aim.

The imp was almost to them now, coming straight at them through the forest. It took Ean a few seconds, but he eventually picked out that subtle blur that gave the imp away. Bran and Jaslen still couldn't see anything of course, so they practically jumped out of their clothes when he suddenly appeared at their feet.

"Zin!" Jaslen said with a relieved laugh. "You nearly scared me to death! That wasn't very nice of you to –"

"There are men coming," the imp said, cutting her off. "A lot of them. All dressed the same and looking very serious."

Bran and Jaslen, who had started to relax, immediately tensed back up. Jaslen whispered the word Ean had been thinking.

"Seekers?"

Ean shrugged. It could be anyone but better to play it safe.

"Time to move camp. Bran, help me drag the pot deeper into the forest. Jaslen, grab the supplies and follow behind us. We'll come back and grab the rest of our stuff then cover up any signs of our camp. All right?"

They nodded and immediately got to work.

"How much time do we have until they're here, Zin?"

"Not much," the imp said, rubbing his hands together. "I would expect them to come into view soon."

"Fine, fine." Ean left the imp's side and began helping Bran move the pot. By the time he had moved the pot far enough back for his liking, Jaslen had put out the fire and Bran had moved the rest of their things behind a group of trees.

Crouching behind a tree, Ean hoped they had hidden their campsite well enough. For all he knew, this group could be friendly but no point in taking any chances. They would stay hidden and hope the group passed without incident. As long as the group weren't Seekers, which Ean doubted because of the large number of them, they should have no way of finding the four of them hiding off the road.

They didn't have to wait long to find out, as a line of people came into view marching down the road. Zin had been telling the truth; there were a lot of them, walking two-by-two down the road. They all wore the same dark crimson robes with black trim running around the wrists and up and down their open fronts. The black trim also ran around the front of their hoods, which were up hiding each person's face. Even though they were all of different heights and weights, they marched in unison.

By the time the group had rounded the corner and were almost parallel to where the four were hiding, Ean could see the end of their line. A quick count revealed that there were thirty-two of the robed figures in total. As they started to pass by where the camp had been just moments ago, Ean tensed. The sharp intakes of breath behind him signaled the tension his friends were feeling as well. Ean only let himself relax once the last two robed figures had moved past where their site had been. Of course, that was too soon.

As one, without even the slightest sound or motion from any of them, the entire column came to a halt. Ean readied himself to sprint off into the forest. It would be a shame to lose their pot and the few other supplies they had gotten out, but at the very least they had kept the food close by. Those bags might slow them down, but it didn't look like this group had good runners anyway.

So Ean waited.

And waited.

And waited some more.

After a decent amount of time, Ean risked a look back at his companions. Bran was staying perfectly still, but Jaslen shrugged with a confused look on her face. Turning back, he watched the still immobile group stand in the road. Not a single person had moved a muscle since they had stopped. It couldn't be coincidence that they would stop near where their camp had been. Not a single one of them had turned a head as they marched by, though, so he doubted they had seen anything that would cause them to stop. Which left one possibility.

The group could sense them in some way.

Sense him.

Seekers.

Ean was about to turn and signal his companions to run when a single robed figure three rows from the back end stepped out of line and turned to face where they were hiding. Raising his hands to his head, the man pulled back his hood and revealed a face much younger then Ean had expected. The man looked to be in his late twenties or early thirties, with straight black hair hanging down to his neck. The only distinguishable mark was a scar running down from the left side of his lower lip to the base of his chin that detracted slightly from the smile he was wearing. The smile held nothing but warmth and friendliness, but his sea blue eyes were hard as he looked directly at them.

Lifting both of his hands into the air, palms out, the man took a few steps until he was at the edge of the road. "The three of you can come out," he called out. "We mean you no harm."

How did he know there were three of them hiding amongst the trees? Well, three humans at least. If he didn't realize Zin was there, that meant he couldn't sense him, which also meant he probably wasn't a Seeker. Unless of course he was trying to trick them. Ean looked to both of his companions to see what they were thinking.

This time it was Bran's turn to shrug, a bit of the tension gone from his body. He still had a tight grip on the hilt of his sword. They turned to Jaslen, who was looking at the man with a slight tilt to her head. After a few moments, she got to her feet and began walking towards the man. So much for deciding what to do together. Ean stood and began walking after her, while Bran was already up and almost to her side.

The man watched as they approached, lowering his hands while keeping the smile on his face. He backed up and gave them space as they walked back onto the road. If he was going to attack them, his demeanor certainly wasn't revealing. He stood there in a much more relaxed state compared to the men he was with. Maybe he was harmless. This close, Ean couldn't see a threatening thing about him. Even the scar looked plain enough, as did the rest of his features. He wasn't a handsome man, but at the same time, he wasn't ugly either.

"My name is Kel Savorian," he said as they finally settled in front of him, "a member of this group of Soulbearers on our way to Rensen from Lurthalan. Have you recently left Rensen?"

Even though Ean barely knew the area at all, a couple of lies jumped into his mind. Unfortunately, Jaslen was a bit more trusting and spoke before he was able to say anything.

"Yes, we just came from there." Flipping her hair lightly out of her face, she returned his smile with an apologetic one of her own. "But were only passing through. We're originally from a small village south of here. My name is Jaslen, and these are my friends Bran and Ean. If you don't mind me asking, what exactly are Soulbearers?"

A slightly raised eyebrow was the only indication that the man was surprised by the question, but Ean caught it. Were Soulbearers well known outside of Rottwealth? Kel took a moment to fold his hands behind his back before speaking again.

"We," he said with a look that took in all of those behind him, "are servants of Kaz'ren, Goddess of the Soul." He waited a moment, looking at each of them in turn then continued on. "Good. By your expressions, you know her at least. It is our duty to retrieve the husks of those that have passed and make sure their souls have departed from their bodies. That is why we are on our way to Rensen right now, to retrieve all of those that were recently killed or are close to death."

That raised quite a few questions in Ean's mind, but of course Jaslen beat him to it. "But all of that just happened two nights ago. How did you even find out, let alone make the journey this quickly?"

Shaking his head, Kel ran a hand through his hair before speaking. "I find it so strange that at your age you know practically nothing about us. Ah well, we can blame your parents for that I suppose." He let out a small laugh, showing no annoyance at their ignorance.

"As soon as a death occurs," he continued, "or is about to occur, our Goddess sends us to recover the dead. If the soul is trapped, which can happen for a number of reasons I won't go into, we do our best to free him or her, so that they may join Kaz'ren in the afterlife. Once we no longer have to worry about the soul, we can take the body back to be stored in the catacombs beneath Kaz'ren's temple in Lurthalan."

"You collect everybody after they die?" Bran cut in. "But that doesn't make any sense. We cremate our own in our village, and we've certainly never had any of you —"

"You burn your dead!"

The man's demeanor changed to anger so fast that Ean felt himself start to draw in energy from the Abyss before he even realized what he was doing. He quickly pushed it away as he took a step back from the man. It wasn't as if he even knew what to do with that energy and just that slight touch of it had been exhilarating.

"Yes," Bran said. His hands were on his hips, but the one near the hilt of his sword was tensed. "That's what we've always done in Rottwealth. In all of my years I've never seen one such as yourself set foot in our village."

"Rottwealth," Kel spit the name out like it was poison. "I should have known. The Voices in Lurthalan bar us from your village, although none will tell us why. Our Voice was the only one to vote against the decree."

Lowering his head, a tint of sadness touched his voice as he mumbled to himself. "How many souls remain imprisoned in the ashes of their bodies, unable to join their families with Kaz'ren?"

"We … we had no idea," Jaslen said, her voice matching Kel's in sadness. "We have always been taught to bury our dead."

"Why hasn't anyone been told about this before?" Bran said, his voice low. "My grandparents … my cousin Matt … the poor little boy, Sten, who got sick and passed … we incinerated them all. They all could be trapped."

Kel gave her a sad smile and shook his head. "A decree made by the Voices of all the temples has never been overturned. I do not know why your village has been secluded from the rest of the workings of the realm, but for whatever reason, those poor souls will likely be trapped forever."

He paused and gave them a quick look over. "This is not the reason that we stopped. I have been instructed to warn you not to continue on. There is a Scar ahead. We took great care to avoid it as we made our way to Rensen, otherwise we would have already reached the village. You should wait a few days for the Seekers to remove it; you do not want to run into them, I assure you."

"We have no intention of going anywhere near it," Ean said quickly before the other two could speak. "The people of Rensen warned us about the Scar and what it does to people and animals. We certainly wouldn't want that to happen to us."

Giving him a long look, the man tilted his head slightly as if he was listening for something. After a moment his eyes widened but he spoke in a normal tone.

"If I were you," he said, "I would fear the Seekers more than the Scar. The Seekers kill anything and anyone that they believe have even the slightest connection to the Abyss." The man's eyes dropped to Ean's right arm for an instant and then shot back up, taking in each of them. "Best just to turn around and wait in Rensen until they have come and moved on."

Did the man really just look at his arm or had he imagined it? Could Kel have been speaking directly to him? The thought made Ean nervous, and he shifted around slightly where he was standing. No one spoke for a time, which made it worse.

"We can't do that," Bran said, breaking up the silence. "We need to get to Lurthalan as quickly as possible. Some kind of lizard monster has taken up residence in our mine that has already killed a number of our people and a few men calling themselves Heroes in their attempts to rid the beast. We are hoping to either find help or at the least find out how to kill it. Either way, we can't waste any more time."

With a sigh, Kel nodded. "I suppose that is reason enough to risk it. Well, if you are going to follow the road, I would move off it onto the east side as you make the journey north. Although I did not see it as we traveled, I have heard the Scar is somewhere on the west side of the road. Sticking to the east side should give you a better chance of avoiding the Seekers."

"Sound advice," Jaslen said. "We will be sure to stay on the right side of the road."

"Excellent."

Ean caught the man glancing at him again! It certainly hadn't been his imagination this time. What did the man know? He was about to say something but Kel continued on.

"I must be going. We are already behind caring for the poor souls in Rensen. Good luck in your journey."

In one smooth motion, Kel turned and raised his hood back over his head. It only took a few quick steps for him to resume his position in the line of Soulbearers. Without the slightest sound or command, the columns began to move as soon as he was in place. Ean, Bran and Jaslen watched the scarlet robed figures go until they were properly out of earshot.

"We're sticking to the road." That had been Ean's thought, but surprisingly Jaslen had been the one to voice it. "We'll move faster if we stay on the road, and if we're lucky, the Scar will be close enough for Ean to sense it. You can sense it, right Ean?"

"What?" Bran asked, moving closer to Jaslen. "You heard what he said. We don't want to be anywhere near that thing when the Seekers arrive, if they haven't already."

"Bran, we've talked for years about how we want to have some connection to Ze'an. I know we can finally talk to Ean about him now, but this is something more physical." She turned to Ean and gave him a weak smile. "Not that you aren't connected to the Abyss in your own way, but this is something completely different. How can we not at least try to see it?"

Ean nodded. "I completely agree, we should —"

"Of course you agree," Bran cut in angrily, rounding on Ean. "You would agree to anything she says."

The silence that followed was deafening. Bran apparently had not forgotten their conversation from the previous night, and the fact that he had even mentioned it in anger meant that he probably wasn't too happy about how it had ended. Ean's mouth opened, but he had no idea what to say. He just stood there, mouth agape looking like an idiot.

"I didn't mean that," Bran finally said, breaking up the awkward silence. "I just meant you've heard everyone talking about how dangerous it is. We shouldn't be risking it."

Taking a few steps away, he began to pace, the start of a scowl beginning to form on his face. Jaslen took a quick look at Ean, then the ground, and finally brought her gaze back up to Bran.

"Of course, we ..." she paused for a moment and frowned. "I mean, I understand how dangerous it is to try to get close to one of these Scars. I don't take the warnings of practically everyone we have met lightly. But we'll have Ean there ..."

Mistake.

Rounding on her, Bran let out a harsh laugh. "Ean? Ean can't even control the creatures he brings into our world. How do you expect him to keep us safe? To protect you!"

The last words came out in a shout. Ean couldn't help taking a step back. He had never seen Bran this upset before, and it was a little scary. Ean couldn't even be upset. Everything he said was true. What would he do if something dangerous was around the Scar? What could he even do if the Seekers found them?

Jaslen, however, was unperturbed. "He'll do the best he can to protect us. Just like I know you'll do the best you can to protect me."

Her voice had dropped to a soothing tone, one filled with affection. Stepping over, she cupped Bran's face in her hands and kissed his lips. When she pulled back, he was smiling. "We can't live in fear now that we are out in the world, love. Especially if we want to openly worship a God that most men fear."

"You're right, of course," he said, any trace of anger gone from his voice. "I think I'm just tired is all. I'm sorry for snapping at you, Jaslen. You too, Ean." He extended a hand in Ean's direction. "Forgive my small outburst?"

Ean certainly didn't consider the outburst a small one, but he had to forgive him. They would be traveling together for a while still. It would be uncomfortable to be spiteful towards him for one crack in his usually positive attitude. Plus, he did sound sincere. Taking his hand, Ean gave him a small grin.

"Good," Jaslen broke in. "If that's settled then, we should get moving. As interesting as Kel and his Soulbearers were, they have slowed us down quite a bit. I say we try to salvage whatever we can from the stew, pack up and get moving again."

"Sounds like an excellent plan." Bran quickly moved off towards their supplies. Ean looked over and caught Jaslen staring at him. He gave her an uncomfortable shrug and moved to follow Bran.

They spent the next few moments eating as quickly as they could. They had lost about half of the stew in their mad dash to hide the campsite and its contents had grown cold. So to keep up their strength, along with a meager bowl they each took a small stick of jerky out of their supplies to eat while they traveled. Once they had finished with the stew, Ean stored most of their things back in his Pocket. With everything ready to go, they climbed back onto the road and started north again.

As they traveled, the three remained silent. Ean wasn't sure if there was still awkwardness from Bran's outburst or if the other two were deep in thought. Regardless, he wasn't going to try to get them talking again. If they started asking more questions about Ze'an that he couldn't answer, he would look like a fool. Especially without Zin to help him out. The imp, of course, had disappeared again. He must have snuck off while they had been talking to Kel, because Ean couldn't feel him anywhere nearby.

Ean had always been able to count on Zin to provide some kind of distraction to get him out of trouble. Maybe Zin was still holding a grudge about how mistrustful Ean had been. If that were the case, Ean would make sure to give him a sincere apology the next time they rested.

Unfortunately, the imp hadn't returned by the time they stopped for the night. They set up camp a little further off the road this time, all three still going about their tasks in silence. They cooked another stew, this one with a bit of meat, and sat around without saying a word. Bran and Jaslen ate their meals quickly and walked off together, leaving Ean alone with his own thoughts for a time.

As he gazed into the fire, Ean thought about the Abyss, or more specifically, the tattoos slowly growing up his arm. He had to stop questioning Zin's motivations and just take his word that he had no idea the extent of what the tattoos were capable of. So, what did Ean know? He checked off each fact in his mind:

He could now sense anything with even a remote connection or infused with a little energy from the Abyss as long as they were close enough.

Magic runes and summoning circles appeared at a thought and no longer had to be painstakingly drawn or carved into something.

The tattoos channeled energy directly from the Abyss, and he could release that energy into someone or something.

It was that last fact that really gave Ean pause. He had seen what happened when a large amount of energy was pumped into a living creature. The change was permanent, or at least he had to think it was permanent, going by the corrupted troll that they encountered between Rottwealth and Rensen. Did that mean he could change anything permanently with the power? An even more troubling question was, could he somehow figure out a way to control how he changed things?

Dark thoughts and images began to drift around in his mind. Bran transforming into a much less attractive man. Krane reduced to some whimpering, toothless dog creature. The Mayor of Rottwealth wallowing around in the mud, hooves replacing his hands and feet and a snout where his nose used to be. A dozen other faces of people that had wronged him distorted and deformed, bowing down to him.

No, that was not the type of man Ean wanted to become. It was true, part of him wanted some measure of revenge on the people that had wronged him throughout his life, but he couldn't imagine it at the cost of inflicting pain on others. At his core, he really was a Healer, someone that brought relief from pain, not added to it. A part of him even felt that smallest bit of remorse about the bandit he had changed, and that man had probably done some horrible things. Ean wanted to be someone people respected, not feared. His revenge would be finding success and acceptance, despite what his enemies tried to do to him.

Holding on to that thought, Ean threw some dirt onto the fire to put it out, then moved into his tent. He wouldn't let his newfound power turn him into the same type of person as Krane. Wrapping himself up in both that thought and his blankets, Ean let his eyes close. However, the last thing he pictured as he drifted off to sleep was of people kneeling before him.

CHAPTER 19

MONSTERS AND BEASTS

EAN WOKE WITH A start, forgetting where he was for a moment. His dreams floated about in his mind and kept him confused. Closing his eyes, Ean took in a deep breath and relaxed until he gathered his thoughts. He was in his tent. The tent was off the road north of Rensen. Bran and Jaslen should be in their own tent, not too far away from his own. He was not a monster.

...

He was not a monster.

...

He focused on that thought for a long time. He needed to, in order to dispel the dream that was even now twisting his stomach.

In his dream, he had been a huge, hulking creature, shaped like a man but much larger than any he had seen before. Larger even than the Taruun he had seen in Rensen. His body had been covered in some type of armor that was more rock and stone than anything made of metal. A large helmet sat on his head, a single piece of stone acting as a nose guard, dividing his face in half and hiding it in shadow. His eyes had been visible though, a dark purple that glowed out of the shadow created by the helmet. And the things he had done in that dream ...

...

He was not a monster.

...

He got up, needing to do something—anything—so that the memories of the dream didn't invade his mind. He changed quickly out of sweat-soaked clothes into fresh ones, even putting on a fresh pair of gloves. He tried not to look at his tattoos, which were giving off their usual dull glow. It was probably just all the talk the past few days about the energies from the Abyss changing things and what he himself had done to that man that had given him the nightmare. No need to dwell on it.

He kept quiet through breakfast even though both Bran and Jaslen tried to get him talking. By the time they had everything packed up and were moving again, he probably hadn't said as much as a dozen words to anyone. Bran and Jaslen took the hint and gave him some space as they continued on down the road. He should just put the dream behind him and go talk to them, but he couldn't let it go.

The images from his dream, so real that they felt more like memories, continued to run through his head. Horrible things. At one point, he had been changing normal people into deformed creatures, laughing the entire time. At another time, he had been savagely beating one of those creatures to the point that he killed it, all while the others watched.

What bothered him most was that he recognized some of the people he had changed, including Bran and Jaslen. In the dream, Bran had sprouted a coat of shaggy black fur. He sat up on his haunches like a begging dog. Jaslen had become some sort of reptilian creature — curvy like a snake, but with stumpy legs and arms. There was no adoration in her eyes — only fear. And in his dream, he felt no shame about what he had done to them. No, Ean looked down on his creations and felt strong, unstoppable. He felt like a god.

That's what bothered him the most. To actually feel good about terrorizing other people was sickening to him. But what if that's what his new powers were doing to him? They were making him powerful, that he knew, but what if they were twisting his mind as well? Or what if that horrible monster was who he really was inside, and the power was simply bringing it out?

And his fears of changing Bran and Jaslen hadn't originated with the dream. Ean knew his control over the power was limited at best. He certainly hadn't meant to change that bandit. What if he slipped while he was helping one of them up? Or contaminated their food in some way? It was clear the glove he wore offered absolutely no protection. Ean didn't think he could live with himself if he did something to Jaslen.

But even with all of those fears, a part of him still wanted to grab that power, have it flowing inside of him. Ean knew it was wrong. It made his body ache, like eating way too much food. And it wanted to come out of him in a flood; it was a struggle just to hold it in and a flat-out death match to be rid of it. Yet it still called to him now, and he found it hard to say no.

Those thoughts blanketed his mind, to the point that he had no idea how long they had walked when he first felt a tug inside of him. He stumbled a bit as a sudden fear gripped him. Had he grabbed the power without realizing it? He took a moment to steady himself and quickly realized it wasn't that.

Bran and Jaslen had stopped. Bran seemed ready to draw his sword and Jaslen had her bow off her back. They were both staring at him intently. Had the fear been easy to see in his face? Giving an embarrassed laugh, he raised both of his hands apologetically.

"Sorry, must have tripped over a rock or something in the road. No need to worry." The tug was probably just Zin getting close, but best to be sure. Could he tell the difference between the feelings he got near Zin and a Scar? He tried to make himself relax as he stood up straight. It must have worked because both Jaslen and Bran seemed to relax as well. "I guess I was thinking a bit too much. What time of day is it anyway?"

"Probably about midday," Bran said. "You seem a little dazed. Are you alright?"

"Yes, yes, I'm fine."

"Are you sure?" Jaslen narrowed her eyes in concern.

"I'm sure."

"You've been gloomy all morning. Between Bran yesterday and you today, I would almost believe that you snuck some Burnbeer last night and had a little too much." She gave Bran a warm smile. "Although Bran did look a bit more pained." That got a small chuckle out of the other boy.

"I swear I'm alright. I was just thinking about those Soulbearers." Well he had, very briefly, in between brooding over his dream. "I just find it extremely strange they would be banned from our home."

Ean's real concern, though, was the tug he had felt. When Zin was nearby, he could feel the life of the little imp, like a small flame. This new feeling was different; it was more like a pulsing or a throbbing. Curiosity began to override all of the doubts and fears he had been feeling all day. If it didn't feel like a living creature, the only thing Ean could come up with was that he was feeling the Scar. Even if it wasn't the Scar that they were looking for, it had to be something from the Abyss.

"… mentioned something about not being allowed into Rottwealth as well." Bran's voice cut through his thoughts. Had he been speaking the whole time? "It's very strange that we have talked to two people now that have said they were barred from coming to our village. Who is making these rules, and why do they want our home cut off from everyone else? And what about The Merchant that comes every year or the Heroes that started showing up?"

All good questions, and another time Ean would want to try and figure them out as well. The tugging at his body, though, had a tight hold on his attention No point in beating around the bush.

"I feel a strong power off the road," he said, pointing off to the left of the road and into the woods. "It's hard to describe, but it definitely has a connection to the Abyss. If it's the Scar we heard about, it means we're close." He wasn't exactly sure about that last part. There was no way to judge distance from the feelings, but they didn't need to know that.

Bran looked skeptical, but Jaslen's face lit up with excitement. "Wonderful! From what that Soulbearer had said, I thought it was much further up the road." Grabbing Bran by the arm, she began to drag him in the direction Ean had pointed. "Come on, Bran! Just think, we're about to see a direct connection to the Abyss."

Dragging Bran along, Jaslen began to hum happily as she started off the road. Bran looked skeptical, casting questioning glances back at Ean while he tried to keep up. "I think we should be a bit more careful in approaching this," his voice cut off with a grunt as he kicked a rock he hadn't seen on the ground.

Ean caught up quickly and placed a hand on Jaslen's shoulder. "He's right. We don't know if the Seekers are there, or some kind of mutated animal like that troll, or even something dangerous from the Abyss itself." Zin's warning about the Nar'Grim flashed through his mind and was gone. "Best if we approach it slowly and try to keep quiet as we do so."

Jaslen nodded, her smile diminished. "Fine, we'll take it slow, and from now on we won't talk. But if nothing is around when we get there, I'm not making any promises that I'll remain calm."

She gave a self-satisfied nod then stared directly at Ean. After a moment of no one moving, she grunted and raised her hands. "Well? If you can feel this thing, then you should take the lead. Let's go already."

He couldn't argue with that. Stepping around the two of them, Ean began to walk off in what he thought was the direction of the Scar. Or at least the direction of whatever was causing the tugging at the back of his mind. Glancing back, he caught Jaslen just as she was snatching Bran's hand up into her own.

Ean picked up his pace. The further away from the road they got, the thicker the forest grew. Thorny plants grabbed at his boots or hid logs or rocks for him to trip over. Here, where trees and vines grew uninterrupted, a beam of sunlight was rare.

The closer they got to whatever it was that was causing the sensation, the more defined the throbbing in his head became. He almost tripped twice in a matter of a few paces apart because of it.

Finally, when the pounding in his head was almost unbearable, they circled around a huge tree, and found it.

The Scar.

Hovering about fifty or so paces from where he was standing, the purple outline of an oval floated in the air a pace or two above the ground. Triple the height of the average man and twice the width, it sucked up the light around it, creating a black void at its center. Small streaks of dark blue energy shot off of it at random, creating jagged bolts that cut through the air. It really did look like a scar in the world.

A gasp behind him let him know the other two had caught up, but he couldn't pull his gaze away from the floating mass of energy. The area around it looked as if an enormous force had pushed out from the Scar in every direction. Trees were either leaning away from the Scar or had snapped as if from some great pressure. The devastation reached about halfway between where Ean was standing and where the Scar was hovering.

"It's beautiful," he heard Jaslen whisper. "Let's go closer."

Even though Ean could hear the desire to do so in her voice, she didn't move.

"Is it safe to move any closer?" Bran's voice was so low that Ean could barely hear it over the throbbing in his head.

"I'm ... not sure."

A large part of him wanted to go running up to it, touch it, feel its power. But the image of the bandit, mutated and deformed, made him stop.

"I think getting too close could be dangerous. I wouldn't want any of us ending up deformed like that troll we came across."

"True," was Bran's only reply.

So the three of them stood there, looking at a doorway to another world. The realm of Ze'an, a place of strange creatures and unnamed horrors. How easy would it be to walk up and touch it? Ean knew deep down they were dangerous thoughts.

Dragging his gaze away from the Scar, Ean took another look at his companions. Bran was still watching the Scar with a grim determination. His body seemed tensed and he was making no move to get closer. Jaslen was a different story. She was leaning forward as if even the slightest word would have her heading towards the Scar. The only thing that was keeping her in place was Bran's hand holding firmly onto her own.

Zin had said Ean's tattoos would protect him from being affected by the energy of the Abyss, but they offered no protection to those around him. If Ean went, he was sure the girl would follow. So no, it was best to just observe the Scar for a time and then leave.

The dimming of the light in the forest only seemed to make the Scar grow brighter. The usual sounds of a forest thriving with animals were gone, replaced by silence and the occasional crackle of energy from the Scar itself.

Until a loud pop made them all jump. Bran's sword came out. Jaslen's bow was drawn. Heads swiveled anxiously about until they realized it had just been a twig snapped by Bran shifting his weight. The three laughed a bit sheepishly at each other, blushes filling their faces in unison. Ean thought that if they were this jumpy, maybe it was time for them to get going. He was just about to say as much when a man's scream echoed through the forest.

"Noooo, pleeeaaase!"

Ean dropped down without thinking. Bran and Jaslen had crouched down as well, although both had moved closer to him and the large tree.

"Please let me go! Let me go!"

The yells were coming from ahead of them. Either straight ahead or to the right, it was hard to judge the direction of sound in the forest. It had sounded like an older man, a mixture of hoarseness and a quavering fear.

"No, I didn't go anywhere near it! Please don't hurt me!"

The voice was getting closer. Was it a Nar'Grim? Should they run, or should they try and hide? Thoughts were almost impossible to hold onto with the Scar so close.

"No, no, no! We can't be this close to it, it's too danger ... mph ..."

The man's voice cut off after Ean heard a loud thud followed by whimpering. He glanced back at his companions, who returned his look with blank stares. Did they really expect him to decide what to do? So be it. He motioned them with his hand to get lower and move more behind the tree. Getting into a prone position, he lay there and watched.

The whimpering grew louder and louder, but it wasn't an old man that came into view first. The complete opposite actually. The man that came into view maybe a dozen or so paces from the Scar was young, although he looked like he had a number of years on Ean. Standing at a height halfway from the ground to the Scar, the giant of a man was covered from shoulder to toe in white leather armor that gave the illusion that he had been chiseled from marble. He had a shaved head and a square jaw that jutted out over his chest. His nose was thin and pointed, and his deep-set eyes looked like pools of black ink.

The man walked straight towards the Scar, stopping only a few paces from it. His right hand dropped to his side, coming to rest on the hilt of a sheathed dagger. He stood there examining the Scar, seemingly unafraid of the pulsating energy shooting off the hole to the Abyss. Motionless, he stared at the Scar, his face growing darker with each passing second.

While the man was huge and imposing, the woman that joined him was much shorter, similar in size to Jaslen, and yet still walked with an air of confidence. Sleek, white armor covered her torso and limbs. A sword swung from her waist, the scabbard plain. She had a slim face, a small, upturned nose and slanted dark-green eyes. Her face was framed with black hair that was cut short to the bottom of her ears. A thick, blood-red strand trailed down the right side, a sharp contrast to her serious demeanor.

The woman stood next to the man for a time, her mouth moving as she addressed him. Unfortunately, she was speaking too quietly for Ean to hear from his position. He could tell though from her expressions that she was unhappy about something. At one point she placed both hands on her hips and Ean could just make out what she was saying.

"...have to do something about EliZane. He is getting worse."

When she only received a curt nod in reply from the man, she grimaced and shook her head, then sat down heavily on an old log.

The giant pulled out a dagger unlike anything Ean had ever seen. The hilt was nothing like metal, wood, or leather, but white and smooth as glass. There was no hand guard to protect its owner from the wickedly curved blade. Ean struggled to make out the etchings along its edge, but it was too far away. A round blue gem decorated the blade's base, the Scar's lightning bolts reflecting on its surface, making it sparkle.

Holding the dagger out like a shield, the imposing man moved closer to the Scar. As he approached the glowing tear in the world, the light coming off the escaping bolts of energy seemed to reflect more and more off the dagger's gem. The white-armored giant reached the Scar, the light shining off the gem in every direction, so bright now that Ean had to shield his eyes slightly even from his spot.

The large man thrust his blade straight into the Scar. A blaze of light erupted from the portal to the Abyss that made Ean, Bran and Jaslen throw their arms up to shield their eyes. An incredible force nearly bowled Ean over, knocking the breath right out of him. Then, just as quickly as it had appeared, the blazing light vanished.

Ean's eyes swam with dark colors as he tried to catch his breath. The throbbing in the back of his skull was completely gone. When his eyes cleared, it was exactly as he had thought. The large man stood there, either already recovered from the dazzling lights and force or unaffected by them. The dagger still rested in his hand, the gem sparkling even now. Brushing leaves and twigs from her armor, the woman wore an annoyed expression but seemed unaffected as well. The Scar however was gone, which meant only one thing.

A chill ran down Ean's back, a cold sensation like dunking your head in a bog in the middle of the Chill season. Only one group was capable of seeking out Scars and closing them.

Seekers.

Ean began crawling backward. He only got a short distance before he ran into Bran and Jaslen. Why weren't they moving? Jaslen was pointing back at where the Scar had been, which caused Ean to swing his head back around in panic.

Two people had joined the Seekers. The first was a man of average height, dressed in the same white armor as the other two Seekers, except it seemed to hang awkwardly on his much thinner frame. He had short brown hair that was long enough to hang in front of his eyes, hiding a good portion of his face. His mouth was visible, giving such a humorless grin that even from as far away as Ean was it gave him the chills. A variety of different tools hung at his belt, most being wicked-looking knives. Some of the other tools were foreign to him, but a few Ean recognized as tools a trapper would use. In one hand he held a small knife, and in the other he was dragging the fourth person by the shirt.

The last man looked haggard. The small amount of white hair that remained on his mostly bald head was sticking out in every direction. His shirt and pants looked as if they had been gray at one point but now were covered in mud. The older man's wrinkled face was bruised, and he was bleeding from a few small cuts on his face. From his appearance and how the thin man was manhandling him, the older man was clearly the source of the cries they had heard earlier.

"For an old man, this one gave me quite the run." The newest Seeker said loudly, a dark chuckle escaping from his lips. "Ended up being a random root that brought him down. Go figure."

"Please sir, I don't want any troub …" the prisoner began before a swift blow from the thin Seeker shut him up.

"EliZane!" The woman pushed the thin man away. "You do not need to be so rough with the poor man. He is obviously scared." Reaching into a pouch at her waist, the woman pulled out a cloth and began dabbing at the wounds on his face.

"So? He should be scared," the thin man named EliZane said, shrugging his shoulders.

"You always make things worse than they need to be. There is no need to hit …"

"And you always try and coddle people we find when you know that most likely we'll end up …."

"I treat them like they should be treated, EliZane, like our God Alistar would want us to treat …"

"I'm pretty sure our God wants us to end this man's life, Kaytlin. Treating him well before doing so is probably just as painful …"

"Enough!"

The larger man's voice was an explosion of sound, silencing the two bickering immediately. Ean had almost forgotten about him, but from his commanding voice it was clear he was the leader of the three. With measured strides he moved between the two, giving each a gaze that made them both wilt. Their captive was near hysterics at this point, his head in his hands, large sobs escaping from his mouth.

"Stand aside, both of you. We will end this now one way or another."

The other two Seekers quickly stepped back, giving the leader and older man a decent amount of space. Kneeling down, the larger man began to speak quietly. After a time the older man began to calm, his sobs softening until they finally stopped, and he was nodding at whatever the other man was saying. When the larger man stopped talking, the older wore a peaceful expression.

The other two Seekers watched the whole exchange with different reactions. EliZane watched with a wicked grin at first, but it slowly changed into a sour one as the older man calmed down. When the man stopped crying altogether, the thin man scowled and let out a disgusted sigh. The woman, Kaytlin, on the other hand, relaxed along with the man, her grim demeanor slowly disappearing. As the man stopped crying, she cast a pitying smile on both the old man and the Seeker at his side.

A tug at the back of his shirt almost made him yell out, but he slapped a gloved hand over his mouth as if he could physically hold it in. Turning his head, he scowled at both Bran and Jaslen, not sure which had almost caused his heart to stop. They both backed away from him slightly, but it was Jaslen that motioned for him to follow. So they wanted to leave now? Not likely. Ean's curiosity had won out against his fear. With a curt shake of his head, Ean's attention returned to the Seekers.

EliZane was pacing now, his mouth working slightly, as if he were struggling to hold in his own words. The woman, Kaytlin, was sitting again with her head bowed, eyes shut, and lips moving. The huge Seeker moved. Still kneeling next to the old man, he brought his hand up that held the dagger. Ean was surprised to see the old man look at it without the slightest hint of fear. The Seeker held out the blade for what seemed like an eternity, until the gem on the hilt again began to sparkle with the faintest light.

Without warning, the Seeker thrust the blade directly into the man's chest. The gem flared and then blinked out, mirroring the life that the blade just took.

Jaslen gave a tiny squeak behind Ean, but he didn't dare turn. The Seekers thankfully didn't seem to hear. The giant of a man gently lowered the old man to the ground, removing his dagger and laying him onto his back. Placing his hands over the old man's eyes, he uttered a prayer loud enough that Ean could hear.

"Alistar, God of Justice and Light, please forgive this man his curiosity. Allow Kaz'ren to claim his spirit and carry him to reside with his ancestors."

Rising, the Seeker turned his back to where Ean hid and motioned for the other two Seekers to join him. They did so and all three stood around the man, conversing quietly with their backs to Ean and his companions. Still shocked at how quickly the Seeker had ended the older man's life, Ean decided it might be a good time to sneak off. He certainly didn't want to be around those three any longer. Placing his hands on the ground, he was about to back up when he saw the huge man raise the dagger over his head.

The dagger was still covered in blood, but what caught Ean's attention was that gem on the hilt. It was still glowing, pulsing being a better word, an almost hypnotic rhythm to its dark blue flashes. He couldn't move, he could barely breathe. It felt like his entire body was made of stone. Ean felt something tugging on the bottom of his pants, but he couldn't even turn his head to look. Numb. That was all he felt, cold and numb.

"Ean, I really think we should go."

Jaslen's voice sounded muted to his ears, as if someone had stuffed them with cotton. The giant man still had his back to them, but the other two were slowly looking around. For what, Ean had no idea but he didn't want to find out. His mind strained with the effort to get his body to move, but nothing happened. With nothing left to try, he did the only thing left that he could think of to do.

The energy from the Abyss flooded into him. He had only meant to take in a small amount at first to see if that could free him, but with his numbed sense he apparently had no control over it at first. Warmth flooded his body, the feeling returning to previously petrified limbs. His body felt like it had been run over by a wagon, all of his muscles sore from being locked in place for even such a short amount of time.

At the same time as his strength was returning, the gem on the man's dagger flared to life, the glow brightening to the point where the three Seekers had to shield their eyes. After a few moments it lessened, but the pulsing of the light grew faster.

That was enough to get Ean to back away on hands and knees, keeping an eye on the Seekers the whole time. If they could just get a little further away without being noticed, hopefully that gem wouldn't lead the Seekers to them. Ean had almost made it behind the tree when EliZane's eyes came to rest on him. The man's eyes widened and his mouth spread into a wicked grin, leaving Ean no doubt that he had been spotted.

"Run," Ean said harshly, pushing himself up onto his feet. The other two followed suit, taking off in the opposite direction of the strangers ... and also away from the road.

CHAPTER 20

FLIGHT OR FIGHT

WITH A GRUNT EAN took off after his companions. It was probably better they didn't go back towards the road, but he had no idea how they would find it again. The other two pulled ahead of him, both being in much better shape. But it was only for a moment. With the energy of the Abyss still flowing in him, he found an extra supply of strength and speed. In a matter of moments he had caught his two friends and passed them. He dodged around trees and over stumps with ease, not feeling the slightest bit winded.

Enjoying this new feeling of freedom and prowess, he got quite a ways ahead of his two friends before stopping and turning around to check on them. They were still running hard, but thank the gods, the Seekers weren't in pursuit. Both Bran and Jaslen were breathing heavily, but Ean felt like he could run all night without getting winded. He was about to call back for them to hurry, when he saw Jaslen stumble and fall to the ground.

At first Ean thought she had just lost her footing or had gotten caught on a wayward branch. As he sprinted back to where they were, however, he found Bran trying to unwrap something from around her ankles — a piece of rope with weights attached at the ends. Once he got it off of her, Bran held it up for them to see. Ean was about to ask what it was when another one wrapped itself around Bran's ankles, knocking him over.

"Now, now, little rabbits," a baritone voice called out from the shadows. "Don't scamper away without introducing yourselves. That would be incredibly rude."

The man called EliZane approached them confidently, his chin held high and a swagger in his step. His hands were empty, but they hung in easy reach of any of the knives strapped around his waist. The Seeker was trying to put on a friendly expression, but Ean wasn't buying it.

"My name is EliZane, and as you can clearly see," he said, moving his hands to outline his armor, "I am a Seeker. Your parents should have taught you never to run from the Seekers, children. It's very rude, and makes us think you have something to hide."

Jaslen was still on the ground, watching the man with cold eyes as she rubbed at her ankles. Bran had paused in the middle of untangling his own ankles, a defiant look on his face. Ean hoped that Bran didn't do anything rash. As for himself, he tried to put on a relaxed expression. He held on to some of the energy of the Abyss though. Just in case.

"Now," the Seeker continued, "if you would be so kind as to accompany me back to where my two friends are waiting, I would appreciate it."

The tone of his voice made it clear that he wasn't asking. Ean took a good look behind the man. The other two Seekers were nowhere in sight. Once all three Seekers were together again, they would be impossible to overcome. This might be the last chance for them to escape.

EliZane laughed as he caught Ean looking around. "No, boy, the other two didn't come running after you as well. They know I can handle two scrawny boys and a little girl easy enough."

"We are older than we look," Bran said, rising to his feet. "And I see no reason why we should follow you anywhere, not after what you did to that poor man."

Ean grimaced as his foolhardy companion placed a hand on the hilt of his sword. Instead of getting tense or angry, EliZane smirked.

"If you want to go about playing like a man with your weapon, feel free. But I doubt you will enjoy the game, boy."

Ean swore he could see the anger bubbling out of Bran. EliZane was trying to goad him into a fight and was succeeding. Of course, they couldn't go back with the man, or at least Ean couldn't. Facing the man with the jeweled dagger meant death at least for him, and Jaslen and Bran might just get killed for being with him.

No, a fight was their only option.

Jaslen rose to her feet and readied her bow. Bran and Ean spread out to circle him. EliZane seemed more amused than concerned about their efforts to surround him. He stood still, picking dirt from beneath his fingernails.

"So," EliZane said. "We're going to do this the hard way? Very well, I suppose a bit of exercise won't hurt."

Letting out a laugh that held no warmth, he let his arms drop to his sides casually. "Well, here is hoping you will surprise me."

EliZane's hands moved so fast Ean almost missed it. In a blur, the man snatched two finger-sized blades from his belt and hurled one at Jaslen and the other at Ean.

The energies from the Abyss enhanced his reflexes enough that he dropped back before the blade hit. He felt it whiz past the tip of his nose. Missing its intended target, the blade sank into the tree behind him with a loud plunk. At the same moment, Jaslen let out a startled yelp.

Rolling to his feet, Ean scrambled to go to Jaslen's aid but quickly realized that she was more scared than hurt. The second blade had sliced through her bow string, leaving her unscathed but weaponless. The rasp of a sword blade coming unsheathed made Ean shift his attention again. Bran was holding his sword defensively in front of his body. EliZane was sauntering toward Bran with that same amused expression.

Jaslen had recovered from her shock and was on her feet as well. She had discarded the bow and instead held a single arrow in her left hand. She took careful, deliberate steps, not making a sound as she tried to catch the Seeker off guard.

"This really is foolish," EliZane said to Bran. "You're just going to make me hurt you more than needs be. Best if we just get you back to my companions so we can test you for the corruption and then act from there. If you haven't been touched by the Abyss, you will be sent on your way. If you have, then you have to die. It's as simple as that."

Bran grunted and moved towards the Seeker, keeping his blade aimed at Elizane's chest.

"Very well," the Seeker said with a feigned sigh.

"You're going to leave us alone," Bran said, a mixture of anger and hesitation on his voice. "We just want to leave and don't want any trouble."

"Listen to you, trying to sound all tough." EliZane still sounded at ease. "Are you trying to impress someone? The girl, perhaps?"

He waved a hand in the direction of where Jaslen was trying to creep up on him. "Is she your girl? Oh that's a shame. Especially if one of you is corrupted and the other one isn't. Then you'd have to sit and watch while the other one was put down."

"Don't you threaten –"

In one swift motion, the Seeker knocked Bran's blade aside with one hand and delivered a strike to the boy's throat with the other, effectively cutting him off midsentence. The younger man dropped to the ground, a gurgling noise coming from his mouth as he gripped his throat with both hands. EliZane stood over him, shaking his head.

With a yell Jaslen charged in, holding the arrow in both hands like a spear. The Seeker easily dodged out of the way of her clumsy charge. As she stumbled past, he stuck a foot out and tripped her. She fell, face first, the arrow thankfully flying from her hands instead of ending up embedded in her stomach. Hitting the ground hard, she let out a muffled moan. She immediately tried to push herself up with her hands to regain her footing.

EliZane stomped down hard on her back with a muddy boot, pinning her to the ground.

"Are we done with this foolishness?" Frown lines creased the Seeker's forehead and mirrored the scowl he directed down at Jaslen, but his voice sounded anything but annoyed. "I would hate to actually break a limb ..."

Ean's mind raced. Clearly they had no chance against this man in a fight; he was far too quick and skilled. Which meant they had to try something else.

"Please, don't hurt us anymore," Ean said, trying his best to sound pathetic. The pain in his gut certainly helped, but it was fading. "We'll go with you."

"No, you can't Ean!" Jaslen cried out. Her words earned her another stomp from the Seeker. A small whimper escaped her mouth, but she still turned her head enough that her gaze locked on Ean's eyes.

"Quiet, girl," EliZane said menacingly. Leaning forward, the Seeker pressed down with his foot harder and harder until a squeak escaped her mouth. Satisfied that she wasn't going to speak further, he turned his attention back to Ean. "Finally, someone with a little sense. Hopefully your friends will follow your lead and come peacefully as well."

"I'm sure they will. We clearly don't have the training to stand against you." Ean was only a few paces away from the man now. He just needed to get a little closer ...

"Now, here is what's going to happen." EliZane's voice had lost a bit of its scorn and had a more commanding quality to it. "I'm going to take my foot off the girl, and then the two of you are going to help your other friend to his feet. If he isn't able to walk, then the two of you will carry him. The sooner we see if you're corrupted, the faster I'll be able to get out of this stupid wilderness and get back to the city."

"We'll do whatever you say." Ean tried his best to sound sincere, and after staring at him for a moment, the Seeker nodded and removed his boot from Jaslen's back. Reaching down, Ean helped her up to her feet while keeping his back to the Seeker. As she rose, Ean carefully slid the glove off his right hand.

He took a step in EliZane's direction. The man was looking down at Bran with a disgusted look. All Ean had to do was get close enough to touch him. If he could do that, maybe they would have a chance. Ever so carefully, Ean reached out towards the man ... EliZane's hand shot out, catching Ean's wrist well away from the Seeker's body. How had the man even seen him? His attention still seemed to be on Bran, and yet he had reached out and snatched Ean's wrist as if he were staring right at it.

"You really didn't think I would believe you had given up so easily, did you?" The contempt and scorn in the man's voice was palpable. "You three have the nerve, the nerve, to attack a Seeker and then you suddenly turn meek as a mouse?"

With a dark laugh, EliZane jerked Ean closer. "I hope this isn't your writing hand boy, because I'm about to snap your little wrist."

The thought of the pain the man was about to inflict pushed all remaining doubt out of Ean's mind. He grabbed the older man's wrist with his right hand and unleashed all of the energy coursing through his body. Ean felt the power flow out of him, into the man and then "hit" something.

An explosion tossed both Ean and the Seeker into the air and a dozen wagons lengths away from each other. It felt like Ean was flying for an eternity, the explosion dulling his senses and the wind rushing around him from the speed he was traveling. When he finally came down, he hit the ground hard enough to knock the wind from his lungs. His shoulder made a popping sound and pain lanced down his arm. The force made him lose his connection to the energies from the Abyss. The power drained out of his body in a way that left him feeling like a spilled waterskin. When he was finally able to sit up, he saw chaos all around him.

The Seeker was on his stomach, quite a distance away and trying unsuccessfully to get to his feet. Ean could see the path EliZane had been tossed. Bark stripped from the trunks of trees and broken branches marked the Seeker's path through the air. The damage made Ean glad he had been lucky enough to miss hitting anything during his own flight. And yet the man was still moving. No wonder people feared the Seekers; this one seemed to be incredibly hard to stop.

Looking to his right, he saw that Jaslen and Bran hadn't escaped the blast either. Jaslen was only a few paces from where she had been standing before, lying on her back. Bran was still down in the same spot. Ean took only a moment to watch Jaslen rub the other young man's chest quickly before trying to climb back onto his feet.

A blur whizzed past Ean's left cheek accompanied by a sharp pain. He touched his face and felt wetness. There was blood on his fingers. He immediately switched his attention back to the Seeker and found the man on his feet, bent over and leaning against one of the trees.

If EliZane could kill with a look, Ean would be dead ten times over by now. The man's eyes were cold, their intensity enough to make Ean gulp. A small stream of blood dribbled down from EliZane's head, branching off at his nose and running around both sides of his mouth. A mouth set in a snarl. The man's trembling hands reached for his belt. It faltered for a moment, than half-heartedly flung another projectile in Ean's direction.

Falling to the right, Ean watched as a tiny blur flew past where his throat had just been. He tried to follow the fast moving object but lost it for a moment only to find it again as it hit a tree. A tiny blade, about twice the length of Ean's longest finger, was embedded up to the hilt in the bark. Rising to a sitting position, Ean knew he was running out of time. He had only come up with one plan of attack, and it had failed. The power of the Abyss had rebounded somehow. He drew it back into his body as he struggled to come up with something he could do before the Seeker recovered ...

The Hound!

Lost in his scattered thoughts, he didn't see the Seeker grab something off the ground and whip it in his direction. Pain exploded in his forehead, causing his mind to go blank as it knocked him onto his back. The world grew hazy, but Ean fought to hold on to consciousness. Raising a hand to his head, he quickly located a knot where the object had struck him, but even his slight touch made the world grow dark, so he quickly pulled his hand away.

A bump on his head was much better than a blade sticking out of it, at least. Regardless of whatever reason why the man hadn't used another blade, Ean had to gather his senses. He had to get up.

He forced himself up on his elbows. The world swam as if he was underwater, and he closed his eyes against the nauseating feeling they caused. When he was able to open them again, EliZane was staring down at him, one hand holding his side while another held a small, curved dagger.

"Thought you could corrupt me, did you, freak? Clearly you fools know nothing about the Seekers."

Wincing as he removed the hand from his side, EliZane pulled out a small amulet that hung around his neck. On its surface was an engraving of a sun with bouts of flame shooting off of it. The Seeker held it out for a few moments then tucked it back away before continuing.

"This keeps us safe from the Scar's energies as well as any that might leak off of those that have been corrupted." His face tightened while small amounts of spittle appeared on his lips. "Which is why your little trick backfired. I don't know what you tried to do, but now I'm going to kill you and let Olleander figure out what to do with your dead body."

The Seeker reached down and grabbed Ean by the shirt, yanking him to his feet. The man ground his teeth in obvious pain from the effort, but he pulled Ean close and placed the edge of his knife to his neck.

"I enjoy every kill I get to make under the service of Alistar," the Seeker whispered menacing, "but in all of my years, I think you're going to be one of my favorites."

As the blade began to slide across his neck, Ean closed his eyes.

In his muddled state, he was confused when he heard EliZane scream and found himself suddenly released. Ean fell to the ground and crumpled to his knees. It took most of his effort to raise his head and what little energy remaining to open his eyes again. The Seeker stumbled back and continued to scream, spinning in circles, trying to reach the back of his neck.

Zin!

The imp's teeth were sunk into EliZane's neck. The Seeker struggled to grab the imp, but Zin was too fast. He scrambled around on the man's back, sinking teeth or claws into any joints or exposed areas of the man's armor. EliZane raged and stumbled around. It would have been a hilarious scene if lives weren't hanging in the balance.

Ean had felt Zin's bites before, and although painful, were nowhere near strong enough to bring the Seeker down.

Reaching down inside himself, Ean grabbed onto the energies of the Abyss and let them flood into every corner of his existence. It filled his bones and made him strong. Gave new life to his muscles.

Cleared the cobwebs from his thoughts. He could act. He would act.

"Cruxlum!" the imp yelled from the Seeker's back. "Bring forth a Cruxlum! The four armed creature! Hurry!"

With the energies flowing in him again, Ean's mind was clear, but he had no idea what creature the imp was naming. What in the Abyss was a four-armed Cruxlum? Images flashed through his mind of the different pages from The Abysmal Tome until they finally came to rest on the page with the runes he needed.

Placing his hands palm down on a flat piece of land, he pictured the intricate design of the Cruxlum's summoning runes. The energies flowed out of his hands again, forming two perfect summoning circles first, one inside of the other and then began to fill in the spaces in-between with runes. Ean focused as hard as he could, trying to make the runes inside appear faster. Snaking around the insides of the circles, the runes sped along, creating a weaving, intertwined design, each one twice the size of a coin.

While the runes flashed along the ground, he heard Zin squeak. Then there was a thud. Realizing his couragous friend might be injured, or worse, Ean's stomach turned to knots, but there was no turning away from the task at hand. It was the only chance to save everyone. Sweat began to dribble down his face as he strained in concentration.

He kept his gaze down on the runes until the last one flashed into place. When the runes finally flared stronger and an opening began to appear, Ean then risked a glance up. Zin was lying on his back with his head in his hands. The Seeker was standing a bit further away, his mouth wide open as his eyes stared at the glowing and misty hole that was in the ground at Ean's feet. A large, four-fingered yellow hand reached out of the hole and clawed at the dirt. A second hand followed ... then a third and a fourth.

And that's when the summoning pain hit. Worse than ever before, he felt the power ripping him apart. Falling onto his side,

Ean wrapped his arms around his stomach as the pain tore at every part of his body. He watched helplessly as the creature pulled itself out of the Abyss. When it freed itself, the hole closed behind it. Ean's pain instantly subsided, but not entirely. Still too weak to move, every muscle tied in a knot, he stared at what he had just brought out of the Abyss.

The Cruxlum was easily three times as tall as Ean, taller than even that giant Seeker, and was mostly torso. Attached to that torso were four heavily muscled arms, two on each side, that ended in four-fingered hands larger than Ean's head. It wore very little clothing, just a small amount of rags around its midsection that covered its groin. Its hairless, dark yellow skin had the texture of a gravel road. Its large bald head was humanoid with two eyes completely black, a stub of a nose, and a tiny lipped mouth. A scar ran from the creature's right cheek down to its chin. The Cruxlum's inky black eyes looked down at Ean in confusion.

The creature spoke in a strange language, using words Ean didn't understand. Its voice thumped like the beat of a bass drum, while Ean returned a blank stare.

"I don't understand what you are saying," Ean said, hoping the Cruxlum at least spoke his language like Zin.

The Cruxlum's mouth twisted into a frown and it placed its lower set of hands on its hips, while crossing its upper set of arms over its massive chest. It stared at him with impatient expectation.

"Um, help?" Ean managed.

The Cruxlum raised his top set of arms in frustration and began babbling away. Its rotund body blocked Ean's view of the Seeker as it waved its arms about. Hopefully the man had run away or was too stunned to move at the sight of the creature. Ean was still trying to recover from summoning such a bizarre creature himself.

To his surprise, he heard Zin speak in the same strange language as the Cruxlum. The two of them began what sounded like a heated conversation. The Cruxlum continued to wave its arms about in annoyance while the words seemed to tumble out of Zin's mouth.

Which was right about the time that EliZane appeared on the Cruxlum's back, one hand gripping the creature's shoulder while the other drove a dagger down right around its collarbone.

The blade stopped as soon as it touched skin, creating a scrapping sound as it failed to even scratch the surface. Unbothered by the attack, the Cruxlum reached back with its two upper hands and plucked the Seeker off its back. It stood there staring at the man for a moment, then with a shrug tossed him aside like a piece of rotten garbage. The Cruxlum resumed its conversation with Zin as if nothing had happened.

That is, until Zin pointed to the fallen Seeker and said a few more words.

The change in the Cruxlum's demeanor changed instantly. It let out a loud bellow and turned to face the Seeker who, despite his injuries, somehow was already back on his feet. Its four hands opened and closed in tight fists, its arms spreading wide in every direction. Its skin color fluctuated from dark yellow to red. Giving a roar, it charged towards the Seeker.

The Seeker threw everything he had from his belt at the creature. Knives and blades of every size bounced off the Cruxlum's bumpy hide. EliZane shrieked as the Cruxlum kept going straight towards him. At the last moment, EliZane rolled to the side and came back up on his feet as the large beast stormed past him. The beast struggled to stop as the momentum of its massive body propelled it forward. Ean couldn't help but admire the Seeker's resiliency. Despite his injuries, EliZane remained quick of mind and feet.

The Seeker locked eyes with Ean. For a moment, it was a standoff. Then EliZane made a motion across his own neck, like a knife slicing it open and then pointed at Ean. Continuing his stare for one last moment, EliZane wordlessly took off into the woods.

Ean gulped, knowing that he had made a permanent enemy this day.

Not satisfied with scaring the man off, the Cruxlum gave chase. It was able to keep up with the Seeker fairly well. The only time it fell behind was when EliZane slipped through an area of particularly dense trees, but that only slowed the beast for an instant. Instead of trying to go around to a spot where it could get through the trees, the Cruxlum simply flexed its arms and swung them out, knocking aside the thicker trees and uprooting the smaller ones. If Ean wanted to, he could easily follow the pair just by following the path of destruction the Cruxlum left.

But Ean had no desire to follow after them, or had any energy to do so for that matter. Between all the blows he had received and the strain of summoning such a large beast, he could barely stand. Jaslen and Bran appeared at his side. They each took an arm and helped him to his feet.

"What was that?" Jaslen whispered, her voice a mixture of exhaustion and excitement. She was looking off in the direction the creature had went, as was Bran.

"It was a Cruxlum," Ean said hesitantly, the aftereffects of summoning such a large creature still taking a toll on his strength. "A very powerful warrior."

He hadn't been able to decipher much else from the pictures in the Abysmal Tome about most of the creatures that he had found. In all honesty, he had only known what it was from its inaccurate depiction in the Abysmal Tome and Zin yelling about a four-armed creature.

"What made it so angry?" Bran asked. "It seemed to go from annoyed at being brought here to enraged in a matter of moments."

Bran was still looking in the direction the Seeker and the Cruxlum had gone, but while Jaslen seemed genuinely fascinated by it, Bran looked concerned. He also kept glancing over at the still glowing runes of the summoning circle.

"And will it come back for us?"

"No?" Ean tried to keep the question out of his voice but he couldn't help it. He moved on quickly to the first question Bran had asked. "As for what made it so angry, I have no idea. You were talking to it, Zin. Did you say something to set it off?"

The imp got up slowly and limped over to where the three of them were standing. When he got next to them, he sent a swift kick to Ean's shin. The spiteful little thing had stuck out the claws on his foot and caught Ean with them as well.

"Ow! What was that for?"

"Always questions, and never even a thank you for saving your life." The imp's teeth were bared and his little yellow eyes had narrowed into slits. "For once I would like to be appreciated for everything I do, especially when it involves risking my own neck."

The pain that the summoning had caused Ean was disappearing, but it was being replaced by guilt. Ean really had taken the imp for granted since the day he had first summoned him. Shaking his head, he realized that he was no better towards Zin then the bullies at home had been towards himself. Of course, Jaslen was also shooting him a disappointed look, her hands on her hips, a clear indication that she was on the verge of giving him a piece of her mind. Well, at least he could try to make things right.

"You're right, Zin. You're absolutely right. I'm sorry." The imp's eyes widened for a moment but then returned to glaring just as quickly. "I know I take you for granted most of the time,"—Zin grunted at 'most'—"but I promise I'll treat you the same as I treat Bran and Jaslen from now on. As an equal."

That finally got the imp to relax, his eyes softening and a slightly embarrassed look crossing his face. "Yes, well, that would be appreciated. After all, I was the only one to actually do any damage to that skinny fool. That makes me the best warrior out of the four of us." The nervous little laugh the imp gave let Ean knew things were okay, and his companions joined in with laughs of their own.

"Well," Ean said, feeling slightly better about the situation. "How are you feeling, brave warrior? It looked like the Seeker tossed you pretty far."

"I've had much worse, believe me. One time, down in the Abyss, I got caught by a —" The imp suddenly cut off, his jaw dropping.

"What is it, Zin?" Jaslen asked walking over to him. "Are you alright? No need to act tough around us. If that Seeker really hurt you, you should tell us."

"Ba ... uh ... ca ..." The imp was making absolutely no sense.

"Seriously, Zin, what is it?" Ean was starting to get worried. The pain from the summoning was almost gone now, but he didn't think he could summon anything else. He felt tired and drained and had no desire to pull in any more energy from the Abyss.

Still stuttering, the imp pointed at a spot behind Ean. He turned and finally saw what was causing the imp so much shock. There, on the ground, was Ean's summoning circle, its glow still casting shadows all about the forest. Except now, the glow lessened, grew weak, and then finally disappeared altogether.

Ean's expression mirrored Zin's, shock overriding every other emotion he had been feeling. In the few times that Ean had summoned anything, he had either had to break the item he had inscribed the summoning runes on or physically make the runes disappear. Never before had the runes simply vanished on their own, and he had no idea what it meant. As if reading his thoughts, Zin spoke, his words choppy and the shock and fear clear in his voice.

"It's dead. The Cruxlum is dead." The imp made it sound as if the moons had suddenly disappeared from the skies above. "The Seeker we fought or those other two Seekers killed a Cruxlum. We need to go."

Despite sounding as certain as the sun rising in the sky, Ean couldn't believe what Zin was saying. "There is no way they could have killed a creature like that. The Seeker we faced was clearly a skilled warrior, but his blade didn't even —"

"For the circle to disappear, it either had to be closed by you or the thing is dead," Zin said, cutting him off. "Which means those Seekers could be doubling back right this moment. We don't have time to argue. We have to get out of here now!"

Not waiting for any of them to respond, the imp took off at a run, his little legs moving faster than Ean had ever seen. Bran and Jaslen watched him go for a moment, looked at each other, and then took off after him. Which left Ean standing there for a few moments before he chased after them as well.

What kind of men could kill a creature like the Cruxlum? With the power from the Abyss drained away, coupled with his injuries, Ean found it difficult to run. Keeping up with his friends seemed impossible. Pushed only by his will to survive, he mustered up his last bit of strength and sprinted after them.

CHAPTER 21

LOSSES AND GAINS

THEY RAN.

Ran until the low light of day that penetrated the canopy of the forest began to fade. Then they ran some more. It grew more and more difficult to dodge around trees and over stumps as the day came to a close, but they pushed on. Even when Ean could barely see what was right in front of him, they continued on. They would have kept going all night if Bran hadn't gotten a foot caught in a loose root. He went down hard, letting out a small yelp of surprise, and by the time Ean and Jaslen got to him, he was gripping his foot.

"I twisted my ankle," Bran said, a hint of annoyance in his raspy voice. "There is no way I can keep up our pace now."

"It's ... alright Bran ..." Jaslen said, leaning over with her hands on her knees. "I don't think my lungs can handle much more running, and Ean doesn't look much better off than I do."

She flashed Ean a weak smile which took the sting out of the comment, but Ean knew she was right. His sides hurt, his lungs burned, and he could feel a hundred different stings from where low lying branches had smacked his body. Even the boost the energies of the Abyss had given him was starting to wear out. A rest at this point would serve all of them well.

"What are you all doing?" Zin said, appearing from ahead of them. The imp had outpaced all three of them, even with his shorter legs. Looking annoyed, Zin sat down heavily, his breathing coming in quick wheezes. "I don't know if any amount of distance would keep us safe from those Seeker people."

Jaslen carefully sat down next to the little imp and gave him a charming smile.

"Then it shouldn't matter if we stop here, Zin. Bran can't go any further because of his ankle, and Ean and I were on the verge of collapsing anyway."

Turning to Ean, she raised an eyebrow. "Do you have anything that would help with a twisted ankle?"

"It will be an easy fix," he replied, "just a little Nevbane to numb it, some Garone Powder for the swelling, and then a tight wrap to keep it steady, and he'll be able to put pressure on it by the morning. It will still be sore for a couple of days, but we have plenty of Nevbane and Garone Powder to keep him going."

Jaslen and Bran nodded in agreement, but Zin looked less than impressed. The imp crossed his arms and let out a frustrated sigh, but kept his mouth closed. Not having a biting comment about the average human's lack of endurance was rare for the imp, but Ean wasn't about to question his sudden self restraint.

Helping Bran to his feet, the group stumbled around in the dark until they found a place with enough room to set up camp. They found a clearing of flat dirt free of stones and roots just large enough to fit their small group. Settling in, Jaslen started to help Bran remove his boot from the injured ankle while Ean focused on opening his Pocket and getting their supplies.

"Yes, brilliant idea. Use more energy from the Abyss," Zin said sarcastically, approaching Ean just as the runes flared to life. "Not only is the light it creates easily visible in this gloomy place, but in case you didn't notice, the Seekers have a way of tracking that energy. You might as well set all of the trees around us on fire to help lead them to us."

"I'm just getting out cold food we can eat, medicine for Bran, and a blanket for each of us. We're smart enough to know better than to start a cooking fire or set up the tents in case we have to leave quickly. And it only takes a few moments now to open and close the Pocket."

Zin responded with a growl and took a seat a few paces away from the Pocket. Once it was open completely, Ean rooted around for the supplies they would need, then closed the Pocket with a thought.

With a thought.

Ean shook his head. He had come so far from the boy who had to sit and painstakingly draw in the runes perfectly for any spell to work. Things were coming to him easier and easier now, which was both exciting and scary. Exciting because he could only imagine what he could do as he learned more spells and summoning runes, scary because that one dream of becoming a monster constantly played itself back in his mind. He would hate to end up injuring his friends, directly or indirectly.

His friends. That word also felt strange to him. Bran and Jaslen had always been nice to him, but in the past he had just seen their actions as coming more from pity than anything else. He never complained back then, of course. Bran significantly decreased the number of times Ean had been bullied and beaten over the years. Jaslen ... well, clearly he had feelings for her, so any attention was appreciated, regardless of the reason. But now, after their few weeks of traveling together, he actually felt like they cared about him.

Smiling at the thought, Ean grabbed the healing supplies and walked over to his friends. Zin followed along, a look of annoyance still covering his face but remained silent. With Bran's boot removed, it didn't take Ean long to fix him up. He covered all around his ankle with Nevbane to numb the pain and Garone Powder for the swelling. Then he finished by wrapping the ankle tight with a cloth, tucking the end back in itself to make sure it stayed on.

"There you go, all fixed up," Ean said as he leaned back. "Best to keep the boot off until we leave tomorrow. I'll apply more of the powders and rewrap it before we head out."

"Thanks, Ean. I appreciate it," Bran and Jaslen said in unison. They shot each other surprised looks, then burst into laughter. Jaslen's was rich and full of warmth, and even though it obviously caused Bran's sore throat some pain, he laughed loudly as well. It only took a few moments for Ean to join in. They needed to laugh with everything that had happened today, and if something as corny as the two of them speaking the same words at the same time brought it about, then so be it. Zin did not join in.

After relieving some of the tension, they sat around quietly, eating some of the dried rations. There wasn't much conversation as they ate, but everyone seemed to be in a better mood. When they finished eating, they put away their things and got ready to call it a night. Lying about the clearing with full stomachs, it did not take long for all four of the exhausted companions to drift off to sleep.

EAN AWOKE WITH A start, barely holding in the scream. The nightmare had returned and had seemed more vivid, more real this time around. In it, he had performed countless horrible deeds without the slightest bit of remorse. All he could do in the dream was watch and scream silently in his mind. Ean sat up and shook his head violently, wishing he could shake the dream from his thoughts forever.

Bran and Jaslen were curled up together under a tree while Zin was on his back on a patch of grass, arms and legs spread out in every direction. The imp was snoring. At least everyone else seemed to have gotten a good night's sleep.

Ean got up. His back was sore, although he couldn't tell if it was from the night before or from sleeping on the cold earth. Rubbing at his back, he walked off a little ways from where the others were sleeping. He wanted to clear his head. Yesterday had been a blur, but it had also made something painfully clear. With his power growing, he still knew practically nothing about what he could do with it.

With his companions out of site, Ean found a good clearing to open up his Pocket. Taking a seat right in the middle, he pulled off both his leather gloves; the tattoos on his right arm glowed faintly. Other than the short amount of time the previous day, it felt like days since he had taken either one of his gloves off, and his hands were starting to cramp as well as smell. Once off, he tossed the two elbow length gloves off to the side and took a good long look at his arms.

Both were so completely different now that they felt like someone else's arms. His left, horribly scarred from the Hound's saliva, was pale. The skin looked like a patched-up cloak of different colors where the drops of saliva had hit, a mass of scars where the teeth of the Hound had done their damage. It still made him self-conscious around other people, all of those burns and scars, but they were a reminder of the danger summoning anything from the Abyss posed to everyone around him, as well as himself.

His right arm, covered in twisting and intertwining dark blue tattoos that seemed to flow out of his palm and around his hand and arm, was completely different. Slightly tanner from being exposed more to the sun before he had received the tattoos, the skin was completely smooth and untouched. Even the tattoos did nothing to mar the skin, feeling no different as he ran his fingers over them. He had seen and felt other tattoos before, and the skin had been slightly raised around the outlines. That wasn't the case with his own. Of course, no one else's tattoos glowed either; the light coming off of his exposed arm was strong enough at the moment to create shadows of branches and trees a dozen paces away.

He needed to be quick. Ean opened himself up to the energies of the Abyss, letting them flow and churn into and around his body. The light coming off his tattoos tripled in strength until the intensity bathed the entire clearing with a dark blue hue. Placing his glowing hand on the ground, he pictured the runes necessary to open up his Pocket.

As fast as the image appeared in his mind, light shot out of his hands, tracing out the required runes along the ground. The circle was completed quickly. He had kept it small, and it immediately disappeared as an opening to the Abyss appeared in its place. Ean reached down and felt around until he discovered the small sack that contained his most intimate possessions. Pulling out the sack, he let the portal close and the runes disappear as soon as the sack was clear and pushed the energies of the Abyss from his body just as quick. Zin's warning from the night before about the Seekers was still fresh in Ean's mind, so he wanted to have the portal closed and the energy out of his body as fast as possible.

Opening up the sack, he ignored the other items and grabbed The Abysmal Tome. Book in hand, Ean moved to a spreading oak tree at the center of the clearing. Sitting down, he leaned against its massive trunk, found a comfortable position, and got to work deciphering runes. He was going to keep at it until his friends woke up, no matter how long it took. And he wouldn't let his mind wander either, like it had so often done in the past. He was going to stay focused on the task at hand.

Placing the book on his lap, he closed his eyes, felt for a random page, and then opened the Abysmal Tome wide and looked. A page completely filled with runes and words written in the language of the Abyss. That wouldn't help much; he needed something with at least one picture as a reference. He flipped over a couple more pages until he finally reached a page with creatures he had never seen before.

The creatures had humanoid facial features and bodies covered in flames. One had a curvaceous feminine figure while another had the masculine form of a male. The same name was written in bold symbols below both pictures in the language of the Abyss. He scanned the pages for other symbols he recognized but only managed to pick out a few words. Bond, growth, intelligence — words he had been able to pry out of Zin years ago.

A creature made of flame was certainly interesting enough for Ean to stay on the page. Sentences were written from the top of the page to the bottom instead of left to right. He didn't know the majority of what he was reading and had no idea where one sentence ended and the next began. After running through both pages five separate times, he was unable to decipher its meaning with any degree of certainty. Tossing the book to the ground in disgust, he leaned back and began to knock his head gently on the tree behind him.

"I'll never figure things out at this rate," he groaned softly. Closing his eyes, he let his mind clear and tried to calm himself down. Which was how, in his more focused state, he was able to feel Zin approaching.

Opening his eyes, he kept a neutral face as Zin approached.

"Are the others up?" Ean hoped that they weren't. He wasn't quite ready to grab a quick meal and start moving again. Especially since they had no idea where in the forest they were and which direction they needed to go. "Or did you just wake up on your own?"

"No, the two lovebirds are still asleep," Zin said stifling a yawn.

A playful jab at Ean's feelings for Jaslen, or a hurtful one? Ean hoped it had been a playful one. "Yeah, well, you looked pretty comfy all spread out. Anyway, why don't you try being useful and help me decipher some new words from The Abysmal Tome."

Zin gave a non-committal shrug and walked over, which was strange as the imp usually avoided anything when it came to the Abysmal Tome or the topic of the Abyss. Looking down at the Tome, he gave a small laugh. "You don't want to mess with these. They're quite dangerous to keep around for very long."

"What are they?"

"Brucanima—living flames. Basically, if you gave intelligence and emotions to a cooking fire, you would get a Brucanima." The imp laughed again, clearly amused by something. "They are more emotion than intelligence though. A Brucanima could refuse to light even a spark for something it didn't like. It could also set an entire forest on fire for something it did like and then become confused when the creature it liked died from the flames. All of the living elements are the same, all overflowing with emotion, whether it's a flame, earth, wind, or water —"

The imp's voice cut off sharply at the last word. He glanced at Ean for a moment, then returned his gaze to the book. They sat there in silence for a while, Ean letting the imp's words bounce around in his head until he was finally ready to speak.

"A living water spirit like the one that killed my parents, you mean."

Ean was surprised at how lifeless his voice sounded as he spoke about the death of his parents. Sure, he barely remembered them, and they had been the cause of most of the anger directed towards him from the citizens of Rottwealth, but they were still his parents. He shrugged off the thought. He rarely thought about them, so why should he be surprised at himself for feeling numb whenever he thought about how they had died?

Lost in his own thoughts for a moment, Ean ignored the awkward silence that he had created. Zin refused to ignore it, though, coughing slightly before speaking again.

"I'm sorry Ean. Maybe we should look at some of the other sections—"

"No. It's fine, Zin. I'm not going to let two people I barely knew weaken my resolve. I want to learn."

"Ean, this isn't just about 'two people.' These were your parents. It's ok to mourn and think about them."

"Think about them? Were they thinking about me any of the nights they got drunk at the Golden Coin? Were they thinking about me, or anyone for that matter, the night they got drunk and wandered down to Rottwealth's spring? It was a spring back then, you know, home to one of these living water spirits you mentioned."

"The water ones are called Vunvuanima."

"Whatever they are called, the one living in Rottwealth was peaceful. Helpful even. It kept the spring clean and provided the farmers with water that not only nourished their crops but aided in their growth. This Vunvuanima was a blessing to the village, and my parents thought it would be fun to insult and attack the creature in their drunken stupor."

"I'm sure they didn't mean to—"

"To what?" Ean struggled to hold onto the numbness he felt towards his parents, but anger was starting to break through. "Didn't mean to get killed by the creature? Didn't mean to anger it to the point that it turned the spring into a stagnant marsh that no one could use? Didn't mean to turn the whole village against me when I was too young to even know what was going on?"

"Ean, I..."

"Never mind Zin. Just never mind. It's in the past. I'm going to succeed in helping Rottwealth, show the people there that I'm nothing like them. And if they still can't see that, I'll move on. I know I can now. What happened in Rensen showed me that. So let's just get back to trying to figure out the Tome."

"Yes, well uh, back to the Brucanima. Like I mentioned, they are quite dangerous, even the youngest of their kind." Reaching down, Zin held his hand up to about ankle-high. "The youngest are about this tall and can barely light a campfire. The largest, though, they can grow to sizes much larger than that Cruxlum you summoned, given they have an abundant amount of materials to consume, of course."

Nodding, Ean returned his attention back to the open book. "Can you read any of these runes or words? If you know about the Brucanima, maybe you would recognize some of them."

Ean had expected an immediate denial from Zin, but instead the little imp sat down next to the book and spun it around to get a better look. How many times in the past had Ean asked for help and been denied? Not wanting to look a gift horse in the mouth, he decided not to comment and instead let the imp examine the pages.

"Well," the imp said after a few moments of scanning the pages, "this word here means flame, as does this single rune." He pointed to a word Ean never would have guessed meant flame, while the rune at least he could pick out what looked like a flame inside of it.

"And this one here," Zin said, continuing on "means young or small depending on how it is used."

This continued, Zin pointing out words he knew while Ean tried his best to take it all in. By the time Zin was finished with the words on the two open pages, Ean had learned close to twenty new words. When Zin had finished, Ean's curiosity about why the imp was helping him was finally too much to take.

"Zin, I've been asking you for years now to help me learn the language of the Abyss and you've turned me down or changed the subject each time. What made you all of the sudden so receptive to helping me?"

The imp shrugged uncomfortably, avoiding Ean's eyes. "I was hesitant before for your protection. Can you imagine what might have happened if you gained too much knowledge too quickly while we were still in your village? If you became over confident in your abilities while there, what's to say you wouldn't try and summon something out of your league or even worse, you tried to summon something out of anger. By the Abyss, can you imagine what the village would have done to you if you had summoned something right out in the middle of the town square? If you summoned the wrong creature, it could wipe out the entire village. How would that have made you feel if you survived?"

"I wouldn't have been that upset about— "

"Don't even try to act hard in front of me, boy," the imp said, cutting him off, "I've known you for long enough to know you put up these walls and try to act like you don't care, but I know better. Given the opportunity, you would happily be the savior of Rottwealth, and not out of spite. You want people to like you, no matter how they treat you and how much you may deny it."

Boy? Zin had never spoke to him like that before. He felt like he was five again, being lectured by Old Cleff after knocking over and breaking a container of herbs, and what was worse was that he was feeling bad about it as well.

"Maybe I do Zin, but it doesn't much matter. The more power I get, the more I'm connected to the Abyss, and the more that people will fear me and want to see me dead."

"That's not entirely true. You have the chance to change how people view Ze'an and the Abyss." Frowning, the imp got up and began to pace back and forth. "Do you know why people fear the Abyss?"

"Well, it sounds like its the creatures Ze'an has created and that escape from these Scars cause all of the negative feelings towards Ze'an."

"Yes, yes, that's disturbing for people to think about I'm sure, but I don't believe that's the real reason for the fear."

"And you think you know the real reason."

Zin shot a glance at Ean and nodded, then returned to his pacing. Ean just stood and stared at the imp waiting for more, but Zin didn't break his silence. The forest seemed to be wakening; squirrels were coming down out of the trees looking for food, the occasional bird flew overhead chirping away, and all the while the imp stayed quiet.

"Zin, I need to know." Ean voice was quiet, especially compared to the noises of the forest, but it caused Zin to finally stop moving. With a sigh, the imp hung his head, his hands balling up into fists.

"Many years ago, I'm not sure how long, there was a man who could control the energies from the Abyss like you." The imp's voice was equally low, enough so that Ean had to lean forward to hear him better. "He lived further north, past what is now Lurthalan, where the majority of your people used to live. At first I think this man was considered a hero, but by the time I came into his service something had changed him. All he cared about was his own power, so much so that he eventually turned against everyone in your realm. The humans and even some other races tried to stop him, but he had hordes of creatures at his command. He subjugated most of the people and did horrible things to keep them in line, but with power came the fear of losing it."

Zin paused, giving a slight shudder. Ean couldn't blame the imp. As Zin had spoke flashes of Ean's nightmares had gone running through his head. Was he going to become a monster like that as well?

Zin's voice, though mellow, cut through his thoughts like a knife. "Hoping to gain even more control over the creatures of the Abyss and access to the energies that reside there, the man attempted to cut a hole into the earth and create a direct route straight to the Abyss. This made everyone under his control, those that were constantly being threatened and tormented desperate. I didn't actually see what happened, but somehow, they were able to kill the man before he accomplished his goal."

"And that's why the worship of Ze'an is outlawed now?" Ean wanted to hear more, had to hear more. Was this his future as well?

"No, no," the imp continued, "it's what happened after his death that made everything ten times worse. I'm not sure if it was because

I had been out of the Abyss for so long or because the man had been so powerful, but it took almost twenty days before I was dragged back down to the Abyss. I was able to see the after effects of the man's death."

Zin looked Ean directly in his eyes. That look, of horror and despair, almost made Ean's knees go weak.

"The area around the hole he had dug began to change. It started out small. Green grass wilted and turned a sickly purple. Animals either became more violent or died suddenly. A thin mist began to appear, with anyone touched by it growing blisters and finding it hard to breathe. And that was just the first day. By the second, the sickness had spread almost a day's journey in every direction. People were getting sick, crops were failing, and the mist thickened. By the end of the first week, whatever was happening had spread all the way up to the north coast and had completely covered what was at that time the capitol for your people."

"Two days before I was dragged back into the Abyss, I heard about a call for a complete evacuation to the south. Anyone not effected by what they called the Plague was fleeing south to Lake Melcoi. That's where the main temple to Alistar had been built and supposedly where the greatest magus of the time were meeting. Since I was dragged back into the Abyss before the conclusion of said events, I was left to wonder what happened to the world here. Since we are standing in what looks like unaffected lands, I can only assume it worked.

Zin's gazed dropped again and the imp sat down heavily. He looked tired, which was not a sight Ean was used to seeing. The imp gave a little shudder, then shook his head and continued on.

"That's why people fear and never speak of Ze'an or the Abyss. All it took was one man connected to the Abyss to cause such massive devastation and disease even in his own death."

"How do you know all this?" Ean asked. "If you were in the Abyss for the majority of the worst of what happened, how could you know what the people here think?"

A pained expression painted the imp's face, making Ean feel he had inadvertently put the imp's loyalty in question again. When the imp continued though, his tone wasn't angry or disappointed. It was simply... pained.

"For the majority of the time between when my previous master died and you summoned me, I was in the service of a particularly nasty Nar'Grim called Baran'Grim. I've told you how evil the Nar'Grim can be in general and this one was no different. I don't want to talk about what I had to go through with him, but I did find something interesting in his possessions. He somehow owned this magical orb that allowed him to see into your world. I found it one day while cleaning his various treasures and trophies, and from then on used it whenever I could to see glimpses of your world. For the longest time, being able to look at a world that had provided me with so much freedom, even if it was while I was a slave to another evil being, was the only thing that kept me going."

Ean sat back down, completely taken back by his friend's story. Zin had never even hinted about his past before and Ean had never really thought much about it. To listen to his friend speak about his past, and watch his demeanor change from the sarcastic, rude imp he had known for years to one that sounded defeated and worn out was painful. If Ean had known about the poor imp's past, he certainly would have treated him better throughout the years.

"I'm sorry Zin, I never realized living in the Abyss had been that bad for you."

Shrugging his shoulders, Zin began plucking at the grass around him. "It's nothing, thousands of others of my kind go through just as bad or worse down there. Being a slave had its perks and it kept me from being hunted on a daily basis. But I hope now you can see how tied to you I really am. If anything happens to you, I go back to either a life of fear or a life of slavery. And that's if Baran'Grim doesn't kill me first."

He shuddered, causing his hand to rip out a clump of dirt. He looked at it for a moment, then tossed it aside. "Plus you've never been anywhere near as much of a pain as my previous master. You can actually be nice every now and then. When you aren't being a complete fool."

Rising quickly, Ean moved over to Zin and extended his hand. "I'm not your master Zin. I promise never to think of myself as your master. If anything, I want us to simply be friends. I need a friend like you to keep this power go to my head. Is that possible?"

The imp smiled then, a large toothy smile that returned a bit of mischief to his eyes. "I'm getting permission now to call you out whenever your being stupid and knock you down a peg or two? Oh, I think that's the nicest gift anyone has ever given me."

Ean couldn't help but grimace as he realized how much freedom he had given the imp to verbally rip him apart. But he forced it away just as quickly. Zin deserved that freedom. And if Ean's nightmares were any clue as too what the imp's previous master in this world was like and what Ean could possibly become, he needed Zin a whole lot more then the little creature realized.

"Yes, well, enough of this touchy-feely stuff," Ean said, laughing uncomfortably. "Let's get back to the others. If they are not up yet, then we should get them up and get going. It's going to be much more difficult getting through these woods now that we don't have the road to follow."

Zin hopped to his feet. "Whatever you say, partner."

Without another word the imp rose and jogged off, leaving Ean standing in the clearing shaking his head. He really was going to regret giving the imp free reign to say whatever he wanted.

CHAPTER 22

CIRCLES

BY THE TIME EAN had opened up his Pocket, put his Book away and gotten back to camp, his companions were all sitting around while Bran tried to start a small fire. It was probably safe to make one during the day, and after the night they had had, a warm breakfast would make them all feel a little better. They certainly looked like they needed something to improve their moods.

Jaslen was sitting with one hand behind her, massaging the spot where the Seeker had stomped on it the day before. She kept her eyes down and was jabbing at the twigs and branches of the campfire with a stick until Bran was finally able to get it lit. Every now and then, a shiver would pass through her body despite the fact that the breeze was warm this morning.

Bran was in much worse condition. His throat was bruised from where he had been struck, the deep brown and purple color of his skin coinciding with his still raspy voice. He spoke very little as they made the fire and cooked breakfast, which was for the best as it gave his throat a rest and time to heal. Unfortunately, there was nothing in Ean's bag of herbs that could help that injury.

They ate in silence, even Zin, who must have felt the mood just as Ean did. When their small pot of stew was just about empty, Bran broke the silence first.

"Well, I would be pretty happy if I never saw any of those Seekers again." His voice sounded less raspy and a bit more energetic than it had the previous night. "At least not without a couple hundred of those four-armed creatures you brought out yesterday. What did you say it was called, Ean?"

"Cruxlum." He glanced in Zin's direction. "Can you tell us more about them?"

The imp shrugged, then slurped down a bit more of the broth before speaking. "Cruxlum are fairly intelligent creatures that love to fight, but only if they think their adversary is a worthy one. Or if you get them angry enough." A small smile touched his lips for a moment then was gone. "The one you summoned yesterday was fairly confused. In his mind, no one present was worthy of fighting him. I had to convince him that the Seeker had said some unflattering things about him."

"What did you say?" Jaslen's face reflected some kind of inner turmoil, and her voice was somber, but there was curiosity in it as well. "It sure seemed mad as it tore off after the Seeker."

The imp's eyes widened, and by his expression, Ean thought Zin would have blushed if it had been possible on his dark brown skin.

"Well, I told him that the Seeker had made some unflattering remarks about his mother and ... certain parts of his body. I'm sure it was the comments about his mother that made him enraged," the imp said quickly. "Cruxlum are very family-oriented."

"Oh ..." Jaslen replied looking confused for a moment, and then her eyes widened in understanding, "OH, you mean you talked about his guy part —" She cut off quickly, her face turning red.

"Yes, yes, that part," Zin said as he turned to look in every direction except at Jaslen.

Starting with Ean, laughter spread through the group. Zin resisted at first, but he too began to snicker, succumbing to the overall good feeling of the group.

"I think we needed this," Jaslen said between a last set of giggles. "It feels really good, even if the laughter was at my expense."

"And mine," Zin piped in.

"Well, now that we all feel better," Bran said, rising to his feet. "Maybe we should think about how we're going to get out of this forest."

"Well," Jaslen said, rising as well. "Going by the map we looked at back home, as long as we continue to head north, we'll eventually reach the end. Then it's just a matter of following the edge east until we find the road again."

Ean hated to be the one to put a damper on their newfound good mood, but the question had to be asked. "Sounds like a good plan, but exactly which way is north?

That earned him blank stares from his three companions. Zin shrugged and returned to finishing off his broth. Jaslen began to look around, her long, cherry red hair swinging about as she looked in every direction. Bran looked at the ground, taking a kick at a nearby stone.

Not sure what else to do, Ean turned his attention to the sky, or at least to the leaves and branches above him. Small amounts of light were getting through, but he had no idea where the sun was at the moment. As sure as water was a necessity to survive, Ean knew the sun rose in the east and set in the west, but without actually being able to see the sun, that knowledge offered him little help.

"Well," he said after giving up trying to find the sun. "Maybe if we start moving off in one direction, we'll eventually come to a place that is clear enough to find the sun. Then we just have to see which way it's moving, and from that, we can figure out which way is north."

"That's brilliant, Ean!" The praise in Jaslen's voice warmed his heart. "I never thought of looking for the sun. Although I don't think since we've entered this forest that there has been a place where we could actually see the sky."

As Jaslen grew quiet, Bran jumped in. "It's the best plan we have though, and sitting here won't help us figure anything out. Plus, if those Seekers are still looking for us —"

The woods around them seemed to darken for a moment, although Ean was sure it was just his imagination. Shaking off the sudden chill he felt, Ean began cleaning up. The other two joined him while Zin sat and watched, all four becoming silent and somber again. With the fire out and most of their things stored away in Ean's Pocket, they stood in a circle looking at each other expectantly.

"So, which way should we go?" Ean said at last. "We still have to be west of the road and east of the Skyfall Mountains. If we run into either as we move, we'll be able to figure out which way is north. If we end up heading south, we'll either hit the Skyfall Ring that circles Rottwealth or end up in Rensen again. So regardless of which way we go, even if we never spot the sun, we'll run into something that will let us know which way to go from there."

"Sounds good," Jaslen said, and Ean nodded along with her.

"Alright, then I say we go this way." Bran pointed straight ahead then began to move. Zin, Ean, and Jaslen followed close behind.

They traveled in silence, talking lightly when they stopped to eat again, and then continued on without speaking. Each seemed lost in their own thoughts. It continued this way into the night, with the companions eating a small snack and then bedding down without a word.

Ean chalked it up to the stress of the previous day and being lost. He hoped the next morning would bring warm weather, a break in the trees, or at least a sweet, wildberry bush. Anything to lift their sagging spirits. Even Zin seemed in a melancholy mood. For most of the day, though, the imp kept his head down in thought like the rest of them, saying the least out of the four.

Yes, Ean thought, right before he drifted off to sleep. We certainly need something positive to happen tomorrow.

CHAPTER 23

CUT TIES

BUT NOTHING HAPPENED THE next day.

Or the one after that.

Or four days after that.

Wait, was it four days, or five? Ean wondered. All of the days started to run together.

After breakfast, they would head off into the woods, following a marker they had put up the night before so that they knew they were heading in the same direction as the previous day. Of course, whether or not they were going in the same direction during most of the day was another story and a question that they never discussed. For all they knew, each time they moved around a dense pack of trees or a fallen log they were resuming their march in a different direction than they meant to go.

They moved about in silence, heads focused on what was directly in front of their feet. By the third day, Zin had wandered off on his own. The imp stayed close enough that Ean could still feel his presence, but he never returned to sleep with them at the end of the day.

When it grew too dark to travel across the difficult terrain, they would stop. Again they would prepare the camp and eat in silence quickly, then move off to their tents to drift off to sleep. As the first rays of light finally broke through the canopy overhead, they would get up and start the same process all over again.

BY THE END OF THE eighth day, or at least what Ean thought was the eighth day, they reached a breaking point. Jaslen and Bran looked as tired as Ean felt. The stench of sweat, dirt and other nasties wafted from all three of them. A dip in a cool creek might have raised their spirits, but since there wasn't one in the area, Ean took it upon himself to come up with another way to raise their spirits. Being accustomed to pain and depression in Rottwealth, he had been able to shield off any depressing thoughts, but by the looks on his friends' faces they had not been as lucky. If they were going to continue on, it seemed that it was up to Ean to do something to raise their spirits.

"It can't be that much further until we find something," he said, trying to make his voice sound as believable as possible. "We've been walking for so long, we have to be near an edge of the forest."

"Unless we're walking in circles," Bran snapped back at him. "And unless you know some way to make sure we walk straight that you've been keeping to yourself, we'll continue to walk around in circles and never leave this cursed forest."

Bran's words stung, not because of anything he said but more because of the tone in which they were spoken. For Ean's entire life, Bran had always supported him against the other townsfolk, even when Ean had done his best to push the other boy away. Ean couldn't remember a single harsh word being said directly to him by Bran before. Besides Jaslen, Bran had been a constant pillar of support.

Jaslen's silence didn't help matters either. She was usually the first to jump to his defense, faster than Bran even, in most situations. Now she stared into the fire, either lost in her own thoughts or unwilling to get involved.

"No, I'm sorry, Bran. I don't know a way to make sure we're always moving in the same direction. I don't think a spell even exists that —"

"Well, then what good is all of this power you claim to have?" Bran's voice was growing louder with every word, and the young man clenched his fists. "Why don't you summon something that can lead us out of here, or better yet, why don't you ask your best friend, Ze'an, to deliver us from these woods. The Gods know I've been asking every other Deity for help and have received none. Maybe your buddy in the Abyss can help us out."

Ean frowned and took a deep breath. He could feel the guilt inside of him being replaced with anger, but getting into a screaming match with Bran wouldn't make things any better. So instead of yelling back, he raised both hands defensively and tried his best to keep his voice level and calm.

"I have no control whether Ze'an talks to me or not." That at least was true, the fact that the god had never spoken to him didn't much matter at this point. "And I have no idea what kind of creature I could call that would lead us from the woods. We just need to stay calm and keep our heads, and we'll figure something out."

"Don't tell me to keep calm!" Rising to his feet, Bran began to pace back and forth in front of the fire. "You're probably loving this, aren't you? You hate people so much that getting lost in the woods is probably a dream come true, especially since you get to stare at my girl the entire day."

That finally got Jaslen's attention. Raising her head, she shot Bran a frown before speaking. "Bran, stop it. This isn't helping anything. We need to stick together, not fight."

"Of course you would say that." Bran spat on the ground in disgust. "You want to believe he can help you get close to Ze'an so badly that you listen to everything he says. Well, he can't, Jaslen. He clearly knows next to nothing. That imp that follows him around knows ten times more than Ean does, and where has he been?"

Jaslen turned towards Ean, giving him a perfect view of the doubt in her eyes. "Is that true, Ean? We know you can perform some amazing feats of magic, but have you been making up things about your connection to the Abyss just to try and impress me?"

"I haven't done it to try to impress you —"

Jaslen's eyes watered up and she turned away from him. That action might as well have been a physical blow the way it caused his stomach to tie up in knots. Things were spiraling out of control.

"Listen," Ean pleaded, trying to get a handle on things. "Maybe I don't know as much as I implied about the Abyss, and maybe Ze'an hasn't spoken directly to me, but that doesn't matter. As far as I know, I'm still the most connected person to the Abyss. That has to mean something, right?"

Jaslen ignored him, looking away from both him and Bran. Bran, on the other hand, had other ideas. He marched right up to Ean and got directly in his face.

"This has all just been one big scheme to steal Jaslen away from me, hasn't it?" The anger was painted across most of Bran's face now. His eyes, though, seemed off, not appearing to really focus as he attempted to glare at Ean. "Always saying or doing things to try and impress her, pretending to be this big follower of the God of the Abyss. It's all a show, isn't it? Your way of keeping people away at first, but then you jumped right into the role when you realized Jaslen was so fascinated by the god."

"You mean," Jaslen cut in, her voice low and wobbly, "when he found that both of us were interested in Ze'an, don't you, Bran?"

A bit of the anger drained from Bran's face. "What?"

Rising to her feet, Jaslen walked over, her steps shaky as if she might fall over at any second. "You said that I was the only one interested in Ze'an. But I thought we shared a mutual interest in him."

Her tone had changed from sad to accusatory. When she reached the two young men, she placed her hands on her hips and stared hard at Bran. He just stared at her for a moment, his mouth hanging slightly open, before he tried to speak.

"That's not what I … you know I'm interested —"

Her raised right hand cut him off, as her voice grew firmer. "Don't call Ean a liar and then turn around and lie right to my face. Three years, Bran, it's been three years now since we first started talking about becoming followers of Ze'an. That's three years that you've been lying to me about something I thought made us closer."

"I didn't …" He looked at her for a second and then threw his hands into the air. "Fine, fine, I had no interest in your god, if you want the honest truth. How you can be interested in a god that clearly causes so much pain is beyond me. I didn't think much of it at home, but now that we've been out in the world and have heard how horrible Ze'an truly is, I'm honestly shocked that you still want to follow him."

Jaslen stumbled backwards as if his words had physically pushed her. She sat down hard on the ground and immediately hid her face in her hands. Even though it was clear she was trying to hide it.

Ean had been growing so used to having people around that enjoyed his company, now that things were falling apart, it was worse than his years of being bullied at home. As Jaslen began to cry, the guilt that Ean had been feeling started to change into something else. How dare Bran treat Jaslen this way? Well, he wasn't going to let it continue.

"Bran, I think you've said enough. We should all just give each other some space and get some sleep. Tomorrow —"

"Tomorrow? Tomorrow?! You mean tomorrow while we tramp around in the woods as our supplies dwindle? Oh, I can't wait for another day of that." His voice dropped, taking on a dangerous tone. "Or do you think that if me and Jaslen are arguing that maybe she'll come lie near you tonight?"

"What … I never even considered …"

"That's right. You never considered it, 'cause it would never happen." Without warning Bran shoved Ean backwards. Ean tried his best to stay on his feet, but his heel hit a root and he dropped down hard into a sitting position. Wincing at the pain the fall caused, he looked up at the young man he used to consider his friend and sneered.

"Sounds to me like someone is afraid he isn't man enough to keep his girl." Ean put as much scorn and contempt into his voice as he could. When both of Bran's hands balled up into fists, for a moment Ean thought he had gone too far, but a glimpse at the still crying form of Jaslen made him not care if he had.

"You think you're good enough for her?" The laugh that came out of Bran's mouth did not contain even the slightest bit of humor. "She wouldn't be with you if you were the last human in the realm. The only reason she has ever been nice to you is because her heart is too big and she pities you. She's told me as much countless times in the past."

"Is that true, Jaslen?" Ean demanded, voice tinged in angry accusation. "Have I just been your little pity project?"

Jaslen pulled her hands down away from her face enough so that her eyes could meet his. It only took a moment of looking into those eyes for Ean to realize what Bran had said was true. Pushing himself to his feet, anger and hurt washed through him.

"I don't need your pity. I don't need anyone's pity!"

Jaslen leapt up just as quickly, raising her hands in a calming fashion. "Ean, it's not what it sounds like. When I said that to Bran —"

"You don't have to defend yourself," Bran cut in. "He's better off knowing the truth anyway. Now he can stop looking at you like a love-sick puppy."

Turning his attention back to Ean, he raised a finger and pointed it in Ean's face. "You just stick to being friends with your little creatures and beasts. They at least seem to be able to tolerate you."

Ean felt as if he was going to explode with rage. He had let both of these fake people drop his guard, break down walls he had been putting up for years. What a fool he'd been to ever think anyone from his village could actually consider him a friend. Clenching his gloved fists together tightly, he opened himself up to the energies of the Abyss. They would see exactly how adored he could be by creatures from the Abyss.

Dropping to one knee, he ripped off his glove and placed his right hand on the ground. The summoning runes leapt into his mind. He had only glimpsed at the page containing the creature he wanted, but the picture had been one of a beautiful woman with short hair and scantily clothed. Overall she had looked like a normal human woman, except that she had a pair of wings coming out of her back. The few words he had been able to translate from the page were 'slave' and 'weak,' so she should be rather easy to control.

It took only moments for the circle to flash into existence, the runes flaring out from his hand and across the ground to form a circle. Bran leapt back, almost stumbling into the fire while Jaslen stepped back a bit more carefully. As the runes took hold and flared to life, they moved back even further. Ean simply smiled at them as the circle disappeared and the connection to the Abyss opened in the ground.

And then the pain hit him.

It was worse than anytime he had summoned Zin or the Hound combined. Worse than when he had called the Cruxlum. It was even worse than the "growing pains" he had experienced as his powers increased. Falling over onto his side, Ean curled into a ball and fought to stay conscious, his right hand still on the runes.

Through eyes half closed in pain, he watched as two hands reached out of the hole and grasped the grass. The hands were human, although the skin was a pale blue and the purple fingernails were longer than what you would find on most girls. Those nails dug into the dirt as the creature pulled itself up.

The tops of wings appeared next, small, bony points sticking out of the dark violet membrane of the wings. In the picture they had appeared more like the wings of a bird, but in person, they were leathery like those of a bat. The wings stretched out as they cleared the opening, flapping once and sending a burst of air into Ean's face. That one flutter of wings completely lifted the rest of the creature out of the hole, propelling it slightly above the ground for a moment before its human feet landed right in front of Ean's face. Looking up and doing his best to ignore the pain coursing through his body, Ean saw the most beautiful woman he had ever seen.

Standing about the same height as Jaslen, the woman, or at least the creature that look like a woman, was scantily clad in what appeared to be some kind of dark leather that barely covered her lithe body. Her skin was a pale blue color, with long purple claws stemming from her toes that matched those on her hands. Short, purple hair that matched her wings fluttered about her head as she looked around with pupil-less eyes that were the darkest red Ean had ever seen. Her ears and nose were petite in size compared to a mouth that was almost too wide. All of her strange features however somehow accented her beauty instead of making her look less human.

Ean watched as she glanced over her shoulder at Jaslen and Bran, whom were both gaping at her, before finally turning around and resting her gaze on Ean. A small smirk touched her lips as she looked at him for a few moments. Then she bent down, bringing her face so close to his that their noses almost touched. The glow of the now returned summoning rune bathed both of their faces in its blue light.

"Thank you for the freedom, little one," she said, her voice sultry and playful at the same time. "I have never been out of the Abyss before. I will make sure to thank you properly in a moment as soon as I've had a little snack. It was awfully nice of you to provide me with two."

Opening her mouth, she playfully licked the tip of his nose before standing and turning towards Bran and Jaslen. As she walked over towards them, her hips swaying rhythmically, her words began to sink into Ean's pain-riddled brain. Did she believe Jaslen and Bran were a snack? Fighting through the pain, it took all of Ean's strength just to sit up.

"Wait, you need to stop," he was able to say through clenched teeth.

Barely turning her head enough for him to see the corner of a blood-red eye, she raised a hand and waved him off.

"I said I would be with you in a moment, dear. I have heard so many wonderful things about how a human's essence tastes. I'll try not to get too caught up in feeding off of them that I leave you waiting long. You don't look to be in any condition to enjoy my company at the moment anyway."

Returning her attention to Jaslen and Bran, she took the few remaining steps to reach them. Ean was able to get a glimpse of Bran's face and wasn't surprised to see a bit of fear in his eyes.

"Wait a moment," Bran was able to get out before the creature extended a clawed hand and place it gently on his cheek. As soon as the pale blue skin of her hand touched him, he immediately grew silent. A look of wonder crossed his face for a moment then faded as his eyes glazed over.

"There, there, no need to speak," the creature said as her other hand moved as well. Ean couldn't see where it went but he imagined it was touching Jaslen in the same fashion. Whatever the creature was doing, by Bran's expression, it seemed to be putting them in some kind of hypnotized state.

"Much better," the creature cooed, her wings shivering slightly. "I prefer not to have any noise while I feed." Leaning over, the creature moved her face to Bran's neck, at which point his whole body shivered. As Ean watched, the color slowly began to drain from his former friend's face.

Ean didn't know if she was killing them or not, and for a moment he wasn't sure if he cared. They both had hurt him so badly, why should it bother him if this woman had her way with them?

But it did.

Ean took a step towards the creature. Every movement felt like he was walking through fire, but he pushed on. Ean opened himself up to even more energy from the Abyss, desperately trying anything he could to alleviate some of the pain. As more energy flowed into him, the pain did subside enough that he was able to move faster. When he finally reached the woman's side, he grabbed onto her shoulder and pulled her away from Bran.

She let out a little pouting sound as she was pulled away and turned to face him. Ean couldn't read anything from her eyes, but her downturned lip showed off her annoyance.

"You can't feed off of them. They aren't for you," Ean was able to say through the pain. "Leave them alone."

Before he could say another word, the creature grabbed his shirt and pulled him in close, her mouth immediately going to his. When they touched, it was like an explosion of bliss throughout his body, erasing his pain at first and then pain and pleasure mixed together in such a way that his knees almost gave out. For a moment, he lost his hold on the power flowing through him and the feelings of pain and bliss tripled in strength. His knees did give out then, but the creature held him up with one small, clawed hand.

"There, now you've had a taste," she said, holding him out and away from her. As the pleasure and pain raced through his body, he couldn't help but wonder at the strength this petite creature had. "I promise after I finish feeding, I will make sure you don't even remember these two."

"Now let me get back to it," she shivered slightly, causing Ean to sway about in her grip. "Your kind tastes a hundred times better than I had been told."

Then, with a mere flick of her wrist, she tossed Ean aside. He hit the ground hard, rolling a bit and coming to a stop next to the still glowing summoning circle. The feeling of bliss left him, and he struggled to turn himself so that he was facing the creature and his companions again. As he pushed himself up to a kneeling position, he also noticed that the pain from the summoning was starting to subside as well. Focusing himself as best as he could, he opened up to the energies of the Abyss again.

The energy blunted even more of the pain he had been experiencing, allowing him to concentrate on the creature and his companions. The creature was back at Bran's neck, the young man's face a mixture of ecstasy and pain now. It was a sickly color, his skin waxy and pale, and his eyes were beginning to roll back into his head.

Ean slapped his hand down on the summoning circle and pictured it opening again and the creature returning to the Abyss. Just as the thought crossed his mind, the circle disappeared and was replaced by a gaping and glowing hole. Putting as much strength into the thought as possible, he again pictured the creature being drawn back to the Abyss.

The force of the effort caught her off guard. Her body jerked off of Bran. She tumbled backwards a few times before finally rolling into a crouched position. Digging her feet and hands into the earth, she turned her head and shot Ean an annoyed glare. Ean tried to use even more willpower into dragging her back to the portal, but the creature didn't move.

"You know, little one, this is starting to become bothersome." Her voice still had a twinge of playfulness to it, but her annoyance was also starting to come through. "You're clearly not strong enough to send me back, so just let me have my fun and then you can have yours. These two possibly can't mean that much to you. I could feel the boy's contempt for you as I fed off of him. You can't possibly want to protect someone that thinks so poorly of you."

She could tell all of that from feeding on him? What kind of a creature was she? Would it be so bad to let her take Bran?

He shook his head, erasing those thoughts from his mind.

"You can't have them," Ean said. "They may not think too highly of me, but that doesn't mean —"

Ean was cut off as the woman launched herself directly at him. As the force of her body hit him, it knocked the wind out of him, and he lost all thought of pulling her back into the Abyss. They rolled over each other a few times before coming to a stop with the creature on top of him.

"Are we having fun yet?" She got into a sitting position on top of him and smirked down at him. "You are making this a lot harder on yourself than need be. All this playing around is just wasting time. I'm going to win in the end. I always get what I —"

"Bran! Jaslen! Run!" Ean hoped that his shouting would snap them out of whatever trance they were in. Relief flooded into him as he saw them both blink a few times before looking around with confused expressions. "Grab what you can and get out of here now!"

They both looked at him for a moment, and then in unison got to their feet. Bran reached for his sword, trying to stand on shaky legs while Jaslen looked around for something to use as a weapon. They were going to try and help him? The words 'pity' and 'pathetic' leapt into his mind. Were they helping out of guilt?

"You have no chance against her," he yelled. "Just grab what you can and run, you fools!" It took little effort to lace his words with contempt, and it seemed to work.

Bran left his sword in its sheath and grabbed their bag of food supplies instead. Bag in hand, Bran grabbed Jaslen's arm with his free hand and attempted to pull her away. She paused for a moment, an unreadable expression on her face as she looked directly into Ean's eyes. Then Bran's legs almost gave out and her attention returned to him. Placing an arm around his waist, she took the bag of food from him with her free hand and began to help him move into the forest.

"Blah, now I'll have to go catch them." The playfulness had completely left the woman's voice now as she sat atop Ean. "You're starting to cause me more trouble than I might be willing to forgive, little one. After getting a taste for humans, I certainly have no intention of letting these two get away."

Placing her hands on Ean's chest, she began to push herself up and off him. Ean's own hands shot out and grabbed both of her wrists, pulling the creature back down. A surprised look crossed her face for a second then was replaced with a sly smile.

"Don't want me off of you? Quite understandable, but like I said, I'm going to feed first and then we can have some fun." She began to push off of him again, and despite his best efforts, Ean wasn't strong enough to hold her in place. Unless …

Ean opened himself up to as much of the energy from the Abyss as he could. It rushed into him, more than he had ever held before. He felt like a jar trying to contain a flood as it swirled about inside of him. The glove on his right hand as well as most of his right sleeve burned away as the tattoos encircling his arm blazed to life. Even the grass beneath him withered from the intensity of the power flowing through his arm.

The feminine creature straddling his body stared down at the glowing tattoo in wonder, the blazing light coming off the tattoos made her pale, blue skin shine and put a spark in her pupil-less red eyes. Her violet bat-like wings stopped their flutter. Unfortunately, the light only distracted her for a few moments. The beautiful creature shook her head and tried to free herself from his grasp again. Tried and failed.

She pulled and yanked her arms in every which way trying to get free, but Ean held on tight. They thrashed about on the forest floor, kicking up dirt and leaves. The power raged through him, giving him the strength he needed to keep her from going after his friends.

From his position pinned beneath her, he watched as the creature's expression changed from surprise to annoyance, and ended on anger. She sneered down at him, her dark red eyes seemed to glow as she struggled against him.

Eventually she slowed, a blank expression washing over her face as she looked down at him. Was she giving up? Ean had no idea how fast she could run or fly, but he hoped that he had given Jaslen and Bran enough time to get away. As for himself, he had no idea what he was going to do about the creature straddling his body.

As her struggling eventually ceased, she continued to stare down at Ean, her blank face masking whatever emotions she was feeling towards him. After what felt like a long period of silence, she finally spoke.

"You're an … interesting … human. What's your name?"

"Ean."

"Just Ean? How simple." That sly smile had returned, and her arms relaxed in his grip. "My name is Azalea, Ean the human. There seems to be a little more to you than I originally thought. I find you quite … intriguing."

Her voice had taken on a more sultry tone at the end, and she leaned down a bit so that her face was closer to his own. Ean had no idea what to do. He still kept a solid grip on her wrists, but she seemed much calmer now. Had she accepted that the other two were gone? He watched her as she gazed right back into his eyes. Her lip twitched slightly as she smiled down at him. It was then that he realized the position they were in and could feel his cheeks reddening.

"Well," he said breaking the silence. His voice warbled slightly, causing him to wince before continuing on. "If you think you can handle not killing anyone for a few moments, I'll let you get up."

"Who says I want to get up?" Her fingers curled into his shirt. Using the grip, she slowly pulled Ean up to the point where their faces were practically touching. "I said I found you interesting, Ean. Maybe I want to have some fun with you."

Her tongue darted out, brushing his lips for only a moment before disappearing back into her mouth. Ean knew his face must be red by this point; it felt like it was on fire. His hands relaxed slightly on her wrists as he tried his best to speak.

"I'm ... uh, glad that you have calmed down. It was —"

"Shhh," she quieted him with the sound, but even more so with how she did it, lightly touching her lips to his. He felt his jaw drop slightly but didn't care. "Time for talking is over."

Leaning back, she gave him a seductive stare that melted his resolve. He let the energy from the Abyss flow out of him slowly until it was completely gone. As his hands slipped from her wrists, she let out a short laugh and that sly grin returned.

"Oh, little one, whatever am I to do with you."

Before he could ask what she meant, she pulled him up slightly higher and brought her forehead crashing down into his.

All Ean felt was a sharp pain as she struck but dropped into unconsciousness before his body even hit the ground.

FLOATING IN DARKNESS, EAN struggled against the weight of unconsciousness. As the darkness slowly receded, voices seemed to drift through his thoughts. Although barely audible, the female voice with its impatient tone was loud and clear.

"... better know what you're doing, imp. I have no intention of ..."

"... trust me. In the long run, things will work out well for you, you just ..."

"... and you're sure that he ..."

"... looks young, but has ..."

"... better not betray me ..."

The snap of a twig to his left made him sit up. His vision returned, but cobwebs made it hard to remember where he was and how he had gotten there. Instant nausea hit. Trying to blink away the darkness, he peered into the dark shadows of the trees. His hands grasped at the earth and leaves beneath his fingers. Then that familiar tingling feeling, like pins-and-needles lightly jabbing his skin, caught his attention.

"Zin." The imp resonated a distinct and noticeable presence through Ean's connection to Abysmal energy. "Is she still here?"

He struggled to his feet. His stomach churned and it felt like something was crushing his head, but he kept it together. If only he could clear the cobwebs from his mind and focus.

Zin's presence move a bit closer and then stopped. When the imp spoke his voice, was low and Ean detected a hint of annoyance.

"We're still lost in the woods, in what little moons' light can break through the trees, and your 'friends' have left you, taking the food with them. There are plenty of squirrels and rodents for me to snack on, but I doubt I could catch enough to keep you fed. And then of course, there is our new companion ..."

"New companion? What are you—"

"Aww," a new voice said in the dark. "I hope you're not holding a grudge for the little tap I gave you on the head, little one."

That womanly voice, a mixture of playful and sultry, brought everything back. The fight with Bran and Jaslen. Summoning the beautiful creature. The struggle. Receiving a head butt, then the blackness. Finding her by sight was impossible, but then he felt her, felt the Abyss covering her like a thick blanket and turned his head towards the sensation.

"Can this human see in the dark like us?" Her voice sounded surprised, and a little impressed.

"No, no," Zin's voice said from the darkness. "Apparently he can feel things connected to the Abyss. It's something new, and makes games of hide-and-seek incredibly unfair."

"Interesting." He felt the woman rise and start to move towards him. Ean tried to climb to his feet, but dizziness overwhelmed him and he sat back down. Feeling around in the dark, he tried to find something he could use to defend himself.

"You don't need to worry about her, Ean." The imp said. "She's agreed to join us. Whether or not that's a good or bad thing is up for debate, but at least she promised not to kill us. And trust me, that's a pretty big deal for her kind."

Ean listened, trying his best to comprehend what was going on, but a fog still clouded his thoughts. And she was still moving closer. If only he could start a fire or had a candle he could light, anything that would let him see ...

With a thought, he opened himself up to the energies of the Abyss, letting the power flood through him. The tattoos on his arm lit up, basking the trees of Rensen forest in their blue light. Blurs of movement fled deeper into the woods from the light. When he caught sight of the blue-skinned woman, sitting cross-legged with her leathery wings folded against her back, the name Azalea flashed into his mind. She flinched at the light and held up a slender blue hand to shield her eyes.

"Dim your light, little one," she requested. "Or are you trying to punish me for what I did?"

"Maybe I am."

"Aw, don't be that way. You started it, after all. You got me all worked up over a good meal and then denied it to me. Can you really fault me for being angry? If it makes you feel better, I didn't go after your friends, although that boy's angst and jealousy tasted absolutely delicious."

"You only left them alone because I showed up, Yulari," Zin said with a grunt. Ean could see the imp clearly now. His beady yellow eyes were locked on the woman. A fresh scratch adorned one of his pointed ears, there were scratches all over his brown skin, and his clawed feet and hands were covered in dirt. "I had come back to check on Ean and found him unconscious on the forest floor while you were about to head out into the woods. It took me a bit to 'convince' you to stick around."

The woman shrugged, not bothering to deny it.

"Wait," Ean said, placing a hand on his head. The energy from the Abyss had eased the pain, but putting thoughts together was like trying to carry water in a sieve. "I thought your name was Azalea. Why did Zin just call you Yulari?"

"Azalea is her name," Zin cut in. "Not that you can believe anything she says. Yulari is the name of her race. I figured a healer of your intelligence would have known what you were bringing out of the Abyss before you had the bright idea of summoning her."

Zin paused to give Ean a snide eye roll. "If you recall, I warned you to never summon a Yulari. So imagine my surprise when I saw Azalea standing over you, about to leave you for wild animals to snack on. I had half the mind to leave you there, too. It would serve you right if a wolf came and had a little snack on your foot. Maybe then you would finally learn to listen to me."

"You let your pet imp talk to you like that?" Surprise touched Azalea's voice.

"He isn't my pet. He's ... well, he's my friend."

She let out a laugh, then took a closer look at Ean and grew serious. "You mean that, don't you? You actually consider this little worm a friend. How curious. I think I am starting to understand why—"

"I'm standing right here you know, life sucker," Zin cut in. "You could at least wait until I wasn't around to insult me."

"Life sucker?!" Anger flashed across her face for a moment, and then was gone, replaced by her playful smile. "Little imp, if you're smart enough to be able to talk, you should know better than to call any of my kind that name. You're lucky we have this little arrangement, otherwise I would rip each of your limbs off and beat you with them."

"Enough!" Things were getting out of control again, but this time Ean would stop it. "What do you mean, arrangement? What have you two been discussing while I've been ... sleeping?"

He made a point of staring directly at Azalea and was surprised when she looked away quickly.

"Well, we had quite the lengthy discussion," Zin said, a hint of amusement in his voice. "And to sum things up, she's agreed to help us and follow your orders --" Azalea coughed loudly, cutting the imp off. He looked at her with a frown before continuing. "Agreed to try and follow your orders whenever possible."

Ean looked over at the Yulari and this time received a nod and that same smirk that seemed to be a permanent fixture on her face. Shaking his head, he turned back to Zin. "And how exactly can she help us?"

"The better question," the Yulari said with a hint of annoyance. "Is what can't I do? Or more importantly, what can't you do, little one? Obviously you know very little about the Abyss and how to use that energy coursing through your body. You're also a horrible warrior, so I can handle any fights you get into. Unless of course, that would hurt your ego too much, having a girl fight your battles ..."

She stared at him, expecting an answer, but Ean refused to play her games. Returning her gaze, Ean plastered on a blank expression. Realizing she wasn't going to get a rise out of him, she sniffed indignantly and continued on.

"Well, if none of that sounds appealing, there is one last thing I can do that you cannot do."

Without warning she extended her wings and pushed off into the air. The light from Ean's tattoos silhouetted her in the darkness, the shadows created only seemed to add to her beauty. She hovered for a few moments slightly off the ground, her leathery wings beating just fast enough to keep her aloft. Then, with a wink at Ean first, her wings tripled in speed and she rose into the air. Branches rained down as she shot through the canopy above and disappeared.

Moments later, she came crashing back down through the trees, dislodging even more twigs and leaves from above, before landing in front of Ean.

"So, little one," she said mockingly. "Which way do you have to go in order to get out of this forest?"

His supplies were gone. His friends, well, ex-friends, would be almost impossible to find, and he wasn't sure he wanted to find them. And even if he did want to and eventually found them, they still would have no idea which way to go. Azalea was his only hope now. The fact that Zin seemed to support the idea of having her along cemented his decision.

Ean searched her eyes for any sign of treachery. He saw mockery and arrogance reflected in those blood red eyes, but no treachery. Trust his gut, he decided with a defeated sigh. She meant him no harm ... at the moment. He extended a hand in her direction.

"You swear to follow my orders and not ignore them when you think they're inconvenient?"

She gave his hand a puzzled glance, and then gripped it firmly. Her nails dug into the skin of his hand.

"I promise, little one, that as soon as you make my presence in this world more permanent, I will aid you to the best of my ability."

"It's a deal then," Ean said, pulling his hands away. He grimaced a bit as he noticed small pinpricks of blood where her nails had dug in. "And the first thing you need to do, after telling me which direction to go, is to stop calling me 'little one.'"

"Fair enough, child," she said with a smirk.

Wonderful. Another person that teased him about looking young. Ean was eighteen-years-old, but due to his thin build, smooth complexion, dimpled cheeks, and scraggly black hair, people often mistook him for a much younger person. He found it demeaning when strangers referred to him as a boy, but child was even worse.

"Now make my visit here a bit more permanent." Ignoring Ean's scowl, Azalea turned and walked over to a pile of leaves. Brushing them out of the way, her summoning circle came into view. It still glowed faintly with the power that kept her tied to this world.

Ean took a few deep breaths to compose himself before moving over to join her. Making her time in the realm more permanent meant transferring the summoning rune to something he owned, just as he had carved Zin's rune into the pendant around his neck. It had to be something that he could keep close as well, just in case she got out of control and he had to send her back to the Abyss. It would be much easier to break the rune if it was inscribed on a physical object anyway.

Ean spied a small, flat piece of bark resting on the forest floor. It was about half the size of his palm--thin enough to tuck in a pocket, with a large enough surface on which to draw the intricate summoning rune. Picking up the wood, Ean was about to open up his Pocket to retrieve his carving knife when a thought struck him.

Well, it wasn't so much a thought as it was a feeling. Taking the bark in his right hand, he placed his left one down on the summoning circle. Closing his eyes, he pictured the rune on the ground transferring onto the bark. A chill washed over his body, moving from his left hand to his right, and sure enough when he opened his eyes the summoning rune that had been on the ground was now perfectly inscribed on the piece of wood.

He glanced up to catch Azalea's red eyes studying him carefully. When their eyes met, she broke their gaze and turned to walk away, mumbling under her breath. "He could have at least bound me to this world by something more flattering than a scrap of wood."

Ean was about to call her out, but she spoke again, louder this time.

"If you want to get out of the forest, you need to head that way." She pointed off in a direction opposite the one he would have chosen. "I could fly to the edge of the forest in barely any time at all, but since I'm supposed to follow you two geniuses around, it will probably take us a day or two on foot. Unless you are as weak as you look of course, then I would say three to four days."

"Leave now? I can barely see anything."

"Well, then I suppose I'll have to lead you by the nose, and then you and your ugly little imp will be out of the woods in no time."

"Unless you enjoy being called soul-sucking hag, I would stop with the insults and call me by my name."

"Fine, fine, can we go now?" Azalea was staring at Ean, her hands now on her hips with one foot tapping impatiently on the ground. Ean returned her stare, drinking in Azalea's form. White leather hugged her curves. Thick purple hair hung to her shoulders, framing a face with petite features. Anyone normal man would consider her beautiful ... if they could ignore the bat-like wings spread behind her.

Ean knew better. As alluring and almost hypnotizing as her beauty was, deep down she was no ordinary woman. She was just another denizen from the Abyss. A creature of darkness. If Zin hadn't made a deal with her, she would have killed them both by now.

"Yes, we can leave. There's nothing left to pack. So if you're ready to go, then so am I."

Without another word, the Yulari walked off into the dense forest. Zin and Ean hurried to catch up. The threesome walked single file through the forest, with the light of the moons barely breaking through the canopy and creating dappled shadows on the leafy ground. Azalea took the lead position, while Zin and Ean walked a few paces behind.

Zin had been the one to support the decision of keeping Azalea around after all. It was confusing now to see him frown in her direction. Ean couldn't exactly ask the imp what the problem was with Azalea only a few steps ahead of them. So, all three of them walked on in silence until tiny rays of light began poking through the canopy above, signaling the beginning of a new day.

"NOT TOO MUCH FURTHER now," Azalea said after her sixth check of their position. "You've been keeping up a better pace than I would have thought, and I'm very surprised that the imp's little legs have been able to keep up as well. Guess I underestimated you."

"These leg's don't feel so little when their kicking things, Yulari," the imp responded. "Keep that in mind."

"Such big threats from such a little creature," the Yulari retorted, her expression that of fake concern. "Good thing I have Ean to keep you from hurting me. Oh wait, it's the other way around. It's a good thing you have Ean to keep me from hurting you. But don't think that the fact that I can't kill you because of our arrangement doesn't mean I can't hurt you. So watch your tone when you address me."

Time for Ean to step in before things got bad.

"Azalea, that's great that we are almost out of the woods, but that means villages and other people who have never seen your kind before. They'll take one look at your blue skin, and the wings on your back, and try to stone you to death. It might be safer for you to...". As far as I know, humans don't exactly have your skin color and the wings certainly are a dead give-away that you are not human."

"Oh, by the Abyss," Azalea's voice was a mixture of sadness and condescending. "Don't you know anything about Yulari? Well you are going to learn something today."

Stopping, she turned around to face him. Once she was set, her wings lowered and folded about her body, underneath her arms.

Then her entire body seemed to shimmer, blurring the image of her body and face until Ean was barely able to make her out. Then, just as suddenly as it had appeared, the blur was gone and Ean's mouth dropped.

Standing in front of him now was a woman slightly smaller then himself, short blonde hair framing a petite face, her body covered in what appeared to be a thick cloth robe. The woman's features resembled Azalea's but were slightly muted, the thin nose a bit more rounded out, the mouth smaller but with lips just as full, her eyes slightly slanted and a dark green color with actual pupils. Her hair was cut the same, but was a dirty blond color. Her skin had taken on a lightly tanned tone, like someone that spent most of their life out in the fields but had just spent the Chill season indoors.

But there was something else. That shimmering effect was still slightly there, although it didn't blur her appearance any longer. It was the same effect that Ean saw on Zin any time he became invisible.

"Well?" Azalea asked, lifting her arms up and slowly spinning around, "would I pass for human?"

"Yes absolutely, unless normal people can see that shimmering effect as well."

She stopped spinning abruptly and turned to face him. "What shimmering effect?"

"I think I can see the spell or whatever it is that changes your appearance. The same thing happens when Zin tries to turn invisible."

"Oh really? How peculiar." Shrugging, the Yulari spun one last time with a laugh before dropping her arms. "Well I'm sure it won't be a problem."

Raising her arms again, the shimmering effect washed over her once more and in an instant she had returned to her pale blue skinned self. "All that spinning made me forget which way we need to go. I'll be right back."

Taking off into the air once more, Azalea was only gone for a moment before returning to the ground. With a casual wave of her hand she motioned for Zin and Ean to follow. The three of them walked on in silence again, with Zin shooting daggers with his eyes at the Yulari while Ean pretended not to notice.

"Here you are," she said, spreading her arms wide, "delivered from despair and starvation by your wonderful Yulari guide. Just a little bit further and we'll be out of these woods and hopefully to more populated areas."

She flashed Ean a smile and patted him on the head.

"Not that I've found your presence boring, of course. It's just that you stink of depression, and it leaves a sour taste in my mouth."

Ean pulled away from her hand, making sure he kept his face and the scowl he wore clearly in her view. It was one thing to put up with all of her demeaning pet names for him, but he wasn't about to stand there while she patted him like a disobedient puppy.

"I'm not depressed. It's just been a long journey."

"You sure?" Tilting her head, Azalea gave him a quizzical look. "I'm pretty sure I've been smelling depression wafting off of someone, and it certainly isn't the imp."

"How do you know it isn't Zin?"

She flashed Zin a wide grin. "The only emotion that I've been smelling from him is distaste, and I'm sure is directed at me."

Returning her grin, the imp began making his way towards the end of the forest. "Finally something we agree on."

Azalea followed after him, forcing Ean to have to follow along or be left behind. They both caught up to the imp as he cleared the forest.

What lay out before Ean was something he had never seen before. To the North and Northeast were rolling hills of dark green grass, a welcome change from the brown dirt of his home and the overgrowth of the forest. To the West he could see the Skyfall Mountains, not that far off in the distance. It was what he saw to the East though that made his eyes go wide.

A huge stone wall traveling from North to South towered over the land. It stretched up into the clouds and out of sight and seemed to travel in the horizon without end. When Ean was finally able to shake away his shock, he turned to his companions.

ABOUT JAMES

JAMES VERNON was born and lives in eastern Pennsylvania. He enjoys reading, writing, most types of music, and anything in the fantasy and sci-fi realm. Often stuck in long commutes for his job, James's imagination was free to create new worlds and stories. Through the assistance of family, friends, and some generous backers, James has been able to pursue his dream to spread his stories to more then just his own mind.

For more information about James and the Three Moons Realm, visit us at jamesrvernon.com!

THE FOLLOWING IS A LIST OF MY VERY, VERY
GENEROUS KICKSTARTER BACKERS.
IT'S THANKS TO THEM THAT THIS STORY IS
SEEING THE LIGHT OF DAY.

My Strath Haven Family: Tara Flynn, Pat Walsh, Chris Buhler, Kate Woodruff, Megan Shell, Vanessa von Hagen, Maureen

Rob and Angel Logan, Mary and Michael Hahn, Amanda Johnson, Sarah K. Greybeck, Jennifer L. Pierce, Eric Camil Jr., Nathan Briley, Robbie, Alexandra N. Walters, Laura Stephenson

Christopher J. Markus, Brent Day, Keith Hall, Christopher Sneeringer, Silence in the Library Publishing, Nick Tyler, D-Rock, Kate Scott, Daniel Engstrom, Robby Thrasher, Butch Shomph, Edward Earl Duggan, Don, Beth, and Meghan Ferris, SwordFire, Benjamin Abbott, Vanessa Chalub, Bob Whitely, Stephen Cheng, Paul D., Paulina Stefanek, Pamela Wayne

www.ingramcontent.com/pod-product-compliance
Lightning Source LLC
Chambersburg PA
CBHW060539180626
46817CB00002B/648